Copyright © 2024 by Leslie Bates

All rights reserved.

This is a work of fiction. Names, characters, places and incidents either are the product of the author's imagination or are used fictitiously. Any resemblance to actual persons, living or dead, events, or locales is entirely coincidental.

No part of this book may be reproduced in any form or by any electronic or mechanical means, including information storage and retrieval systems, without written permission from the author except for the use of brief quotations in a book review.

Copy editor & proofreader: Taylor Robinson (Instagram: @tayloredtext)

Formatting: Kristen Hamilton (Instagram: @kristenreadswhat)

Cover Designer: Sarah Hansen (Instagram: @okaycreationssh)

Map Artist: Hannah Truelove (Instagram: @centaurmaps)

Character Art: Vii More (Instagram: @viimorte)

TRIGGER WARNINGS

VIOLENCE/DEATH
GRIEF
CHILD ABUSE
DOMESTIC VIOLENCE
MENTION OF SUICIDE OR SELF HARM
SEXUAL ASSAULT
MENTAL HEALTH THEMES
PROFANITY

This book is a NA Dark Fantasy Romance meant for audiences of 18+ with explicit language and sexual scenes. Where Darkness Blooms is the first book in the series and does end on a cliffhanger.

The characters may be fictional, but their feelings are very much real. I know a lot of the topics I mention in this book may hit home for some readers. Please know you are not alone, and if you ever find yourself in need of someone to talk to, there are people who are wanting to help and will listen. My

DMs are always open to those who may need it, or want more information about the trigger warnings. With that being said, please read at your own risk.

To all those who have entered their villain era, this one's for you.

PRONUNCIATION GUIDE

Almeria (Al-mare-e-ah)
Alessians (Ah-less-e-ans)
Atro (Ah-tro)
Calydan (Cal-e-den)
Cardosian (Car-dose-e-an)
Cecinia (Say-sin-e-ah)
Dakar (Da-car)
Elysium (E-lee-see-um)
Eretum (Air-e-tum)
Lachyses (La-kuh-suhs)
Klatho (Klath-o)
Minas (Min-is)
Riyadh (Ry-add)
Sorrena (So-rena)
Veritas (Ver-e-tas)

Cardosian Mountains
Bajna Castle
Koscet
Calydan Kingdom
Bakrem Alps
Northern Red Oak Forest
Hangman's Chasm
Bloodwood Forest
Minas Kingdom
Kismet Inn
DeVero Castle
Phantoms Keep
Rhone River
Aros Castle
Proteus Mountains
Eralan Lake
Dakar Exile
Eretum Kingdom
Riyadh Kingdom
Elysian Peaks
Mohren Castle
Basalto
Cerona Mountains
Almeria Kingdom
Coventry
Cecinia River
Veritas
Romera Castle
Sorrena

ELYSIUM

NAROS
LAYETTE
PALMANA
SALER
ASTORA
CAPRYNA
KERES KINGDOM
KALANI SEA
VEMOND CASTLE

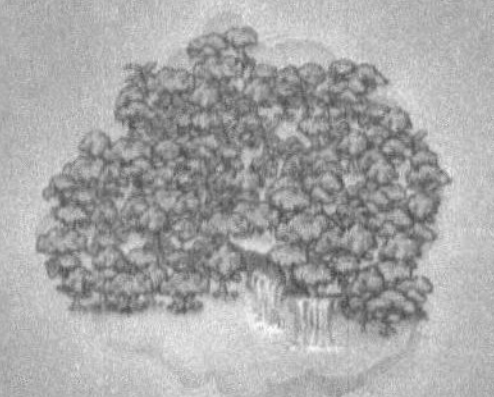

WHERE DARKNESS BLOOMS

LESLIE BATES

PROLOGUE

10 Years Ago

SHE WAS sixteen years old when she murdered a man, and the crazy thing was, she liked it.

She watched as the light in his eyes slowly started to shrink in on itself, his eyelids fluttering like a butterfly's wings as he realized in that instant that he was dying.

She heard him take his last breath as his broken body crumpled to the floor, his warm blood staining her hands crimson. She felt darkness consume her, and she felt invigorated and powerful—she was in control. The darkness wrapped her up in its embrace like they were old friends, and maybe they were. She savored that black abyss and breathed it in. It now lived inside her. Alive. Waiting. And just as it appeared, it was gone.

She didn't think that this body that lay motionless on her bedroom floor could be a father, a husband, a son—all she knew him as was the man that murdered her parents, leaving her an orphan.

Blink. Her hands trembled.

Blink, blink. The shard of glass used to slice the man's throat open was still clutched tightly in her hand, shades of red pooling in between her fingers. Hers and his.

Blink. She couldn't move. She was paralyzed, and she felt herself lose her senses one at a time. She couldn't feel the pain in her hand anymore; at some point it had become numb. She couldn't smell the smoke and blood that lingered in the air, and she couldn't taste the salt of tears on her tongue. She hadn't realized she had started crying. She couldn't hear. Not her own heart beat, the only one still beating in the room. Not even the chaos that was ensuing downstairs distracted her from her inner turmoil. There was just silence.

Everything became so blurry that she couldn't see her own hands in front of her face. She became so unaware that she didn't see or hear the man enter the room.

By the time she realized she was going to die, there was already a blade to her throat, and she was pinned between him and her dresser. Her vision swam, but she could see enough to see right into her killer's piercing, cerulean-blue eyes. The only thing visible on his body. He was covered head to toe in black gear and to complete his shadow-like look, there was a black scarf masking his face, leaving his eyes her only focal point. His grip on her was unnerving. Before she could beg for mercy or a quick death—at this point, she didn't know which one was better—he put his free hand to her mouth. He was pressed so tightly to her, she could feel every hard, rigid line of his body.

"Don't scream," the stranger ordered her. "I'm not going to harm you. Blink once if you understand me."

His voice was muffled by the scarf, and it took her a second to put the words together. She blinked once. *Her only option.* Her heart raced a million miles a minute. Judging by his voice and his build, he was young. Maybe a few years older than her, give or take.

"I'm going to take my hand off your mouth and put my

dagger away." His hand lingered as he withdrew his blade from her throat. "Don't try anything stupid. Blink once if you understand."

She blinked once.

He stared at her a little longer, his eyes searching hers consideringly before he removed his hand from her mouth. He released his hold on her and she stumbled sideways away from him, backing as far away as she could go, until she stumbled over the dead bodies.

That's when she realized what she had done. She was a murderer.

She was a killer. An orphan. Her parents had been slaughtered. For a moment, she forgot about the man in the room and finally looked over at her mother, her blood running over the hardwood floors. And that's when she started to scream.

She can't be dead. She was just here. I can still feel the phantom touch of her hand on my cheek, her soft lips on my forehead, her lovely angelic voice saying goodnight. She can't be gone. But all that blood. No, no, no!

The man was on her within seconds. His hand flew to her mouth, and they collapsed onto her bed. She didn't even struggle. She surrendered. Surrendered to the pain, surrendered to the darkness and the hollowness in her heart. She was empty. That night, Kieryn Rhodes died along with her parents. This shell of a girl had no idea who she was, or what she would soon become, but she didn't want to know. So, she surrendered her fate to her killer.

"Do it! Kill me! Just get it over with. It's what you came for," she spat at him. She then dropped her voice, whispering softly under her breath, "I have nothing left to live for."

The last thing she saw was him kneeling over her body, those discerning blue eyes gazing down at her in sympathy. Pain flooded her head and consumed her consciousness. Heavy tension was pulled to the point of impact as if magnetized, and her eyelids fluttered close. All she could remember as she faded into black were his eyes.

She had grown up in the countryside of Coventry—just outside the city of Veritas, the capital of Almeria Kingdom. Almeria was her home; it always had been. It was all she knew.

It wasn't grand like the neighboring provinces, but it was the isolation and the unspoiled land that charmed her parents into settling here. The people of Almeria had nicknamed Coventry the "Green Heart", for the surrounding land was a plethora of greens, from the hunter green cypress trees to the emerald-colored fields that blossomed with lavender in the late summer. Lush vegetation even grew alongside the open country lanes that led into the capital. Coventry was spread out over acres of vast, open land, cocooned by mountains and valleys, vineyards and rolling hills. It was a place of serenity, and Kieryn loved it.

Her home sat perched on top of a cliff, where she could see over the valley and the walled city in the distance. There was a courtyard at the main entrance by the front gates that came alive in the springtime, her favorite season here. That was when explosions of colorful flowers would burst from the soil and the fragrance was so prominent she could smell it from her balcony. The courtyard was her favorite place in the château, other than the library. On rainy days, she would hole up inside the library curled up on the blue velvet couch with any book she could get her hands on, the fire roaring for hours. It was her happy place. She would spend all day there if she could, but her father thought it best that she trained.

The Queen of Almeria's Alessian warriors were an elite army of dangerous and lethal women known for their brutality and strength. As their Chief Commander, danger was part of Elijah Rhodes' job. While he looked the part with his short military-style amber hair, icy blue eyes, and well-defined muscles from years of training, he had a heart of gold. Queen Nyla had such a fondness for Elijah's war strategies and training tech-

niques that she gave him the title of Chief Commander of her greatest assets.

Being the daughter of the Queen's Chief Commander, at the ripe age of sixteen, Kieryn was adept at wielding an assortment of weapons: sword, bow, and daggers. But most importantly, her father made sure to teach her hand-to-hand combat, her training took up most of her days and she wasn't allowed to venture off too far by herself, which left her without friends besides the house servants and her books. She never understood why she had to learn how to fight if her life was never in danger, or why she couldn't join the Alessian warriors, but she never disobeyed her father's rules. Except for the one time she did. The most important rule. And it was what got her parents killed.

She was never permitted to leave the grounds without her father, but on the night of the Harvest Equinox, Kieryn snuck out of her room, descending the stone wall with the ivy vines next to her balcony. She had no idea that she was being watched. She had no idea that would be the night that led to this very moment weeks later.

She woke up on the bench of a carriage—her father's horse carriage. A quick, subtle glance to her left revealed that the man she thought would be her executioner had become her abductor instead. His mask was off, that much she could tell in the ray of moonlight, but the hood of his cloak was raised, obscuring his features. His fists were clenched so tightly in his lap that they were deathly white. The carriage was going too fast, but he didn't seem at all concerned about the speed.

Why would he want me?

She wondered if this was just a nightmare. If she would wake up any minute now and go downstairs to her parents sitting at the dining room table that overlooked the vineyards, the smell of coffee and the sound of her father's faint humming in the air. But she saw her white nightgown drenched in sweat and her hands stained crimson.

Is that blood? Is it mine?

And then she remembered. The sound of steel ringing downstairs that had woken her, the petrified look on her mother's face as she willed her magic to the surface, her eyes scanning Kieryn's room for the threat in a last attempt to protect her. The smell of ash and smoke that permeated the air, and then the smell of blood of the man that she had killed. Her mother's lifeless body next to her killers'.

Where is he taking me?

If she had to guess, they were heading north, following the coastline based on the smell of salty air and the sound of the waves from where her right ear was pressed against the window. Piercing Eyes glanced over at her, and she pretended she was still unconscious, trying to calm her nervous heart from exploding out of her chest. Either luck or recklessness on her captor's part meant she wasn't tied up.

What a fool.

She would bide her time and figure a way out of this, but she had no idea where she was heading or who she could even go to for help—her family was dead. When the stranger turned his head away, she slowly reached down with her right hand underneath the seat and looked for the small knife her father always stashed there.

"Always be prepared," he had told her.

Would I be able to kill him? Could I kill again—even to save my life?

All she could see behind her eyelids was her mother's bleeding body and the man's eyes slipping away. Before she could get lost in her grief, the carriage finally stopped. She opened her eyes slowly; all she could see out the window were soaring mountains, their peaks swallowed by the night clouds. He still hadn't made a sound since they had left her home. She heard the closing of his carriage door, and the opening of her own. He was leaning in to lift her out when she withdrew the knife from underneath her gown and aimed upwards, underneath the rib cage by the heart, like her father had shown her. When he stumbled back, taken off guard, she ran like hell.

She didn't know where she was going, but she ran as fast as she could. She was in the middle of nowhere. There was nothing but a black lake, an empty field, and a towering mountain looking down on her as if it pitied her. Like it knew what her fate would become. She could feel the sharp slices of pain as her feet were ripped apart, and hot tears pricked her eyes. The wind had a bite this far north, and it tossed tendrils of her golden locks out of her braid as she tore through the fields.

She heard the man's labored breaths as he chased after her. She hadn't killed him, she realized with terror. Instead, she just buried the only weapon she had into his side, leaving her with nothing to defend herself with. She didn't know if she should be thankful that she hadn't killed a second person in one night, or if she should be afraid because if his wasn't the next death of the night, hers surely would be.

His steps were getting heavier, and she knew if she turned around to look, she'd see that he was gaining on her, and fast. If she wasn't so full of adrenaline, she would've collapsed by now, but *the Fates* had other plans for her. She stumbled when he lunged for her, and they both rolled down the hill towards the lake. She tasted blood, flakes of dirt and grass as they tumbled. She braced herself for the impact, her head smashing into the side of a sharp, jagged rock. The rippling waves from the lake lapped at her fingertips in the sand, carrying her pooling blood with them. The fall knocked the breath out of her and she gasped for air. She felt the weight of his body over her then. She could smell his blood from where she'd stabbed him, the weapon itself dripping from where he held it in his hand.

She was pinned, and for the second time that night, she

surrendered. It was over and she was as good as dead. She didn't want to die; she knew that now. But she was tired of fighting.

She knew her father would be disappointed in her for giving up so easily, instead of fighting for her life. But he was gone—dead and could no longer protect her now. And she was just *so* tired.

She wondered how he'd kill her. Would it be fast, or would he make her suffer? A knife to the throat like she did to his fellow soldier? Drowning? Choking? Maybe he'd take the rock that split her head open and finish the job.

He stared at her, his breaths coming fast yet shallow. His hand with her father's knife was shaking as if he was at war with himself. His hood was still up and the only light she could see was from his eyes. For a second, she thought she glimpsed a morsel of regret buried deep, and she felt his body start to relax. She wiggled underneath him, but he tensed again, and the flicker of emotion she had seen disappeared as he raised his hand and struck.

No one had informed him that his mission tonight would involve a young girl. *Gods Above*, she couldn't have been any older than sixteen. The assassin had his targets, and she was a complication he was not expecting. He knew exactly who he was dealing with when he led the mission to execute the Rhodes family. He expected a heavily guarded fortress and a fight, not a frazzled kid on the verge of a breakdown. He knew there were three targets, but he didn't know the third was a teenager. He had no idea why his father wanted this family erased off the maps of the realm, and he hadn't asked. Perhaps it was due to the rumor that the Queen's Chief

Commander had a weapon comparable to the strength of the gods.

He saw her from the hallway as she sliced Warren's throat wide open with a shard of glass. She didn't even hesitate, and her cut was clean and precise. She knew exactly where to cut a person's throat so that he couldn't make a noise. This was a huge problem for him. He had to eliminate her. It went against everything he stood for. *No kids.* And then he saw the swirling darkness that surrounded her—impenetrable darkness.

Holy gods.

He took a step towards the door as silent as he could.

It couldn't be.

She didn't even hear him when he snuck up behind her, and before she could react, he had her pinned, trapping her against the furniture in her room. The glass slipped from her hand at the sudden movement, and he had his knife to her throat before she could blink. He had every intention of killing her, but one glance into her eyes and he hesitated.

A deadly mistake.

He couldn't kill her, despite knowing *what* she might be, and before his mind could catch up to his mouth, he had already told her that he wouldn't hurt her.

Now here he was, carrying her bloodied and tattered body up a long pathway into the side of a mountain. After seeing the utter devastation on the young girl's face as she took in her mother's lifeless body, he started to question why he did the things he did in the name of his father. Then when she had told him she had nothing to live for, how broken she looked because of *him*, it all but tore his heart in two.

His feet dragged him up the mountainside as if they knew where they were going, as if fate was driving him forward and he prayed to the gods that he was doing the right thing by sparing her life. After a few miles up the rugged mountain, he came upon what looked like a monastery. His feet guided him as he ascended the three flights of stairs to the big oak door. The wound she had given him luckily wasn't deep, but it would leave a nice scar. The pain from carrying her lanced through his side like lightning. He slumped to his knees and placed her on the edge of the gate and prayed that whoever resided here would look after her.

He strode down the stairs, his hand coming up to clutch his side to stanch the bleeding, and took one last look at her. He didn't even know her name, but he hoped to the *Gods Above* that he would never see her again, for her safety. When the rest of his father's soldiers met him at the meeting point between kingdoms, he would declare the entire Rhodes family dead.

If her shadows were any indication of what she could grow to be, what she could eventually do … he prayed he wouldn't have to bear witness to it, for it would be a full-out cataclysmic war with major fatalities. As he turned back to the stairs, he wondered again if he was making the right choice.

PART ONE

ONE

KIERYN WOKE up immersed in sweat. She couldn't force any breath into her lungs after tearing herself from her nightmare. She was so hot that she stripped off her slip and swung her legs out of bed. When she stood, her whole body trembled. Shockwaves traveled down her arms to her toes. She stumbled sideways into her nightstand, trying to catch her balance. Her heartbeat seemed to pound harder and faster with every step she took. The more she tried to calm herself down, the shallower her breaths became. Her vision was blurry and as she finally stumbled into the bathroom and turned on the light, she saw herself in the mirror.

Her eyes were narrowed slits, and there were fresh tears running down her face. Rivers of sweat cascaded past her breasts, and she followed one down to her navel.

"You're dying," her reflection whispered to her.

"Is this what death is like?" she muttered out loud, her reflection blinking back at her in response.

No!

She was not that scared and helpless sixteen-year-old girl anymore. It was only a nightmare, she told herself as she slowly sank to the cold, tiled floor. She curled up into a fetal position and tried to let the bitter cold of the tiles bring her back to reality. She kept muttering under her breath, and she didn't know how much time passed. At some point in the middle of her breakdown, she ended up back in her bed on top of the sheets. Some time later, she rose with the sun, the rays covering her body in golden beams of light.

She sat up in bed and looked towards the window, watching the sun's light reflect off the lake beyond the mountains. The night her parents died felt like it was only yesterday. It felt like that every time she had the nightmare. That nightmare was her life, and she never forgot any of the details from that dreadful night. Ten years ago today, Kieryn Rhodes died along with her parents, and on that night a new version of her was born.

She was an assassin now—one of the deadliest for the *Santuario del Corona e Sangue*. The Sanctuary of Crown and Blood.

Kieryn should've died down by Eralan Lake. The killer with the piercing eyes spared her life, for reasons unknown to her. It was that thought that kept her up most nights.

Why did my parents die, but he let me live?

When she came to that night, she was bleeding, shivering, and disoriented, lying at the top of a flight of stairs that was wedged in a cliff in the very mountains that loomed over her. She was taken in and trained by a group called *The Guild of Phantoms*. No one knew how she had gotten there, but they took her under their wing nonetheless, and she had been there ever since.

She climbed out of bed and threw on the robe hanging off her bedpost before stepping out onto her balcony. It was a long drop from where she stood. At least 2,500 feet above sea level and on a clear, sunny morning like today, she could see the lake from here. The terror never faded, forever haunting her.

She didn't know why out of all the places, the killer with the piercing eyes brought her here. A place where they trained people to become deadly weapons.

She was taken in for questioning and forced to tell her story repeatedly, until her voice was hoarse and her lips dry and cracked. They wanted to know who she was, where she came from and how she got there.

No one just showed up at Phantoms Keep. The location was a secret to all. Assassins were selected for their unique abilities and extended invitations.

She was held in a room while they interrogated her and sent scouts to her childhood home, or what was left of it. *The Guild of Phantoms* had later informed her that the house had been reduced to ashes. But they had discovered that she was the daughter of Elijiah Rhodes and had taken that into account when deciding her fate. Maybe they too had heard the rumors of what her father supposedly possessed. Kieryn had heard the assassins whispering about her family, but she was just in the dark as they were. If the rumors were true, if her father had possessed this weapon they all feared, she had a feeling it was what got him killed.

When they were satisfied with her answers, they released her to the room she currently occupied now, and she began her new life as an assassin. She had no other option. So, she dedicated her life to finding her parents' killers. She chose revenge.

She was a ghost, just like every other assassin in the Keep. Their lives were no longer their own. None of them had a life to go back to outside these walls, even if they wanted to. They were all orphans, forgotten, wanted by the law, or presumed dead. *Phantoms.*

She was already ahead of some of the apprentices in her class, thanks to the training her father had drilled into her. In a matter of years, she added more to her repertoire, such as learning how to infiltrate kingdoms, becoming a master at creating and detecting different poisons and learning their antidotes, disarming, and creating bombs, and using her body and beauty to manipulate men and women of nobility. While the realm of Elysium may not know her real name, they knew her by reputation alone.

Deathbringer.

She watched the sun crawl its way into the sky, feeling the remnants of that late summer warmth on her golden skin. Autumn was knocking on their door, but summer weather was still digging its claws in, not wanting to leave. Kieryn didn't want autumn to come either; it only brought about more desolation.

Colder weather would be here soon. She could feel that slight chill in the breeze, and anticipate the explosion of colors on the trees that would soon grace her eyes. Feast of the Dead was right around the corner and every year she looked forward to it. It fell a few days after the Harvest Equinox, and the timing was all too perfect. Legend had it that the veil between the dead and living dropped then; she wasn't sure it was true, but it made her feel closer to her parents, nonetheless.

Her stomach rumbled, and she headed back inside to get dressed and headed down to the Hall. Her four-poster bed sat in the middle of the room, the sheer, white curtains cascading down in waves. The bedframe was carved from walnut wood and the designs embedded into the pillars were of the Old Gods. The furniture around her room matched the bed, from her nightstand—which was home to her tower of books—to her wardrobe and dresser. Her favorite part of her room, apart from the balcony, was the living area. It was filled with bookcases that towered to the ceiling, a hearth with a couch big enough for two to lie on, and a piano sitting in the corner by the floor-to-ceiling windows. She didn't play that often anymore, hadn't let herself in years, but it was nice to look at and reminisce. After her first year here at the Keep, she sat down to play a song her mother would sing while her father stared longingly at her. But when her hands pressed down on the first note, the anguish of losing them so violently tore through her, until she was leaning over the toilet in her bathroom. She hadn't touched the piano since.

The library here wasn't much compared to the one she had back home, but over the years she had collected all her favorites again, hoping to find some comfort in them with this new life.

She quickly dressed and headed out into the hallway. Today was going to be difficult, that much she knew. It was the Harvest Equinox and people would be out celebrating in their own kingdoms, while she withered deeper into that black abyss. Ten years was a long time, and she was no closer to the truth. Every year she went not knowing who assassinated her parents was another failure in her book. Her footsteps echoed on the marble floors as she made her descent through the Keep. The hallway was already flooded with light from the arched windows that lined it, making the ornate gold carvings sparkle in the early morning sun. The architect had wanted to build a monastery extravagant enough for a god, as if they were to waltz through the front doors at any moment. But, everyone in Elysium knew the Gods were gone, asleep in *The Veil*.

A few minutes later, she stood before the Great Hall, a spacious dining hall with three long wooden tables running down the length of it, all occupied by chattering assassins. Upon entering the dining hall, her senses were overloaded with smells of freshly baked biscuits, bacon, eggs, and hot coffee. She quickly loaded up her plate with all the above and turned to scan the sea of heads until she found the seafoam-green eyes that belonged to Grayson Hunt. He was known here as the class clown, and his laugh was contagious. While a lot of the other Phantoms made jokes that he never took anything seriously, there was no one else she'd rather have watching her back out in the field. In their line of work, assassins were bred to not trust anyone, but she trusted him with her life, whole-heartedly.

While he was the jokester inside the Keep, out on a mission, he was known to the surrounding six kingdoms as *The Executioner.* On the battlefield, he was a force to be reckoned with. It was as if a light switched off in him and his bloodlust came singing out, ready to eliminate any threat.

She made her way over to Grayson, who had saved her a spot next to him, and took in his lopsided grin. He was her first friend here. She didn't talk to anyone the first month she got here, but one day he sat next to her in the training ring and just kept talking to her. Every day he would find her and just talk about his day, even when she wouldn't answer. He was persistent then, and persistent now. When she realized he was never going to leave her alone, she had simply asked if he would ever shut up. His response was, "She talks." They became fast friends after that.

She sat down next to him and playfully smacked his arm, ruffling his blonde curly hair teasing him. She had seen his wicked grin from the door and knew he'd be relentless today.

"It's too early, Grayson, don't start. I haven't even had my cup of coffee yet," she grumbled, slumping over her food dramatically.

He smirked, the corners of his bow-shaped lips rising.

"Rough night?" he asked her.

She knew it'd take him less than a minute to ask her how her mission went last night. If you could even call a date a mission. At that moment, Damien Conall strode over to them, leaning across the table to take a sip of her coffee before settling down on the seat across from them.

She glared daggers at him and snatched her coffee back so fast droplets splattered the table.

"Touch my coffee again and you'll end up like my date last night," she threatened.

"Don't tempt me with a good time, Kieryn, you know I can't say no to you," Damien taunted back.

She threw her bread roll at his face, but thanks to his assassin reflexes, he caught it with precision.

"Do tell me about your so-called *date*," he purred at her, taking a bite out of the roll.

She rolled her eyes at him and turned her attention back to Grayson.

"He didn't last long; the guy is too squeamish over blood."

"Can you blame him?" Grayson asked. "You daggered his hands to the table."

She shrugged. "He shouldn't have had his hands in places they didn't belong."

Grayson shook his head, while Damien mumbled something incoherent under his breath, his jaw tense. Seducing the poor bastard had not been her intention, but shameless flirting usually worked for her, especially with what she had worn last night. She'd been attempting to get information from him until he tried to nuzzle her neck and put his hands in between her thighs, where the slit in her dress revealed a lot of skin. He had the knives coming.

The rest was easy. But before she left, she decided to have a little fun. She wondered what the barmaid's face looked like when she came in to find the man's hands nailed to the table and *PIG* written across his forehead in his own blood.

Clarke Ryvers, *The King of Phantoms*, wasn't as thrilled by her theatrics, but he was at least satisfied with the information she had so *nicely* extracted from her date. She hated when Ryvers sent her on missions like those. She didn't want to play the seductress; she wanted to feel the slice of her blade cutting into a man's throat, feel the sticky substance of blood on her fingers like a second skin. She wasn't always like this. She didn't always crave the spilling of blood. But after that night, she did. She was so far gone from that girl, she sometimes wondered if that version of herself ever existed.

Grayson's smile faltered then, as he remembered what day it was and stared at her. He knew her better than anyone else in this Keep, and his tendency to read her face was uncanny. His eyes silently searched hers to see if she was okay. He and Damien were among the select few that knew the true history of that night and what had happened to her. She saw his concern written on his face and knew what he wanted to voice to her. They always had a deep connection. Somehow, she always knew what he wanted to say based on his facial expressions. She could only shrug in response because, quite honestly, she wasn't okay. She hadn't been okay in ten years. She wasn't really living, just existing. Coping. Suffering in silence.

The rest of breakfast passed by with measly chatter and light banter between Grayson and Damien. She sat silently through the whole thing until they headed out to start their training for the day.

The three of them made their way to what the Phantoms called the Pit, a dark, damp underground fighting ring. A slow, steady drip echoed somewhere off in the distance. No matter how long she had been here, she still couldn't manage to get over the musty smell and the blood that constantly stained the ground. The walls were constructed of cement, and it hurt like hell when you were thrown against them. Kieryn would know. Maddox Young, the Weapons Master, was the trainer for all assassins and he was malicious and grueling with what he called training. Maddox had them start with fighting drills today, something she excelled at. Damien sauntered up to her, and she couldn't help the grin that crossed her face. This would be fun.

He leaned into her. "Don't worry, I'll take it easy on you," he whispered into her ear. His hot breath left a trail of goose-bumps on her skin.

"Good to know, because I won't," she managed to reply, their lips inches away from each other.

He readied himself in a fighting stance, but she didn't wait to be on the defensive. She attacked first, which he didn't expect, and her right hook hit its mark. He stumbled back half a step, regaining his footing and winking over at her.

"That's my girl," he chuckled, rubbing his jaw.

"I'm not your girl," she reminded him, her laugh playful.

He charged at her, fists flying, and she met him blow for blow. He'd throw a punch and she'd block. She would land a kick, and he would elbow her in the ribs. It was a dance of flirtation with them. At this point, their banter and fighting were drawing a crowd. He kicked her so hard in her stomach that she doubled over, leaving her face exposed where it met his fist, blood trickling down her nose. He grinned, thinking he'd won, but he had no idea she'd planned it that way. His body was in a forward stance from his hit, and that's when she made her move. She swung her right leg out, swiping his legs out from underneath him. He stumbled to his knees, but not before she had a knife at his throat. She tilted his chin up with the edge of the knife.

"This is a good look for you. You on your knees."

The crowd chuckled.

He smirked up at her. "I think I prefer you in that position."

Despite the hollering and taunting from the assassins at Damien's comment, she didn't waver. "Yield," she ordered him, but he only laughed in response. She pressed on the knife slightly, nicking him, drawing blood.

He seethed. "This time, Kier, I'll yield."

She got eye level with him, emerald meeting bronze.

"Next time, I'd suggest not taking it easy on me. I'm not as breakable as you think."

Maddox Young stalked over from the corner of the Pit. She could tell by the crinkles at the corners of his eyes that he was entertained, but he'd never say anything to show it. She still had the blade to Damien's throat and his blood had already trickled down to his gray shirt, leaving a stain.

Maddox had his thick shoulder-length hair up in a knot today that lay like a crown upon his head. The dim lighting in the Pit made his hair look almost black, but she knew it was a dark golden brown.

"I said hand-to-hand, not weapons, Kieryn." His lips thinned into a hard line as he scolded her, but his opal eyes said something else. He was proud.

"Sorry, Weapons Master," she replied as usual. She wasn't sorry, though.

Maddox continued, "As for you, Damien—you should know better than to let your guard down around this one." Kieryn smirked.

As Maddox walked away and urged the other assassins to disperse and to try to impress him today, Kieryn removed the dagger from Damien's throat. She reached out her hand to help him up, and he took it willingly, but not before pulling her into him. The movement was so sudden she inhaled sharply. His lips brushed close to hers as he muttered in a husky tone, "I'll remember that you're not so easily breakable tonight."

He leaned back, satisfied that he had gotten to her. He lifted the bottom of his tee, exposing his chiseled stomach, years of training on full display for her, as he wiped at the blood that hadn't yet dried. She held his gaze, not daring to blink. He liked playing games, and she found herself enjoying the fact that she was the prize he hadn't yet won. He released his shirt, and she felt herself breathe again. He turned away to continue his training, but not before he looked over his shoulder and winked back at her.

Thank the gods that the lighting down here was dim; she did not want to think about what he would have said if he could see her neck and cheeks flushed red. She took a few breaths to steady herself. Slicing open a guard's throat, daggering a man's hands to the table, sitting outside in torrential downpour caked in mud on a recon mission—no problem. But leave it to charming and cocky Damien Connall to make her lose her sense of self.

"You're not sly, you know," the beautiful raven-haired woman next to her stated.

Kieryn whipped her head around to find *The Wraith* standing behind her, her coy smile spreading across her olive-toned skin. *Damn.* She hated how Ashlyn Delgrer always managed to creep up and catch her unaware, but it was what she was great at, hence the nickname she held here in the Keep.

"I don't know what you're talking about. We just banter and joke with each other, that's all it is," she stuttered, grabbing a towel from the bench, wiping at her bloodied nose and thanking the Gods that he hadn't broken it.

"Kier, you forget we share a wall and I'm pretty sure the night before last there was some interesting noises coming from your room, and—"

Kieryn moved quickly, throwing her hand over Ash's mouth. She dragged her to a dark corner of the Pit.

"Keep your voice down. No one knows, not even Grayson. He knows we flirt, but nothing more. And you know how Ryvers feels about relationships within the Keep," she pointed out.

Ash just shrugged.

"Yeah, yeah, yeah someone will end up with a knife in their eye if things go south," she laughed. "You think anyone cares?

People still do it regardless. And I know that you're not a virgin. I know about your nights out in the town. Damien wants you and he practically drools over you in front of the other Phantoms. Something I've never witnessed him do before. So, what's the issue?"

While it was true what Ashlyn said, she knew her and Damien's relationship was complicated. God knew she liked him in whatever capacity her heart could, and he wanted her, but then after all was said and done, she wouldn't stay long enough for his feelings to be anything more than lust.

It'd mess with their entire friendship. She wouldn't risk that, she couldn't. They were all she had left, and she wouldn't let her feelings get in the way of that. They were two lonely souls, just not wanting to feel alone anymore in this life they shared. That was all.

"The issue is me and Damien are one and the same. We like the chase. It's a game with us and I just don't think it's worth crossing that line." Ashlyn stared at her, her smile teasing as if she knew that was bullshit. "Plus what's the point of labeling things?" Kieryn pointed out, knowing that death was imminent for them all.

Grayson waved them over, but she locked eyes with Damien next to him. Even in the soft light she could see the hunger and amusement in his eyes, as if he knew they were discussing him. She smirked and flipped him the finger.

Whatever her heart wanted, she would not allow herself those feelings for another. Love was a weakness that could be used as a weapon against her. She would not feel that way again. She would not feel helpless. She'd kill anyone before they could even get a chance to use her feelings against her.

TWO

THE FOUR OF them made their way to the Courtyard for weapons training. Going from The Pit to the Courtyard was like night and day. The Courtyard was situated on the backside of The Keep, nestled deeper into the mountain range. Running down the middle of the Courtyard was a 50-foot-long reflection pool. Not only was the pool an artistic touch to honor the gods, but Maddox had utilized its benefits to train them on improving their lung capacity. Kieryn would never forget her second year at Phantoms Keep when the Weapons Master had some brute assassin hold her down underwater in below-freezing temperatures. All part of training, he had told her hours later, as she recovered in medical from inhaling too much water. It was not something she wanted to experience again.

The rest of the Courtyard was a wide expanse of forest-green grass that stretched for miles, only ending when it met the mountains that extended high into the sky. Maddox had them broken up into groups. Damien, Ash, and Grayson were in a group with her, and she thanked the gods for it. She didn't really get along with anyone else in the Keep. They either gossiped about why she was here since she didn't have a "gift" like the rest of them or they despised her because, despite it, she managed to still be the Phantoms Keep's most lethal assassin.

Kieryn was the best at sword fighting, but Ash was her fiercest competitor. She wasn't just *The Wraith*, but she was also from Kieryn's home kingdom of Almeria where the Alessians trained. Why she would become a Phantom after being an Alessian warrior made Kieryn curious, but it wasn't her place to speculate. Everyone here had reasons to run away from their past. She did wonder if Ash had known her father, if only briefly. Her father had taught her how to fight like the Alessians even though he refused to permit her to become one. But if she couldn't label herself as one of them, it was the next greatest honor to know she could fight like them.

Kieryn withdrew her Katana, a gift bestowed on her by Ryvers himself on the anniversary of her parents' murders. It was elegant yet simple. When Ryvers had gifted her the sword, it looked as if it was drenched in liquid gold and ignited in flames. The blade had one sharp edge, the other a dull one. *A sword of mercy*. Because of that, Kieryn had named her sword *Makaria,* meaning "blessed death." It glistened in the fiery honey rays of the afternoon sun as her hands closed over the intricate hilt decorated in swirls that closely resembled a burning ember or an eddy of shadows. It was beautiful and a gift Kieryn didn't think she deserved. She never would get used to the feeling that came over her when she held *Makaria*, the way it felt in her hands, as if it was an extension of her. As if the sword knew it had been forged for her hands to one day use, a song sung for her ears only.

She took a step toward Ash, and Ash mirrored her movements. Ashlyn's sword was of the same material, just aged and worn in from her days as an Alessian, the steel glowing like a thundercloud ready to strike.

Gold and silver crossed, signaling the start, and with ease and steady footing, the two assassins merged into what could only be described as a beautiful, choreographed dance. As one lunged, the other parried the blow. They slashed, ducked, and twirled around each other, finding each other's rhythms. Kieryn ducked from the flying blade and quickly lunged to the side, sweeping Ashlyn's leg out from underneath her. Ash went down, but within a second was on one knee, blocking the swing of Kieryn's sword.

"Neat trick," she teased.

"Thought you'd like that move."

With blades still crossed, Ash lifted and kicked Kieryn in the stomach, creating distance between the two. The two lethal women continued their extensive dance with more striking, kicking, and evasion until eventually they started to tire.

"You would've done well with the Alessians. Your father taught you well," Ash said to her in a voice soft with affection and admiration.

Kieryn gave her a weak smile in return. "Thank you." Her throat constricted, feeling like she was swallowing glass as she tried not to think about the memory of her father.

Ash and Kieryn made their way over to the boys on the other side of the Courtyard, where both were firing arrows at their targets silently in competition with the other. There was no true contest; the winner would always be Grayson. Before Grayson was a Phantom, he had come from the Kingdom of Calydan, where he was an elite *Nightraider*, a prestigious dragon rider in the old king's aerial fleet. Where Grayson was coltish with defined muscles due to his aerial training with the Nightraiders, Damien was his opposite. He was brawny. He had broad, wide-set shoulders, and his muscles along his chest and stomach were chiseled from years of training at the Keep and because of his wolf-shifter abilities. His arms were bulky, and when he pulled the arrow tight, the veins in his arms protruded from his skin.

The targets were scattered throughout the Courtyard and looked like ragdolls on sticks blowing in the wind. The closest target was 45 feet away, and the furthest 100 feet. They weren't entirely stable, the slightest breeze and the whole target changed direction. The drills were designed with precision and accuracy in mind. Damien's arrow released from his bow and soared through the air, making its way to its mark, but at the last second missed by a hairsbreadth. He grumbled to himself, clearly agitated.

"Let me show you how it's done, my friend," Grayson taunted him, just as Kieryn and Ash approached.

Grayson stepped up to the line and waited patiently. It was as if he was listening to the wind before he finally made any sudden movements. With the skill of a Nightraider, he released three arrows, one after the other, aimed at the furthest target. Each sliced through the air like liquid before finding its mark: one in the head, one through the neck, and the last a bullseye into the heart. He turned around slowly, a smile that spread ear to ear lingering on his face. He bowed before them and threw a wink their way.

Damien shook his head, annoyed but laughing all the same. "Showoff," he replied.

Grayson turned his eyes to Kieryn and Ash and tilted his head in the direction of the other targets.

"Want to sharpen your archery skills, ladies? Can't say you'll ever outrank me, but I'll let you try."

The corner of Kieryn's lips raised slightly, her eyebrow lifting with amusement before she replied, "Challenge accepted."

The four of them wandered over to the big oak tree by the

base of the mountain, where Grayson picked up a white sack and dumped a dozen apples onto the ground. He approached her and handed her his bow and quiver before making his way back over to the tree once more.

She strapped the quiver to her back, pulled the arrow free, and nocked it.

"Feel the wind, listen to it," he shouted to her. "When you feel the wind die down, let the arrow go. Accuracy is important here. If you don't hit the apple directly in the middle, it will deflect. Got it?"

She nodded. She stood there and waited, calming her breathing. It was one of the first lessons her father taught her when he had given her her first bow at the age of eight.

If you don't control your breathing, your aim will always be off. Inhale, hold, and exhale. Inhale when you take your aim, hold, exhale on the release.

She did as Grayson instructed. She listened to the wind as it danced around her in the midafternoon sun. While the air was full of chill this high up in the peaks, her body never felt the cold. She breathed in and held her position.

Her eyes opened and with a tilt of her chin Grayson tossed the small target in the air, and she breathed out, releasing the arrow. The small thud and scratch of bark told her she had hit her target. Ash cheered in the background, and she smirked over at Grayson.

"That's all you got?"

"That was just the warm-up exercise, my sweet Kier," he said, grinning. "Get ready."

She stepped back to the line and nocked another arrow. She felt the tension building in her back, like muscle memory. Her arms held steady as she pulled the string flush against the curve of her bottom lip. She anchored her thumb on the corner of her mouth, the condensation from her breath coating the string. When she was ready, she dipped her chin subtly to signal Grayson that she was good. Grayson launched three apples into the air, and she fired off her arrows, meeting each target with the sharp pierced tip of her weapon, sending them to be impaled on the oak tree.

Grayson's jaw dropped, the sack of apples hanging limply in his hand. Ash was cheering even more enthusiastically, and Damien was bent over, laughing at Grayson's defeat.

Grayson quickly recovered and graciously accepted the loss.

"Is that the main event?" she asked him. "I thought a Nightraider would've had a more interesting challenge for me to try," she mocked playfully.

Grayson opened his mouth to respond, but Maddox strode over to them and announced that training was done for the day. Grayson jogged over to where she stood and nudged her shoulder, a smile firmly planted on his face, his arm coming around her shoulders.

"I'm impressed, Kier. Now try doing that from the skies with a dragon moving underneath you," he said with a sad grimace.

Kieryn knew he missed flying and she couldn't blame him. If given the opportunity to ride a dragon like a Nightraider, she wouldn't hesitate.

"Don't worry, Grayson, you still hold your title for now," she replied to him, trying to keep the mood light, squeezing his hand gently.

They followed behind the Weapons Master as they made their way back to the Keep, passing the Phantoms' Crest. The crest of Phantoms Keep lay on either side of the stone pillars: Two swords crossed and pierced through a crown, to signify that no king or queen would have more power than the gods and goddesses who now slept soundly in *the Veil*.

All six kingdoms in the realm of Elysium had been granted great power by the gods themselves.

In her home kingdom of Almeria, Cahira, *Goddess of War,* and Irina, *Goddess of Peace,* had gifted them their brutal strength and useful skills for the battlefield. Both were beautiful women and lethal, the perfect pair.

Alene, *the Goddess of the Hunt and Moon,* had gifted her powers of shapeshifting and everything that came with it to the Riyadh Kingdom.

Then there was Lux, *the God of Light and Life,* who had gifted Minas his powerful magical abilities, which varied based on the bloodline.

But the humans eventually got greedy with the powers they were already given, turning some gods to leave them to be cursed as a punishment.

Those in Keres Kingdom, who were gifted by Kano, *The God of the Sea and Sky,* were cursed with damnation when it came to finding love. Beautiful creatures destined to kill their true loves, if they were to find them.

Eliana, *The Goddess of Revenge and Retribution,* placed a curse on Calydan Kingdom ending the line of dragons. After her death, dragons weren't able to reproduce, and when a dragon died in battle, or faded away from age, they were gone, until one day they would eventually become extinct, making the kingdom vulnerable.

And then there was Shade, *The God of Shadow and Death,* who had once gifted Eretum most of his magical abilities, all but his shadows. When he was bested in the war, he cursed the kingdom to a life of living off of blood to recuperate their strength, turning them into monsters.

Despite the powers the kingdoms had inherited from the gods and goddesses that were passed down from generation to generation, it never stopped them from reaching out to their scouts throughout the realm to hire assassins to avoid breaking the treaty that kingdoms had signed hundreds of years ago. If it couldn't be traced back to the kingdom, then no laws were broken.

Due to its location hidden amongst the Elysium Peaks, Phantoms Keep wasn't ruled by any kingdom, and was therefore exempt from signing the treaty. Though it may have been landlocked by three of the kingdoms, Phantoms Keep answered to no king or queen, only the gods. None of the six kingdoms knew the location of Phantoms Keep due to the wards put in place by the gods hundreds of years ago, but the people of Elysium knew that it existed and that the Phantoms had scouts in every kingdom if they needed their service.

While Maddox and her friends made their way back inside the Keep, Kieryn hesitated by the crest, turning towards the towering mountains. It was eerily quiet, even for a late summer afternoon. High up on the cliffside she would normally be able to hear the music of the birds and the howling winds, but it was as if the world had gone silent.

She felt it then, a dark, looming presence crawl over her skin, burrowing itself into her heart. She wasn't scared of this sudden darkness, but rather felt as if it was a long overdue greeting. Although she couldn't see anything, she did notice her shadow cast on the stairs was darker than before. And like the flip of a switch, the world came back to life with the calls of birds and the faint whispering of the wind. The feeling of being watched left her with goosebumps and the hair on the back of her neck raised as she retreated into the safety of the Keep.

THREE

KIERYN FOLLOWED her friends up the spiraling staircase to the top level of the Keep to the Atrium. It was a large room with floor to ceiling glass windows, and a skylight that filled the room with natural light from the afternoon sun. It only reminded Kieryn of being inside a glass house and every time she stepped foot in this room lately, her skin crawled. There were only a few tables set up throughout the room, the rest of the Atrium was clustered with different plants that they used for making poisons, and on the other side of the room was glass cabinetry where ingredients for antidotes were stowed in glass jars. The air had an earthy smell to it and she felt herself start to relax as the sinister feeling she had only a moment before began to diminish.

The moment of tranquility was brief though, when she realized the only empty seat left was next to Kailah Mayfell. *Lovely.* Kailah's pin straight strawberry-blonde hair swung with the pendulum swing of her head as her bright silver-coated eyes met Kieryn's. Kailah's scowl mimicked her own, as Kieryn closed the distance between them and sat down next to her. Her beady eyes never left Kieryn's face.

"Do you have a staring problem, Kailah, or shall I help you by plucking those eyeballs from your face? The *Gods Above* know I want to," she whispered.

"Funny, I was just pondering what spell I can use to liquify your insides," Kailah sniped back.

Mila Thorne turned to them then. She was tall and slim, and a tinge of pink flushed her cheeks. Her skin was a rich, tawny beige much like golden hour in the Himal Desert in the Southern region. Her auburn hair was woven with strands of gold that framed her oval face and her champagne-hued eyes glared at them from over her spectacles.

"As I was saying," Mila continued, her eyes roaming over them and moving through the students. Her tight, dusty rose-colored dress stretched as she walked through the rows of assassins, stopping at Kieryn and Kailah's table.

"Today you will be working with partners. Each group will have a different unlabeled poison in front of you. One of you will drink the poison, while the other is to identify the poison and create the antidote." She peered down at Kieryn. "Kieryn, you will be drinking the poison, Kailah you will be identifying the symptoms and creating the antidote." The Potions Master turned on her heel and gave the same instructions to the other partners scattered throughout the room.

Kieryn let out a heavy sigh as she watched Ash and Grayson go first. Grayson drank the poison disguised inside the goblet of wine and instantaneously started showing symptoms. He started to drool like a rabid animal until just as quickly it stopped. Immediately afterward, he started to puke into the wastebasket next to his feet. Ash sprang into action, feeling for his heartbeat as she watched for any unnatural movements in his eyes. As Grayson continued to release his breakfast into the trash can, Ash raced to the glass cabinetry, filling her arms with the ingredients she needed. Most poisons would take less than a half hour to kill you if not provided with the proper antidote.

Despite the intense situation, Ash stayed calm. Once she had produced the antidote, she spoke her first words in ten minutes.

"Grayson ingested the venom from a Pandirus scorpion from the deserts of Himal. The antivenom I created should relieve him of his symptoms and he should fully recover by dinnertime," Ash instructed. Grayson took the antidote with trembling hands, and Ash held them steady to his lips as she helped him swallow all the contents in the vial. After he had swallowed every drop, Mila smiled softly and confirmed Ashlyn's theory. The color gradually started to return to Grayson's face as he brought the trashcan to his chest, giving it a bear hug. His face came to rest on the lip of the can.

The rest of the class went on like this for another half hour. One person suffered from Monkshood poisoning, otherwise known as wolfsbane. He started to convulse on the dusty ground as his partner struggled to pour the antidote down his throat. Damien's partner, Wesley, had to endure the effects of Bloodroot. Drinking these poisons and correctly identifying them was a cruel and unusual learning experience, but not every person who was here would make it out alive. Luckily, no one died *this* time. Back in Kieryn's third year here, they had to identify poisons in order of least harmless to deadly. One student mixed up his order and his punishment was to drink the one he deemed the harmless poison, he ended up drinking Bloodbane—a deadly and painful poison. He had collapsed onto the ground and before anyone could give him the antidote, he was dead. Finally, it was Kieryn's turn to drink the wine filled with poison.

She calmed her breathing and brought the cup to her lips and took a gulp of the poison. Instantly, Kieryn felt the effects. She shook her head, trying to clear her blurred vision, but to no avail. Her hands came out to the table in front of her, white-knuckling the edge as her body tensed up as she began to feel the poison work its way through her bloodstream, trying to make its home in its new host. The muscles in her throat constricted as she tried to fight the nausea building inside of her. Her hands slipped from the table as they became cold and clammy, and she struggled to remain upright. Everything was in slow motion. She watched helplessly as Kailah walked —*walked*—to the glass case to sort out the ingredients.

Was she moving slowly on purpose?

Her heart pounded in her ears, and the thought of dying brought her back to that night.

The burning smell of wood and flesh. The sounds of steel clashing. The blood-curdling scream of her mother as a sword ripped through her chest. The hot, sticky feeling of blood coating her hands like honey. The loss of life in the man's eyes. The beat of her erratic heart. The stranger with the piercing eyes.

She shook her head to clear the horrid vision. Hallucinations, disorientation, nausea—she knew the second she thought it she had drunk Bloodbane. The same poison that if not administered the antidote quickly… No, she wouldn't allow herself to finish that thought.

How long has it been?

If she had to guess, she had less than two minutes before she'd start to convulse. Everything hurt. Just lifting her head mere inches to see where Kailah was with the antidote took all her strength. Kailah was mixing the ingredients slowly, a small smirk at the edge of her lips.

She was doing this on purpose.

Kieryn looked down at the ingredients and knew Kailah had purposely retrieved the wrong ingredients for the antidote. That antidote would not save her. It would only enhance her symptoms and make it worse. With all the strength she could muster, she leaned over and swiped the ingredients off the table—glass and liquid shattering on the floor.

In a last effort, she locked eyes with Damien and silently signaled him with her eyes, pleading that hopefully he could read her mind, like Grayson seemed to be able to. She took one step towards him, before she started to fall. Damien caught her around the waist and lowered her to the ground.

"Blood … Bane …" Kieryn whimpered. Her body started to twitch in Damien's arms.

She had less than a minute.

Ash sprinted to the glass case, grabbing the antidote vial she needed and dropped to her knees by Damien's side. Kieryn could barely keep still, her eyelids closing involuntarily. She needed that antidote, but she couldn't force her body to respond. She could hear yelling faintly in the background. A panicked Grayson yelled for Damien to hold her mouth open. She felt his calloused hand on her cheek as he pried her mouth open and poured the liquid down her throat. It hit the back of her throat like a tsunami. It was ice cold, as if she had plummeted into Eralan Lake naked in the dead of winter.

She laid there for what felt like hours. She could feel her body drenched in sweat, and she was shivering, the tears that had built up in her eyes running down her cheeks freely. Her vision slowly started to come back as she took in the scene before her. Ashlyn was beside her, praying under her breath. Grayson was now holding her, his breathing hard and heavy. She peered up, her eyes trying to find Damien among the chaos that had ensued. Her eyes found him across the room, as he stared at her, his eyes filled with agony before they turned to a raging inferno once more. He turned back to Kailah, who he had pinned against the wall, his forearm dangerously close to suffocating her.

"Touch her again, Kailah, and I will pull the cold stone you call a heart from your Gods-damned chest. Do not … fucking … test me," he roared into her face. Kailah clawed at Damien's arm as he increased the pressure on her neck. It took three shapeshifters to pry Damien off her. Kailah collapsed to the ground in a fit of choked sobs.

"It was just a joke," she whimpered.

Half the class snickered, clearly entertained by Kailah's theatrics and Kieryn's demise, while others remained too stunned to show emotion. Mila quickly dismissed the class except for the four of them and Kailah. Kieryn painfully stood up, clutching at Ashlyn's arms to steady herself, her balance still shaky from the effects of the poison.

"If you want me dead, you'll have to try harder than that," Kieryn managed to wheeze out.

Kailah was escorted by Mila to medical, but not before Mila told Kieryn and her friends that Ryvers would be hearing about this.

Damien's steady and gentle hand took Kieryn from Ashlyn's arms and led her down the long corridor and spiral staircase to her room.

"Are you sure you don't want to get looked at?" Grayson asked.

She shrugged and said she just wanted to take a long nap. Ash and Grayson were slow to nod but left her alone with Damien. Kieryn ambled over to her bed and sank down onto the edge. She looked up at Damien, but he was struggling to look her in the eye.

"Damien, look at me," she said in a soothing voice.

He lifted his head, his usual bronze eyes now a molten gold and filled with utter despair.

"Kier, I … I'm sorry," he stumbled out.

She looked at him questioningly.

"Why are you sorry? You didn't try to kill me with poison. It's not your fault you have a psychotic witch as an ex." She laughed half-heartedly.

He barely smiled at her attempt to play off what just happened. Instead, he slowly made his way over and dropped to his knees in front of her. His arms wrapped around the sides of her thighs, and he looked deep into her enchanting, green eyes—the color of them was like laying on the floor of the forest looking through the trees into the summer sky.

"I can't bear the thought of losing you," he confessed, dropping his face into her lap.

She eased back onto her bed, pulling him with her. His random confession sent her into an internal spiral of conflicting emotions for him. He crawled forward, settling into her pillows, resting her head on his chest. She listened to the beat of his heart, willing hers to beat in tandem with his, pretending for this moment that he could be hers, and she could be his. His fingers combed her hair, rendering her sluggish and in a state of bliss.

"Rest up, love. I'm right here. You're okay. I'm here," he repeated soothingly into the crown of her hair. She fell asleep wrapped in his warmth before she could muster up a response to his confession.

FOUR

DISCERNING blue eyes the color of forget-me-nots in her mother's garden haunted her nightmares, and she woke up with a jolt. She felt those eyes on her still, like they were woven into her skin. She could never forget those eyes, even now. They tormented her, angered her, confused her. If she ever saw him again, she would drive her dagger hilt-deep into his heart. She didn't care that he had saved her; he destroyed her. If given the chance, she would return the favor tenfold. And this time, she wouldn't miss.

She sat up in bed, squeezing her eyes shut, as she rolled her neck side to side to loosen the kink she had from sleeping on Damien's chest. She looked around her empty bed and found no one beside her. The absence of light from her window told her it was late; she had probably missed dinner.

She stretched trying to shake off the uneasy feeling of those inquisitive eyes watching her from the depths of her mind and the aftereffects of being poisoned. Her stomach rumbled despairingly, just as a knock sounded on her door. Ashlyn walked in carrying a plate of wrapped food. *Thank the Gods.*

"I thought you might be hungry. You missed dinner," she said in greeting. She carried with her the aroma of lemon roasted chicken, garlic potatoes and corn. The smell of the mouth-watering food practically had her drooling and her stomach grumbling in a happy plea.

"Thank you," she mumbled between bites of food.

"How are you feeling?" Ash slouched back into the bed, her chestnut eyes searching Kieryn's for any lingering symptoms.

"I'm fine," she answered. "How did things go over with Ryvers?"

The weight of her sigh said as much. "Ryvers was furious at Kailah's so-called *prank*, and he ordered her to solitary confinement for a week."

Well at least it was something, she thought.

"And Damien?"

"He understood that it was a reflex to protect you, but he is still to face his punishment tomorrow—but neither Ryvers nor Damien will acknowledge what it is. I've never seen him react that way, Kier. Be careful with his heart."

Kieryn gulped down the last of her food, it now felt like stones churning in her stomach.

Ashlyn saw the troubled look on Kieryn's face and reached for her cold, dry hands.

"He'll be okay. He always is. Don't ask him about it though, okay, you know how secretive he is about his punishments with Ryvers."

Kieryn barely managed a nod, before her door swung open with a bang. Two curly heads of hair poked their way in, devilish grins on their faces.

"Oh, this looks like fun," Damien declared teasingly. He rushed the two girls lying in bed and squirmed his way in between the two of them, both his arms coming around Ash and Kier.

"I can get used to this," Damien chuckled.

Kieryn whacked his arm just as Ash said, "As if."

Feeling left out, Grayson nose-dived them, landing hard on top of all three of them in a tangle of limbs as Kieryn let out a snort with her belly laugh.

"Oh. My. God. What was that noise?" Damien teased her, nuzzling his five o'clock shadow into the crook of her neck. He turned his body towards her, brought his hands to the sides of her stomach, and started to tickle her.

"No … please," she wheezed, struggling to breathe in between laughs. "Stop!"

Damien leaned in, his lips touching the tops of Kieryn's cheeks. "I can listen to that sound for a lifetime. It's a good look on you," he whispered into her ear so only she could hear.

Kieryn peered up at him, "What is?"

"Happy," he replied, his golden eyes peering into her own.

Kieryn stared at him wide-eyed. Ever since that afternoon, Damien's whole demeanor towards her had changed. He had always been a smug bastard who was a notorious flirt, but now he was sensitive and sweet. She didn't know how to handle this version of Damien. Her lips parted slightly, a response on the tip of her tongue when Grayson spoke up.

"Hey, I have an idea." Grayson sat cross-legged, his face lighting up like it was Wintersfest.

"Let's head out for drinks down at Exile."

At the mention of Exile, Damien tensed up, his fingers hovering over Kieryn's stomach.

"Exile?" Damien repeated. The look of dread was written all over his face.

"Yeah, man. I need to get out of this place, it's stifling. Plus I think we could all use a distraction after today. Who's in?" he prodded. After a little coaxing, Damien finally agreed, and the guys left to get dressed.

Later, after the girls had changed, they met the guys in the library before heading out to Riyadh Kingdom. In their fifth year at the Keep, and the first year they could accept independent missions, Grayson and Damien had convinced a witch to create a portal to teleport them far distances. They had hidden the portal under a rug in the cooking section of the library.

Nobody was going to look in that section.

"Ladies first," Grayson teased them.

Kieryn made sure her weapons were still strapped to her black leathers before she smiled. "See you on the other side," she said, saluting them as she jumped. Her warm white sweater billowed up to her toned, tan stomach as she dropped. Her golden hair tied back was the last that they saw of her. Ash went next, her brown strapped sandals slowly wading into the portal like she was testing the temperature of the lake. She held her white skirt that rested high on her thigh tightly. Her midnight hair swayed in the phantom wind as she entered the portal, disappearing completely.

Grayson followed Ashlyn with a dramatic flourish, leaving Damien to dwell in his own thoughts in the library. He used to love drinking at Exile, but now it just tasted like regret and nostalgia. But he'd endure, he always did. He'd turn that side of his emotions off and not dwell in the past tonight. He wouldn't think about that night, he promised to himself as he jumped through the portal.

Once Damien had dropped to the ground out of thin air, the four assassins made their way towards Exile. Riyadh Kingdom was nestled in the heart of the western peaks, in the province of Dakar—a lavish mountain town. They passed the town center clock just as it chimed the ninth hour, and a brisk wind picked up and danced between them, making Ash shiver slightly. Grayson sidled up next to her, wrapping his arms around her playfully. Autumn would soon be approaching and Kieryn suspected that with autumn approaching, Dakar and the rest of the kingdom would be covered in a blanket of fresh white snow. Kieryn gazed up at the clock that loomed over them, admiring its beauty and stability. During the battle, much of Riyadh Kingdom was destroyed, but the one thing that remained untouched throughout it all was the clock. Her father had told her about the Battle of the Gods that took place hundreds of years ago.

There were seven Gods: *Alene the Goddess of the Hunt and Moon, Lux the God of Light and Life, Kano the God of the Sea & Sky, Cahira and Irina, twin sisters – The Goddess of War and the Protector of Peace, Eliana the Goddess of Revenge and Retribution and Shade the God of Shadow & Death.* In the beginning, all seven gods lived harmoniously with the humans, giving them powers, and befriending them, some even becoming lovers. The gods ruled together as one entity. Back then Elysium wasn't broken into six different kingdoms, and no king or queen ruled. Some legends say, the humans got greedy and even though they cherished their gifts and powers, they wanted more, so they formed the six kingdoms known today appointing kings and queens to rule. They wanted to be equals to the gods, not their inferiors making sacrifices and worshiping them with celebrations in their honor. Other legends claim the gods became greedy. They wanted more than just human lovers and parties; they wanted unwavering loyalty. Some gods looked at the kings and queens as competition and started to sacrifice their people as sport. The gods fought amongst themselves. Alene, Lux, Cahira, and Irina combined their powers and sacrificed themselves for the humans and brought the other gods behind *the Veil* with them. Only on certain occasions could you feel the remnants of the gods beyond *the Veil*, like The Feast of the Dead. Kieryn had her own theory as to what happened. She believed both sides became greedy and weren't satisfied with what they were given, and it was an all out war started on both sides.

During that time of war, Riyadh Kingdom had suffered a lot of infrastructure damage, but despite the wreckage, the clock remained intact. If there was one thing Kieryn loved about becoming a Phantom for the Guild, it was the magic of traveling to the neighboring kingdoms. It was as if each kingdom had their own unique imprint to bestow on Elysium. Here in Riyadh Kingdom, King Bjorn ruled, a wolf-shifter like Damien. He had fair hair that he preferred to wear long, with light arctic blue eyes to match. History of his raids and wrath traveled throughout the kingdoms, and he was a king to be feared if you crossed him.

As she walked, her combat boots echoed along the cobblestone street that stretched across the center of town. Surrounding them were cafes, restaurants, bookstores, and clothing shops. But the real beauty laid directly in front of them. The picturesque Proteus Mountain rose majestically over the town guarding it.

She glanced over at her friends as Grayson led them through the throngs of people milling about on the streets. She noticed Damien was still rigid in his movements, his lips stretched thin and the look in his eyes portraying pure anxiety. He caught her staring at him, and she saw the small strain of his lips pull up into a half-assed smirk before he reached out and pulled her into his side. His nose turned into the crown of her head and he inhaled deeply, as if trying to ground himself. Kieryn gave him what she hoped was a reassuring squeeze on his side as they finally stopped outside *Loretta's Apothecary Shop*.

The apothecary shop was the color of black garnet, its paint wearing thin from age and weather. Two windows framed the door on both sides, where herbs, soaps, candles, and crystals lined the display case. Grayson pulled open the door, allowing everyone to make their way inside before swiftly closing the door shut behind him. They made their way through the labyrinth of aisles housing the smells of lavender, mint, bergamot, and a potent wave of sage emanated from the incense candle that was lit in the back corner.

Grayson approached the short but stocky older woman at the counter.

"My friends and I are picking up an order. A vial of butterfly serum, lavender and fig oil, and mint leaves."

The woman's beady eyes glazed over them before she stepped out from behind the counter and led them to a glass apothecary cabinet. It was a spacious cabinet, wide and tall enough to fit two people in and housed nothing inside. She opened the door to the cabinet, and Kieryn and Ash stepped inside. The unsightly woman closed the door roughly behind them and with a flick of her wrist, the inside of the cabinet rotated, making the two girls disappear. Damien and Grayson followed in pursuit and with the same flick and unyielding emotion, the cranky witch sent them on their way as well.

FIVE

THE INSIDE of Exile was located beyond the apothecary cabinet, down a flight of cement stairs that led to the basement. Ever since Damien had mentioned to Grayson that this was his usual haunt when he was in Riyadh, Grayson had been fascinated with the *secret entrance* concept and had begged him to bring him there. No matter how many times Grayson had come back to this place, he could never get over the secret entrance. It was a tad melodramatic for Damien.

Occasionally, the assassins would frequent Exile to blow off steam, which is why Grayson had convinced a witch to create them a portal for easier access. Damien was always on edge when they came this close to Riyadh Kingdom. Kieryn walked through the bar, the exposed brick wall looking grungier with each visit. The bar wasn't packed but had a decent number of customers spread out throughout the mahogany wood tables. Raucous laughter made its way over to her ears from the group of people sitting on the wooden stools, the lighting dim and almost intimate.

She made a beeline for the burgundy leather couch over by the pool table, surprised that it was available. Damien and

Grayson strode over to the bar, grabbing them all a round of drinks as the girls settled in.

Kieryn took in the patrons at the bar. A beautiful blonde with pin-straight hair sat perched on one of the barstools, twirling the straw in her bubbly drink and making easy conversation with Grayson as Damien gave the orders to the barkeep. A leopard-shifter sprawled across his chair at the neighboring table, spots covered him head to toe like permanent tattoos. He had his cards in one hand and a glass of beer in the other. It was his laughter she had heard when she first walked in. He slammed his beer on the table just then, at the same time he laid his cards flat on the wooden surface, a sly grin on his face. His hands reached out to the center of the table where he picked up the gold coins in the middle and pocketed them. His opponent, a lion-shifter, had a scowl on his face. Kieryn knew he was a lion-shifter by the looped L symbol on the back of his ear.

While she waited for Damien and Grayson to make their way over with their drinks, she couldn't help but eavesdrop on the shifters' conversation. She caught a few words from the leopard-shifter's mouth about rumors of the exiled prince of Eretum making an appearance in a nearby village.

"The Exiled Prince," the lion-shifter snickered, "more like the bastard child of *The Mad King*. King Elias kicked out that pathetic excuse of an heir a long time ago. He should've stayed in the shadows," he scoffed.

"It's him though, I swear it. My cousin said he razed the entire village to the ground looking for something and he's different now, ay. He said he's a dark one, just like his old man."

Damien approached, carrying with him an amber beer that was already half drained, a foam mustache coating his upper lip. The other glass in his hand he extended out to her, pulling her from the shifter's eerie conversation.

"Bourbon. Neat. For you," he said. She took the drink with a smile as Damien grabbed her elbow and brought her into his side.

"Let's play," he whispered in her ear. She looked over his shoulder at the brown table, ten round balls, all different colors and patterns neatly confined inside a triangle.

"I don't know how to play," she admitted to him sheepishly. She'd never had time growing up.

Damien reached over to the case that housed a cluster of wooden poles, handing Kieryn one, its length resting just under her chin.

"Here, take this. This is called a cue," Damien said, handing her the wooden pole. He came around behind her, bringing his body flush against hers. His arms wrapped around her body, placing his calloused hands over the tops of her smooth ones.

He felt her lean back slightly and if he listened closely, he could have sworn he heard her sigh in contentment. Damien cleared his throat, trying not to think about how great her ass looked in those tight leather pants that were mere inches from his cock. *Fuck, focus.*

"Okay, place your left hand here," he whispered delicately into her ear, his hand guiding hers down the length of the pole. He wondered shamelessly about how good that would feel if that was his cock she was ... *damn*! He cleared his throat. He took her right hand and slid it gently backwards on the cue stick.

"It's all about the angles. The goal is to take the cue and hit the white ball into the cluster of the colored ones until one of them sinks into one of these pockets." He tapped the middle of her back to signal for her to lean forward and aim. Kieryn did as he instructed. She leaned forward, her ass sticking out and rubbing directly on Damien's leg. She heard him inhale sharply, and just to play with him, she moved slightly, rubbing herself on him until she heard a grunt.

He leaned in close, his lips resting easily on the top of her left ear. "Careful, Kieryn. You keep rubbing that delicious ass on me, I will show you exactly what I will do to it later."

Kieryn's body jostled with his sinful intentions, craving the touch of his lips on her skin again. Instead of responding, she eyed her shot and hit the white ball. Ten balls went flying across the wool top, two striped ones sinking into the side pockets. She leaned back and did a little dance, Damien's breath husky and ragged behind her as she felt the bulge in his pants.

She turned to face him as his hands came down on the table boxing her in his space. She rested her chin on the cue as she gazed seductively up at him.

"How did I do, teach?"

The laugh that erupted from Damien's lips was infectious, and it was one of the greatest sounds she ever heard. He didn't often laugh like that, openly and carefree, and she wanted him to do it again.

"Well, your shot was good, I'll give you that, but …" He dropped his head closer to her lips. "It would be wise in the future to not rest the cue on your face."

Kieryn blinked up at him in confusion pulling the wooden cue stick from her face. Damien's hand came up to her chin, swiping his thumb across the blue mark that was left there. Kieryn saw the blue dust coating his thumb, and leaned her face in, laughing into his chest.

"That's embarrassing," she mumbled into his shirt, the smell of Damien lingering in her nose—pine and spring rain. His arms enveloped her and felt intoxicating yet comfortable. She stared into his bronze eyes, the green of his shirt making the gold specks peek through and shine in the light. They were so caught up in the moment, staring at each other that it took three times for Grayson to get their attention.

Grayson whistled. "Hey, lovebirds. Bring it down a notch with the sexual tension, you can cut the air in here with a knife." He smiled widely, clearly pleased with the look of utter shock on Kieryn's face as she stumbled over her words to deny it.

"It's not … we're not … I mean," Kieryn muttered, taking a step toward the couch where Ash and Grayson were lounging lazily with mischievous smiles.

It only made Grayson laugh more. "Kier, baby. We all know you two are hooking up. Don't deny it. Lying doesn't look cute on you."

"But I do," Damien chuckled from behind her, bringing her body against his. His arms circled around her in a bear hug as he kissed her neck happily. His smile left echoes on her skin.

Kieryn let a smile slowly slip as she leaned back into Damien as they rested against the pool table.

"Let's play truth or drink!" Grayson sat up higher on the couch, his shit-eating grin saying he was already one sip from drunk.

Ash pouted up at him from his lap. "Do we have to?"

"Yes, Ash. It is either that or we watch these two"—he pointed over at Damien whispering into Kieryn's ear as she smiled coyly—"have sex on the table." Kieryn scoffed over at him.

"Mmm, that does sound tempting," Damien purred to her.

She playfully shoved at his chest, her body easily melding to the front of his. He sat perched on the edge of the table, Kieryn between his legs. One hand wrapped around his cold beer, his other coming to wrap around her waist possessively. He was making a statement to all in the bar that she was his. But she couldn't help but second-guess her feelings—was she truly his? She'd never belonged to anyone but herself. She was toying with the idea of being Damien's when Grayson's voice broke into her thoughts.

"Ash, you're first," Grayson slurred slightly. "How many people in this room would you be willing to kiss?"

Ash lifted her head and scanned the room, taking in everyone at the bar before she sat up and sank into the couch, sipped guiltily on her martini, and said, "Two," not going into any further detail.

Grayson looked over at Kier, his next victim.

"Kier baby, what sex act are you best at?

Ash nearly choked on her drink. Kieryn cocked her head slightly to the side, amused.

Damien perked up behind her, "I can answer that for you, she's really good at—"

Kieryn turned, shutting him up with a kiss.

"Do not finish that sentence, otherwise you won't be experiencing that ever again," she whispered breathily in his ear, her hand resting right on the bulge in his pants. She turned around and looked over at Grayson. "I'll drink instead."

"Lame!" he hollered. "Come on, Damien, give me something! Where's the craziest place you've had sex?"

The smile that erupted from Damien's face was lethal. He pulled Kieryn in closer, her body still facing him. He looked at her, a daring look in his eyes, as he answered Grayson's question.

"Right here on this table," he said as he lifted and slammed Kieryn down onto the wool surface, his body coming down on top of her, trailing kisses over her neck and her exposed collarbone. His shifter senses were in overdrive as he smelled her arousal at the mere thought of them fucking right here on the table for everyone to watch.

He leaned in close. "So you like the thought of me fucking you with an audience?" His voice was coated in lust and desire. She licked her lips and nodded. "Fuck, baby, what are you doing to me?!" He leaned down to kiss her when his body suddenly went rigid. She barely had time to blink before he pulled her off the table and threw her behind him protectively. His body was a shield from the imminent threat that had just walked into the bar.

A deep, gravelly voice spoke and the entire bar held their breath.

"You have some nerve showing your face around here," the wolf-shifter growled. "You must be stupid and pathetic, because we all know you're not brave. Not anymore."

Kieryn felt his muscles tense under her fingers, his hands balled into fists. She squeezed his arm, trying to reassure him, and the mysterious stranger noticed.

The sneer on his face put her on edge, as she remained by Damien's side. The wolf stepped closer towards them, his eyes roaming up and down Kieryn's body as if she was his next meal.

"Pretty little thing you got yourself there, Damien." Damien let out a growl from the back of his throat. *A warning.* But, the wolf continued, "I couldn't help but overhear your conversation, and I think I'll help myself to a little taste. You won't mind, right, Damien? We can share."

His three friends reached out, grabbing Damien, and pulled him away from her. He thrashed in their hold, trying to tear at their throats, but he was no match for these wolf-shifters. Damien had given up his wolf pack and with it, the strength that emanated within each wolf-shifter when belonging to a pack. "Lay a finger on her, Emmett, and I'll fucking kill you!" he snarled, saliva spilling from his mouth. He had gone feral.

Emmett waved him off like he was some insistent pest and backed Kieryn into the table. "Maybe I'll be nice and even let *you* watch *me* while I bend her over this table and fuck her until she's ruined, screaming my name instead of yours." He chuckled menacingly, staring at Kieryn with hunger in his eyes.

Kieryn didn't balk from his stare. She'd stared death in the eyes and survived, Emmett would be no different. She refused to be intimidated by his tactics of trying to force her into submission. She would not yield to any man. She brazenly lifted her chin, her eyes darkening as her face turned into stone. Her warrior face. His eyes flickered and she could see how bright and golden they were, almost as if they were two blazing suns.

"I wouldn't touch you with a ten-foot pole." Kieryn's snarky response pierced the air. She discreetly looked around her, taking in her surroundings. Emmett's three bodyguards still held back a struggling Damien, and two other shifters had cornered Ash and Grayson and held Grayson captive with two knives on Ashlyn. One at her throat, the other angled towards her back. One move from Grayson, and they would sever Ashlyn's spine. She knew without a doubt, Ash and Grayson could disarm them in less than a minute, but it's why she also knew they wouldn't risk it with her and Damien also in danger.

"I like this one. She's got some fire in her." Emmett's voice exuded superiority as his lips curled upwards ravenously. As he stepped closer to Kieryn, she could see every speck of yellow in his eyes, the stubble on his chin, and smell the whiskey on his breath. He pinned her between his bulky body and the table, their bodies aligning where she could feel him through his pants. He gripped her throat and slammed her down on the hard surface, the balls digging into her back, a pompous smirk on his face. One of the wolf-shifters holding Damien stepped towards them and held her feet down on the table. Emmett's body loomed over hers, boxing her in with his arms. She could see the intricate markings of tattoos on them as they snaked their way upward, disappearing underneath his sleeves, but more than that she could see all the scars they hid underneath.

She thrashed her foot upwards, kicking the shifter in the face as he went to grab her.

"You fucking bitch," the shifter spat at her, blood splattering the floor around him.

"Hold her still, Tyler," Emmett commanded.

When Tyler grabbed her this time, he wasn't as gentle. Kieryn's chest rose, the tops of her breasts spilling out of her sweater with each calculated breath as she weighed her options. Emmett looked at her with a vicious gleam in his eye. With a hand still on her throat and his muscular thighs pinning her arms to her sides, he leaned down and dragged the tip of his tongue from the crease in her breasts to her throat where he bit down. She could hear in the background, a low, deep growl of pure hatred from Damien as he whimpered and begged Emmett to stop. She tuned him out, tuned everything out, and retreated into herself. She felt Emmett slowly lower himself onto her, his thighs shifting just slightly.

"When I'm finished with you, you'll be begging for more of my cock," he sneered. She closed her eyes for a brief pause and then his lips were on hers. She could taste the expensive whiskey as he forced his tongue down her throat, his hands roaming to her skin underneath her sweater. She gave in to the onslaught of his tongue, eliciting a moan from the back of her throat to satisfy him. The growl that vibrated from his throat told her he was pleased she had finally submitted to him. And just when his hand started to slip further south, she bit down hard on his tongue. She tasted the acidity of his blood as it poured down her throat. Emmett reared back, his hand meeting her face as he slammed her head back into the side of the table.

"Cunt!" he screamed at her. Kieryn's eyes went cloudy as the impact threw her off, but her hands were free, and she grabbed Damien's empty glass and slammed it into the side of Emmett's head, shards of glass raining down on them both. Tyler, who was holding her legs, jumped back in surprise, releasing her feet. Just like Maddox taught her, she used her body to buck Emmett off of her. He fell off the table but was quick to his feet, but not as quick as Kieryn and the round-house kick she slammed into his face.

At that moment, Ash and Grayson moved. Grayson threw one of the guys with the knife into the wall before making his way over to help Damien as Ash ducked and swept the other shifter's legs out from underneath him. Kieryn leapt off the table and went to Ash's side, fighting back-to-back with her. She took a kick to the gut before she and Ash had the other shifter pinned and in a chokehold. She could hear the grunts and more glass breaking as she scanned the room for Grayson and Damien. Damien was finally free and attempting to make his way over toward her, just as Emmett blocked his path.

"I wonder how your slut would feel if she knew the truth of what a coward you are! Does she even know about Natalie?" he inquired. Damien stopped dead in his tracks, visibly flinching at the name, a pure mask of devastation and guilt written on his face.

Every wolf-shifter had stilled at the name of Natalie and they let out a collective howl, and Damien's face shattered. He looked over at her then, his eyes a reflection of his past.

"I …" he stammered. But she didn't get to hear what he was going to say, as Emmett shifted into a wolf, his clothes ripping apart, before he barreled into Damien, sending them through the window.

SIX

THE SOUND of shattering glass pierced the air, the slight chill of the night blowing into the bar. Kieryn and her friends raced after Damien and found him struggling to stand upright, blood pouring from wounds on his chest and face, and his shirt clinging to his body by a measly scrap of fabric.

Emmett's wolf form was majestic and beautiful, yet savage and lethal. His coat was such a brilliant shade of silver, you would think the moon had shed its own skin to coat his. The rest of Emmett's pack shifted into their wolf forms and surrounded their alpha, backing him, but didn't make a move. This fight was clearly personal.

Emmett lunged towards Damien, his daggered claws puncturing his skin, blood cascading down his chest, mingling with pieces of shredded skin. Kieryn watched in horror as Emmett ripped Damien to shreds in front of her eyes. *Why won't he shift into his wolf form?* Come to think of it, in the ten years she'd known him, she had never seen him shapeshift. He would be killed with another hit like that. He may be invincible in theory, but he wasn't immortal. He wasn't a god.

She didn't think at that moment, she impulsively rushed

towards Damien's side without giving a second thought for her own safety. She couldn't watch his death, she wouldn't survive it. All she could think about was getting to Damien. She leapt in front of him, shielding his body with hers right as another swipe of Emmett's claws came, piercing her skin. Kieryn's agonized scream ripped through the night air, the back of her sweater tearing apart, exposing the bloodied slash marks across her back. Her knees buckled as she fell into Damien, his weak body barely holding them up.

"What the hell are you doing, Kieryn! Why the fuck would you do that!" he cried out, tears slipping from his bloodshot eyes. His left eye was already swollen shut, and a huge gash ran across it, cementing it over with his blood like armor.

She took in slow, short breaths as she found her voice through the searing pain, "I wasn't going to stand by and watch you get killed."

She heard a rustle behind her as Emmett shifted back into his human form, his full nudity on display without a care. She turned and locked eyes with him, hissing through her teeth.

"This isn't your fight, little girl," Emmett seethed, spit flying from his mouth. "Damien doesn't need anyone to fight his battles for him. He wouldn't need to fight me if he would just shift," Emmett fumed with fire in his voice.

He continued his verbal lashing of Damien. "Tell her Damien! Tell them all why you refuse to shift. Why you refuse to acknowledge your past, the pain of it all, your deadly mistake. Tell her how you got Natalie killed, my little sister!" He choked on the last three words, and wore that emotion on his face for the world to bear witness to. "Tell them how you're too cowardly to face yourself in the mirror, how you walked away from your pack rather than be a man, a leader."

Damien took every assault thrown at him, every word, a stab in his heart as he hung his head in shame at the truth in

Emmett's words. He didn't try to deny it. He was a coward. He knew that, and he fucking hated himself for it.

"Natalie was your wife, your mate and she loved you and her love for you got her killed! She would be ashamed of the person you are today." Emmett closed the distance between them, and his golden eyes bore into Damien's over Kieryn's slumped body. "If you ever show your face again in Riyadh, I'll kill you on sight and anyone else that defends you," Emmett said with conviction, his eyes gliding over to Kieryn on the tail end of his words, and with that he shifted forms again and took off into the woods, the rest of his pack slowly turning and darting after him, the echoes of their howls bouncing off the evergreen forest.

Blood dripped down the side of Damien's face, where he held the makeshift rag to his face. Kieryn's sweater was ripped to shreds and she had torn off a piece and handed it to him wordlessly. He had seen her try not to wince when she raised her hand to give him the scrap of fabric, but he could see it all over her face. She was in pain and in usual Kieryn fashion, she never said a word about it. Just bottled up her emotions, put on a brave face and pretended the pain wasn't knocking the breath right out of her lungs. He could say the same thing about himself. He too bottled up his emotions and shoved them down his throat, hoping the suppression would prevent them from emerging. She was in pain because of *him*. Everyone always seemed to get hurt because of *him*.

Every slice of Emmett's claws on his chest Damien savored, as if his body knew that he deserved to feel that lick of pain. That pain was nothing like the pain that Natalie had endured. The pain Emmett unleashed on Damien was justified in his eyes, although his friends wouldn't agree. If Damien was still alpha he would've ripped a wolf to shreds for what he'd done, and then the rest of the pack would've gotten a hit in, until the wolf was begging for their life. It was what they did for a beta that disobeyed the alpha, that put their pack in danger, that turned their back on the pack. Damien was lucky that they didn't do worse to him tonight.

He stumbled up the dirt path that would lead them back to the witch portal. He dragged behind everyone else, too ashamed to look them in the eye. Damien glanced up, his right eye squinting from underneath his long eyelashes and like a magnet, finding exactly what he couldn't stomach the sight of: Kieryn's shredded back. Ash and Grayson held her as if she was a fragile doll, and he knew she was cringing internally. She didn't like to burden people with her pain, they had that in common. She had pushed them away, but when she faltered in her footing, they had latched onto her like parasites. Ashlyn had attempted to shoulder his weight, until he had given her a look that said *don't you dare*, and she had gone back to aiding Kieryn.

The four gashes were about eight inches long and two inches deep, the blood carving its way across her back like a river. It shone brightly in the night, like a beacon in the shadows that surrounded them. It glared at him, taunting him. *He did this.* The skin on her back peeled backwards, curling like a wave of the ocean, and he looked away, sickened with the thought that he was the reason she was hurting.

He dabbed the blood that had caked his face, the white fabric now saturated in his dark blood.

Ryvers would have his head on a pike when he heard about the fight, and he *would* find out. Damien had at least two broken ribs, if his labored breathing was any indication. Every step was like a knife gliding in and out of his skin repeatedly. He breathed in through the pain, favoring the physical over the bottomless ocean of emotional despair he was in. Luckily for him, the broken ribs and the shattered cheekbone would be healed by morning, thanks to his shapeshifter abilities. He didn't have to shift into his animal form to heal, the healing properties of shapeshifters were in his blood. Although at times, he wished the scars would be permanent. He wanted the bruises to linger longer than one night. He needed that reminder. Kieryn wouldn't get off so easily. She'd be lucky if the scars left behind were minimal and just raised pink, jagged lines. She had a tattoo that ran along her spine. Words in the language of her people, she had told him, but he never asked her what they meant.

He had known Kier for almost half his lifetime and he could tell you how she took her coffee, that she was such a silent sleeper you would think she wasn't breathing, or that she tossed and turned like the waves in a storm but would never admit it was her nightmares waking her. He could tell you she smelled like vanilla and books, a scent that reminded him of happier days at home with his family or the first time he shifted and he ran like he was one with the wind, darting back and forth between the oak trees of his land. She was as beautiful as Alene, *the Goddess of the Hunt & Moon* and a walking nightmare like Eliana, *the Goddess of Revenge & Retribution* all at once. People only knew what she wanted them to know. Her mind was an enigma, a labyrinth of memories and secrets, desires and fears and he spent his days and nights trying to figure her out. She never let anyone in. She never let *him* in, and maybe that was a good thing; he'd only dim her light. His thoughts of Kieryn terrified him for it was the first time he had admitted to himself that he may like her more than he was letting on, and that made him feel guilty as hell. Emmett wasn't lying, Natalie was his mate, and with shapeshifters, that was your person for life. When a mate died, especially in the way Natalie did, you didn't survive the loss. You were a walking shell of yourself, a husk of the person you once used to be.

Damien knew he wouldn't ever love another woman like he did Natalie, but what he felt for Kieryn, well, that was troubling. She made him feel. She gave him hope. And he feared what came next for either of them. He wanted her, but he didn't deserve her. Not if he couldn't love her fully, like she deserved.

They made it through the witch's portal, Damien hesitating over the threshold. He didn't know how he could face his friends. How he could face Kieryn. *What will she think of me when I tell her the truth?* She would probably spit in his face, or bloody up his other eye for what he allowed to happen. He wouldn't blame her if she did.

For a minute, he contemplated leaving the Keep, his friends, his home. But he knew he couldn't make it out on his own, not without them. They were his safe harbor; he was the ship and they anchored him to shore. Where one went, the others followed. He couldn't leave them; they were the closest thing he had to family even though he wasn't worthy of an ounce of their love or loyalty. With his heart shattering into slivers in his hand, he stepped through the black abyss, letting it swallow him up.

They traipsed their way through the halls of the Keep, the sounds of assassins reverberating through the open-air windows. The glow of a fire in the distance luminated the bridgeway, a guiding light. They ended up outside Kieryn's door, where Ashlyn dug out the key from Kieryn's back pocket and slid it into the lock. He followed them inside her room, still mute and lost in his thoughts.

Grayson turned on him quickly, shoving him against the now closed door. His fists gathered in what was left of his t-shirt, the venom in Grayson's eyes lethal.

"What was that back there? You're a fucking shapeshifter, man! A ten-foot wolf for fuck's sake and yet you stood there like ..." he couldn't finish. Damien knew Grayson was angry, he had every right to be. "You put all of us in danger! You put Kieryn in danger!"

Damien stared down at the floor, refusing to answer Grayson's accusations.

Pain built in his cheek as Grayson's hand found its mark.

"Stop being a coward and fucking look at her. Look at her back. Look at the damage you ..."

Damien's anger erupted and he shoved his best friend off him. His chest rose and fell in waves, his nostrils flared as he tried to restrain himself from throttling him.

"You don't fucking think I see that?! You don't think I wish I could've protected her? I should've! Fuck man, I know ..." His words came out choked and he was sobbing. "I failed her. I failed then and I failed now. I can't protect anyone I love, and it eats me up inside. There's nothing but pain and emptiness. I can't stare at her back because if I do, I will go mental.

I'd give anything to take away her pain. I will have to live with seeing those raised scars on her back, while my wounds heal. And trust me, I know that isn't fair. No matter how many times I try to keep the marks on my body, they always heal."

Damien's throat hitched at his confession, and he sank to his knees.

"Enough!" Kieryn yelled. She emerged from her bathroom in a black slip, one of her loose-fitting ones that was open in the back, so she could let her wounds breathe. Ash had to help her pull the sweater off that was plastered to the dry, sticky blood on her back. She quickly tossed that in the garbage, there was no saving that sweater, unfortunately. She had only stepped away for two minutes to rinse the blood off in the shower and came out to a fuming Grayson and a broken man on her bedroom floor.

"Everyone out, please."

Grayson swiveled his face toward her like a pendulum, his eyes bulging from his face as if he wanted to lecture her too.

"I appreciate you guys helping me, but I got it from here. Go! Get some sleep, I want to be with Damien for a bit."

Ash silently nodded and gripped her hand as she made her way across the room, she kissed the top of Damien's head before leaving. She waited outside for Grayson, motioning for him to follow her, but his feet remained frozen.

"Grayson, I'm okay. I have survived worse. It's just a scratch," she laughed lightly, playing off the severity of her injury.

Grayson berated her with a killing look, and something crossed his face that for once Kieryn couldn't read.

"Don't joke about that, Kier. We need to talk about this."

Kieryn nodded. "And we will, but not tonight."

Grayson released a heavy weighted sigh and kissed her on her forehead, his lips lingering on her skin.

"I love you, Kier, you know that. I'll always want to protect you, even if that is from one of us," he whispered for her ears only., although with Damien's keen sense of hearing he prob-ably heard, but showed no sign.

"I know," she said.

And with those parting words, Grayson turned away, but not without looking like he wanted to say something more about the situation, and followed Ash from the room.

Kieryn exhaled what felt like her first breath after the fight had broken out. She looked over at Damien, who still had his face in his hands, kneeling on the floor of her bedroom. She crouched down directly in front of him, covering his hands with hers.

He looked up then, the ghosts of his past swimming in his eyes, drowning him in misery. A broken shell of a man blinked back at her.

"Can you ever forgive me, Kier?"

His head dropped as if weighted down by stone, like he couldn't bear to read her reaction to his question. She gently grabbed his chin and tilted it up until his eyes met hers once more.

She leaned in closer to him, the smell of blood and sweat and the smell of him mingling.

"Believe me when I say this Damien, there is nothing to forgive you for." He started to shake his head to disagree, but she gripped his chin harder. "This"—she pointed toward her back—"is not on you. This wasn't *because* of you. I need you to believe that. You didn't do this to me. I would've jumped in front of you hundreds of times if it meant saving you. I'd do it for any of you."

He didn't respond to her explanation. She grabbed his hands and lifted him from the floor and led him to her shower. He collapsed on the ground, his eyes glazing over, a tear slipping from his eye. She let him cry and she held him stroking his back, murmuring to him that *it was okay, she was here,* just like he had done for her. And while he sat like that, vulnerable on the floor of her shower, she took a wet cloth and wiped the dirt and blood from his body and together they silently watched it all go down the drain as it would wash away their sins.

He didn't know how long her voice had soothed him into a trance, but he knew it was probably hours. He woke up to the brightness of the moon, as it illuminated them on her bedroom floor through her balcony doors and bathed them in a white light. He peered up at Kieryn, her face serene, peaceful. The moon's light wrapped her in a blanket and her skin looked so milky and translucent, he thought she was glowing. *A burning inferno in the darkness.* As if she sensed his wariness, her eyelids fluttered open, like a baby opening its eyes for the first time. Lost, unaware, and disoriented, but content. It was mesmerizing watching her vulnerable like this. When she registered her surroundings and looked down at him, a smile slowly crept on her face and stayed there. But he knew it would be short-lived when he told her the truth. He owed her that much. He owed her *everything*.

As if she could sense the change in the air, she adjusted her body, a bare twitch of her lip the only sign of her revealing the pain in her back.

Damien sat up and reached for the salve, where she had left it earlier. He turned back to her, his hands shaky. She went to grab it from him, as if she was going to do it herself, and the jerky movement broke his stupor.

"Please," he begged. "Let me do this for you."

He uncapped the lid on the tin, taking a generous amount of the healing salve. She nodded mutely, spinning around, and brushing her golden waves to the side. His hands were warm and comforting, like sitting next to a fireplace after a long day out in the cold, winter air.

Gentle, like the fluttering of an eyelash on a cheek, he spread the salve on her burns, the gel the opposite of his hands. It was cooling, a phantom wind on her skin and it felt like her open wounds were sighing in pleasure at the glorious taste of relief.

When Damien was done rubbing the salve into the grooves in her skin, his fingers remained, a faint whisper of a touch. She could hear his beating heart. She stayed silent, not wanting to push him. He had to do this on his time.

"Kieryn," he said with dread in his voice. "I owe you the

truth about what happened tonight. Everything Emmett claimed I was and did was true, I don't deny that."

His fingers stilled on her shoulder. His heart skipped a beat. He took a long, deep breath.

"It's time I tell you about my late wife, Natalie, and how a reckless mistake I made got her killed."

And so, he began to unravel the truth, his skeletons plummeting from the pits of his mind for her to bear witness to. He only hoped she wouldn't look at him differently. Maybe then he could start to forgive himself.

SEVEN

DAMIEN'S HAND fell limply to his lap, leaning all of his weight to rest on Kieryn's bed, as if the truth would pull him down through the floorboards. He never told anyone the truth about that night. Even Ryvers only knew to an extent, no more than the basic facts of what happened.

Kieryn faced him now, her legs folded under her curvy figure, looking at him intently. She reached out her hand and squeezed his leg lightly, a reassuring gesture. He took a deep inhale, and as he let it out he brought her back to the night he tried so hard to forget.

"I was the youngest alpha my pack had in centuries. My father was alpha, until he was fatally wounded in combat and then I became alpha shortly afterward at the age of fifteen. I had no idea what I was doing at the time. I was forced to grow up sooner than I wanted to. No longer could I be the wild teenager who partied in the woods with the other locals and shifters or have pointless hookups. I had to be a leader, which meant I had to start acting like one. For a while, my younger self resented my father for dying in battle. I didn't want to be alpha, at least not at first. I thought I had a few more years of messing around before following in my father's footsteps. My father was a legend in my pack, and I knew I had to continue his legacy and live up to those standards that my pack expected out of me."

Damien's voice trailed off into the dead of night in Kieryn's room. He still didn't make eye contact with her. He hadn't even told her the worst part, yet his heart was already on a sprint to rip through his chest. He could feel a pain in his head, a warning that his headaches were coming back.

"I was alpha for only six months, when during one of our meetings the Elders suggested an alliance with one of the other wolf packs. Our pack was still one of the strongest in the Kingdom, but our numbers were dwindling, and the Elders deemed it necessary to marry into another pack for power and territory purposes."

Damien's eyes glazed over, a look of loss in his eyes as he remembered her.

"I was livid that night. The thought of being forced into a marriage that I didn't want. The fact that I was alpha, and yet I still had no choice in the matter unraveled me. I shifted and ran through the warm summer night. I didn't stop until I reached the edge of a lake. That's where I first saw Natalie. I was mesmerized watching her float there in the moonlight. Her skin glowed, and I remembered thinking to myself she was the most beautiful woman I had ever seen."

He had shifted and waded into the refreshing lake water, making enough noise so that she would be aware she wasn't alone anymore.

Her back was still turned to him, her head tilted up to gaze at the canopy of stars above her when she spoke aloud to him.

"Are you going to continue to stand there like a creep, or are you going to join me, Damien?"

He treaded water as his name fell from her lips. She said his name so sweetly, like honey. Her voice was like a siren's song. He floated over to where she was, the water coming to rest peacefully above her breasts so that her bare shoulders were the only thing visible. He stared at her from the side, noticing the scar on her left shoulder, and a constellation of freckles gracing her back. She looked so serene under the moon's radiance.

"You know who I am?" Damien asked.

She had turned to him then and he was impaled instantly by her beauty. She was an angel in human form. The moon's lover. Her hair glistened in the water, a bright white with hues of gray, her eyes a stunning ice blue. Her tongue darted out to catch a drop of water falling down over her lips, and his eyes followed. He felt the urge to lean in and rub his thumb across those lips of hers. He wondered if they would feel as soft as a rose's petal. If they would taste as sweet as honeydew.

"Of course I know who you are. You're to be my husband, are you not?"

He was so enchanted by her beauty, he almost hadn't heard the last thing out of her mouth. He forgot how to breathe. *This was my betrothed?* He expected literally anything else, but the *Gods* must have been looking down on him, because looking at her, he could only think that she shone brighter than the moon itself. She was beautiful in every way, and he wanted to trace the constellations on her back with his fingertips. He wanted to know the noises she would make if he kissed her scar. Would she moan at the contact? Would she shiver at his caress? Would she get goosebumps? He wanted to know every sound she would make, and he wanted to be the one that extracted it from her lips.

"I … you … you weren't what I was expecting," he said, stumbling over his words. Gods, is this how he was going to react to his future wife every time he talked to her? He was usually a lot smoother than this, but her very presence made his tongue feel swollen, like it tied itself into a knot, choking on his attempts to string together a sentence.

She examined him fully then. She turned her body to face him, the water sloshing in her wake. Damien kept his eyes pinned on hers, not daring to look down at her milky skin on display. She was confident in her skin, most shifters were, but on her it was devastating.

"And what did you expect from a wife that is forced to marry you despite her wishes? Did you expect that I would just keep your bed warm at night and cook and clean for you during the day? Did you expect your future wife to fall at your feet because you're the big bad alpha? Because if so, Damien"—she had a bite this time when she said his name—"you are sadly mistaken and a fool," she scolded angrily.

"She was feisty and she gave it to me straight. No sugar-coating, no barriers, and it was the first thing I fell in love with," Damien rattled out loud to Kieryn, smiling back on the memory, before he forced himself into it again.

"Actually, my darling wife, I do expect those things from you. I expect the bed to be warm, because you'll be sleeping in it, just sleeping," he reiterated, catching the look she threw his way. "I don't expect anything else in that regard, but just know I'd never force intimacy on you, unless I hear the request spill from your lips. I do expect you to cook, not for me though. I can handle myself and my cooking is superior, but I expect you to eat and to be healthy. As for cleaning, something tells me I will be the one cleaning up after you."

She scoffed at that, raising her chin slightly.

"And as for the kneeling at my feet, that is a whole different conversation for another time," Damien said slyly. "I do not expect anything from this marriage, other than the fact that this is to solidify both our pack's strength and power. I do expect open communication and at least a friend from the marriage though, even if that is all we amount to, but …" he swam closer to her and gently cupped her face in his hand, "I will not force anything from my wife. You will have full rein, I just expect loyalty and I will do the same for you. There is only you, no one else. I don't *want* anyone else."

Damien's eyes locked with hers and waited, a game as to who would blink first. He won. She searched his eyes, finding the truth in the weight of his words. She leaned into his touch, putting her small hand over his.

"Well then, hello, husband, I'm Natalie. It's nice to officially meet you," she said with a mischievous grin. "I think we will get along just fine."

Damien got lost in his memory of her. A time where they were nothing but two teenagers falling in love in tough circumstances. But, to him, Natalie was the smell of cinnamon and fresh baked pies, running through the forest at dawn, belly laughs and butterfly kisses, not an alliance.

"We fell in love over time, slowly and then one day we knew we set each other's souls on fire, she was my *mate*. She was the light in the darkness, my anchor—a lifeline when I strayed too far.

"About three years into me being alpha, our pack's century-long feud with another pack came to light. They were infringing into our territory and slaughtering villages—torching them and doing unspeakable, unfathomable things to the women and children. My right to be alpha was in question, and so I led the charge to their front door. We attacked when they were vulnerable. It was my call to make and I chose to retaliate for everything they had done to our people. My mistake that day was not killing off that entire line of wolves when I had the chance. My retaliation just fueled the fire for them to burn down my world. They lit the match, but I dropped it.

"The next day, I was away for meetings about increasing security around our borders, when Emmett, my second at the time, came barreling through the thick layer of trees. He was wounded, and when he shifted he was in bad shape."

"Arlo and the Shadow Crescents are in Basalto, he ... they've obliterated the village, Damien. Everyone is dead. Natalie ..."

"My heart ceased to exist at that moment. Seeing the look of devastation in Emmett's eyes as he said his sister's name paralyzed me to the core. Natalie was there, and I could feel this hollowness start to spread throughout my body. That invisible thread that tethered me to her, I couldn't feel its presence anymore and I *ran*. Emmet's voice of, *"Everyone is dead "* a constant echo in my head. My heart trembled with the more ground I covered. All I kept thinking was *please be alive.*`

A tear escaped and Damien allowed it to slip down his cheek.

"I smelled the rotting bodies and smoke before I saw it," he started to tell Kieryn, "The village was coated in blood, ash, and body parts. They ripped them to shreds, and left no one as a witness. I couldn't look any closer at my pack that laid dead at my feet. I couldn't. I raced to my front door to find it wide open and a message for me written in Natalie's blood ..."

He started to hyperventilate, sweat pouring down his face, his shirt soaked through. He felt the warmth of Kieryn's touch on his skin, but it was white noise. The flashbacks were overwhelming. He spent endless nights in fitful sleeps, never really sleeping for fear of seeing that day on a loop. His obsessive thoughts consumed him and he tortured himself with different scenarios of what he could've done differently. But it never changed the outcome, Natalie was still dead.

When he found the strength to speak again, his voice was barely above a whisper.

"Our house was painted in her blood. I found her lying naked on the floor, the evidence of what they … what they did to her on display for me to see. They tortured her for information, but she never broke. She never sold me out even when she was dying. She saw death on her doorstep, and she went out swinging *for* me. She died *because* of me. She died without my voice in her ear, the last touch wasn't one of love by my hand, the last face she saw wasn't one of adoration. And Arlo made her suffer the most. She deserved better."

Damien had let out an inhuman scream that echoed throughout the kingdom. An agonizing howl ripped from his chest as he sat there rocking Natalie's lifeless body back and forth, her blood staining his skin. His wife, the love of his life, his mate.

"Emmett found me hours later, still holding her, my head bent over her body."

Emmett wobbled his way over to Damien, his body still in the process of healing his injuries, and kneeled next to his baby sister, breathing deeply through his nose, trying to hold it together. Emmett reached out his hand and rested it on Damien's shoulder.

"Natalie is gone, D. We need to regroup and figure out what we do next. None of their deaths will be in vain, I promise you, but you have to be the alpha now. Not Damien, not her husband—alpha. Everyone from around the borders are here to stand by you and back you in whatever you decide, but they need a command from you."

Damien blinked through the haze. He heard Emmett's words, but they sounded muffled. He knew he had to act, this couldn't go unpunished. Arlo wanted a war, he would get one. Damien would surely end this fight.

Damien laid Natalie gently on the floor of their cabin. He reached up, removing his shirt and laid it over her body. He didn't want her body on display for anyone to see. He reached over her, closing her eyelids, memorizing those big beautiful blue eyes. He kissed her lips one last time and whispered into her ear, "Until we meet again, my love." And then he stood up slowly, robotically. With a deadly gaze and a switch of his emotions, he voiced the command that would destroy him, "No one makes it out alive. I want everyone dead … everyone, Emmett! I know that goes against our personal code, but we can't have anyone retaliating."

"What are you saying, Damien…" Emmett prodded. He knew exactly what Damien commanded of him and his face said everything.

Disagreement. Disgust.

Damien felt those things too, but it had to be done. Damien was alpha, not Emmett.

"I want the Shadow Crescents wiped from the face of this realm. Their line will die with them—everyone, Emmett. And I do mean everyone. We can't be looking over our shoulders. No prisoners! Leave Arlo for me. I will deal with him personally."

Emmett hesitated on the threshold.

"Think about this, Damien, they have children, babies …"

"Your alpha gave you a command, second! I want them extinct, *erased*. Am I fucking clear?!"

Damien growled viciously. Emmett whimpered in response, his head falling down in a bow, and he slipped out into the night to pass along the command. Howls rippled through the air, until they faded through the trees, leaving Damien alone with his demons.

"I followed my pack, letting them do the dirty work I couldn't bring myself to do because I was a coward. I had a one-track mind that night, and it was revenge for Natalie. My one and only target was Arlo. And I got it. Slowly and painfully. I made him watch as his own pack, every last member, was slaughtered—torn to pieces, burned to death, skinned alive. I told my pack to be creative. They had no problem with that. The women and children were a different story and I can see the haunted looks in my pack's eyes. We made their deaths as quick and painless as we possibly could, but I could barely even stomach the scene. A lot of my pack members had to disassociate, otherwise they couldn't live with themselves. Some couldn't and ended their own lives months later. I live with that regret too.

I took my rage out on Arlo. I never shifted after I saw Natalie. I couldn't. Wolves feel emotions ten-fold when they shift and I knew if I shifted into my wolf form, I would feel that night all over again as if I was reliving it. The pain I feel now, that's nothing compared to what I would feel in my wolf form. And who wants an alpha who refuses to shift? So, I made Emmett alpha and I left my pack behind, no goodbye and no explanation."

Kieryn remained silent the entire time Damien slipped into his old skin from the past. She felt his pain down to her bones. She knew what he was going through. The survivor's guilt, the anxiety, the agony and heartbreak of not being able to save the one you loved. She knew that pain intimately.

Damien looked up at her through bloodshot eyes, his hands twitching in his lap.

"I had as much blood on my hands as Arlo. I'm just as bad as he is, if not worse. I've lived with that choice for ten years, but it wasn't just revenge for Natalie, I was avenging my entire pack. I was preventing another war from rising. I struggled with my morals then and I still do now. When I close my eyes at night, I don't just see Natalie laying there, I see my neighbors legs strewn across the town square, a member of my pack's head spiked through the wooden fence, and a young girl's skin completely torn from her flesh. I see all of their faces, I know all of their names by heart. But, it is not their faces that haunt me the most—it's the bloodline of wolves I erased into nothing. It's their faces that haunt my sleep. I was in denial for a while. I bargained with the *Gods*, hoping they'd hear my prayers, begging to bring back Natalie, take me in her place instead. I deserved it, after what I did. But they never listened. They never do."

Kieryn spoke up, her voice strained from not speaking.

"You are not alone, Damien. You're allowed to grieve for her, for your family and for the innocent, and for yourself. A part of you died with her that night too. You allowed your grief to swallow you whole for all of those years, and now you need to fight back. Fight for your life now. Natalie sounds like a wonderful woman, and I'm sure she'd be devastated to know how you're beating yourself up for her death. You didn't kill her, Damien! Arlo did. You were lucky in the fact that you found a love so pure, so selfless. Natalie didn't die in vain, even if you'd never got revenge. She died *for* love, not because of who she fell in love with. That's admirable."

Kieryn went to him then, settling in Damien's lap. Her legs wrapped around his hips. She kissed his forehead, his nose, his lips, in sweet soft kisses.

"You have to accept the past for what it is. You can't change it. All you can do is find a way to cope with the pain living in your heart and find the things that make you happy. Remind yourself of that happiness, because you do deserve to be happy again. You deserve to live and for the right reasons. You have to allow yourself to forgive yourself, Damien."

He stared up at her, a look of understanding, not pity, shining in her forest-green eyes. Forgiveness for his past but also for tonight's events was written on her face. He made a sound between a whimper and a strangled sob and his arms wrapped around her small frame, burying his face in her neck.

"You are the light in my life now, Kieryn. Please don't leave me in the dark. I can't go back there again, I won't survive."

"I won't," she promised him.

Kieryn gripped him harder, her own tears slipping down to mix with his as they sat on her bedroom floor, two broken assassins trying to fix each other with bandages and promises.

EIGHT

KIERYN WOKE up in her bed to the morning sun coating her in its warmth. Wait, not the sun, Damien's body. Their limbs were tangled together under the sheets, his arm wrapped around her waist protectively. His light snores moved the wisps of her hair on the back of her neck. She didn't remember falling asleep last night, but for the first time in years, she slept soundly. No nightmares. Last night came back to her in waves: Exile, her scarred back, Damien's confession. She slowly lifted Damien's hand off and made her way to the edge of the bed. She felt Damien shift on the mattress behind her.

"Good morning, love." His voice was raspy as he slowly woke. She turned to look over at him, his hair disheveled and sticking out in different directions. His eyes were still bloodshot and red-rimmed from opening up his wounds last night, and bags sat heavily under his eyes.

"We should get going, breakfast will be over soon," Kieryn replied. She felt scattered this morning, not used to waking up to a man in her bed, especially Damien. They never stayed the night with each other, and she didn't know how to go about it, let alone how to act after the fact.

Without a backwards glance, she headed to her bathroom to change clothes. When she emerged some time after, Damien was already dressed and waiting, a strange look flitting across his face.

Damien was about to speak when there was a knock at the door. She walked over, pulling the door open to find an assassin she didn't know well standing outside. She thought for a moment, trying to remember the girl's name. She believed it was Elena.

"Ryvers needs to see you both right away in his office," Elena said and then quickly ambled down the hall and out of sight. Kieryn watched her leave, and as she was about to close the door, she saw Ash and Grayson walking toward her from the opposite side of the hall.

"I assume you got the same message from Ryvers?" Grayson questioned.

She nodded.

"Do you think this is about what happened last night?" Ashlyn voiced.

"Who knows. But let's not keep him waiting."

Damien came up behind her then, his hand brushing her hip as he closed the door silently behind them. His expression weary as he faced Ashlyn and Grayson in the hall.

"I'm sorry about last night," he croaked out, his eyes lifting to meet theirs.

Grayson grunted and turned down the hall, but Ash gave his arm a little squeeze and they followed after Grayson to Ryver's office.

The four assassins made their way inside The King of Phantoms' office. Ryvers sat regally behind his oak desk, a stern look on his face.

"Sit," he demanded as they entered. "Reports came in last night of you four entering Riyadh Kingdom and getting into a bar fight with one of the alphas. Explain yourselves." His voice was deep and authoritative. His bronze hair shimmered in the golden light pouring from his floor to ceiling windows, the light making his jaw look more defined. He had sharp facial features, and his pale-blue eyes radiated displeasure at the assassins before him.

Damien spoke up.

"I ran into Emmett, a member of my old pack last night. Words were exchanged and I let him get to me. I didn't think, I just reacted and I attacked first. It was my fault, sir." A lie to protect the others from punishment.

Ryvers let out an aggravated sigh, shaking his head in disappointment.

"We will discuss that later, Damien."

Kieryn side-eyed Damien, watching a lump form in his throat as a look of dread crossed his face. Though Ryvers was a fair and understanding man, no one wanted to be on the bad side of his punishments.

The King of Phantoms continued, "I called the four of you in here because I need my best assassins for this new job. It came late in the night from one of my scouts."

The assassins sat taller in their seats, curious as to what the mission would entail.

"I need the four of you to attend King Luc's masquerade ball in two day's time," he ordered, throwing four intricately decorated invitations onto the desk.

Kieryn reached forward, picking one up and looking over the details. The front of the golden envelope featured beautiful calligraphy, spelling out *An Enchanted Affair.* She turned the envelope over to find the sealed bronze wax of Minas's emblem —a sun on fire, a phoenix with its wings spread out in front. She delicately slipped her finger under the wax and lifted, pulling the invitation out.

The invitation itself read,

You are cordially invited to attend King Luc's An Enchanting Affair—a masquerade ball.

Kieryn read over the details, the rest of the assassins already tearing through their invitations as well.

"We're actually attending the ball this time?" Kieryn asked.

Ryvers glanced her way and nodded.

"Yes. You will each have different roles to play, your attire has already been picked out, and I have a few attendants already packing your bags as we speak for a few days. You leave by midmorning today."

Ryvers sat back in his chair and continued.

"The scout has told me this person would like to remain anonymous, but that he has it on good authority that there will be an attack on the masquerade ball. They didn't say how, just that there will be one. They also passed on the guest list, blueprints of King Luc's old residence, and the security patrol for that night."

He handed over the papers to Kieryn. Her eyes skimmed the papers, the other assassins reading over her shoulder.

"Ash and Grayson, I will need you to make your way to the rooftop where there should be ten guards. These guards have a full view of the ball below, take them out quietly."

He looked over at Damien and Kieryn.

"And you two," he started. "I need you to blend in this time. Socialize. Keep your ears and eyes open. Study the guest list and know who could possibly be a threat, and get rid of them discreetly." He sucked in a breath. "There will be lots of big names there. Not only will the King of Minas be there, but he has extended invitations out to all the monarchs in Elysium. If this attack happens, it would be catastrophic."

Kieryn nodded, an uneasy feeling forming in her stomach about this mission. Something didn't add up to her, and she was suspicious about who this contact was and what his or her endgame was. Usually missions required their own research and took time to plan out, and Ryvers was taking the word of some stranger and going off of information they hadn't confirmed, nor could they on such short notice. It seemed off.

The assassins stood and made for the door.

"Not you, Damien. We need to discuss a few things," the King of Phantoms instructed. "The rest of you may go, grab some breakfast—it's a long journey. You can wait for him by the carriage."

Kieryn looked at Damien, giving his hand a small squeeze as the rest of them exited Ryvers' office and headed to the Hall before they took off on their journey. The last image Kieryn saw was Damien's rigid body, fear paralyzing him in the doorframe.

NINE

THE DENSE FOG cloaked their carriage in an eerie light, the sun's journey settling over the mountains. Kieryn couldn't help but think that today's weather would be a promise as to what awaited them out there. As soon as Ryvers had given them their mission, she had a peculiar feeling that something was off. The Keep's carriage wasn't anything fancy, like the ruling six kingdoms were. It had no recognizable symbol or intricate markings. The Keep used a commoner horse-carriage to blend in with the townsfolk. Kieryn made her way to the carriage, Ashlyn sauntering up to her, looping her arm through hers. They walked in silence for a while before Ash asked, "How are you feeling today?"

Kieryn made a slight shrug with her shoulders, the ointment only a conductor for speeding along the healing process, but doing nothing to obscure the pain she still felt. Any big movement would stretch her skin to a point of excruciating pain that felt like the alpha that attacked her was digging his claws into her back and peeling the layers of skin off her body.

"I'll manage," she replied, not wanting to divulge any more. After Damien's confession about his past last night, she understood better why he refused to turn in front of Emmett. It was guilt and shame that held him prisoner, and Emmett knew that and preyed on that weakness of his. She was proud of Damien for having the courage to tell her his trauma. She knew it was a difficult moment for him to dredge up his past to her, knowing it would paint him in a bad light, but she knew from experience that even telling one person your story took tremendous weight off your shoulder. She knew the pain he suffered from, and he had a long way to go to healing and finding forgiveness. She would know, she was still trying to find hers.

Ash took Kieryn's muteness as a sign she didn't want to talk about last night anymore and changed the subject.

"Despite the reason behind our mission, I am excited that we get to dress up in extravagant ball gowns and attend King Luc's celebration," Ash said with a twinkle in her eye. It was a rare occasion that they got to attend these elaborate parties that were reserved for the higher classes of the kingdoms. They were usually on the outskirts of the celebrations, watching from the outside waiting for their target to leave, or they were sneaking in through underground tunnels with a quick in and out mindset. They didn't get to walk through the front doors playing dress up.

"That makes two of us. I am curious as to how the elite spend their nights celebrating. Time to partake in some debauchery, wouldn't you say?" she replied mischievously.

The two girls shared a secret smile before catching up to Grayson who awaited them outside the carriage doors. The tension was thick in the air, Grayson not ready to forgive Damien's actions as quickly as Kieryn.

"Your chariot awaits, miladies," Grayson stated with a devilish smile, opening the door for them. Ash politely chuckled, placing her hand delicately in his bear-like hands and making her way inside. Kieryn took her time ascending the stairs, careful not to cause herself any more pain. She saw out of the corner of her eye that Damien was jogging over, his eyes trained on the ground as if he found the dirt mesmerizing. Grayson glanced over at him and gave him a look of death as if he fantasized all night how he would kill him. Kieryn locked eyes with Grayson and slightly shook her head, signaling him to drop it. Grayson mumbled under his breath before hopping in after Kieryn, leaving Damien the last one to enter. He took a seat next to Ash, with Grayson and Kieryn facing him.

Shortly after the door was closed, the two horses took off, the carriage jolting over the terrain leading down the mountain. Even after a decade of being an assassin, Kieryn was still enchanted by the magic of the Keep and the surrounding kingdoms. Their carriage was spelled by a witch informant of theirs to travel without a person directing the horses, they just knew the path they were to take. Kieryn drowned out the conversation between Ash and Grayson about what the party would entail and peered out the window, watching the trees blur past. She saw Eralan Lake glistening in the distance, a feeling of unease coursing through her body from memories of that night. She fell asleep, her head resting on the window while piercing blue eyes stared back at her from the reflection in the glass. She wasn't sure whether it was a trick of her imagination or a memory.

Kieryn startled awake to a roaring thud and the snorting and whinnying of their horses. She immediately drew her knife sheathed to her thigh on the outside of her leather pants and stood to a crouching position. She looked around and didn't notice any movement outside the carriage. She looked to her friends, who all had some form of weapon drawn and faces masked with calculation and determination. She signaled to the boys to exit from the back while her and Ash would exit from the side. They nodded in agreement, not one uttering a word. Kieryn opened the door softly, and dropped to the ground, avoiding the squeak in the footboard. Ash followed closely behind her, the two covering each other's backs as they circled to the front where the horses were shaking their heads and pawing the ground. She scoped out the woods, listening intently for any rustling of footsteps, but heard nothing. If there had been an attacker, they weren't there anymore. The boys circled the other side of the carriage concluding the same; there was no one out here. Kieryn reached up behind one of the horse's ears, scratching slowly and delicately trying to calm Whiskey down, before moving on to do the same to Duchess.

"I found the problem," Damien called from the rear of the carriage. "The axle broke off the carriage, causing the back wheel to bend and break off."

Grayson bent down examining the issue, as if he had to confirm Damien's suspicions.

"Damien is right, the axle has snapped in half."

Ash stepped up towards the horses, surveying the area, looking for any markers as to where they were.

"If I'm not mistaken there is an inn a few miles up the road. We can get a room for the night and see if anyone can come back tomorrow morning to fix our carriage," she suggested.

Kieryn nodded her agreement.

"Let's unhook the horses from the carriage and grab our bags and weapons from the cart, and then drag it off to the side," Kieryn replied, already starting to untie Whiskey and Duchess. The assassins made quick work of unloading their bags and saddling up the two horses to continue along.

"You're with me," Grayson said to Kieryn as he pulled himself up onto Whiskey.

Damien gave a grunt in response to Grayson's command, but otherwise said nothing. Kieryn looked over at Ash who just shrugged and made her way to Duchess, putting her foot in the stirrup and swinging her leg over, situating herself in front of Damien. With a shake of her head, Kieryn climbed up Whiskey, careful not to jostle her wound. They traveled side by side, but with some distance between them, Ash mentioning sporadically that they were getting closer to the inn as dusk neared the horizon.

Grayson peered down at Kieryn, taking in the slight twitch of her mouth as if she was biting back pain.

"You forgive him too easily," Grayson commented, his voice low so only Kieryn could hear. Kieryn remained silent, but Grayson wasn't finished. "He put you in danger, Kieryn," he said angrily. "And you're sitting here in pain acting so nonchalant about the fact that you have a gaping wound in your back. You don't heal like we do, Kieryn. You don't have to pretend like you are okay, I know you're in pain." Grayson body slumped in defeat at his words. "You don't always have to be the protector of others, especially him."

"I appreciate you looking out for me, Grayson, I do. You've been my defender since that first day, but there is more to what happened that night. There's more to Damien's story, but it is not my story to tell. But, I understand the *why* of Damien's actions. I jumped in front of him, though, he didn't put me in danger, I did. And I'd do it for you as well. I forgave him, but please do me a favor and go easy on him. He's already distraught as it is from the incident, and trust me when I say he's nowhere close to forgiving himself," she managed to answer despite the pain in her back, the material of her shirt scraping her skin, putting her in agony.

Grayson didn't answer, but after a minute of silence, he acquiesced to her request with a nod. The rest of the ride was in silence, and to take Kieryn's mind off the pain, she took in the view before her. The evergreen trees extended high into the sky, and in the distance she heard the distinct sound of a river. She took a deep breath in, inhaling the fresh scent of pine and the faint whiff of rain.

Ashlyn's cry broke her out of her reverie.

"There it is!"

Kieryn followed Ashlyn's direction, and there in the distance she could faintly make out the small ragged wooden sign that read *Kismet Inn and Tavern.*

"An inn devoted to fate, this should be fun," Kieryn mumbled under her breath.

The assassins approached the inn and tethered their horses to the post outside, making their way inside. To her surprise, the Kismet Inn was surprisingly clean and warm, yet old-fashioned in a way that made her feel at ease, like she was coming home.

Ashlyn headed over to the desk where a lady with jet-black hair had it wrapped tightly upon her head and dark makeup greeted them with a playful smile.

"Hi, our carriage broke down a little ways down the road. We were hoping to get two rooms for the night while we have our carriage tended to in the morning. How much will it be for the rooms?" Ashlyn asked the eccentric woman.

"Your money's no good here, my dear. I take payment in tarot readings."

The assassins exchanged a look of confusion.

Ashlyn cleared her throat. "Tarot readings?"

The woman chuckled. "Each of you will do a tarot reading. You simply shuffle the deck and pick out one card. This card holds great meaning to your life and what shall come," she said matter-of-factly.

"What the hell! Why not? Sure, yeah. I'll go first," Grayson said enthusiastically. "The sooner we do this, the quicker we can start drinking," he mumbled to Kieryn and Damien, passing by Ashlyn and taking a seat at the desk. He sat down, legs spread and arms wide on the table, his entire mood indicating that he thought this was some entertaining gimmick.

The raven-haired witch took the seat beside her and placed the deck of cards in front of Grayson. She lifted her hands, words slipping from her mouth of an unfamiliar tongue. A sheer film surrounded them.

"Shuffle the cards, my dear child, and when you're done, lay them flat on the table face-down and spread them out. Once you've done that, pick one card that you feel speaks to you," she instructed.

Grayson made a show of shuffling the cards, a teasing smile plastered to his face, his eyebrows raised as if this was the highlight of his day. After he shuffled the deck and laid out the cards, he selected a card closest to the middle directly in front of him and turned it upright.

"The Fool in its upright position. Interesting card indeed, my child."

"What does the Fool mean?

"In its upright position, the Fool represents new beginnings. You will embark on a journey that you and only you alone can endure. But do not be frightened by the destination, as you will soon discover that what awaits you is what you've been looking for. Be bold and take risks when you find what it is you've been seeking. You may fear rejection, but that is where you need to be courageous with your words, as you'd be surprised by the answer you may find."

The seer took Grayson's hand in hers and closed her eyes.

"You sought adventure in your days, a thrill-seeker. I can see the happiness it bestowed in you, when you felt free and alive in the skies. You crave that feeling once more, which is why you yearn to travel the kingdoms and beyond. You want more of that life again, and you should, child. There is so much more beyond this land. You're a storyteller, I can see that within your soul, and you will have marvelous and terrible stories to tell in your future. You're honest with the ones you love, even if it's brutal, but you are loyal nonetheless. You have enthusiasm for life and while you may feel the darkness in your own life, don't let it win over the light that shines from within."

Grayson drew his hand back, his face a mask of perplexity. He swallowed three times before he slowly rose, a bit off-balanced, from his seat and walked over to the bar without a sound.

"Who's next?"

TEN

ASHLYN STUMBLED FORWARD, cautiously lowering herself into the seat. She gracefully picked up the deck, shuffling a few times and spreading the cards across the table. Her finger lifted unconsciously to her chin and she tapped three times, before her hand dropped and hovered over a card to the left. She grasped the card in her hand and turned it around.

"Just what I expected with you. The High Priestess in its reversed position. Doesn't come as a surprise to me," the seer divulged.

Ash stuttered, "What do you mean that you expected this card with me? What does it mean?"

"The High Priestess in its reversed position means you have a lack of direction in your life. You are full of secrets and knowledge, but you feel lost with no sense of purpose—and something tells me that this is a normal feeling you've had for a while. You serve as the mediator in your personal life, but come off mysterious even to those closest to you. You're scared of showing your true self, so you bury the truth of your past by remaining quiet. You wear a shield around you to keep others from seeing in, but you will soon learn that those you love the most will still love you despite your past. But, I do not believe you think it'll be your friends that won't accept you, but rather yourself."

She reached out and grabbed Ashlyn's hand and continued, "My poor child, despite the darkness of what you have been through, you will soon become the beacon of light in someone else's darkness. Don't let the fear of your past prevent you from shining your light on them, as they will need it." She leaned in closer to Ashlyn and whispered, "You will find love again, my dear. Be open to it, trust it; she will not be angry with you."

Ashlyn's face turned white as a sheet and she ripped her hand back viciously. She stood up, the chair sliding backwards on the wood floor. She pulled the hand the seer held tightly to her chest, tears welling up in her eyes as she turned on her heel and followed the direction that Grayson had gone.

"You're up, handsome," the seer indicated, waving Damien over to the seat.

Damien's eyes widened in fear, terrified of what this seer would read from him if Grayson and Ash were stunned speechless with their readings.

He slowly dragged the chair forward back to the table, sitting on the very edge of the seat, readying himself for an attack.

He cautiously picked up the deck and shuffled them in his hand, never taking his eyes off the curious woman. Without breaking eye contact with her, he laid the cards back on the table and selected one without a thought and turned it upwards.

"The Towers card in its upright position," the seer said with a troubled look on her face.

"You have had a traumatic past, and soon you will come to a revelation about what this will mean for your future. You have suffered a tragedy and you carry that loss with you here."

She tapped gently over her heart. "But do not let the pain overwhelm your thoughts. Especially when you come face to face with your past again in the near future. Not everything you see is what it may seem, you'll do well to remember that."

She leaned back in her chair before continuing.

"There's a raging inferno in you and if you're not careful containing it, you'll set this world on fire including destroying and betraying the ones you love around you. Learn to control your temper. You have a good heart despite what you may think. You are passionate, ambitious, daring to do things others wouldn't. You're a natural born leader—-remember that."

Damien recoiled in his seat. The trauma of his past made its way to the forefront of his mind as he sprung up from his seat, nearly knocking the chair over and following the other assassins into the bar without a second glance.

Kieryn looked over at her friends as they drowned themselves in alcohol. The seer had put a silencing charm around the table for each assassin, but whatever she told them, they looked terrified.

"Don't be scared my child," the seer called to her, beckoning her over with her crooked finger.

To be honest, Kieryn would rather sleep outside in the woods than sit down at this table and listen to what this seer predicted for her future. But, if her friends could endure what they were told, she could too. It couldn't be that bad right? It's not like she believed in fate, per say.

She put one foot in front of the other and sat down across from the seer. She wasted no time shuffling the deck, wanting to get this over with. She spread the cards out on the table and like a beacon, her hand hovered over a card. She could feel the warmth of the card as if it was on fire, and flipped it over.

The seer leaned back in her seat, gasping at the card that lay before them. Not one part of her body touched the table, as if she thought the card was going to jump up and attack her.

"Death," she stammered out, "in its upright position."

Kieryn yawned. "Is that bad?"

The seer sprung forward, reaching for Kieryn's hands, closing her eyes.

"You're a fighter. You're passionate and loyal, to a fault. You lead with your heart and pour your soul into the ones you love. You'd die for them. Your heart is your greatest weapon and your biggest weakness—lead with it wisely, guard it fiercely."

She swallowed an inhale.

"The answers you've been seeking lies in your death. I see an ending in the near future for you my child, but that is just the beginning. Be careful who you trust." Her eyes fell to the card laying on the table. "Where there is death, the devil lies in wait and he is very tempting, but remember that the devil always has a secret agenda."

The seer stood up from the table, collecting her things, cautiously picking up the Death card as if it would magically grow teeth and bite her hand.

"Good luck, my child," she whispered to Kieryn before heading around a corner and disappearing into the night. Kieryn watched her go, a little shell-shocked at the message she had received.

Kieryn sank into the chair, unmoving as she poured over the conversation she just had with the peculiar woman. Did she actually believe what she told her? Could the Seer have truly meant that she was going to finally find out why her parents were slaughtered, only to die because of it? And who was the devil supposed to be?

Kieryn rose to her feet, already storming over to the corner where the seer had disappeared and found an empty room. She ran out of the inn, hoping she could catch up with her outside to give her a piece of her mind, but she saw only a few patrons idling outside the inn, mugs of beer in their hands and their horses nodding off at the post. The seer was nowhere to be found, as if she never existed.

The four assassins spread out at the bar top, drowning their unspoken thoughts in their drinks. Damien stared blankly into his amber liquid, while Ash sat to the right of him, the color not yet returning to her face. It was as if life itself had drained from her eyes. Grayson stood resolute, leaning into the bar, swirling his drink around and around in his hand, staring off into space. Kieryn kept stealing glances back at the table where the seer did their readings, wondering if she would appear out of thin air.

Grayson broke the silence of their pity party.

"That was weird right? Her fortune telling was just for entertainment and not …" he trailed off, not truly believing what he was saying.

"She … she knew things about me that no one else knew. That can't be a coincidence," Ashlyn spoke up, her voice barely audible.

"It's not real. The inn is literally named after fate, and it's probably part of their act. She's a seer, she can easily read people's emotions. I refuse to believe her words of what my fate is, because if I did …" Kieryn's voice grew fainter. "No, I'm not going to let her words define how I live my life. I will not let her words make me afraid to live and have me looking over my shoulder for the rest of my days. I am the master of my own fate, I control what I choose to let affect me."

Her friends continued to stare at her wordlessly, lost in their tormented thoughts, struggling with their reality and untold futures. She shook her head, throwing a few coins down for the barmaid and grabbed her drink.

"I am going for a walk," she announced to them and walked out the door to the inn, not even knowing if her friends had heard her.

It was dusk when Kieryn exited Kismet Inn, the smell of

cedar permeating the air. She followed the trail behind the Kismet that led to a garden with a beautiful variety of flowers. She crossed the wooden bridge, fireflies lighting her way in the blue hue of night.

Her hand grazed the Minasian Daisies lining the path, the splashes of sunset in her peripheral. She felt the velvet touch of the flower's petal in between her fingers, grounding herself back in the moment. She glanced up at the vast colorful garden before her and gasped, nearly dropping her glass of whiskey.

The garden was a plethora of different colored flowers. A burst of life surrounded her, making her feel a sudden rush of calm. There were the bright red hues of the tropical flower known in Minas called the Lilies of the Valley, and the whimsical, frilly Blue Kalmia flowers. Purple, star-shaped flowers blanketed the path around her, along with pops of white, gold, and pink. The aroma was overwhelming, and she drank it in, her senses in overdrive. She followed the beautiful scent of flowers through the garden oasis until she stumbled upon an opening hidden beneath the trees. Lanterns hung from branches, coating the place in a mystical light. A bench sat at the forefront of the big willow tree, a haven in the midst of this magical place. She laid her head on the bench, bringing her feet up to rest on the arms, and taking in the sounds and sight of the magical garden she'd stumbled into.

But even the magic of this place couldn't silence her thoughts about the seer's message and that Death card. She wasn't lying when she told her friends she didn't believe in fate, or the fortune the seer had told her. Kieryn wasn't afraid of death. She was afraid of living, living was a lot more difficult. At least in death she'd find peace again and she wouldn't feel guilt or pain, she'd feel nothing at all. And she would rather feel nothing than be consumed by her dark thoughts. If death came for her, she'd be ready, but she wasn't ready to go until she got her answers and had her vengeance. Only then would she welcome death's embrace.

After what felt like hours of getting lost in the beauty of staring up at the blanket of stars in between the wisps of trees, she felt a presence, and like a flame roaring to life in her bones, Her shadows surfaced to her skin, surrounding her in a black veil.

My shadows only made their presence when I killed a person, why were they appearing before me now?

Her shadows danced around her as she looked around the garden, trying to see into the depths of the forest beyond the faint glow of the hanging lanterns. She was just about to chalk it up to her imagination when a firefly went off near the base of a tree fifty feet away and she cursed out loud. There staring back at her was a figure in black with electric blue eyes. She stared back, unmoving, her shadows inching forward, curious about the person before them, when she snapped out of her stupor and ran like hell after the figure. She saw him turn and duck behind the tree, and she could hear the rustling of leaves beneath his feet and the snap of twigs as she took off after him. When she rounded the area he had been, he was nowhere to be found. She listened intently, waiting for the sound of foot-steps running through the forest, but only heard the echoes of birds whistling in the trees and the beating of wings. She stood there, unwavering, her skin on fire after what her eyes had perceived.

The figure that haunted her sleep was now haunting her in reality. After all this time, why? If he wanted to play games and toy with her, let him. She would beat him at his own game. She turned to head back to the inn when her eye caught something at the base of the trunk. She picked up the foreign object and observed it in her hand. Inside her palm she held a black feather, about six-inches long.

ELEVEN

HER FRIENDS HAD LEFT EARLIER that evening to scope out the location of the ball, but Kieryn was still in turmoil from what she had seen last night. She felt like she was being haunted. She had this sense that overwhelmed her, a notion that someone had been following her for some time now. She was certain now that someone was the stranger from her past. The question was why was he following her now, after all this time? Or had he always been there?

The inn had a carriage that picked her up, while theirs was being fixed and brought her to the Venetu Canals.

She was the last one to arrive at the king's chateau where the king hosted his annual masquerade ball. She left the comfort of the carriage and made her way over to the narrow, elongated row boats across the cobblestoned street. Both ends of the wooden boat curved up and inwards. The gentleman rowing the boat took hold of her hand and helped her aboard.

The man was short yet stocky, with jet-black hair and soil-brown eyes. His arms were tan and toned from his line of work, and he sported a mustache that drooped low over his upper lip. He wore a wide-brimmed straw hat, black pants, and a simple white tunic. He took the oar in his hand and used it to lever them away from the wall and into the canal waters. His stature remained straight and at attention, his body barely shifting as he rowed their boat towards the ball.

She nestled into the plush, velvet cushions and gazed up at the bustling streets to the sides of her. She tasted the bitter scent of magic on her tongue, like sulfur from a match. She loved visiting Minas Kingdom, or *The Floating Kingdom*, as most of Elysium knew it as. All of Minas Kingdom was constructed of hundreds of canals that crisscrossed throughout. The main transportation of the kingdom was either by boat or walking over the 200 bridges scattered throughout. For the number of canals and bridges, Minas Kingdom was the smallest of them all, but what they lacked in geography they made up for in ambience.

Minas was home to witches of all kinds: seers, folk-healers, and the mortarri. Seers they had unfortunately come across at the inn, people throughout the realm remained wary of them. As Kieryn had experienced, they didn't necessarily want to hear the insights seers bestowed on them about their future. Folk-healers on the other hand were amongst the friendliest and coveted. They were elemental witches who used the resources nature provided. Each kingdom across the land had folk-healers. It was a lucrative and sought after position of power and status. And only the best were employed by the monarchs. Those who weren't as fortunate remained humble and offered their services to the villages they resided in, opening up shops and helping those in need.

The mortarri were a coven of witches that combined their magical powers and unique skill sets to create stronger and bigger spells. They always traveled together and were sometimes known to be ruthless in getting what they wanted. They were feared and with good reason, even by Kieryn.

Minasians graced the promenade with their opulent

costumes, some witches had glamoured themselves to look like they were dripping in actual gold, while others walked on stilts through the streets, and some had glamoured their makeup to resemble galaxies of stars. The capital of Minas, Venetu, was portrayed as *The City of Dreamers*—poets, artists, musicians thrived in a place like this. Kieryn envied them and the life she could never have.

The man escorting her came to a stop by a bridge that looked just like the rest and helped her step onto the floating dock.

"Enjoy your night, miss," he said in his Minasian accent as he pushed off the dock. She thanked him and made her way across the stone bridge towards the king's chateau.

It was the king's old residency before he built an even larger castle. Now he uses it to host celebrations and masquerades. The chateau loomed over her intimidatingly, its spires touching the heavens. He'd spared no expense for the chateau: the palace glowed in the sun's golden hour, the large, curved arches casting shadows across the labyrinthine gardens filled with statues of the gods. Columns twisted around the complicated shapes until it was a perfect paragon of Minasian beauty.

The interior was just as luxurious and ornate. Even with her designer dress she felt out of place being in a space saturated with opulence. After presenting her invitation, she was escorted through the pale grayish-white marble foyer lit with crystal chandeliers and frescoed ceilings. She passed an open courtyard to her left with four long obelisks that stood like knights on a battlefield.

She approached the sleek marble doors and stepped into the main ballroom. Aerial performers greeted her as they dropped from the domed ceiling in red silk, their bodies twisting with the fabric as they climbed and fell like a spider spinning its web. She froze at the top of the stairs in complete awe of the elaborate decorations. She scanned the ballroom, crossing over fire breathers on raised platforms swallowing poles of fire and blowing it above the crowd, unfazed. Exotic dancers swayed naked in cages, their bodies painted in gold like a second skin. Jugglers were dispersed amongst the crowd, creating a wide berth as they juggled knives.

The music carried her down the marble stairs, a sensuous beat that played from a nearby musician and his violin. She found Damien from across the room and strode over to where he stood.

Damien had seen her enter from the stairs and was left speechless. He was enraptured by her ethereal beauty as she walked towards him in a floor-length green silk dress the color of her eyes. The straps of her dress rested lazily off her shoulders, showing off a deep plunge between her breasts, while a slit up to her thigh allowed for easy access to the dagger he knew she had hidden there. When she strode through the crowd, people turned their heads, her toned, golden legs flashing through the slit with every step she took. Her honey-light hair hung loosely off one shoulder, a gold comb and what looked like gold leaf foil in the strands. Finishing off her look was a gold filigree mask that was decorated with tiny swirls and leaves.

She looked so sublime that no goddess or starry night could compare to her beauty.

"Everybody ready?" she asked them upon approaching. Ashlyn, dressed in a wine-red dress with a full skirt and heavy, gold embroidery, a bright red ruby placed delicately in the valley of her breasts, nodded and left them with a silent salute. Grayson winked at Kieryn and gave her a subtle kiss on the cheek, his hunter green suit hugging his broad frame elegantly as he retreated into the crowd after Ashlyn.

Her eyes took in Damien dressed in a sapphire suit. His usual curly, ebony hair was slicked back, making him look older and handsome, his black mask making his bronze eyes glisten in contrast.

He opened his mouth to speak, but the clinking of champagne flutes echoed throughout the room as King Luc took to the stage. His own dark, curly hair was also brushed back, and his eyes the color of the finest whiskey peered out into the crowd at his guests. He was dressed in an indigo and silver brocade suit, his amethyst crown reflecting off the crystal chandeliers.

"Welcome, friends, to *An Enchanted Affair.* Minas is pleased to have so many of you join us here to celebrate The Feast of the Dead. Let's raise a toast to another year of prosperity for all our kingdoms." He raised his glass of champagne in the air as butlers swarmed the room, passing out champagne flutes to those in attendance. Damien handed Kieryn a flute, but they both knew neither would drink it.

Could never be too careful.

Damien gazed at Kieryn, his half smile appearing, the upper left corner of his lips raised slightly. "Kieryn, you look absolutely …" he started to say.

"Beautiful," the stranger behind him finished.

Damien turned, agitated at this random stranger for stealing the compliment that was his to give.

"And who are you?" he snapped.

The stranger had thick, curly onyx-colored hair and eyes just as dark. His attire was no different. He was in all black from head to toe, including his mask. *Mysterious.* He was tall and had high, sharp cheekbones, a strong, chiseled jaw, and from the looks of it, a toned body underneath all that material. He exuded danger and darkness. A true enigma.

The stranger smiled then, cold yet lovely, like frost on a winter morning.

"Who am I?" He glared threateningly at Damien. "Well, I am a man of many names—*Angel of Death, Reaper of Souls, Prince of Darkness*—but tonight, you can call me Callian," he said with conviction and a tinge of humor.

Damien's eyes glazed over as he came to terms with who was standing before him. They had both heard of the Angel of Death. He made the Phantoms Keep look like a monastery with the acts that he had committed. Rumors stated that he had been with almost every woman across the realm, burnt down entire villages with a flick of his wrist, and took torture beyond what was necessary. The latest rumor was that he had maimed some drug lord's fingers and shoved them down his throat until he asphyxiated on them. Each rumor was just as outlandish as the next.

"And tonight," Callian continued, "I would like to dance with the most beautiful woman in the room."

Kieryn looked at him, utterly perplexed. She looked death in the eye and laughed.

"Not interested," she responded to his offer.

Gods, do I have a death wish?

The disinterest and blatant *no* didn't even faze him, let alone deter him. Within a blink, he was inches from her, his chin level with the top of her head as he peered down at her with a devilish grin.

"It's cute you thought that was a request," he chided as he grabbed her hand leading her to the dance floor. As he did so, he whisked her champagne flute out of her hand and handed it off to Damien without a word.

He twirled her into his waiting arms just as the violinist started to play a seductive and enchanting number that required close body contact filled with twirls, dips, and lifts.

Kieryn saw Damien's seething look from the side of the dance floor, rage written in his eyes. She gave him a shake of her head and communicated as best she could to finish the job they came here for.

"Your pet seems awfully jealous. Hope I didn't cause any problems," Callian chortled, no hints of remorse in his voice.

His hands were large, one folding completely over hers, the other gliding to the small dip in her back, causing a jolt to run through her even with her dress as a barrier. He drew her flush against his body, making her jerk her head up at him, killing him softly with her eyes as her left hand floated right above his shoulder, barely touching.

"Your body was meant for mine, puppet. How enticing," he purred into her ear.

"None of me is yours, let's set that straight," she fumed.

They stared at one another, a fiery gaze in each of their eyes as he stepped backwards leading them around the dance floor, his eyes never once leaving hers.

"Don't you worry, you'll soon realize you were made for me."

She scoffed incredulously at the stranger's audacity. But, before she could muster a retort, he continued.

"I came here to warn you."

He turned, his hand lifting from her back as he spun her in a circle repeatedly before drawing her close to him. He dipped her low, her breasts rising and falling dramatically in her tight dress. His eyes dipped lower, a blush rose to her cheeks and he grinned when she noticed where his eyes had strayed to.

He leaned forward, his lips brushing the shell of her ear. "You were led into a trap. This masquerade ball was an opportunity to lure you here," he whispered, his hand slowly dragging up her exposed thigh. He straightened, bringing her against his body once more. Kieryn dropped her hand, feeling for her dagger—only to discover that it was gone.

"Looking for this, puppet?"

She was still locked in his embrace, her dagger sitting pretty in the palm of his hand.

He tsked at her. "Were you going to stab me?"

"It crossed my mind," she returned with a fiery snap.

He grabbed her wrists and scooped them into one hand, raising them above her head. With his other hand still clutching her dagger, dragged the tip lightly down the inside of her arm, featherlight, a bare trace of mockery in his movements.

"You'll get this back when I know you won't stab me with it," he snickered, running the tip of the blade across her exposed skin above her breasts, smiling at the shiver she struggled to hide, before he pocketed the dagger.

"Who …?" Kieryn started to ask, but she never got to finish her question. At that moment, an ear-splitting blast erupted, sending shards of glass through the ballroom as the room exploded into chaos. The last thing she saw was Callian twisting his body, shielding her from the incoming blast.

PART TWO

TWELVE

SHARDS OF GLASS fell from the ceiling like a spring downpour, coating the pristine white marble with blankets of blood. Kieryn blinked rapidly, her vision hazy, and a high-pitched frequency kept ringing in her ears. The more she shook her head to clear it, the worst it became. She felt a heavy pressure on her chest, and her eyes settled on his.

"Are you hurt?" he asked her, his voice muffled by her ringing ears. She stared up at him blankly. He didn't wait for her response, he started to feel up her arms and legs looking for any injuries, not satisfied until he had gone over every lick of skin exposed. Besides superficial cuts and bruises, she felt okay. Her dress was ruined, but she remained unscathed. He helped her to her feet as he towered over her, blocking her from the mayhem ensuing.

Everything was in slow motion, as if she were swimming through mud. The waiter that had handed her a champagne glass earlier lay decapitated on the floor, his blood pooling like a halo around him. She stumbled away from the rolling head. The chaos and decimation around her reminded her of that night in her childhood home, the feeling of helplessness as she took in the sight before her. If it weren't for Callian's arms around her holding her body upright, she would've sank to the floor and allowed herself to shrivel into the darkness that had a chokehold on her. All these years later and she was still fighting her demons.

"Hey! Look at me," he said, grabbing her head between his hands, his thumb brushing away a silent tear. "We need to leave, NOW!" he yelled over the blood-curdling screams of despair around them. She glanced over to her right, where one half of a woman's face was burned severely from one of the fire breathers, her cries unbearable. Her face was shrunken in, the skin completely melted off. Her face resembled fiery coals sitting at the base of a roaring fire. Her screams eventually faded away, her eyes glazing over and her mouth frozen in a wordless scream. Another guest had a glass shard through her eye, and a man's legs were the only thing visible under the pillar that had collapsed on him.

She choked back a sob.

"My friends, I … I need to find them."

Callian released her, but grabbed her hand gently, firmly sheltering her under his arm.

He reached into his suit pocket to hand her back her dagger. "Just don't stick the sharp end into me, please." His face was locked in a grimace.

She took her weapon back and attached it back to her thigh holster. She couldn't lose anyone else.

Kieryn and Callian searched the ballroom together. She looked for Ash's shiny velvet hair, strained to hear Grayson's rowdy voice above the chaos, and chased down people who had Damien's dark, slicked-back hair, but she came up empty.

"Oh gods, Kieryn is that you?!" a faint, feminine cry came from the stairs.

Kieryn wrestled her way through a pile of moving bodies

to the woman who radiated her sanctuary, a sister who she confided in, laughed with, would kill for.

She nudged aside people, struggling to get to Ash, who was sprawled on the stairs.

"Ash, what happened? Are you hurt?" she pleaded, begging the gods above that she was unharmed. Besides the gash above her right eyebrow that would leave a scar, she remained intact.

"It's Damien. He found me and he … he … he pushed me out of the way. I didn't even see the chandelier falling …" she couldn't finish, hysterical sobs spilling out her mouth.

Kieryn looked behind her friend, following the line of sight of Ash holding someone's hand. Not just someone's hand, Damien's hand. And then she heard it, the unmistakable sound of his labored breathing, a suctioning sound coming from his lungs. She scrambled up the stairs to him, her knees hitting the marble floor with a thud, as she gauged his wounds, praying that he'd survive. Callian came up behind her just as Damien started to cough up dark blood. Kieryn went to work tearing a piece of her dress off to stanch the gaping wound in his chest. He was bleeding out, fast.

No, this isn't happening. I can't lose Damien.

Damien reached out his hand, closing over Kieryn's.

A dying wish.

"Kier … I … just wanted … to … say," he leaned to the side coughing up more blood.

"No! You don't get to say your goodbyes," she sobbed, hot tears rushing down her face. "You don't get to do that. You are going to be okay," she promised, blinking back any remaining tears.

He coughed, blood spilling out between her fingers splayed on his chest. *Blink.*

Do not go back there. Not now.

She couldn't think about losing Damien as he bled out in front of her. She tried to remember her father's lectures about remaining calm, it's when you become frantic that you make mistakes, but for the life of her, she couldn't get her mind to function. Her heart was winning this battle.

Callian rested a hand on her shoulder gently. "Kieryn, we must go."

She shook his hand off, not budging. She wouldn't leave Damien here to die alone. Over her dead body would she leave him here. She prayed to whatever God would hear her, begging them for mercy, for help, for anything.

Damien leaned forward as best he could, kissing Kieryn on her forehead, *a farewell kiss.* His eyes fluttered close, and one last breath escaped his lips before his body gave up. His head fell back to the tile, his hand went limp, and suddenly the blood stopped flowing like rivers between Kieryn's fingers, turning slowly into a trickle.

Kieryn sank back onto her heels and let out an unnatural, soul-shattering scream, her shadows emerging from her skin like flowers springing from the ground. She breathed in the darkness, for she *was* the darkness, and then she and Damien were engulfed in a cloud of shadows.

THIRTEEN

THE DARKNESS SWALLOWED her and Damien into its hungry depths. Kieryn felt her lungs constrict and she started to shake. She was losing control again. Her skin quickly felt clammy, a sheen of sweat already coating her arms. She looked down at her hands, only to see utter blackness. She had never seen anything like this before, not even the night was as dark as this.

She swallowed down her fear and staggered forward, feeling for any type of purchase. *Am I still in the castle? Where exactly am I?*

She didn't want to know what her friends would think of this side of her. She didn't even know where her shadows came from, just that they first emerged the night she took a life, the night of her parent's murders. All she knew was that when she first laid eyes on the shadows hovering above her skin like a ghost, she felt giddy inside. Like she had awoken from a dead sleep and that the darkness was opening its arms, welcoming her home.

This was different. The times that she had embraced the shadows, she let her curiosity take over, but this time it was as if the shadows that erupted from her were controlling her. Leading her somewhere, or to *someone*.

As if the lights were thrust on, light filtered through the darkness, a beacon. She looked up to find a full moon illuminating the sky, and a forest before her, its tall oak trees rising high into the skies, never-ending. She braced her hands on her knees, hoping to force her trembling hands to still. She gradually stood up, her body going into fight mode as she took in her surroundings. It looked like she was in Riyadh Kingdom, but not.

Out of habit, she reached for the dagger strapped to her thigh, and surprisingly found it still there. She wasn't dead, but she didn't know where she was. She tasted sulfur in the air—magic. Someone had used magic to bring her here, but, *who?* A distant howl graced her ears, and her mind instantly knew. *Damien!*

She ran blindly into the forest, the glow of the moon her only source of light. Her silk dress shredded into pieces as she stumbled her way through, her foot catching on a tree root. Her knees took the brunt of her fall and her hands came out to catch herself. Her palm sliced open, blood dripping into the soil and dissolving like hot mist. It was then the forest came alive, reaching out to her. Skeleton trees bent in the wind, extending toward her with contorted fingers steeped in shadows. She quickly stood and started to run in the direction of where the howl originated from.

Damien, he's here!

She dodged swaying branches and jumped over writhing roots until she reached an opening in the trees, where she stumbled upon a village. She was in Riyadh, just outside Dakar

—Damien's home of Basalto. A glow of orange light poured out from homes, laughter trickling from open windows. People pranced around the streets without a care in the world. She approached a burly man with a mane of hair that ended below his shoulders.

"Excuse me, sir?" she reached out her hand to tap him on the shoulder, only to find that her hand went straight through his body.

A ghost?

How is this even possible? Where has this person taken me?

You could only see ghosts if you were dead, otherwise she would've had endless conversations with her parents. She would maybe remember more of her parent's faces. Each year was tougher than the last, more pieces of them seemed to fade into the background. She still remembered her mother's laugh and her father's smile when he stared at her mother, hopelessly in love. Those things were harder to forget. But she couldn't remember if her mom's eyes were the shade of a summer blue sky or the deepest midnight blue like that of the ocean.

She saw a tall, broad figure at the corner of her eye just then. She whipped her head in that direction and chased after him. She followed him down a street, right to his front door, where a woman with bright white hair and arctic blue eyes met him in a passionate embrace.

Her legs wrapped around his waist, and he pulled her in by the back of the head for a body-melting kiss. This was *her.* This was *his* Natalie—and she was stunning. Her hair glided down her back like a waterfall, the texture looking softer than spider silk. Her hair was a beam of moonlight, blinding. She was dwarfish in size to Damien, but she carried herself well. You could tell she was confident from the way she had approached him, and the love that shone from her eyes as she took him in, as if it was the first time.

Does she realize he's dead?

They broke apart, but his hand still cradled her face, committing it to memory. Reacquainting himself with his lost love. Kieryn broke a bit inside, watching him with her. She was his anchor, and Kieryn was just a buoy barely tethering him. But she was happy for Damien too. Happy to see Damien smile like that. He never smiled like that with her. A tear fell from her bottom lash onto the street, hissing as it dissolved.

The hair on her neck rose just then, and she felt the air drop in temperature. It was as if all the oxygen had been sucked out of the room, an eerie shift in the night air making her shiver down to her bones. A shield of shadows and ice consumed her. She reached out toward Damien, only to be met with resistance. A shimmery veil encased her, cocooning her inside the barrier. The crunch of footsteps on gravel alerted her of an unknown presence behind her.

She pivoted where she stood, dagger ready to strike. It was then she came face to face with a stranger, his hood pulled up, shadows dancing around him like puppets on a string. His movements were graceful, calculating. He towered over her, his shadows begging to come closer, curious.

She found her voice, though it was feeble in pitch.

"Who are you?" she demanded with a raspy tone, a lick of fear under her tongue as she tried to remain in control in front of this cold and domineering stranger.

He stalked towards her, his actions meticulous, and she couldn't help herself. She leaned in, transfixed. He moved with such precision and grace; it was as if the wind bent to his will.

The shadows bowed in the darkness to its master, forming a barrier. He controlled the shadows like they were pets.

His voice carried over to her like the strum of a cello, musical and haunting.

"I've been waiting for you," the stranger answered with a sinister smile, blue eyes holding hers captive.

His shadows swirled around him, like wisps of curling smoke. Her own shadows itched underneath her skin, wanting to tangle in his. They too felt a connection or familiarity with him. That realization alone paralyzed her to the core. She felt it then, this was the stranger that had been stalking her, haunting her nightmares—it had to be.

"I like to make an entrance," she drawled. "Hope you weren't waiting too long."

She wore her *Deathbringer* smile like a mask, hoping her confidence would overshadow the anxiety that was vibrating underneath her skin. The vibration inside her body buzzed like a million insects crawling their way through her veins.

The stranger smirked at her cheeky remark, a demonic laugh escaping from his lips and sending a wave of icy shivers down her spine.

"Charming one, aren't you?"

Her eyes narrowed to slits as she took him in.

"I've heard worse," she answered with a nonchalant shrug.

His shadows burst from his fingertips, wrapping around her like a snake ready to slaughter its prey. His shadows held her in a vise-like grip, unrelenting and merciless. He stalked forward, the air growing colder as he closed the distance between them. Despite being nose-to-nose with her, he still hid his identity behind a hazy glamour.

"You're not in any position to make demands from me, little girl. I am in control here."

His words sliced through the murky shadows, each word a sharp blade. He tightened his hand into a fist and the shadows obeyed, squeezing her limbs roughly.

"I can cut the oxygen to your brain ..." On command, her body went rigid, her lungs frozen. "I can make you swallow your own tongue until you asphyxiate on your own blood." Like a puppet, her teeth sank into her tongue with brute force, blood spilling from her mouth. She choked on her own blood, the taste of iron and salt filling her mouth. Her eyes protruded and the first tear spilled down her cheek.

With a flick of his wrist, he ended her torment. She coughed up blood, her lungs finally functioning once more as she took a deep breath in. *Breathe in, hold, breathe out,* her father's voice echoed in her mind.

She found the strength to lift her head and looked up at her jailer.

"What do you want from me?" she whispered with a note of defeat, her eyes falling back to the ground, afraid to look at him any longer than what was necessary.

His answer was immediate.

"Your soul."

Those two words struck her down. Paralyzing fear had her in its chokehold and she unraveled.

My soul? I can't. Who would I be without my soul?

Her eyes shot up to his. "I … I can't."

He laughed, like he had simply asked her the day of the week. Another flick of his wrist and the shield of shadows dropped, her body falling limply to the forest floor. The shadows disappeared back into him and suddenly she saw Damien again, still holding on to Natalie like he would never let go again.

His dark presence loomed over her, and he bent at the waist, a sneer on his face.

"You care for him; I can see it clear as day. It is written all over your face."

His hand seized her chin, forcing her head up at an awkward and painful angle.

"I'll give you some advice—your feelings will be the death

of you. Love will get you killed. Mark my words, little girl. Best to not have any."

And with those words, he released his grip on her. Her head drooped low, hanging idly. Her nails dug into the soil as she absorbed his words. That was the second time someone told her love would get her killed.

"He's dead, you know."

He said it so matter-of-factly, as if he was telling her the weather. Soulless.

She choked out a sob, quickly trying to muffle it into the back of her hand.

He let out an agitated sigh. "Humans and their emotions. Such a waste … so weak," he mumbled.

"I'll make you a deal, little girl."

With all the strength she had left, Kieryn rose to her feet and stood, guarded, waiting.

She swallowed the lump in her throat, her stomach hardening into stone at what she was about to do. She rolled back her shoulders and took a deep breath in.

Hold.

"What's your deal?"

His left eyebrow raised slightly, almost as if he expected her to refuse him, but just as quickly he regained his composure.

"Your soul in exchange for his," he said as his hand waved over to where Damien was lingering. She followed the movement of his hand, her eyes taking him in. He looked happy with her, it was written all over his face. Happiness to Damien was Natalie, but happiness to Kieryn was him alive, with her and their friends. What it came down to was happiness—his or hers? She knew the pain he felt, she too suffered from survivor's guilt. She would give anything to be reunited with her parents again. To have that chance to embrace them and be happy like she used to be.

Can I take away his happiness?

That was essentially what she was doing, she was taking his choice away from him. She knew Damien would stay with Natalie even if that meant he was dead, but the more Kieryn thought of a world without Damien's humor or laughter, the more it made her soul ache. It would be like living without a piece of her heart, and she couldn't have more of her heart shattered. He would hate her for this. Deep down she knew this fact, and accepted that fate. She had to push him away, to stop his growing feelings for her. In a way, she felt relief at the fact that he would hate her. She would do this to save his life, in more ways than one. Loving her was death itself.

She locked eyes with him, determination written in her face.

"Deal."

The smile on his face was pure sin. "I need to hear you say the words." His voice was full of death.

"You can have my soul, in exchange for Damien's."

And with that sentence, she gambled her soul away to the devil in black.

FOURTEEN

KIERYN WAS SWALLOWED up by the shadows as the stranger portaled her back to the masquerade ball, the weight of what she'd done barely registering before she could blink. Instantaneously, she registered the frantic chaos she had left behind, as her own barrier of shadows started to fall away. She saw Ashlyn first. An expression of shock and terror crossed her face as she took in the sight before her. At some point, Grayson had arrived at her side, his suit stained with blood. Kieryn prayed it was not his. He too was in disbelief.

Grayson spoke, "What in the *Gods* name did you do, Kier?"

She blinked rapidly, trying to readjust to reality and the nausea she felt. Like an embodiment of a nightmare, the dark looming figure behind her emerged.

Callian.

She turned her back to him, hovering over Damien's still lifeless body.

Wake up! Please don't let it be for nothing.

Her hand was caked in dirt and dried blood, but she reached toward Damien, cradling his head. "Please wake up, Damien. I need you," she begged.

She felt Callian's eyes on her.

"He's dead, Kieryn. He's gone and we must …" His words were cut off as his eyes glanced over at Damien's rising chest.

"It can't be, there's no way."

His eyes darted over at Kieryn's face, his expression morphing from confusion to shock to alarm. There was a look of fear in his eyes, as if he knew the bargain she struck. She turned away from him, focusing on Damien. Ash and Grayson reached out for their friend at the same time, a sigh of relief falling from their lips.

"You're alive," a sob ripped from Ash as she gripped Damien's hand. "You're alive," she repeated to herself. Grayson looked down at his friend in disbelief. He had no idea how his best friend was alive given the circumstances, but he was grateful all the same.

Damien turned his head, disoriented at first. He looked down at his body, his bottom half ripped open and covered in blood from a gash that had started to stitch itself back up. He remembered finding Ash in the madness, reaching her at the stairs. It was then that he'd felt the shaking and the slight rattling of glass above his head. He saw the ceiling start to crack and the chandelier seconds from impaling them and he had reacted. He remembered the piercing pain of needles stabbing him every time he took a breath. The pain of dying and saying goodbye to Kieryn.

But then he saw *her*. He had seen Natalie again and he held her in his arms. That had to have been real, he couldn't have just imagined that. He had felt her strong legs wrapped around his waist, the smooth touch of her porcelain skin, the warmth of her breath as he kissed her. He knew he saw her. She was still as beautiful and magical as the first day he had seen her. He still smelled her on him. Cinnamon and apples, the smell so overpowering. He knew he had seen her like he knew his own heart. He died. He had died and she had come to welcome him home, yet he was at the masquerade ball, and yet it was Kieryn crying over him, not Natalie.

The realization hit him and without hesitation, his hand shot into the air and wrapped around Kieryn's throat. He lunged forward, toppling onto her, his hand never wavering.

"What did you do? What did you do? What did you do?" he spat at her. Grayson struggled to pull him off Kieryn, but Damien latched on.

Kieryn struggled to breathe, her arms coming up to push Damien's face away, but he pushed down harder, her airway constricting.

"I saw Natalie again. I was with her when I suddenly felt a tug, a shift in the air around me. Someone was pulling me away from her. I don't know what you did, but I know it was you who took me away from her."

Kieryn fought him relentlessly, her vision spotty and fading. She was going to blackout from the loss of oxygen. *She was getting tired of being choked to death today.* She scanned Damien's face and only saw wrath and devastation. His head jerked back and suddenly she felt weightless as his body was knocked sideways. She choked, gasping for air as she realized what happened.

Callian had punched Damien, the sheer force knocking him off her. She shot to her feet, ready for Damien's attack, but he sat there, his heart in his hands.

"You should've let me die, Kieryn. I was happy with her. You took that choice away from me. Are you really that selfish?"

Ash looked between them.

"What does he mean by that, Kieryn? Is that what those shadows were?"

Kieryn ignored her questioning, instead reaching out a hand to Damien. He smacked her hand away from him.

"Don't. Fucking. Touch. Me!" he ordered.

"Damien ..." she sobbed, knowing she broke him, that she destroyed their friendship because of her selfish tendencies. She just ... she just didn't want to feel abandoned, not again.

"I want nothing to do with you," he spat out at her, his words like venom. "I will never forgive you. You're dead to me, Kieryn."

Every sentence was a death blow. She visibly shivered at the sheer intensity of his wrath, knowing he meant every word. And he was right. She took away his choice, but she couldn't bring herself to regret it. She bargained for his soul, and she would live with that guilt and his hatred if it meant he was alive. He didn't know what she had sacrificed in return for his life, and he never would.

"Damien," Grayson coaxed, approaching his friend, "You don't mean that. Kieryn is your best friend. She saved your life."

Damien stared up at Grayson with death in his eyes.

"She didn't save my life, Grayson. She ruined it."

Kieryn faltered back a step, into the waiting arms of Callian. His strong, firm hands gripped her shoulders lightly, steadying her.

"I hate to break up this loving reunion, but we need to go."

Ashlyn and Grayson finally took in the stranger before them and shared a confused, hesitant look.

"And who in the hell are you?" Grayson prodded, his hand coming to rest on the hilt of his dagger.

With a roll of his eyes, Callian replied, "I am tired of people asking me that question today. I am your worst nightmare or your temporary savior. Choose! And if I were you, I'd choose the latter."

As if Grayson knew he was looking death incarnate in the eye, he solemnly nodded. He lifted Damien to his feet and herded him and Ash up the stairs to safety. Kieryn was on his tail when Callian reached for her arm.

"He's in pain now, but give him time. He will forgive you," he said consolingly.

She was taken aback by Callian's voice of comfort, but she shook her head sadly.

"No, he won't."

Callian slowly let go of Kieryn's arm and she turned, hiked up her dress, and ran after her friends. In her twenty-six years, she was at a point where she didn't know her next move, and that was more frightening to her than the *Angel of Death* behind her.

FIFTEEN

THEY RACED THROUGH THE CHATEAU, Callian taking the lead. They rushed by more of the wounded, as they all tried to make an escape from the devastation behind them. The streets of Venetu were just as bad. Those without an invite who mingled on the outskirts were caught in the crossfire of the attack, and some were embedded with flying shrapnel. It was a battlefield.

Ashlyn hesitated as she took in the scene before her.

"We need to stop and help them," she said in a small, panicky voice.

Callian faltered in his step, briefly, but kept moving.

"We can't help them. We need to keep moving!" he demanded of the assassins.

They had reached one of the side streets that led to a dock overlooking the canals.

"There is a small door hidden by the barrels on the dock. We need to move fast, they are probably already looking for you." Callian motioned to the stone steps leading down to the docks.

"Who is looking for us?" Kieryn demanded of him.

"The Minas Army."

"And why would they be looking for us?" Grayson questioned the towering figure of darkness before him.

Callian looked down at Grayson without blinking.

"That explosion killed the King of Minas and the Minas Army got word that four assassins were in attendance at the ball and that it was you four that triggered the explosion. You are all wanted for regicide and treason. They will have your heads if they find you. Not to mention, half of that ballroom saw Kieryn's shadows."

Callian's words were like a knife to the gut. The four assassins were stunned speechless, neither one knowing what to say at that revelation. Distant shouting in Minasian echoed from around the corner, and Callian beckoned again for them to follow. With no other choice, they followed him to the hidden door and they entered one by one. Callian was the last to enter, and with a flick of his wrist flames flickered from the sconces on the wall, creating a path of light for them. With another flick of his wrist, the door they had entered through vanished into thin air like it never existed.

"Explain yourself, now!" Kieryn's voice rang throughout the tunnel.

Callian sidled up next to her, a threatening look in his eyes.

"I really don't like being told what to do. Do not forget who you are speaking to," he snapped.

Kieryn stood taller, her shoulders arched back.

"I know exactly who I am talking to, *Angel of Darkness,* or should I say the exiled prince of Eretum," Kieryn said with conviction.

Callian took a step back, surprise flickering across his features before he recovered.

"Why would you assume I am the Prince of Eretum? The rumor is that he's been gone with no trace for over a decade."

His eyes locked onto hers, waiting to call her bluff.

"Call it a lucky guess," she revealed to him, not wanting him to know all the cards she had to play. *The Exiled Prince* and *The Prince of Darkness* were one and the same. The rumors of what she had heard in the bar that night were true.

They continued with their stare down, until Grayson broke the tension.

"Why are you helping us?" Grayson directed his questioning to Callian. "Given your reputation, helping us seems beneath you."

Callian finally released his gaze from Kieryn and acknowledged Grayson directly for the first time.

"I tried to warn Kieryn tonight when I asked her to dance. The mission you were sent on was a trap." He chuckled to himself then. "Let me guess, you were told there would be an attack on the ball and you had to stop it before it could occur."

The assassins said nothing in return. The silence was all the answer he needed.

"I thought so," Callian continued. "Your informant is the one who set you up to fail. He was the person who hired your services, set the explosion, and then rigged it so you would take the blame for it."

Damien's head shot up and he spoke for the first time.

"And how do you know all of this information?" he inquired.

Callian turned his head slowly, death incarnate, and when he spoke there was venom in his voice.

"I know this because your informant works for my father, the King of Eretum," he replied. Callian smiled to himself, a wicked grin forming in the shadows. "Well, I guess I should say, *worked for*."

Ashlyn gasped, her hands coming to her mouth to stifle it.

"I interrogated one of his men on his council, and he informed me of what my father had planned rather vocally," he said, smiling to himself menacingly as he relived the torture he put the councilman through.

"I knew something felt off about this mission," Kieryn mumbled out loud to herself. "It didn't make sense why we were just sent here without vetting the information and without extensive surveillance ourselves. We never confirmed the information given to us by Ryvers."

Grayson roughly rubbed his chin, taking in the information.

"But why set us up?"

Callian looked at Kieryn like she was the answer.

"My father wants Kieryn, and he's willing to wage war with the surrounding kingdoms to get her in his grasp. He is prepared to slaughter monarchs and their subjects to obtain her. And what better way to do that than to stage an attack on King Luc's party where he invited all the kingdoms to attend, pinning the blame on her," he said, pointing at Kieryn, "and having all six kingdoms be his eyes and ears to hunt her down in retaliation? It's a genius plan really, I'll give my father that."

Damien laughed, amused at this admission. Grayson and Ash, on the other hand, looked perplexed, and glanced over to Kieryn, who was staring at Callian, stupefied.

"What does he want with me?"

"Ah, my sweet little puppet, that is the question of the night and I have a wager that it has to do with those shadows of yours."

The group of assassins swung their heads in unison towards Kieryn, a questioning look in their eyes. She stared down at her disheveled dress, which was now torn into pieces. Her legs were caked in dirt, pebbles had embedded themselves into her skin when she fell in the forest chasing after Damien, and she had cuts up and down her arms and across her chest from either the falling glass or the tree branches she ran through. She stared down at her ruined dress, her hands fumbling with the torn garment.

She looked up at Callian, not risking a glance at her friends as she confessed what she'd kept hidden from them.

"I barely know anything about my shadows," she disclosed. In the faint amber glow, Kieryn could see Damien's emotions written across his face. He felt betrayed. She knew his tells—the tightness in his jaw, the crinkle by his left eye, she knew she had disappointed him once again tonight.

He spoke up then. "How long have you known?"

"What …?" she whispered.

He stared icily at her, the bitterness saturating his words like daggers digging into her skin.

"How. Long?" he emphasized, spitting the words, the anger bleeding through.

She flinched at the ferocity of how he spoke to her. In the corner, Callian fisted his hands discreetly by his sides, the look in his eyes screaming of death.

She finally spoke the words aloud, the last nail in her coffin.

"I've known since the night my parents died. Since then, they never emerge, unless … unless I kill. I think they get stronger each time."

Damien flinched back at Kieryn's confession, his head slowly shaking back and forth as he finally forced an exhale from his parted lips.

Callian fixated on Kieryn, his eyebrows drawing together.

"You have no idea what you can do, do you? What you're capable of?" he asked her.

Kieryn glanced away from Damien's retreating figure and shook her head.

"No. I don't even know what my shadows mean or where they came from."

Callian believed her. How could she have trained when she had no one to guide her or explain to her what her shadows meant? Until now.

"You're a Shade Walker. Shade Walkers are force wielders —you can conjure the darkness and shroud yourself in shadows, bend the shadows to your will, and weaponize them to give you immeasurable power. It's not a power that many have. It is a very rare, unique power to behold."

"If it is rare, where did it come from?" Grayson spoke from the shadows of the tunnel.

Callian didn't take his eyes off of Kieryn as he answered Grayson's question.

"The only one I know who could wield that power is the *God of Shadow and Death* himself, Shade."

SIXTEEN

THE DEAFENING SILENCE of the assassins echoed in the dimly lit tunnel.

"The *God of Shadow of Death*, ruler of the Shadow Realm?" Kieryn questioned, the tone of her voice surprisingly calm for just being told she wielded the same power as one of the most ruthless gods, a bedtime story told to children to keep them out of trouble, or he would summon them to the pits of Hel through their nightmares. She wondered if the shadowed man she had seen in Riyadh was that god. For she didn't just make a deal with a devil, she made a deal with *the* devil. If she had promised her soul to the god of the Shadow Realm ... she couldn't begin to finish that thought.

"The very same one." Callian grinned, an uneasy feeling washing over Kieryn at his lack of surprise.

"You just keep getting more and more interesting, puppet."

She ignored his taunting.

"How do I have the same powers as the *God of Shadow and Death*? All the gods are gone. And I can't Shade Walk, I just have these shadows that reside inside me like a living thing. I don't even know how to use them, I can't even heal like everyone else," Kieryn muttered quietly. "I am just normal."

Callian scoffed at her remark.

"You are far from normal, puppet, and as to how you have the same power as Shade, that is exactly what I intend to find out." His eyes bored into hers as he continued, "And who said the gods were gone? Don't believe everything you hear."

He turned his head, acknowledging the other assassins in the room.

"You need to split up. I have a contact in Keres Kingdom that can aid us in this war that will soon break out, Kieryn and I will head—"

Kieryn never allowed him to finish that sentence.

"I am not leaving my friends. I am not running away from this fight."

"You're not running away from it, you're running to it. You and I are going to head to Keres Kingdom and lead the armies away from your friends, so they can get a head start trying to gather reinforcements from other Kingdoms," he addressed her.

"I don't like this at all," Ashlyn spoke from the shadows.

"What do you mean we will be gathering reinforcements?" Grayson questioned.

"My father has one of the largest armies in Elysium and his …" He wanted to say monsters, but they felt like more than that. Finally, he spoke a word that was as close as he could get to what they resembled: "Abominations." His abominations roamed the Bloodwood Forest, vicious creatures he created with dark magic, monsters beyond what parents warned their children about.

"The stories are true, then," Ashlyn voiced.

"All the stories are true," Callian confirmed. "As I said, I have a powerful connection in Keres Kingdom that can be of use." Callian sized up the black-haired beauty then and came to a realization. "They call you *The Wraith*, do they not?"

Her mouth opened and then closed at his directness.

"Yes, they do," she replied.

"The Alessian Warriors will follow you into the battlefield, of that I have no doubt. I wouldn't waste your time traveling to Almeria, but I would send word to any of your contacts there to speak to *The Fair Queen*. She will aid you against my father. She always loathed him. Head to Riyadh Kingdom instead with the mutt," Callian demanded with a jerk of his head towards Damien.

"We can't step foot in Riyadh without death waiting for us on the other side, and I won't allow anyone else to get hurt," Damien spat. "I will go alone."

"No, mutt," Callian hissed venomously, his powers crackling to the surface of his skin like a lightning storm in the middle of a summer night. "You will not. You will need *The Wraith* by your side. End of."

He moved on to Grayson without hesitation.

"You need to go to Calydan Kingdom and convince *The Savage Queen* to come to our side and not my father's. She is the wild card, but her dragons will be a key player in this war."

"That might be difficult to do," Grayson mumbled, his eyes straying to the ground.

"And why is that?" Callian stalked toward him. He stopped directly in front of Grayson. Close enough that Grayson could feel the power of Callian and why he was deemed the *Angel of Death*. Almost like he was under compulsion, he raised his head and met the glare of the demon in front of him.

"If I step foot into Calydan, I will be killed on sight. There is a bounty on my head because my people believe that I killed the King of Calydan."

Callian glowered fiercely at Grayson.

"And did you kill the king?" he spoke through his teeth.

Grayson didn't flinch when he finally spoke.

"I killed my father, they just happen to be one in the same," he spat at the ground. "Not even my position in the Nightraiders or being the rightful heir to the throne could've saved me, so I ran."

The assassins blinking was the only indication that they were blindsided by Grayson's truth, but Callian forged on.

"Sounds like a problem for you, but I am sure you can get creative."

Kieryn stepped up to Callian, crowding his space.

"And who is to say I'm going to go with you? I don't like you."

Callian's hand whipped out, caging Kieryn's body into the cave wall, his hand coming up to grip her chin. The sounds of three blades being pulled from their scabbards reverbated in the air, but he was *the Angel of Death,* none could best him.

"If you'd like to give your friends the best chance at surviving, you will listen to me and follow my instructions. I can keep you safe, against my better wishes," he seethed. He leaned in closer. "And for the record, I don't like you either."

He loosened his grip on her chin and turned to face the readied assassins behind him.

"Shall we?" Callian beckoned them further into the tunnel.

The tensions were high between the assassins and Callian, but they followed him silently through the tunnels. His power radiated off him in waves, causing the air to drop in temperature, the only warmth being the fire coming from the wall sconces.

After an hour or so, they finally reached the end of the tunnel, where with another flick of Callian's wrist, the door swung open with a blast, revealing a forest beyond.

Callian broke the silence.

"We're close to the inn. You don't have much time, so grab what you need and get out. It'll only be a matter of time before the Minas Army arrives," Callian explained.

"How do you know this is where we were staying?" Grayson accused him.

"I know everything. You assassins like to stay off the grid, plus no one willingly stays at the *Kismet Inn*."

The assassins exchanged a look, remembering their form of payment for a night's sleep in a bed. Kieryn shuddered at that thought and what it dredged up for her.

"You have five minutes, make them count," Callian directed towards Kieryn.

The four assassins left Callian in the woods, making their way through the forest back towards the Inn.

"I don't like that guy," Grayson spoke out loud, swiveling his head to make sure he wasn't following them. "I don't trust him. And I sure as hell do not like the fact that you'll be with him, Kier. He's dangerous. You know his reputation."

Kieryn reached out, squeezing Grayson's hand, hoping to comfort him just a little bit.

"I don't either. As much as it pains me to admit it, though, he's right. His father is after me, not you guys. The best plan is to draw them away from you, and I can take care of myself, you know that. And strangely, I have a feeling that he's not going to hurt me."

"You can't be serious, Kier. He's *the Prince of Darkness*, he's leveled cities and disemboweled those who even looked at him wrong. How can you know he won't do the same to you?!" Grayson replied frustratingly.

"Call it a gut feeling. He needs me alive, not dead—which is why I know I'll be the safest with him. And ..." she trailed off, not daring to voice the rest.

"And what? What were you going to say?" Ash prodded.

"I feel like I know him. Like there's some connection between us. I don't know what it is or what it means, but my mind and body can feel that he's familiar. I can't really explain it."

She could feel their judging stares as she crossed the threshold of the inn. She knew they wouldn't understand. She barely understood it herself. She had heard the gossip in Exile, and she didn't have to meet him to know that all of those stories were true. But whether it was her soul or her shadows reaching out towards him, she didn't know. All she did know was that there was something between them, and she didn't like that one bit.

They followed her into the inn, all four on high alert as if expecting the Minas Army to pop up from behind the bartop. No one peered up at them from over their mugs of beer, the news from Venetu hadn't reached them. Yet. They slipped quietly up the stairs and changed out of their dress attire and back into their assassin leathers.

By the time they had dressed and grabbed their bags it was nearly midnight. Just then, Callian emerged from the darkness on top of a black stallion as dark as the night itself, its only marking a white crescent moon shape just above its nose. The stallion's eyes were a beady red, as if the horse came from the pits of Hel.

"Say your goodbyes," Callian said, as he dropped down from the horse.

Grayson stepped up to Kieryn first, giving her a tight bear hug.

"Stay safe, Kier, please. I love you."

Those three words sent a crack as wide as a chasm through her heart. She wasn't used to people's feelings and being told she was cared for, let alone admitting them out loud herself. She hugged Grayson tighter at those words. He was always the one to openly express his feelings. Discovering his secret tonight sent her on an internal spiral that she had no choice but to tuck away to process another time.

"I …" she wanted to finish that sentence, but couldn't bring herself to say those words back, even though she felt them. So instead she said, "Stay safe, Grayson. I have faith that you will be okay in Calydan. Stay alert, and stay hidden," she said, giving him another squeeze, wondering how she missed the fact that he was the lost heir to Calydan. The entire realm believed him to be dead, or at least that was the announcement Calydan Kingdom had made back then. Now she knew they were trying to cover it up. Everyone had their secrets: her with her shadows, Damien and his refusal to shapeshift, and Grayson being the heir to a lost kingdom. What was Ashlyn's buried secret?

"You've been like a sister to me. I can't lose you," Kieryn began to say to Ashlyn. "Keep him safe, okay? Watch over him, make sure he's …" Kieryn trailed off, not knowing what to say.

Ash nodded into Kieryn's hair, understanding all the same. "I'll take care of him. Stay safe out there!"

Kieryn turned to Damien, taking a step forward as he took a step back. He put up a hand to stop her.

"Don't."

He crossed his arms, turning to the side slightly.

"Take care of yourself," Damien grumbled before walking toward the horse, turning his back on Kieryn.

"Give him time, Kieryn. I'll get through to him," Ashlyn expressed, her voice full of concern and a sliver of hope.

Kieryn nodded and watched her friend walk towards Damien. She prayed to the gods that it wouldn't be the last time she saw all of their faces.

Finally she willed herself to face Callian. He stood there staring at her with an expression on his face that she couldn't exactly place.

"Let's go, Princeling."

She walked towards him and his demon horse, dressed in her leathers and vest, her cape blowing behind her in the phantom breeze. She was armed, *Makaria* strapped to her hip and her dagger holstered to her thigh. Another knife was sheathed and laid on the underside of her left forearm.

She ignored the hand that Callian held out for her, and grasped the saddle. With her foot in the stirrup, she swung her right leg over the horse and moved as far up as she could. She felt his looming figure as he settled in behind her. One arm snaked up around her, as he gripped the front of her waist and pulled her flush against his hard-muscled body. His hand left her hip, his touch faint but gradual as he grabbed the reins in both hands, caging her in.

Kieryn squirmed in his grasp, trying to put some distance between their bodies, but it was no use. A growl rumbled from his throat as he leaned forward to speak into her ear.

"Keep doing that, and you may just like what you find," he said with a deep and lilting tone.

With a move like lightning, Kieryn had unsheathed her dagger strapped to her forearm and brought it to his throat.

"Say that again, and my hand may just slip," she said icily, as she started to bring her hand lower, to what was no doubt his favorite part.

His hand shot out, gripping her dagger by the blade, his blood pooling in his hand where he sliced it.

"Careful, puppet, violence turns me on," he said with desire, his eyes dilating as he took his bloodied hand and smeared it over the top of her breasts before bending down and licking it clean, his tongue lingering on the swell of her breasts.

"You are a delicious and deviant little demon."

Kieryn was at a loss for words as to what just happened, her voice leaving her, and her mouth opened in utter disgust and shock, shock at the heat between her legs.

He leaned in, dragging his tongue across her neck, licking off more of his blood that he missed.

"I'd close that pretty little mouth of yours, before I find a better use for it," he purred into her neck before sheathing her dagger back into its rightful place and maneuvering her in one move, bringing her back tight against his body.

Kieryn sat rigid in the saddle, not wanting her body to touch Callian's in any capacity, because she didn't want to admit to herself—no couldn't begin to fathom—that his voice, his actions, that wicked tongue of his had made her toes curl in her boots. Her labored breathing sure as hell wasn't because the *Angel of Death* sat behind her, his reputation notwithstanding, but because his touch lit her skin on fire and she craved more of his violent tendencies. Her blood sang for him, her shadows danced underneath her skin, wanting more, and she didn't know what that meant about her.

SEVENTEEN

KIERYN AND CALLIAN trekked through the forest in silence. The stillness in the air made Kieryn's body tense up in response. She could feel her shadows flowing idly under the surface and she willed her mind to keep herself calm, to keep them at bay. She couldn't afford to lose control. Not out here where creatures of the night roamed, including the walking nightmare sitting behind her.

Breathe in.

Hold.

Breathe out.

She repeated the process until she felt her muscles relax and the shadows simmer, but still close by.

One day. That's all it took to completely turn her life upside down. The psychic reading of her imminent death, being told that the King of Eretum and all the kingdoms were on a manhunt for her, selling her soul and learning her shadows came from the very devil himself—she could use a fucking drink right about now. Maybe three.

She shook her head, clearing the dark thoughts that emerged, instead trying to focus on her surroundings. She had parted ways with her friends back at the inn, Damien and Ash taking Whiskey and riding towards Riyadh Kingdom, where she prayed for their safety entering that territory again. She had seen Grayson hesitate before he got on Duchess, the dread washing over his face like a tidal wave. It looked like he was afraid of more than just the bounty on his head.

"Stay vigilant. We're coming into territory that not many people tread through, and for good reason," Callian warned.

She looked around at the trees. There was no breeze and she felt the unease of the forest around her. There wasn't a sound to be heard besides the horse's hooves on the dirt path.

"Why? What is out here?" she questioned him, her eyes darting back and forth watching the trees ahead of them for any signs of danger.

When he spoke, it was barely the hint of a whisper, as if speaking the word would draw them in.

"Nightwalkers."

Kieryn's eyes strayed from the forest and peered back at Callian; horror seeped into her eyes.

"One of your father's creatures?"

"Unfortunately, so. He was always fascinated by the Dark Arts. He prided himself in learning sorcery to create such things, evil things that lurk in the shadows, the monsters parents warn their children about so they don't stray too far from home."

Kieryn thought back to the stories she had heard from her time in the Keep. If anyone had seen a Nightwalker, they almost never lived to tell the tale. Those who had survived, barely existed after that. Their minds were so far gone. It was hard to say what Nightwalkers looked like as everyone's stories were different.

Callian continued, "Nightwalkers can take the form of whatever the person fears the most. They have no exact shape as their chosen skin is visible only to the person whose dread they are representing."

Kieryn whipped her head around, her senses on high alert and her shadows breaching her skin underneath.

Callian leaned into her body and warmth.

"You need to remember one thing when dealing with them. This is important."

Kieryn angled her body towards his, a mere few inches between their faces as he looked directly into her eyes.

"You need to remember that the fear you feel is not real. It is an illusion that the Nightwalkers use as their weapon. When you allow your fear to take over your senses, your psyche becomes unstable, overstimulated. Your body will start to shut down and it feels like you are being drained of your very soul," he murmured, his eyes looking pained as he spoke the last of his words. "If it gets to that point, there is no coming back. They'll take you and torture you brutally over and over again, then heal your mind just enough for you to come to consciousness, only to repeat the process until they are bored and kill you."

Kieryn leaned back at his admission.

"How do you know so much about the Nightwalkers?"

A look of shame flickered across his face, as his gaze met her curious emerald eyes.

"Because they were my idea."

Kieryn stared at him in bewilderment. Of course these heinous abominations would be his idea. Like father like son, she supposed. After she got over the shock of what he had told her, she glared at him with a sinister look in her eyes.

"You're just like your father."

Callian slumped back in the saddle, as if he was physically slapped by her truth. He wasn't always like this, a monster in human skin. He lived a relatively normal life, before everything …

"No, puppet, I am worse than my father and you will soon realize that. But understand, it was not my intention when I first thought about these creatures that they would be unleashed into the realm of innocents. They were to be an army—a last ditch effort if we were attacked. They were supposed to be a weapon, yes, but used only on our enemies."

Kieryn took his words in, but refused to acknowledge his reasoning. Regardless of what his true intentions were, he created them and his father unleashed them.

"I will protect you, at whatever cost," he whispered.

She allowed his words to roll over her, refusing to dissect the meaning behind that sentence and why he felt like he had to protect her. Instead she chose to focus on what possibly awaited them. She could feel his body tense around her, the muscles in his arms rippling. She could see the swirls of his tattoos peeking out from his sleeve, as if they too sensed the danger that lurked beyond the trees. Her shadows licked at her skin, begging to be unleashed. Her shadows felt like a person, she could feel their agitation of being trapped. Caged.

Suddenly, they stopped.

"Why are we stopping?"

Callian closed his eyes and listened intently. When he opened them, they were velvet black and sinister.

"They're already here," he gritted through his teeth, launching his horse into a full gallop.

"Hold on tight and don't let go," he yelled over the air roaring around them. Her golden hair whipped across her face, obscuring part of her vision.

Between the wisps of her hair, she could see a black mist gliding across the forest floor coming towards them. A tree branch up ahead tumbled to the ground, spooking the horse. Callian's horse reared up on his hind legs, knocking off the two riders before taking off at a sprint through the woods. Callian wrapped himself around Kieryn as they fell, taking the brunt of the fall. They landed hard, but that was the least of his concerns.

He looked at her wide, scared eyes.

"Run!"

She didn't hesitate. She sprinted through the forest as fast as her legs could carry her. She didn't dare look back at what was following her. She only knew that Callian was on her heels from the sound of the crashing brush and snap of twigs under his boots.

They came to a clearing that backed up to a cliffside overlooking a ravine. She peered over the edge, getting lightheaded at the sheer drop below. There was no way down. They wouldn't survive that drop, and the water had to be below freezing.

She turned to find Callian, sword already drawn, fighting what seemed to be air. He was sweating profusely, torment on his face as he struggled to fight what was attacking him. She was so focused on Callian that she didn't feel the cool touch of spindly fingers wrapping around her throat from behind and flinging her into the air. She crashed hard by the edge of the cliffside, her breaths strained. She rolled onto her back, right as the Nightwalker straddled her. For a brief second she saw the Nightwalker's true form. They were human, but not. It was as if it had been skinned alive, its jaw was unhinged and she could see the bones poking from beneath the flayed skin. A putrid smell came from the rotting corpse on top of her and she nearly gagged. Then suddenly, the figure changed and became her worst fear.

Suddenly, it wasn't skin and bones, but actual flesh. It was the mysterious figure from that night. He was still masked, but this time he wasn't going to save her. She struggled underneath him, as the creature's claws dug into her side, piercing her skin. Her cry rang out as she wrestled to free her hand out from under her body to reach her dagger.

The acidic smell of the creature's breath wafted over her as it leaned in.

The voice itself had no tone to it, it was neither male nor female, but what tore from its unhinged mouth incapacitated her.

"You should've died that night. I should've killed you when I had the chance," it hissed.

The vision that dropped over her eyes was her living night-mare. She saw her mother's death, the thud of her body hitting her bedroom floor echoing from behind her eyelids, her blood pooling around her. She screamed in agony.

"Stop! Please!" she begged.

"You beg so pretty," the creature crooned, its claws coming to scrape across her cheek.

"I think I'll take my time with you. You have a very inter-esting mind, indeed."

She looked up into her attacker's eyes, but saw nothing but black, coal-like eyes. *That wasn't right.* The man that night had stunning, beautiful dark blue eyes, eyes she could never forget.

"You need to remember that the fear you feel is not real. It is an illu-sion that the Nightwalkers use as their weapon." Callian's words rang through her ears.

"It's not real. It's not real. It's not real," she chanted over and over again. When she opened her eyes again, it was no longer the man from that night, but the Nightwalker's true form. She reached up and smashed the pommel of her dagger into its skull. The creature reared back, a scowl on its face as it turned into black mist once more and circled the air around her.

Callian crossed the grounds towards her, a slight limp in his gait.

"We can't stay here. They will keep attacking us."

He looked over the edge of the cliff.

"We need to jump."

She stared wide-eyed at him, quickly glancing back at the swirling obsidian mist surrounding them.

"Are you out of your damn mind! We won't survive the fall. We will die upon impact," she protested. She swung her eyes back to the faceless monster in front of them.

"I'd rather take my chances with the Nightwalkers."

Callian grabbed her by the waist, pulling her into his body, cradling her body against his.

"You'll just have to trust me," he said sweetly into her hair. The smell of vanilla and cedarwood hit him in the center of his chest.

She peered up at him, then over to the black mist, and before she could think it through, she placed her hand in his, right as he flung their bodies off the side of the cliff and into the rushing water below.

EIGHTEEN

THE RUSH of the wind left a trail of goosebumps up and down her skin. She forgot how much she loved the freefall, the feeling of time standing still, a time where the noise faded to the background. She was afraid of heights, but the freefall was an exhilarating rush to her—she was untouchable in that moment. She felt her stomach jump to her throat as gravity forced her down.

She knew the height of the cliff could potentially kill them, but Callian had told her to trust him, and she did blindly, surprising herself. She didn't dare open her eyes for fear of seeing her death when it came to meet her. She'd rather remain ignorant in that matter. While her stomach remained lodged in her throat, she didn't feel the dragging pull toward the ravine below them. Instead, she felt like she was gliding through the air, like she was slowly being lowered. Right as she opened her eyes and went to pull her head back from Callian's chest, gravity kicked in and she felt the impact of the icy rush of the water, and she took a giant breath.

The impact of submerging into the freezing water caused Callian and Kieryn to be forced apart. The sheer force of the water dragged her lower and lower into its black abyss. She pried her eyes open, trying to assess how deep she had gone. She willed her legs to move, and she swam toward the surface. She broke through the water, barely getting a breath into her lungs. She looked around frantically, trying to find Callian in the dark.

"Callian!" she struggled to scream. But it was no use. The onslaught of the river drowned out her voice. She heard a splash behind her, and she twisted around to see if it was Callian breaking through the water to her. She turned her head, just as something latched onto her foot and dragged her down through the murky water. Kieryn swallowed water as she struggled to disentangle herself from whatever had grabbed her. She looked down to discover an outline of a figure. The creature blended in with the shadows, but she could see a webbed hand wrapped firmly around her ankle.

Selkies.

They were ghastly creatures who lived in the deepest and darkest depths of the water. A distant and estranged cousin of the beautiful and alluring sirens. They were skeletal with webbed hands and feet that formed so they could adapt to their new surroundings. They had no teeth, instead their mouths consisted of a pronged tongue that was more like a razorblade. They would wrap their tongues around their prey, decapitating it before swallowing it whole.

Kieryn started to panic and reached for her dagger hidden in her leathers. Trying to move through the water made her slower in her movements but she was finally able to unhook her dagger from its casing. She arched her right arm downwards, slashing at the webbed hand holding her hostage underwater. Through the roaring of the water in her ears, she distinctly heard the hissing of the selkie as it howled in pain. It released her, its blood circling the water between them. Kieryn didn't hesitate, she kicked back toward the surface, her lungs on fire, wanting to explode from the pressure. She was almost there.

Just ten more feet to go. Her lungs started to constrict, and her vision blurred. All she saw was black before her lungs collapsed and in one last attempt, she shot her hand through the water, praying to the gods to help her.

Callian's heart skipped when Kieryn had placed her hand in his, her blinding trust in him almost gutting him where he stood on the precipice of the cliff. They had jumped together, his arms coming around to embrace her and guide her gently down. He would've survived the fall, but he knew she wouldn't. He had told her to close her eyes, not from the fear of jumping into the dark oblivion and the rush of the water coming to greet them, but so she wouldn't see him. He was the *Angel of Death* for a reason, in more ways than one.

The impact of their bodies shot through the water, and he lost his grip on her, the water dragging him further away from her. He swam toward the surface, hoping to catch a glimpse of her. He could see in the dark, better than anyone else could, but all he saw was darkness and the jagged cliff rising towards the moon. He tuned out the lapping of the water as it glided along him and listened intently for her voice. He heard nothing. He swam with the current, desperately looking for the bright halo of her hair only to come up empty.

He had to find her! He needed her to be alive …

He smelled the blood in the water and swam towards the scent, praying that it wasn't her blood.

He saw a faint outline of a hand through the dark bloodied water, and he dove below the waves, chasing after her. He reached Kieryn, relieved to find the blood wasn't hers, but distraught to find her unconscious. He circled his arm around her waist and brought her back through the water. He dragged her toward the rocky shore, carrying her in his arms as he gently lowered her to the ground. He palmed her chest and started to press down repeatedly, before finally tilting her chin upwards and breathing into her mouth. He repeated the process, only stopping to put his ear to her chest to see if she was alive. She wasn't breathing, but she had a faint heartbeat. Just as he was about to lean down to breathe into her mouth again, water spilled from her lips as she began to cough up water. He turned her to her side and he let her body lean against his knees as she hacked up all the water from her lungs.

She rolled back onto her back and saw Callian leaning over her face, too close for comfort.

"Did you just kiss me?" she asked, a show of revulsion on her face.

Callian stood to attention and let out a belly laugh.

"My sweet puppet, you're welcome for saving your life by the way, and no, I did not kiss you." He leaned down until his lips hovered inches from hers. "If I kissed you, you would certainly know." He lingered there, a sultry smile forming, and her eyes dilated, coated in lust. "And something tells me you would enjoy it."

He stood then, surveying the rocky shore, seeking out shelter.

"Let's go!" he ordered. "I believe there is a cave nearby that we can hide out in until the morning. The Nightwalkers won't risk coming this close to the water."

Kieryn got to her feet and scoped the area out herself, finding nothing but jagged cliffs and a waterfall. What cave was he talking about? She strained her neck looking back up at the edge of the cliff and was rooted to the spot. There was no way they should've survived that jump, yet here they both were. She was pondering this when Callian spoke from the darkness.

"Today, *puppet!*"

She gritted her teeth, wondering when she would have the

opportunity to stab him in his neck. She followed behind him mutely, curious to see where they were heading. Callian strode over toward the hundred-foot waterfall towering over them like a giant.

"This is the cave?" she questioned.

Callian didn't so much as turn around. "You ask too many questions. The cave is behind the waterfall."

She peered over his shoulder, only seeing darkness and hearing the thunderous sound of the roaring waterfall plummeting down the side of the cliff.

They scoured over the slippery rocks, until Kieryn saw the opening to an underground cave. With a snap of his fingers, Calian had made a bag full of supplies materialize from thin air. He went to work pulling things from the bag and looked around the dark and damp cave to start a fire.

"What kind of magic do you possess?" she asked while roaming the cave, fascinated.

She saw the orange glow of flames illuminate the cave, and could see the outline of the shadows on Callian's face. He was really handsome to look at, and she was sure he knew it too. His face was chiseled like stone, as if a sculptor created him to resemble a god. She came closer to the fire, not sure if she was drawn to the heat of it or the way Callian's eyes looked when he had hovered over her earlier.

"I have dark magic in my blood along with being a *Bloodling*," he replied after a bit, as if debating what to reveal to her. Dark magic wasn't uncommon for those of Eretum. It was another form of magic different from those who resided in Minas. And with Callian being the *Prince of Darkness* it made sense he practiced dark magic like his father, but a Bloodling—that was interesting indeed. Bloodlings were rare, but not uncommon. They possessed the magic to manipulate blood, meaning they could control any living thing. Bloodlings were extremely powerful and a deadly weapon, but the downside was they also craved the taste of blood.

She removed her coat, wringing out the excess water and laying it out to dry, when she winced.

"You're bleeding," Callian said matter of factly.

Kieryn looked down at her white shirt, stained in her blood and molding to her stomach. She touched the wound and hissed.

Callian stood at attention, his nose wrinkled and his eyebrows sitting low on his forehead. Was he concerned?

"Take off your shirt!" he commanded her.

Kieryn looked up at him, shock written across her face. "Excuse me."

"Did I stutter? Take off your shirt."

Kieryn hesitated, her hand lightly gripping the underside of her shirt. Callian's demeanor changed from concerned to agitated.

"*Puppet,* if I wanted to see you naked, I wouldn't have to ask."

She rolled her eyes, begrudgingly removing her shirt. She felt a small inkling of fear having him within arm's length of her blood.

Callian watched as she removed the soiled linen from her body, captivated by her perky breasts nestled in that pretty black lace bralette of hers. He cleared his throat.

"Lay down," he instructed her, laying a blanket he grabbed from the bag down on the cave floor for her to rest on.

She did as he said, her eyes never leaving his, the moss green of her eyes holding questions she wanted to voice out loud.

Kieryn lowered herself to the blanket on the damp cave floor, wary of irritating her wound more, and slowly leaned back. Callian moved closer then, coming to kneel before her, like he was when he had brought her to shore.

His jaw was clenched, and his eyes were a darker shade than they usually appeared as he assessed her injuries.

He reached around for his bag, digging out the tools he needed to close the wound. He pulled out a needle, thread, and a flask and her eyes narrowed. He handed over the flask.

"You're going to want this for the pain," he insisted.

She tipped the flask back to her throat, the taste of whiskey burning as it glided over her dry lips.

Callian grabbed the flask from Kieryn's hand and poured it over the open wound, cleaning it out as best he could. She bit down hard, gritting her teeth and sucking in a deep breath from the pain. His jaw clenched, as he made eye contact with her, as if hurting her hurt him in the process.

"You ready?"

She nodded, swiping the flask back, opening her lips and pouring more of the fire down her throat.

Callian took a white cloth and dabbed at any remaining blood, clearing the area. He looped the thread through the needle, and then pushed the sharp object through her skin and rotated his wrist for it to pierce her skin again.

Kieryn thought her jaw was going to shatter from how hard she was clenching it tightly. She saw starbursts behind her eyes, and she tried to breathe as best she could through the agonizing pain. She had been through worse, but she still wasn't a fan.

She tried to distract herself from the pain by watching Callian while he was distracted and concentrated on fixing her up. Despite his large hands, he was meticulous with his work, his fingers deftly working the needle in and out through the opening in her side. He may be the *Angel of Death*, but his touch was the opposite. He was soft and gentle as his long fingers laid spread out on her bare skin. She couldn't tear her eyes away from his fingers.

As he worked his way suturing up her wound, the faint

touch of his fingertips glided close to the underside of her breasts, where his fingers met lace and his body tensed. His hand was hot to the touch, and he swept his thumb soothingly back and forth, almost reflexively, right underneath the material. They both inhaled sharply, and his eyes met hers, tension mirroring in both their eyes. Her breathing was labored, his hand still splayed underneath her bralette that didn't really hide what lay underneath, and the caress of his thumb kept up its steady movement.

His eyes dropped, watching the rise and fall of her chest, the valley of her breasts a temptress for his cock that was growing hard in his pants. The black lace was doing nothing to hide the pale pink of her perky nipples. He leaned back, breaking the trance that he felt like he was in and turned away from her, putting away all the materials.

"You're all set," he mumbled almost incoherently.

Kieryn cleared her throat. "Thanks for that."

Callian grumbled and handed her one of his shirts that was still dry. "I'm going to see what else I can find," he said to her, turning and walking further into the depths of the cave, leaving Kieryn at a loss for words.

Callian stumbled through the labyrinth of tunnels, putting distance between him and Kieryn. Being close to her and her blood was maddening. He was in pain the entire time he closed up her wound, while the temptress lay underneath him, her body and the smell of her blood a seductive siren's call. He wondered what her blood would taste like—would it be sweet or tart? It wasn't until he knew he was far enough from her that he punched the cave wall with the full force of his powers, making the rocks shake and crumble. Blood didn't affect him like it would other Bloodlings. He had decades to control that hunger, to suppress that demon side of him. But *her* blood—it called to him. He sank to the ground, burying his face into his hands when he smelled it. Her enticing scent, her blood. He looked down and for the first time he registered he was still clutching the bandage he used to clean the blood from her side.

Without any hesitation, he brought the cloth to his nose and inhaled her blood. His eyes flared, and his tattoos rippled beneath his skin. His inner demon dared him to take just one taste. He warred with his conscience, on the brink of bloodlust for the first time in his life. The smell of her blood made his mind weak. Made him weak. Maybe one taste wouldn't hurt. He could control it, he had been ordered not to harm her, so what was the harm in giving in to temptation?

He inhaled her blood again, before lowering the cloth to his lips. His tongue darted out where her blood was still wet, and when her blood dripped onto his tongue, his one thought before he saw darkness was that her blood was like honey— sweet and addictive.

NINETEEN

WITH EVERY STEP Grayson Hunt took towards Calydan Kingdom, he felt like he was one step closer to his death. He had watched Ashlyn and Damien steer their horse back towards Riyadh Kingdom, the feeling of regret weighing in his stomach like an anchor. He had watched his best friend die. He saw the blood. He observed the light in his once bright eyes fade as Kieryn knelt over him, choking on her emotions. In that moment, Grayson felt like a piece of him died with Damien. His best friend had entered *the Veil*, and Grayson knew he had lost his opportunity to make amends. Upon being initiated into the *Guild of Phantoms*, one of the main objectives they drilled into the assassins' heads was to not get close. What they did was dangerous, and they were bound to lose people; and they had. Lots of them. But people still formed bonds despite knowing that truth. How could they not? It was a lonely life to live, and Damien, Kieryn, and Ash were all he had left in this life.

But then Kieryn had screamed, a bloodcurdling scream, and shadows erupted from her like branches extending from a tree. All he could do was watch, rooted to the spot in horror, as the cloud of darkness swallowed his two best friends whole.

The stranger that appeared with Kieryn tried to penetrate through the shadow barrier, but was met with resistance. When the mysterious figure extracted his hand from the shadows, his face was stone and the look in his eyes portrayed death, as if he had seen something that haunted him. He stood like a statue, waiting for a sign. Of what, Grayson didn't dare ask.

After what felt like hours, he heard Damien's heartbeat before he had even opened his eyes, and Grayson felt the muscles in his shoulders sag with relief. He vowed to make his friendship with Damien right, regardless if he disagreed with Damien's actions. But as he and Duchess trekked through the forest, he knew he would never have that chance now. Another regret and goodbye he never had a choice in.

The last time Grayson had seen Calydan Kingdom was ten years ago, the last memory he had of his homeland was of desperation and betrayal. He closed his eyes briefly, letting his mind wander to his past and to the kingdom he had lost.

Perched high up on the Cardosian Mountains sat Bajna Castle, its very presence looming over the town of Koscet in the valley. Bajna Castle was known as an enigma to those who had never set foot inside its walls. Even those who were lucky enough to grace the interior of Queen Ambra's residence would never know what lay beneath the surface. That the castle itself was settled directly over a lake, and that the water that surrounded the castle ran underneath its foundation and directly into its underwater caves, which was where Queen Ambra's aerial fleet of Nightraiders and their dragons resided.

Grayson didn't mind living underground back then, despite

it always being damp and musty, he loved the smell of the earth seeping through the stones, and the brief escapism it allowed him. The caves were forged by dragonfire and the hard labor of those who came before them. The tunnels were designed to run deep within the mountains, where there was a hidden cave entrance on the side of the Cardosian Mountains. The castle itself was pentagon-shaped with guard towers at every corner, and trees lined the borders, shrouding the walls from outside intruders. A courtyard ran adjacent to the castle, and below the courtyard was the cistern where they stored their water supply.

If Grayson concentrated hard enough, he could smell the burning wood coming from the chimneys of village homes, the moldy leaves as the seasons changed, and the aroma of nutmeg and hazelnut as people sipped on their coffee in the early light. It was his favorite time of the year there, with the Cardosian Mountains looming over Bajna Castle like watchdogs in the background, the combination of marigold, crimson, and vermilion painting the heads of the Northern Red Oak trees, the air crisp and fresh.

A feeling of melancholy washed over Grayson as he remembered his home. He hadn't realized how much he missed being back in his kingdom, but as he made his journey there, a wave of despair wrapped around his heart and dragged him into its depths. All the good memories were easily swallowed up by the grim ones he had thought he had locked away in a box never to be opened again. The stillness of the unsettling darkness in the small closet under the stairs, the piercing sound of shattering glass, the muffled sound of a deep, furious voice and the distinct noise of a hand hitting flesh, the muffled whimpers of his mother, all slammed into the forefront of his mind. The onslaught of his trauma-filled childhood knocked the breath from his lungs, as he fought the emotions building in his chest.

His mother was young when she married his father, three years younger than he was now. She used to talk about their whirlwind affair with affection and adoration in her eyes. She was to be married off to someone in her village, when she had met his father, who was passing through with his men. His father was king back then, but preferred to fight in the front lines in the aerial fleet with his men, and his mother a barmaid in the tavern they frequented. According to his mother, his father was smitten and relentless in winning her over, and win her over he did. Grayson was born two years later. The position of king changed him overtime. He wasn't sure what altered his father's personality, whether it was the stress of threats from neighboring kingdoms, or his panic-driven attacks from when he was younger and fought in battles, but he went from a passionate husband and devoted father to a raging alcoholic and an abuser.

His mother tried to protect him from the worst of it, but those moments were few and far in between. His father locked him in the closet for twelve hours once and when he finally freed him and realized that his son had soiled his pants, he whipped him senseless. His mother tried to escape with him, he remembered that. He was ten years old when his father caught them trying to sneak out of the castle while he was in one of his drunken stupors. They never made it to the front door. He tied his mother to a chair and beat her senseless, but he was always careful to never leave bruises where onlookers would see. He made Grayson watch the entire time. His mother was left with three broken ribs, a fractured collarbone, and a broken wrist that night.

The next day, his mother held his hand and enlisted him in the Nightraiders. She knew his father couldn't touch him while he was under the eye of the Nightraiders. He loved his mother for that, because his family there saved him. His dragon healed him. But he also knew that in saving him, she had forfeited herself to the abusive hands of her former lover. He resented her for that, too. He felt helpless that he couldn't do more to protect her.

The Nightraiders made him stronger, resilient, and brave. He still saw his father when he made an appearance at training, but he grew to no longer fear him, but to be better than him and stronger. He stood up to his father in all different ways, even if he still ended up punished for it. One of the worst punishments was preventing him from seeing his mother. It was six years until he saw his mother again, at the age of sixteen, the night where everything went to Hel.

Grayson shook his head, trying to clear his mind from that dreadful night. Instead he tried to focus on the task at hand—making it to Calydan without getting killed on sight. The easiest way of getting to Calydan from Minas was through the Hangman's Chasm, a deep fissure that ran through the snowy Bakrem Alps. While it was the easiest way for traveling purposes, he would be out in the open for any Nightraider guarding from the skies to spot him, which only left him with one other option. *The Bloodwood Forest.*

The Bloodwood Forest bordered Calydan and Eretum Kingdom and was filled with lethal and vile creatures that the *Mad King* had manufactured. Luckily, he didn't need to go deep into its bloodthirsty web of terror, he could remain on the outskirts of the treelines, enough to remain unseen and under cover from the skies above.

Grayson trembled with every step Duchess took closer to Calydan, knowing he couldn't just waltz right into the queen's castle and ask for her aid, even if she was family. He had to be meticulous, calculating, and cautious in his approach. And then it hit him, like an arrow to the chest. He knew exactly where he could go that remained on the edges of the border of his kingdom. A place where he could sneak off to and remain under the radar, plan his reappearance from the dead or possibly his death. One of the two was bound to happen. But going back to that place, to his sanctuary that he shared with her, was going to bring back memories he didn't want to dig up. He sighed in defeat, his body sagging into the saddle as he started to dig his grave, and the image of *her* crossed his mind.

TWENTY

WHENEVER THERE WAS a dull moment in time, Ashlyn's thoughts always fell back to her. Her porcelain skin and rosy cheeks, the freckles that framed her button nose, those sweet, innocent doe-like blue eyes the color of the ocean. Not the deep sea blue, but the color of the waves as they recede back into the sea, the in-between of blue and green—that was her eyes if she had to put a word to it. The in-between.

She saw Damien's rigid body tense up as they got some rest in the carriage. He was still torn up over what occurred at the masquerade ball. She didn't blame him for his reaction. He had mentioned he had seen Natalie again and was reunited with her once more. She didn't know who Natalie was to him, or what she had meant to him, but she could only imagine the despair he was in. She couldn't imagine the irreparable damage that must have been done to his soul. If that were Ivy, she would've dug her fingers into the patchy dirt and held on for dear life. She also blamed herself for the state that Damien was in. He never would've died if it wasn't for her. He died protecting her. She had to live with the fact that he was hurting because of the actions he took for her. She understood Kieryn a little bit better at this moment. She reflected back to their earlier conversation days ago down in the Pit. Maybe Kieryn refused to be anything more with Damien because she was afraid that she'd one day lose him in this life they chose. She understood that more than anyone else. Damien died protecting her, Ivy did the same and Ashlyn had dealt with the fallout, the spiraling, the aftermath of her noble but senseless death. Her and Damien, they were the same.

They teased her about her love life, how it was non-existent. But, they didn't know it was intentional, and she kept it that way because Ashlyn didn't believe she could find someone she loved as much as she loved Ivy. What they'd had was special, and she worried that if she began to feel that towards anyone else, it would taint Ivy's memory.

Alessian warriors were all beautiful, but it was Ivy's fiery spirit and bright light that drew Ash into her orbit. In a way, she guessed that's why she was drawn to Kieryn from the start as well. Kieryn and Ivy had similar personalities, but Ash never saw Kieryn as more than a friend.

The friendship they formed, she'd needed it back then. In a way, becoming friends with Kieryn all those years slowly healed Ash. In some ways, she felt close to Ivy's ghost again.

She knew her friends wouldn't judge her based on who she loved, but she just couldn't bring herself to bring up that traumatic moment in her life. She wasn't ready to dig up her past, not yet.

Her hands gripped the dagger in her hand until knuckles turned white. Glimpses of sunlight through the window penetrated her closed eyelids, reminding her of the way Ivy's hair fell around her like a halo on her pillow. The blinds that cast patterns of light on her nude body, her limbs tangled up in the sheets. Her sleepy smile as she slept peacefully next to Ash. A stark contrast to Ashlyn's dark silk hair and olive-toned skin. It gutted her to think back on those moments in her life.

Damien had no idea they shared similar trauma, similar tragic love stories, but she didn't know how to comfort him with that knowledge without revealing who she was. After what happened back then, she didn't trust anyone with her secrets.

The thought of Ivy stirred up her time of training as an Alessian warrior. It felt like a lifetime ago, an old version of who she was, but it was only seven years ago.

Gods, seven years?

Had it really been that long since she had felt hollow, like she just merely existed? She missed the female warriors, her other family. They were fierce, loyal, and protective. She knew without a doubt, they'd come running to help her if she asked. She also knew they would do anything to help Elijiah's kid. To the Alessians, Kieryn was already one of them, even if she hadn't trained with them. She had the heart and soul of one, and just as they would be loyal and protective of Ash, they would be of Kieryn, a kindred sister they never had the opportunity to know.

Ashlyn remembered Kieryn's father well. He was a good-looking man with chestnut hair cut close to his head, and a piercing icy blue stare. He was stern and strict with his training, but not overbearing, a sweet man that made sure his warriors were well taken care of for Queen Nyla.

The Fair Queen was what many people referred to the Queen of Almeria as, but her warriors knew her to be a fierce fighter and one of the best Alessian warriors in history. Many people had forgotten over the years that she was a warrior first before she was queen. Many didn't realize that you could be both. A woman could be anything she set her mind to.

Ash tried to control her breathing, twirling the dagger between her fingers. She wondered if she would fight alongside her fellow warriors once more. Deep down she pondered whether she actually wanted to. She had loved being an Alessian warrior: talking into the late night with each other, the power of wielding a sword, feeling in control and powerful in her body, but with it came a deadly cost that she had paid.

She couldn't be an Alessian, not without Ivy by her side. It was *their* dream. Leaving her family behind was the second-hardest thing Ashlyn did in her life, but becoming an assassin was the next best thing. Being a Phantom for the Guild wasn't tainted with her past and bad memories. It was a beginning, a new life of starting over as someone different, so long as she hid her true identity behind a mask.

TWENTY-ONE

KIERYN WOKE up to the lingering scent of cedar and sage. She took a deep breath of the woodsy aroma before slowly opening her eyelids to the damp dark cave she was in. For a brief moment, she completely forgot where she was. She peered down at the oversized white tunic shirt she was wearing, fingering the material of the shirt that skated just above her mid-thigh, and lifted the warm leather jacket covering her bare legs. *Callian.*

She sat up slowly, taking in her surroundings. The makeshift fire that Callian had assembled last night was down to the embers, the red coals glowing in the gloomy cave. She noticed he was gone, and she couldn't help but wonder if he had left her behind.

Her thoughts drifted back to yesterday: Damien's stricken face at her betrayal, the look of confusion and awe on her friends' faces at her shadows, the bargain she struck up with the devil himself, the truth of her shadows, the Nightwalkers … but it was their jump off the cliff that was on a consistent loop in her mind. There was no explanation as to how they had survived that fall. She should be dead, but she wasn't.

How did I survive?

This thought ran rampant as she pondered the possibilities, when she heard footsteps approaching. She lunged for her dagger and sprung to her feet, her body melting into the cavern walls, the darkness of her shadows shielding her from the intruder. Weird, she thought to herself, she had never been able to do that with her shadows before. She waited in silence, not daring to breathe. The footsteps stopped just shy of where she was hiding, and she didn't hesitate, she struck.

Except, Kieryn ended up being the one pinned between the cavern rocks and Callian's muscled body, her dagger to his throat, as he stared down at her with those obsidian eyes, the dark circles casting a shadow over his high, sharp cheekbones. He wore a smug expression that should not be as distracting, but was, his eyebrows shooting upwards, disappearing underneath his curly locks of hair.

Kieryn was wedged between two solid forms, his body a welcome weight. He was close enough that she could see the jagged, protruding scar that ran diagonally over his right eye. Why didn't she notice that before now? She felt the urge to lift her hand and trace its path.

"I can kill you, you know."

His smile grew as he laughed, his arrogance penetrating through his icy exterior.

"I'd love to see you try, puppet."

Kieryn wanted to wipe that smirk right off his face with her blade, she wanted to see him bleed because of her. She craved that feeling of power, and it seemed like her shadows agreed with this decision. Maybe it was because of that feeling, she pushed him away and lowered her weapon. But Callian pulled her body flush against him and purred into her ear, "I like seeing you like this."

She didn't move an inch. "Seeing me like what? her answer falling from her lips faintly. Her mind only now registering that

Callian was shirtless, with nothing but his black leathers on. She tried not to notice how warm his chest was, or that there was a trail of hair that glided over his ripped stomach and how the path went lower …

"You, provoked and seething wearing nothing but my shirt." He pulled back slightly and glanced down at her. Her body arched backwards from the position he held her in, betraying her thoughts and making her nipples pebble at his attention. That and the goosebumps that trailed along her arms were the only indication of what his words did to her. He smiled then, knowing the effect he had.

She bristled and forcefully took a step back, her body chastising her in the process.

With her arms folded across her chest, she demanded to know where her clothes were. His eyes grew darker as he drank in her appearance. His white tunic rose higher with her arms crossed, and a knowing smirk graced his face.

"Right over there," he remarked with a nod in the direction of the fire. She glanced sideways to where he implied and saw her bag laying there.

His hand reached out, and he made a gesture as if to come closer, but she remained frozen.

"What?" she said in a dry tone.

"I'd like my shirt back. Hand it over."

She grunted her displeasure, as she ripped his shirt off and threw it at his face. She stood there half-naked in her under-garments, simmering with rage as she strode over to where her bag lay and crouched down to grab her clothes. She discreetly looked behind her to see if he was still observing her, but once again he had disappeared without a sound. She felt disappointed when he was gone.

She quickly dressed, throwing on her black pants and top, and finally lacing up her boots. She tied back her hair into a braid with a strap and followed him out. She found him gazing out beyond the waterfall, lost in his thoughts. The sun's light blinded her briefly, before her eyes adjusted to the light change.

"We have a long walk ahead of us, we need to move," he stated.

She gave him a terse nod and followed him out of their safe refuge and back into the danger.

It was late afternoon by the time Callian and Kieryn made it towards the outskirts of Eretum Kingdom. They had walked in silence since leaving the cave, but it was a comfortable silence. They walked along the bank of the river, sticking close to the rocks for protection, before the river opened up and the dark woods before them beckoned them into their waiting arms. Luckily, they didn't run into any more creatures along the way. They were just cresting the hill when they came upon a cottage nestled among the trees.

"We can rest here tonight before we set sail tomorrow. The port we need to get to is just beyond those trees," Callian explained to Kieryn as she shielded her eyes from the sun, trying to get a glimpse of the cottage before them.

All around them, the world seemed to slow down and go quiet. Too quiet for her liking. She followed him, her steps light and cautious, her hand resting on the hilt of her sword, just in case, as they approached the cottage. Callian's hand reached for the handle on the door, finding it unlocked. They exchanged a wary glance before they both unsheathed their weapons and made their way inside. They cleared the cottage in less than a minute, finding the place dusty and undisturbed for quite some time.

Kieryn dropped her bag and sheathed her sword, taking in the little cottage in the woods. She could tell that the cabin was a cozy sanctuary once upon a time. The cabin looked like it was built by hand and with love, using the oak trees around them. She could picture the fireplace being lit, filling the cottage with warmth and happiness, the smell of the burning wood wafting through the chimney into the open air. There was a wall filled with books that had collected dust, and a couch lay hidden underneath a white sheet. She grabbed hold of the sheet and tossed it to the side, a cloud of soot blanketing the air as she did. She coughed at the onslaught of dust and saw a brown leather couch still in good condition.

She heard Callian rummaging around in the kitchen, looking for food. She made her way over to the fireplace, kneeling before it, curious to see if there were any logs they could use to start a fire. Night would come soon, and it was getting colder with the sun sinking below the treeline.

"I am going to go look outside for any logs to start a fire. Want to see if you can find some matches to light it?" she called out to Callian.

He mumbled something, and she took it as a yes. She peered outside from behind the curtain, checking for any movement, and saw no one. She stepped outside, shivering down to her bones with the darkness descending. The sun's light cast a beautiful golden glow over the trees, making it look like the trees were on fire. She started to make her way around the side of the cabin, and finally saw what she was looking for. A small shed stood tall before her, its door slightly off its hinges. She stepped closer to the building, peeking in through the dirty window, and found dry logs. She pushed the door to the side, bending to collect the wood. When she couldn't hold any more, she turned and started to make her way back to the house, only to hear a twig snap somewhere off to her left in the woods. She stopped and listened. Everything was still too quiet. She didn't hear anything else and started to step forward when something came barrelling into her from behind, and a scream tore from her throat.

Callian rummaged through the kitchen, trying to find anything that would get them through tonight. Food, running water, some matches, even. He tested the faucet and discovered they had running water, surprisingly, so that was in their favor. Food was a different story. There was nothing of substance besides moldy bread, a few cans of beans, and soup that they would have to make work for the night. He was just checking the nightstand in the bedroom for matches when he heard Kieryn scream.

Fuck!

He reached for his sword and ran outside to find not the Minas Army, but ten mercenaries from his father's kingdom. *How did they find them?* There was a small carriage he knew was a prisoner transport, and saw two soldiers standing guard. Three of the men were wrestling with Kieryn, half dragging her towards the awaiting prison.

He briefly watched her, mesmerized by her unique fighting skills. One man was at her back and had her arms pinned between them, while another man struggled to remove her Katana from its sheath, and a third was attempting to grab her legs. He watched her kick the man in the nose, breaking it. He heard the insults he muttered under his breath before coming up to spit in her face. As the spit hit her directly on the cheek, he saw a wide smile crest her face, as she threw her whole body towards him, head-butting him and sending him to the ground. Her momentum forward caused the man holding her to loosen his grip. She used that to her advantage to remove her arm from his grip and threw him over her shoulder to the ground before easily sliding her dagger into his heart in one clean swoop. The soldier who a moment ago was grabbing for her sword started to retreat, but she was on him instantly. Her knife cut across his neck so swiftly, he barely had time to react as he sank to his knees, his hands coming up to his throat, as if he could stop himself from choking on his own blood.

Kieryn glanced up and saw Callian lingering by the doorway, blood splattered on her face and her hair disheveled. She looked monstrous, and he felt his cock twitch in his pants at the sight of her unhinged like this.

"Feel free to help at any time," she yelled over to him, as the other guards started to run over, weapons raised.

Callian walked over to her, his own sword drawn.

"I think you had yourself handled," he said, his voice coming out strained and husky.

Her gaze swung his way, perplexity crossing her features, before she released her dagger, the rush of air whipping past a hairsbreadth from his ear before burying itself in the eye socket of one of the soldiers that had tried to come up behind Callian.

"The question is, are you, *princeling?*"

They faced off with the other four mercenaries that came barreling down at them from the woods. They both raised their swords, fighting back to back. Callian was a fierce fighter, and his death blows were swift and efficient. With one graceful swipe of his sword, he severed the head from one Eretum soldier, before twisting his body to meet the blade from the other. He blocked the man's blow, before pushing back and spearing him on his sword. The smell of blood permeated the air. Kieryn couldn't help but be in awe of the way Callian killed. *Reaper of Souls* indeed. Where he was brute and muscular, she was light on her feet and moved with finesse. Sidestepping one soldier to bury her sword in the man's stomach, she quickly dropped low to the ground as another attempted to cleave her head off. As she dropped to the ground, she swung her leg, catching his. Before he could move an inch, she had already speared his heart with her dagger.

With blood still painted across her skin, she found Callian among the carnage.

"Your father's army, I take it."

"Yes," he spat the word, his upper lip curling in disdain. "I …"

She saw the arrow spiraling toward her too late. She heard Callian yell, but it sounded far off in the distance, like an echo. She was shoved to the ground out of harm's way, just as the arrow ripped through Callian's body, the arrow protruding from his shoulder, centimeters above where his heart lay. She rose to one knee, and launched her dagger in the archer's direction, her weapon hitting him right in his throat. She turned back towards Callian just as he collapsed into her waiting arms, dragging them both back down to the ground.

TWENTY-TWO

CALLIAN CLUTCHED HIS CHEST, where the arrow still protruded from his body. He had seen the arrow spiraling through the air, and like a force was controlling him, he pushed Kieryn out of harm's way. He had been badly wounded before, but that still didn't make the pain any less excruciating. He felt a cold chill wrap around his body, as if ice ran through his veins. The pain throbbed from his shoulder like it had its own heartbeat, and then he felt the lick of flames burning him from the inside, before he sank to his knees, collapsing into Kieryn's arms.

Blood rained down around him. He remembered the smell of iron and salt as the lifeless body that bled out before him assaulted his senses. His first kill for the man he despised more than his own father. Callian's life was forfeited by his father in exchange for glory and power beyond his wildest dreams. King Elias didn't even flinch at the price he had to pay for that kind of power, he simply handed his own son over, as if his life meant so little. Now Callian was a slave to this man, doing his bidding and killing for sport. An endless cycle of blood, regret, and pain. He couldn't even remember the last time he felt an ounce of freedom.

Callian faded in and out, images flashing before his eyes,

from his past to the present. He focused on the sound of Kieryn's heartbeat, as he tried to forget about the burn ripping apart his insides. He could feel the flames burning a path through his bloodstream, caressing his vitals like a longtime friend. He felt Kieryn's hands lift him from under his arms, dragging him backwards towards the house. She kept mumbling *"I'm sorry"* over and over again, as if she felt responsible for the arrow sticking out from his skin. Callian bit down hard on his bottom lip to prevent himself from crying out, but he knew she could see the agony written across his face as he hissed through the pain of her jostling his injured arm.

She managed to get his body through the door, and he felt himself being propped up against the couch as he heard her rummaging through cabinets and drawers, looking for materials to tend to his wound. His vision started to turn hazy, and his body was burning up, which told him all he needed to know. This arrow was laced with poison.

This will be fun.

Kieryn dropped to her knees before him. It felt like such a struggle for him to lift his eyes to meet hers, and he almost wished he hadn't, because all he saw in her jade-green eyes was anguish and remorse, guilt. Her eyes darted back and forth searching his, and he saw her lips moving, but he couldn't register the words. He was fading. Kieryn grabbed her dagger and shredded his shirt down the middle, leaving him bare before her. His scars were on display for her, and he was thankful that he was in too much pain to care if she thought he looked like a monster. He was a monster, and his scars unveiled the truths of his sinister past. She flinched slightly, but quickly recovered. The blood on her face had dried, but she made no attempt to clean it off, and he found himself still turned on it. She looked like a warrior. He might be delirious at this moment, but he had never seen her look so *god damn* delicious.

"This may hurt," she told him, as she pushed the rest of

the arrow through his shoulder. Callian swore to the Gods as he breathed slowly through his mouth. He felt the arrow tip shred through his skin, and it was like a million needles doused in fire prodding him. He felt his whole body catch fire at the movement.

"I need you to hold still."

She reached behind her, grabbing his flask of whiskey and passing it to his free hand. He lifted his hand, his arm feeling like it was being anchored to the floor. She leaned over him, wrapping her hand around his that held the flask, and helped him lift it to his mouth to sip. Once he was able to hold the flask without dropping it, she removed her hand, and he immediately missed the warmth of her touch. As he tipped the sweet burning liquid down his throat, she placed one hand on top of his shoulder to brace herself, and the other grabbed the arrowhead and snapped it in half. The movement made the flask slip from his mouth, and a few drops slid down his chin.

Kieryn wiped the liquid from his chin with her thumb, her fingers lingering close to his mouth. Their eyes caught and she saw his eyes dancing between her eyes and lips. She couldn't help but part her lips, licking them when she felt a moan fall from his lips.

She pulled back, recovering from that heated, intimate moment and focused on cleaning his wound and treating it for any possible infection.

"It's laced with poison …" he managed to choke out.

Her head jolted, peering at him with terror.

"What kind of poison?" she asked him.

"Liquid Death if I had to venture a guess. My father always had a fondness for that poison."

She remembered from her potions class that *Liquid Death* was a deadly poison. She grabbed her dagger, cleaning it of the blood, sterilizing it.

Luckily, she had stanched the wound, and the blood had

stopped pouring. She stood up and ran outside to collect the logs, and came back inside to light the fire. She explored the cottage, opening up every cabinet, every drawer, every door, until she found some matches and lit a fire for the both of them. Her dagger hovered just above the flames, and she turned back towards Callian, a grimace on his face.

"Deep breath," she said in a calm tone, as she squatted down, leaning over him. He breathed in her scent, vanilla and cedarwood, as she laid the hot dagger over his wound, cauterizing it. His teeth clenched, but he savored her intoxicating smell, letting it soothe him. It felt like a warm hug.

She stood and started to look around for the proper ingredients, and prayed that whoever lived here previously carried what she needed. After a few minutes she discovered the glass cabinet towards the back of the house, filled to the brim of herbs. Thank the gods, she muttered inwardly to herself. The old tenant must have been a witch.

She mixed the ingredients in a grinding bowl and added water to the mix. She made her way back to Callian and sat next to him applying the poultice to his wound, covering it with a leaf she found outside to help keep it moist. With a poison like *Liquid Death,* she would have to keep applying the poultice every hour or so. She just hoped she'd have enough of it to get him through the night.

If he survived the night.

Kieryn checked Callian's pulse, holding steady for now, and felt his head for any fever. It was high, she could tell, but it seemed to be going down. She grabbed the blanket off the chair, and wrapped it around him to help with his shivering. He had nodded off at some point, so she grabbed her sword and headed back outside to take care of the mess they had left.

After over an hour of dragging the dead mercenaries into the woods and hiding them under a thicket of leaves and roots and stripping them of their weapons, including the poisonous arrows, she headed back inside to check in on Callian.

Callian was still where she had left him and sound asleep, his breathing steady. She removed the leaf and took inventory of his wound. It didn't look like it was infected, which was a good sign that he was healing correctly. She reapplied the poultice and covered the wound again with a new leaf from her supply. After grabbing a damp towel from the kitchen, she dabbed at the sweat glistening on his chest and face, trying not to get distracted with how her own body lit up with heat when she touched him.

She spent half the night cleaning his wound and tending to the fire, trying to keep both alive. She turned his body so that he was able to lay down, his head resting in her lap. Out of habit, she stroked his hair back away from his face, humming a song that her mother used to sing to her when she was sick.

She couldn't help but watch him while he slept, taking advantage of the only time she would be able to take in his appearance without him catching her staring.

He was the *Angel of Death*, but at this moment he just looked angelic. His hair glistened in the firelight, and she watched his eyelids flutter, making her wonder if he dreamed at all, and if so, what was he dreaming about?

She thought back to the small white scars that covered his chest and arms. Some were small and inconspicuous, while others marred his skin, vile and thick. She got lost in her thoughts, wondering about their stories and who tended to his wounds then.

Had he had someone that cared about him?

She knew all scars had stories and secrets of their own; hers did as well. They said a lot about the person who bore them. She knew not all scars were visible, but people wore them on their skin like a barrier between them and the world. She wondered what his said about him. She glided her fingers over the ones on his chest, and she felt his body shiver beneath her touch. As she thought about their scars, she thought back to the attack that transpired.

The poisoned arrow was meant for her. She was supposed to be dead, and she knew Callian had no obligation to save her, let alone take an arrow for her, but he had. She hadn't seen the arrow in time, yet he did, and his first thought was to save her with no thought to the consequences of his actions. His only thought was protecting her.

Why did he save me?

He had no reason to, yet Kieryn spent the rest of the night taking care of him and staring intensely at his face, willing his mind to spill his secrets.

When Callian came to, it was early dawn. He slowly peeled open his eyes, blinking rapidly as he took in his surroundings. His body felt warm, not because he was overheating from the after effects of the poison, but from the deviant little demon above him. He slowly tilted his head upwards, and glimpsed the divine beauty of Kieryn, sleeping peacefully. At some point during the night, she had cleaned the blood from her face.

What a shame.

That version of her was engrained into his fucking soul.

Her head rested on the lip of the couch, and her light snores grounded him back in reality. A ghost of a smile rested beautifully on that heart-shaped face of hers. He cataloged where they were, and the simple fact that this woman had taken care of him last night. His heart ached at the thought. She wasn't at all who he'd imagined her to be. He felt a twitch and realized it was her hand on his bare chest, her fingers sprawled across his body in a protective and possessive way.

Her other hand was woven in his hair, as if she couldn't bear to let go.

Callian's hand reached up and cupped her face, taking in the significance of this moment, painting it into his memory. He felt a kinship of sorts with her that he couldn't yet explain, and he wished they could stay in this moment. But as if she felt his touch, she started to stir. Just as quickly, he pulled back his hand, and a smile graced his face.

Kieryn jostled awake, as if visibly shaken, like she hadn't meant to fall asleep on him. She glanced down at Callian, guilty for being caught asleep, to find not only him smiling up at her, but her hands on his half-naked body. She reined her hands back and instantly felt hollow afterwards.

What is happening to me?

Callian was still smiling sheepishly up at her.

Her sleepy voice had a bite of agitation when she spoke.

"What are you smiling for? You threw yourself in front of an arrow last night, or did you forget."

His smile grew wider at that statement.

"I think I was dreaming."

His face fell momentarily, before he quickly recovered. "You were in it, smiling at me."

She scoffed, barely suppressing the smile that wanted to break free from her lips.

"If I was smiling at you, it was most definitely a dream."

Callian laughed so abruptly, even he was shocked by the noise that came from his throat. But Kieryn savored that sound for a rainy day. It was a beautiful melody to her ears, and she almost asked him to do it again before she caught herself. Her feelings towards Callian were slowly toeing the line of an infatuation of sorts, and that began to worry her. She couldn't develop feelings for this mysterious stranger. But gods, she would make it her mission to hear him laugh again.

Callian sat up slowly, slightly wincing at the pain in his

shoulder. There was no raging inferno licking his skin, but there was still a dull throb where the arrow had pierced. He got to one knee and stood up, stretching the kink in his neck. Despite his sleeping position, he finally had a good night's sleep for the first time in years, and for once, his nightmares didn't wake him up. In fact, when he told Kieryn he had a dream, it wasn't a lie. He couldn't remember the last time he actually dreamt, and was not stirred awake by a nightmare.

He heard Kieryn get up behind him and she laid a hand just over his injury.

"You should let me dress the wound again before we head out."

He didn't look back at her, but she saw him nod his head.

She stood flush to his back, applying the cool ointment to his wound, before coming to face him.

She was standing so close he could see the specks of gold in her emerald eyes. He cleared his throat, erasing any thoughts of her from his head.

"That's twice now I saved your life." Even though he meant to sound smug, his voice came out gentle, with a hint of concern.

She stopped applying the dressing and glanced up at him, her eyes blinking up through her long eyelashes.

"Why did you save me?" she questioned.

He studied her face, and lifted her chin up toward him, wondering how she could possibly ask him that question. As if saving her was beyond imagining. Like her life didn't matter.

"Don't ask stupid questions, little demon. There was no choice in the matter. I swore to you that I would protect you at all costs. I saved you and you saved me, we're even. Don't read too much into it."

She recoiled from his touch, his hand still lingering in the air where he had gripped her chin. A look of hurt took root in her dark eyes. He couldn't dwell on that. As it was, he was already getting soft around her, and he couldn't be blinded by her or the effect she had on him. He had to keep whatever feelings he had for her out of it.

Before she could respond to his comment, he spoke up again.

"We need to get moving. We need to make it to the port by midday," he told her, rummaging through the cottage before he found a black tunic shirt hidden in the depths of the stranger's closet. He started to gather up materials, and snuck a glance her way. She was staring into the flames of the fire, a look of contemplation on her face, before she shook herself out of her reverie and doused the flames. She cleaned up the mess of bloody bandages and threw them in the sink, before making her way back to him and picking up her pack.

He started to reach out to her, to apologize or comfort her, he didn't know, but she brushed right by him and walked out the door, leaving him to stare after her.

TWENTY-THREE

KIERYN AND CALLIAN walked in silence through the dark woods, the canopy of trees so thick, the sun's light barely penetrated through the small openings. What light did sneak through cast shadows of the forest, and if Kieryn looked hard enough, they began to dance into monsters of her creation.

Kieryn kept a watchful eye on Callian to make sure he wasn't showing any lingering signs of the poison. She watched him carefully, studying his movements. She noticed how he kept rolling his shoulders back, presumably to relieve the tenderness in his shoulder. He alternated what hand held his sword, always on alert in these woods after their brushes with death the past few days. Her mind began to wander, wondering how her friends were faring with their own missions.

Is Damien still furious with what I did? Will he ever forgive me? Do I even want him to?

Is Ash keeping him from edging the line of self-destruction?

Did Grayson make it to Calydan Kingdom—is he even alive?

She hated that she didn't know, that she had no form of communication with her friends. It was eating her up inside. She would never admit it out loud, but she was grateful for

Callian's presence. As unbearable as he may be, she was glad that she was not alone, even if she did feel lonely.

They stumbled their way over tree roots and overgrown branches, Callian occasionally helping her over the large fallen trees. His grip on her was tight, but he never lingered with his touch as he did before. She began to miss it, like a child who'd lost its favorite blanket.

They finally came to a clearing upon a hill and peering down she could see Redaia, a small port village of Eretum. The sleepy harbor below them was beginning to wake with the bustle of fisherman and merchants tending to their work. The waves collided against the docks as a large, three-masted sailing ship anchored to the harbor, making its temporary home in the port.

The fog slowly dispersed, revealing more of the narrow streets and the rustic buildings that lined the entrance to the docks. The buildings and homes were as weathered as the fishermen's faces in the high sun after a long day's work. They made their way down the dirt path that ran behind the town's homes. Most of the houses lit up with the villagers out and about. Just as they crested the bottom of the hill, sun-kissed light poked out from behind the gloomy clouds, the reflection bouncing off the water.

The streets were animated with the town now awake, making two mysterious strangers easily noticeable. Kieryn shot Callian a glance, wondering if he noticed. If he did, he didn't acknowledge the unease of the stares around them. Either these people knew who he was, or they could sense the darkness in him. *Death* had entered their village, and they knew.

Callian didn't even have to weave through the crowd, they dodged out of his way, clearing a straight path to the docks, where a ship was anchored, its skull flag billowing in the breeze. She followed behind him closely, scanning their surroundings and keeping her right hand low by her thigh, in close range of her dagger.

Callian's footsteps echoed along the wobbly dock, the discolored wood bending to his weight. He passed by pirates who looked like they had seen better days. A pungent mix of fish, low tide and the body odor of the men permeated the air, making her gag. He came to a full stop in front of a man who looked to be in his early forties, a gold medallion clipped to the front of his shirt, a symbol of captain status. His olive-toned skin was dark and leathery from long days out at sea. His brown eyes were just as dark, lethal-looking as he scrutinized the *Prince of Darkness.* To her surprise, the captain stood his ground. If he was intimidated, he did a good job of hiding it. Maybe he too had a death wish.

Callian wasted no time getting straight to the point.

"I am commandeering your ship. We will need you to accommodate two more passengers and we're looking to go to Keres Kingdom. Do we have a problem?" he said, his tone of voice threatening on the backend of his statement.

The captain glanced over at Kieryn, and back at Callian.

"Yes, I believe we do."

His accent was strong, most likely from the lands further out west, she couldn't place where, though. She was instantly envious of the captain, the places he must have seen outside the continent of Elysium. She wondered what lay beyond their six kingdoms.

Callian stepped closer, invading his space.

"Do tell."

Their pissing match drew a scene from the townspeople, but the pirates easily surrounded them. Kieryn's fingers grazed the handle of her dagger as she stared directly at one of the pirates, a vicious snarl escaping, his response a wicked toothy smile.

"We are not heading to Keres Kingdom," he responded

with certainty, his eyes looking towards Kieryn, a satisfied smirk on his face. "And women aren't allowed on the ship unless they're whoring around for me and my crew."

The pirates that surrounded them laughed maliciously, their intentions clear as day as some started to make crude gestures.

"Touch me and I will feed your cocks to the sea creatures and make you watch before I throw you over," she seethed towards the captain.

The captain stepped towards her menacingly, his ego deflating at her snide remark. Callian's hand seized the captain's arm, ripping him back towards him, before driving him hard against the ship, the captain's teeth rattling at the impact.

The pirates took a step forward, but with one hand raised by Callian, they all stopped dead in their tracks, their hands flying to their throats. Kieryn whipped her head back towards Callian, shocked at the power he just unleashed. The captain's eyes blew wide as he finally realized who was before him. The *Angel of Death* was a befitting title he wore like armor, and Kieryn secretly hoped to see more of this side of him.

"I can kill you all with one flick of my wrist, but I prefer to not steer this ship, I'd rather get drunk instead. So here's what's going to happen. You are going to bring us aboard and take us to Keres Kingdom, no questions asked. If any of your men even look at her the wrong way, I'll let her enact her revenge before I make you choke to death on your own blood. Do you understand?"

Kieryn continued to stare at him in bewilderment. Out of the corner of her eye, she saw some of the pirates drop to their knees, still clutching at their throats, lips turning blue.

"I can't hear you, Captain. You may want to decide quickly before you have a dead crew at your feet. And I will make sure you join them."

"... Yes, okay, I'll do it," he sputtered out.

Callian let out a haughty laugh, as he dropped the captain back to the dock, and with a flick of his wrist, the crew inhaled roughly, coughing up their lungs as they gasped for fresh air.

Callian looked at Kieryn with a shit-eating grin on his face, reaching out his hand for her to take.

"Let's go, puppet."

And without hesitation, she placed her hand in his for the second time in days.

TWENTY-FOUR

AS SOON AS they were out of earshot of the captain and his crew, she dropped his hand and whirled on him.

"What the hell was that!" she demanded.

"Did you not like my neat little party trick?"

"Your party trick," she scoffed at him. "Is that what you call being a Shieik? Why the hell didn't you do that when we were attacked by your father's men, would've saved you a hole in the chest."

"Because, puppet, it drains a lot of my energy, and I like the feel of blood on my hands."

Her shadows danced at that confession, but her eyes told a different story. For once in her life, Kieryn had no words, instead she bit her tongue and kept quiet as she came to a realization about the man that stood before her. Callian was a bottomless well of raw pure magic.

Shieiks were dark magic wielders that practice mind altering, forcing someone to perform whatever actions the wielder commands. They were no longer in control of their bodies. Callian had made them hold their breath for as long as he said. There was also rumors that stated they could *dreamdive*.

Suddenly, she felt herself mentally building blocks around her mind, protecting herself. Those kinds of shieks were very rare, indeed.

"Where am I sleeping?"

"I say we take the Captain's Quarters after how rude he was, what do you say?"

She grinned ear to ear, and without a backwards glance, she followed him.

The room was spacious for a Captain's Quarters. The room was toward the stern, and its windows rose from the floor all the way to the ceilings, giving Kieryn unobstructed views of the sea before her, the sun shining beams of light through the room.

Burgundy curtains cascaded down over the windows, parting slightly to the side. The room was painted in reds and golds. The bed to her right looked plush, and was set up so it was partially hidden and in a little alcove, and two wooden bookcases stood on both sides of the bed. An oak desk sat parallel with the windows, and perched on top sat maps of the oceans and lands beyond Elysium, a compass and a decanter of a dark colored liquid.

Yeah, she could make do with this room. She turned around to ask Callian where he would be sleeping, but he already answered her question.

"I will be through that door, also known as the Right Hand's Quarters. But, I wouldn't say no to you if you'd prefer to have me warm your bed instead."

"I think the bed would freeze with your cold heart in it," she jested.

"Deny it all you want, puppet, but you'll soon be begging for it."

And with those parting words, he left a speechless Kieryn in his wake. She felt an ache low in between her legs at his words, and she scolded herself for how her body reacted to him. Despite how forward he was with her, she found their playful banter a nice distraction from her life. She stripped her clothes off and sauntered over to the captain's bed. It looked like the Captain had already had his sheets changed, thank the gods.

She'll never take sleeping in a bed for granted again after sleeping in caves and upright against a couch with a semi-dying prince in her lap. She sank deep into the plush satin sheets, and despite her better judgment, her fingers drifted lower, to the opening between her legs. She replayed Callian's words over and over in head.

Her fingers gently brushed along her slit, not surprised to find herself wet at his words. She plunged two fingers inside, and her eyes closed as her head sank into the pillow behind her, as she fantasized about the brooding devil with the midnight eyes in the room next to hers. As her fingers stroked against her clit like a musician strumming his instrument, her legs locked and her orgasm swept her deep under the waves of self-loathing and ecstasy as his name slipped from her lips like poetry.

It wasn't soon after that her orgasm lulled her into a glorious sleep.

She woke up parched and famished. She had only sipped on soup the night before, more worried about trying to keep the idiot from dying in her hands. She ran her fingers through her hair trying to tame the knots that made their home there while she slept. She threw her hair in a bun and checked herself out in the bathroom mirror, wiping smudges of dirt from under her eyelids. She had an afterglow, rosy cheeks and a brightness to her eyes now that she had finally slept well after five days.

She pulled on tight leather pants that hugged her curves, and threw on a white tunic that laced in the front, before pulling on her boots and knocking on Callian's door. She heard a grunt from the other side of the door, taking it as his permission to enter. She turned the handle and pushed open the door, only to stand wide-eyed, mouth hanging open at what she saw.

Callian was mid-stroke as he pleasured himself with his hand, his full Adonis body on full display. She didn't dare look at what he held in his hand, even though his hand barely even covered what was there. She trailed her eyes upwards at the chiseled V-shape that opened up to his abs and chest hair. She could see his forearm flexed with the movement and her eyes finally made it to his face, where he peered at her, half in shock, half with lust. His hand stilled.

"Well, don't stop on my account."

She kept eye contact with him, refusing to look anywhere below his chin, because at that moment, she could already feel the pool in between her legs.

A devilish grin appeared on his face.

"Wouldn't you rather finish the job, puppet?"

She clenched her legs tighter, fighting the urge to actually give in to that offer. She cleared her throat before answering his proposition.

"I think I'll stand over here and enjoy the show. Do continue, princeling."

His mouth dropped slightly, his lips looking like a beautiful place where she wanted to rest, but she didn't break eye contact. He wouldn't win this round. His lips twitched slightly, as he started to move his hand again.

"So you enjoy watching, do you? Take it in, love, because when I come all over myself, it'll be your face I'm thinking of, wishing it was you between my legs, stroking my cock with that bratty little mouth of yours."

He must have liked what he saw on her face, for his eyes lit up with lust as he went back to stroking his cock. Kieryn normally wasn't so bold, but she was utterly transfixed by what transpired before her. Callian's face was beautifully sculpted, his jaw tightening with every stroke he made, so close to erupting.

He bit his bottom lip as he looked up and continued to stare at her as she watched him. She could feel herself getting turned on at the sight of it, and knew she would probably be thinking about this moment later on in bed.

"You like that, *little demon*. You like the reaction you get out of me," he moaned in between kneading his fingers over his veiny cock.

She couldn't even utter a response to him, she just simply nodded, as she found her body drawing closer to his.

"I'm going to come, and you're going to keep your eyes on me as I do."

"Okay," she answered breathlessly. What on the *Gods'* green earth was happening to her? He was an enemy as far as she was concerned, she didn't trust him, not really, but yet she couldn't fight this draw toward him.

He started to stroke faster and harder, his coal eyes never leaving hers, as his mouth dropped open, an orgasm ripping through him as he finished. She couldn't help her body's reaction to the intimate moment they shared as she licked her lips

"Still think we both would have enjoyed it more if you did the work. Do you mind grabbing me a cloth though, love?"

She snapped out of her trance-like state and exited his room to his washroom to grab him a towel, catching her reddened cheeks and smirk in the mirror. She needed to snap out of this feeling, whatever this connection was between them, because clearly they were attracted to each other.

She hurried back into his room, throwing him the towel before she turned her body away from him.

He laughed mercilessly at her.

"Don't get shy on me now, sweetheart."

"Hurry up and get dressed, we should find some food and see if the captain kept his word about taking us to Keres Kingdom."

Callian stood up, his glorious, god-like body on full display, making her blush harder and turn her body fully to the door.

"Come on," he said from behind her, "let's see who I can threaten into giving us food."

TWENTY-FIVE

KIERYN WALKED out to a sky on fire. She took everything in around her as she tried to get her bearings on the ship. The sun-warmed planks beneath her boots were worn through with the years of hard labor of pirates on their feet, and she could smell the pipe smoke permeating the deck from the crew milling about, to the waves crashing against the hull of their ship. She could hear the caws of the birds soaring high above her head, their silhouettes crossing in front of the setting sun. She walked towards the port side of the ship, admiring the sinking sunset, when Callian came stumbling up next to her.

"Drink for your thoughts?" he asked, handing her a tin cup of a dark liquid exuding sweet aromas of vanilla and syrup.

She took the drink from his hands, and for a brief moment their hands touched and their eyes locked. Her face instantly flushed at the feel of his hand under hers.Knowing exactly where that hand had just been, and flashbacks of the look of pleasure on Callian's face she had witnessed was enough to make her almost lose her grip on the cup. She cleared her throat and grabbed the cup from his waiting hand, and let it hang loosely from her hand over the side of the ship. She waited until the sun sank below the horizon, before she took a sip of the sweet drink. Her face revealed her thoughts of it.

"Ugh, why do pirates drink the terrible shit? Haven't they heard of whiskey?"

Callian chuckled, and Kieryn took notice. She kept count of how many times she could make him laugh. She internally chastised her heart for feeling something towards him. She couldn't deny the attraction she felt for him, and that thought alone paralyzed her to her very core. With Damien, they had happened organically over time. They were friends once, who'd just happened to fall into bed with each other one drunken night after a mission, and instead of talking about it, they just used one another. For what, she had no idea. The companionship, the craving to not feel alone in their line of work, or maybe just to feel wanted. Regardless, what she started to feel for Callian was different. And that scared her.

"You're right." A devilish smile appeared as he glanced over at her. "I can think of something sweeter I'd rather taste."

The cup almost slipped from her hand at his innuendo. She felt her cheeks warming, and prayed he couldn't see with the way the sky had darkened, now that the sun had slipped below the horizon.

Before she could answer his taunting remark, something in the sky caught her attention.

"Look! It's a comet," she called out, grabbing his arm and pointing up towards the sky. Her face lit up at the beauty that glided across the black velvet night, a streak of fiery blue that ghosted across the sky. "Make a wish," she exclaimed to him.

He stared openly at her as she continued to stare up at the starry sky, her eyelids fluttering shut for a fraction of a second.

"You are an interesting woman, I'll give you that."

She slowly opened her eyes and looked towards him at his statement.

"How so? You don't find it beautiful?"

"Oh, I do. I think there is beauty in madness and chaos, and that is exactly what that comet represents."

"What do you mean?"

"Comets are known for being the messengers of the gods, some believe they are the *Harbingers of Death*. If you see one, it's meant to be a bad omen intended for you by the gods. So, little demon, what god did you piss off?" He laughed heartily.

The wonder vanished from her face in an instant, as she thought back to that seer who predicted her death in those cards, and now one from the gods this time.

Who did I piss off?

And just like that, her mind threw her back into her past, to the last time she thought something barreling through the sky was beautiful, yet too was a stark reminder as to the havoc it would soon wreak. The night of the Harvest Equinox and what was the beginning of the end of her life.

The entire city was alive and in full swing celebrating the evening. Shops and market stalls had shut down early that night for the celebration and the streets were packed with all sorts of people, from the merchants and drunkards to the high ladies and noble lords. Bonfires were being lit all over the green, and little kids dressed up like the old gods played in the fountain. Wine flowed endlessly, and people danced well into the night as they waited for the stars to announce their presence.

The Almerians celebrated from dusk to dawn, reveling in another year of prosperity. Every year people would wish on the falling stars for forgiveness, power, love, whatever it was that they desired from the gods. Kieryn had never celebrated with her kingdom, but tonight she would. She had never traveled to the neighboring kingdoms like her father did, but tonight she felt like she was celebrating with the entire realm of Elysium. Her father had once told her each kingdom celebrated differently, and she longed to experience that for herself one day.

Kieryn had made her way into Veritas and was stunned by the chaotic beauty of the walled capital. Veritas was the opposite of Coventry. She walked along cobblestone streets instead of dirt roads, and she passed ornate churches and underground tunnels that ran below the city rather than green fields and livestock. While Coventry was quiet, Veritas was its raucous counterpart. Streets were bustling with people dressed lavishly, as if they were trying to impress the gods. Kieryn was dressed in a simple ivory gown that stretched over her long, lithe frame and brushed the tops of her feet where they poked out from her golden sandals.

She walked along the narrow alleyways that led into the heart of the city, where it opened into a wide square. The entire city had congregated to see the queen make her entrance. Kieryn had just climbed the stone wall that bordered the open park when she spotted Queen Nyla arriving on foot, of all things. She was surrounded by her Alessian warriors, but from Kieryn's vantage point she could see clearly. Queen Nyla had chin-length hair the color of espresso beans, light hazel eyes, and porcelain skin that looked as if she barely ever stepped out in the sun. She was petite and her smile stretched to her eyes—a genuine smile. She was sweet-natured, but just in her ruling. She was well-loved and respected by her people, and it showed in their reactions to her. Men bowed with respect, women gazed at her with love and children squealed in delight as the queen made her way through the thick crowd, shaking hands as she went. Her golden-hued dress billowed in the breeze behind her.

After the queen had passed, Kieryn climbed to the top of the open park that overlooked the celebrations and settled in. The gods were finally arriving. Falling stars shot across the sky by the dozen. It was one of the most magical nights of her life, and for a while she allowed herself to get lost in the beauty of the starry night. She drank the fruity and strong wine; she danced around the bonfires and sang the songs of her people, blessing the gods and getting drunk off the magic of the crowd.

The memory of reveling in that night's activities and the freedom she felt for that lapse of time, made her feel guilty. That feeling was tainted by what she experienced later. Her parents had kept her so sheltered from the world, she'd craved just one ounce of normalcy, and she hadn't been prepared for the events that unfolded later that night.

Callian saw the light in her eyes drain as her face started to lose color.

"Don't dwell too much on it, love. It's just myths and legends that people have believed for years. There's beauty in a death like that," he finished pointing back up the comet that was sinking below the stars, disappearing as if it was never there.

Kieryn brought the sugary liquid to her lips, chugging more than she intended at the turn of the name Callian used. She poured more of the drink down her throat as the seer's Death card burned in the back of her eyelids like an iron.

Callian drew her attention to the top deck where there was a bench big enough for two. They made their way over, laying down on the hardwood, their heads resting on the lip of the ship, his body a warm beacon next to her as they gazed up at the blanket of stars.

"See those three bright stars running diagonally upwards?" he asked her, trying to distract her from the dread that coated her moments before. He had no idea where she had gone inside that head of hers, but he knew it was dark based on her expression.

She followed the length of his finger until she found the bottom star and saw what he was pointing to. She nodded next to him, still silent.

"That's the Orion constellation. Myth has it that he was born of Kano and searched the world over for a human girl he came across one night as she was walking the beach. He spent every night searching for her, hoping to profess his love and offer her the moon and the stars. He hunted the skies, trying to find that missing piece of him. Soon everyone referred to him as *The Hunter*. He eventually found her."

"Did he ever tell her he loved her?" she asked him.

He turned his head, taking in her profile from the side. Her long hair flowed effortlessly down her chest, the ends curling up in the salt air. She looked serene, if not a little somber. She turned her head, meeting his eyes, before he spoke again.

"Unfortunately, no. Once he found her, he realized he could never speak with her, not directly at least. He was bound by the night, and while she came out to the beach every night and spoke her truths and confessions to the night sky, he could never respond. He watched her come every night, over the span of her lifetime. Sometimes she would bring someone with her, and a few years later a third joined them. She had married and they had a beautiful daughter, and Orion watched over them from the skies, listening to her tell him about her life, and he watched as she got older and he stayed young, until one day she stopped returning."

"That's tragic," she whispered to the night.

"How so, love?"

She thought for a minute before she responded.

"Orion loved her from afar and selflessly. He could've been jealous, he could have made a deal with his father or the other gods to be with her, but he chose her happiness over his. He watched her live a life without him in it, all the while she never knew he loved her, even in death. That's tragic. She could've loved him, and they could've had an epic love, if only she knew."

"I guess when you put it like that, it is pretty tragic."

"Love is weakness though, it blinds your judgment," she said matter-of-factly. Callian peered over at her, his eyes searching for the lie beneath her words.

"You and the mutt? You didn't love him?"

She took a deep breath and let it out before answering him.

"His name is Damien. And things with him were compli-cated." She sighed heavily. "At first it was just a physical need. We were attracted to each other and we were friends, but he was emotionally unavailable and I don't do relation-ships, so it worked out. There were no expectations, we were harmless to each other, but things started to shift between us, and I wasn't sure what to make of any of it, so I shut it down. I shut down. I distanced myself before I could get hurt."

Callian nodded.

"And then he died." He didn't say it to be mean, it was a fact, a true statement of the events that had transpired.

A tear rolled down her face, as she remembered that moment, the feeling of grief ripping through her insides.

"And then he died," she whispered.

"Kieryn …" Callian started to say. The use of her name stunned her. He never called her by her name. He continued, "What did you see when those shadows surrounded you?"

Her mind wandered back to running through the forest, her blood spilling and the night reaching out towards her like it was welcoming her back into its fold, and to the mysterious dark figure. The devil himself, and the bargain she made. She wondered when he would come back to collect his debt. She tried to mask the terror on her face as best as she could, but she knew Callian saw something there.

"I was outside Riyadh Kingdom, searching for Damien. And then I found him with her, his lost love, his mate."

It was the truth, in part. She felt like the deal she made was supposed to be kept secret, and she didn't want to risk divulging that to Callian. She wanted to protect him from that kind of evil. If he knew, he'd try to help her, and she didn't want him involved. She had grown close to him, despite her reasons not to. She didn't want to risk his safety because of her decision.

"Nothing else, you're sure?" he pushed her.

They both knew she was lying, but Kieryn wasn't going to tell him. Honestly, the thought of speaking it out loud frightened her, that if she did *he* would appear from the shadows.

"Positive," she lied, swallowing back the rest of the contents in her cup. She swung her legs off the bench, sitting upright, her hair a tangled mess in the salt air.

"I'm going to head to bed. Goodnight, princeling."

"Goodnight, *alora*," Callian whispered behind the brim of his cup, swallowing more of the sweet liquid.

She made her way back towards the Captains Quarters, pondering what *alora* meant. She made a note to ask him tomorrow.

The gentle sway of the ship and the sweet drink quickly pulled her to sleep. It wasn't long before the night terrors creeped into her mind. Her nightmares piled on top of each other like dead carcasses in battle. It started off with the bargain she made.

"You can have my soul, in exchange for Damien's."

The words that forfeited her soul.

The Death card from the seer and the burning comet in the skies flashed before her eyes, and like clockwork, her demons brought her to the night of her parents' murder, only this time the dark stranger with the cerulean blue eyes finished the job.

She was back down by the lake, her head bleeding from where it smashed into the rock, and the man was straddling her, his hands wrapped around her neck like a necklace. Her lungs felt constricted, and her body thrashed side to side, trying to shake him off, but he was too heavy and she was too weak to care. She felt the muscles in her body go slack, her eyes beginning to roll to the back of her head. Her hands were fighting with the man on top of her, losing their strength before they fell limply to her sides.

Kieryn jolted awake, the screams ripping from her throat making her voice hoarse.

"*Alora*, it's me. You're okay! You're okay," he consoled her.

Kieryn looked frantically around the room, trying to get

her bearings. Her breathing was erratic and shallow, her chest rising fast in the aftermath of her night terrors.

"*Alora*, you are safe. I'm here. I got you," Callian repeated in her ear. He had heard her frantic screaming from his room, and didn't even think twice before toward her. He didn't know what to expect when he crashed his body through the door. If he had found one of the lowly pirates forcing himself on her, he would've seen red and he would've made their deaths slow and painful. What he found was her drenched in sweat as her body thrashed side to side, the sheets getting tangled. He brought her face into his chest, his strong hands coming up to cradle the back of her head, running his fingers down her hair.

After a few minutes, Kieryn finally managed to control her breathing enough that she was able to pull back from Callian's embrace. She peered up at him through her tear-soaked eyelashes.

"Do you want to talk about it?"

She shook her head delicately, as if the slightest of motions would rip her to pieces. Her breathing was normal, but her anxiety had her hands trembling.

"Will you stay with me?" she asked.

"Of course," he said without hesitation, surprising both of them. "Lay down and I'll tell you a story," he instructed her.

Kieryn tried to empty the thoughts from her mind, and she laid back down on the bed, getting lost in the sound of his voice. Callian laid down next to her, nothing but the blanket and her night slip between them. Her head rested on top of his bare chest, his hair tickling her nose, and she inhaled the scent of him. He smelled like the woods after dusk, cedar-like and smoky, and the smell alone soothed her chaotic thoughts. He continued to play with her hair, as his deep and angelic voice told her a story about a prince who grew up in a faraway land and his adventures, until eventually she fell asleep feeling light and safe.

TWENTY-SIX

KIERYN WOKE up cocooned beneath the blankets, her pillow carrying the lingering scent of cedar. Memories from last night assaulted her as she remembered her vivid nightmare, only she seemed to have more demons haunting her mind now.

She tossed and turned restlessly, her fingernails leaving half moon divots in the palms of her hands. She faintly recalled the bed dipping with the added weight of Callian. He had come barrelling into her room, eyes wide and alert, and his dagger raised as if he expected to find one of the captain's men in here. He had held her in his arms and weathered the storms that were brewing under the surface.

She was grateful for his presence. He kept her demons chained to the floor, and distracted her from the pain breaking through her icy exterior with tales of an arrogant prince who cared more for adventure than politics in his faraway kingdom. His velvet-smooth voice had carried her into a comfortable dream-like state. She felt a newfound appreciation for him. She didn't expect to get along with him, let alone tolerate his presence at all, but she was glad that she was wrong in that assessment. However, it still didn't make her feel better about the strong feelings she was developing for him. He didn't have to console her or care for her, but he had stayed and picked up her broken pieces without a lick of judgment and that was more than she could have hoped for.

She opened her eyes, praying to awaken to his body wrapped around hers, but she knew before opening her eyes that he was gone, and if it weren't for his lingering scent, it would be as if he was never there.

She gathered her belongings and stepped out into the glaring sun, her eyes adjusting to the light before taking in the view around her.

Keres Kingdom. A kingdom known as *Tidal Islands.* The kingdom was made up of five islands: Layette, Capryna, Palmana, Astora, and Naros. Vemond Castle, where Queen Calista resided was on the island of Capryna. Despite the grueling travel to Keres, Kieryn was absolutely captivated by the beauty of Capryna.

She knew that each island was uniquely different: from varying delicacies, geography of the islands, to the architecture. Capryna itself resembled the shape of a crescent moon, and Vemond Castle sat in the middle of the sea. The inn that Callian had mentioned was in the center of the island.

The first thing Kieryn noticed was the transparent aquamarine water and sandy beaches, home to white-washed homes with terracotta dome roofs that hugged the rugged coastline. Pure paradise. She felt the balmy air kiss her skin as she stepped off the boat that they had occupied for the last three nights. While the journey by sea had her covering herself in layers, the temperature in Keres had her shedding them. A trickle of sweat was already making its way down the side of her face, falling behind her ear.

"The inn is this way," Callian said in a dry tone. She peered over at him, watching the sun's beams of light radiate off him, casting him in an angelic-like glow. *Gods above!* With the bright light as a halo around him, his white tunic drenched in sweat revealed his toned stomach underneath, and his chiseled jaw clenched in concentration, you could almost mistake him for a god. *Almost.* Until he went and opened his mouth.

His arms tightened as he threw their belongings onto his back and briskly started walking through the sand to the road. She followed him, struggling to keep up with him on the uneven ground beneath her.

"I can carry my bag, you don't need ..." her voice trailed off as he whipped around to her, his scorching glare pinning her in place.

"I got it!" he snarled back, his lips pursed in suppressed rage before turning back towards the hill. She knew it was childish, but she stuck her tongue out at him. This version of him was entirely different from the kind soul he allowed her to see last night, and she wondered if that was the reasoning behind his sudden change in demeanor towards her this morning.

"I saw that," Callian grunted, but she swore that she could hear the hint of a smile behind those words.

As they made their way up the ascending cobblestone streets, Kieryn took note of everything around her. The cobbled streets were lined with quaint cafes and restaurants with the smell of fresh lobster and baked bread pouring out the open door, drawing customers to their colorful terraces. Boisterous bars were filled with sailors and their raucous laughs as they enjoyed the flow of wine after a journey out at sea. She took in the ivy-covered walls that gradually chased the cliffs into the skies. It was idyllic. She felt at peace, a feeling she hadn't experienced since she was a little girl in the lavender fields behind her childhood home.

This place could easily seduce her, and she knew that she would happily fall to her knees for it. She was so taken with the beauty that Capryna was flaunting, she hadn't realized Callian had stopped in front of a rustic, picturesque inn that looked like it had been plucked from the pages of a fairytale. The entire inn was constructed of Arcadian stone and the roof was the color of a burning sunset. Pillars circled the structure and there were a few balconies overhead that looked out over the charming, sleepy port village.

Kieryn followed him willingly into the enchanting inn. A nimble man looked out over the edge of the desk, his tired eyes crinkled as he gave them an affectionate smile. The man had gray hairs poking through his hair, and his skin was weathered from the caress of the sun over time.

His gentle eyes took them in, eyeing their weapons warily.

"Welcome to the *Siren's Call,*" the man with kind, light eyes greeted them as Callian approached him. The man squinted up at Callian, his body slowly shrinking inward, unnerved by Callian's demeanor.

"We would like two rooms," Callian addressed the wide-eyed man.

"We ... un-unfortunately don't have two rooms, sir. I ... I do have a suite that may be to your liking," he stumbled. "It has a large bed, a stone fireplace, and a private balcony that grants you unparalleled views of the sea and the Queen's Castle."

Callian's body went rigid at the thought of sharing a room,

but before he could rip out the man's throat, Kieryn swiftly stepped forward and offered the man a genuine smile.

"Thank you, uh …" she trailed off.

"Sebastian."

Kieryn placed her hand over his. "Thank you, Sebastian. We appreciate that generous offer and we would love that, wouldn't we?" she said, nudging Callian's foot. "He'll cover the bill," she added, her voice dripping in honey. Callian's eyes narrowed menacingly at her, but she ignored him. "What room would that be?" she asked Sebastian.

"It … It would be the third floor, miss. All the way down the corridor to your right," he stuttered, handing her over the key.

"Thank you kindly." She picked up her bag that Callian had at some point dropped to the ground, turned on her heel and strode up the stairs leading to the third floor, leaving a flustered Sebastian and an irritated Callian behind.

Kieryn opened the door to the suite that she and Callian would be sharing for the next couple of nights, and dropped her bag in a startled gasp. The suite Sebastian had given them was lavish. The room was spacious and had an intimate glow from the sconces on the walls. The flames licked the sides, casting dancing shadows across the room. The bed was big enough that they could fit their bodies twice over, and the tangerine sheets looked as if they were woven of the finest silk in Elysium. She blushed just thinking of what those plush sheets would feel like on her bare skin.

I will be sharing those silk sheets with Callian, the last thing I should be thinking about is my bare skin wrapped up in a cloud of bliss.

She turned away from the bed, avoiding where her

thoughts had gone and took in the rest of the suite. The walls were a rich, creamy white, and there was a stone fireplace nestled in the corner of the room next to a cart of Keresian wine and an amber liquid she was well acquainted with. She strode over to the bar cart and poured three finger lengths of the liquid devil in a short glass. She savored the oaky vanilla flavor that glided down her throat, her body feeling warmer with the liquor burning inside. Calming her nerves, she opened the wide, double doors that led out to their private balcony. She stared in awe at the vision before her.

Sebastian wasn't exaggerating when he said their balcony gave panoramic views of Capryna. The slanting rays of the setting sun cast Kalani Sea and Vemond Castle in a warm, orange glow as the sky was set ablaze in brushstrokes of indigo, vermillion, and a golden yellow.

"It's beautiful," she said softly, afraid her words would taint the moment.

She sensed him before she heard his approaching footsteps.

"What's beautiful?" he inquired.

"The quiet beauty of the sunset. The palette of colors setting the skies ablaze as if the gods themselves painted it. My mother would tell me that it's a promise of a new dawn. That the sunset is the sun's burning kiss to the night sky, a token of his love for the radiant moon. And I found that to be beautiful. Do you not think so?" she found herself asking.

He gazed at her in silence as she stood there, enchanted by nature's final act of the evening, the smell of bourbon dripping from her lips. He wondered if he tasted those lips would she taste like smoke and sugar. The more he studied her, the softer his eyes became.

She glanced over at him then and their eyes locked like a pull was drawing them in. She licked her lips, and his eyes dropped following the movement like a man thirsty for the first taste of water. His eyes found hers again and he stepped towards her with intent.

"I prefer things that are *real*, like the steady beat of a woman's heart"—he took another step closer towards her—"or the warm stroke of a woman's hand on my skin"—he grasped her hand and laid it on his chest, the touch igniting a burning desire through her veins—"or the soft, buttery feel of a woman's luscious lips between my fingers ..." His deep voice was saturated with smoke and desire. His hand came up to her plump, rosy lips taking her bottom lip between his thumb and forefinger, stroking back and forth. "That's what I define as beautiful, *alora*," he muttered into her ear before pulling away.

She felt like her body was liquifying from the inside. His touch was like sticking your hand in the fire. You craved the warmth of the flames, but the burn was a lick of pain. Her lungs felt like balloons expanding, wanting to jump out of her chest and sidle into the comfort of his arms. And gods above, her heart was treading water and he was a riptide pulling her under.

If she was being honest, she'd gladly drown in those dark eyes as if they truly were the deepest parts of the ocean.

Twilight crawled its way across the night sky, and the street-lights blazed on, pulling Callian from his reverie. He cleared his throat and swallowed violently before collecting himself to speak.

"We're going to be late meeting my friend." He paused for a beat. "I'll let you have the bathroom first to get ready." His voice came out raspy, as if he had just woken up.

Kieryn blinked, snapping out of whatever spell she fell under with those words of his. He seemed perfectly at ease, as if he hadn't realized his words just cracked open her heart. He remained wholly unperplexed while she silently fumed.

"Yeah, okay. Sure," she managed to say before swallowing

the rest of her drink. She maneuvered past him back into their room, grappling with her thoughts of how much she loved his fingers on her lips. And that she wanted him to do it again, so she could bite down on it and roll her tongue over his callouses.

Fuck, I am screwed.

An hour later and her thoughts were still scattered, left presumably on the balcony with her sanity. She showered off the sweat and salt that clung to her skin and combed her hair with a fine-toothed brush. She threw her hair up and allowed it to air dry in the humidity as she lathered her face in rose water. She grabbed her accessories from her pack and applied kohl to her eyes, making her green eyes look bigger. She finished with a ruby tint to her lips to make them look fuller, and pinched her cheeks for color. When she was satisfied with how her hair curled slightly at the ends, she slipped into her black sheer dress and nude heels the Keep had also stowed away for her.

Without a backward glance, she exited the bathroom. As if his soul knew the sound of her steps, his eyes found hers across the room. The look on his face was captivating. He sat with one leg crossed over his knee, one hand resting on the cinnamon leather armchair with a glass of bourbon. His other hand came up to his mouth, and he bit down on the flesh. He clenched his hand in between his teeth so hard, she was surprised he didn't draw blood.

"What's that look for?" she probed him, watching his eyes darken with unmistakable hunger.

He looked her over. His ebony eyes traveled from her hair that was curling from the sea air, a shine to it that reminded him of golden hour in autumn, her eyes a darker shade today, more jade than her usual bright emerald. His gaze traveled lower to her sultry smile before his eyes took in her shimmering onyx-colored dress that clung to her curves as if it were made specifically for her.

The straps were beaded, the bodice scooping dangerously below her breasts, and a high slit came up to her thigh where he knew her dagger was strapped. His eyes made his way back to her, but he quickly recovered and winked at her.

"Don't ask questions you don't want the answers to, *alora*."

Before she could ask what he meant by that statement, and why he kept calling her by that name, he was out of the chair and already walking past her and out the door. She followed on his heels, taking in his attire for the evening. While she was getting ready, he must have changed. He wore a black, fitted velvet tunic that matched his eyes, brocaded with silver and dark pants tucked into black boots. She couldn't help but silently appreciate the view.

She caught up to him, determined to know what his reply meant. She reached out to grab his wrist, and at the same time he turned, grabbed her by the waist and pressed her against the wall. Their bodies aligned like the missing pieces of a puzzle. He dropped his head so that his lips brushed her ear. The sudden movement caught her off guard, the cold cement wall pressing in on her bare skin making her gasp in surprise.

His ethereal voice embraced her body in a wave of euphoria, her blood pulsing at the faint whisper of the desire in his voice. "You look delicious, and that dress ... is driving me wild," he growled. "It is taking everything, *everything* in me, not to ravage you right here against this wall."

He tilted his head slightly, his lips inches from hers. Maybe it was how he smelled like cedar and pine, or the way that despite him warning her that he wasn't a good man, he had defended her, killed *for* her, and shielded her from an arrow to the heart. So, she leaned forward until their lips were almost brushing.

A future promise.

"What's stopping you then?" she asked breathlessly.

Just as he leaned forward to close the distance, loud voices started to drift toward them, and he broke away from her suddenly. The expression on his face was jarring, as if he was in physical pain. Clearing his throat, he suggested they make their way to the meeting and with that, he quickly closed himself back off to her and hastily retreated down the hall.

One step forward, two steps back.

She remained against the wall, stunned. His icy cold demeanor was colder than the chill her body now ached with without his touch.

Gods above, what was he doing? *Stupid,* that is what he was. He was falling for her. Why her? This mouthy, sarcastic seductress of a woman was leaving him paralyzed with fear. They were toeing a dangerous line, one that he promised himself he wouldn't cross. He couldn't. She was freedom, his salvation, but in turn he'd be her damnation. But he would gladly dance with the little demon before him for what she did to him. Seeing her in that sheer, translucent dress reminded him of a star-filled night sky.

Beautiful, magical, unattainable—just out of reach.

And he wasn't worthy of her. She was a comet, *his* comet.

Callian thought he finally understood what she was saying before. Seeing her in that dress, he knew he'd rip the stars from the sky one by one and deliver them to her on a silver platter, if only she would look at him again the way she did out on that balcony. And it was that thought that made him realize he would do everything in his power to protect her. From who was coming after her, but also from himself. And in order to do that, he needed to break a vow first. He would obtain the impossible, for her.

TWENTY-SEVEN

THEY MADE their way in silence to the bar where Callian's friend was waiting. The bar was at the bottom of the hill, burrowed between the beach and the towering cliff adjacent to it. Descending the cobblestone street proved to be rather difficult in her heels, and she stumbled a few times. Despite his cold attitude toward her, he remained close to her side, his hand coming to rest on her lower back.

"So you don't show up looking like a Helhound ripped apart your face," he told her, when she shivered at his sudden touch on her bare skin.

The beachside bar known as *Divinity* was crawling with every islander within a mile radius. Divinity sat perched on a stilted rise over the sea and palm trees stood outside the entrance like bulky bodyguards, swaying in the breeze. Callian led her inside and she was bewitched by the hedonism that was scattered through the bar.

This was the kind of place where the party lasted into the early hours of the morning. Keresians were dancing seductively on the dance floor, a whirling blur of skin and body parts as they swayed to the trance-like music. Long wooden tables took up residency in the back of the bar by the open-air pavilion that sat high over the jagged rocks below. On the lower deck, couples were partaking in intimate activities in semi-private tents that were on full display for anyone to watch.

"Don't take anything that is offered to you," he warned her. "Keresians like to party and their drugs are not for the faint of heart and some are addictive. Just stick to the wine and you'll be okay," Callian instructed her as they made their way to a side booth in the corner.

Kieryn nodded as he handed her a glass of sparkling wine. Their fingers touched briefly, and their eyes met, neither one of them moving or looking away. She swallowed the lump that crawled its way up her throat.

"Am I interrupting something?" came a sultry voice from behind them. Kieryn reared back and feasted her eyes on what she could only describe as the most beautiful woman she had ever seen.

She was a *siren*, women known for their beauty and alluring voice that could lure any man or woman into doing their bidding.

The narrow strips of satin hugged her breasts before criss-crossing around her neck, and she had a slim waist, yet curva-ceous hips. Her bright wine-red hair was long and voluminous, and even with it held high in a pony, the tips of her hair touched her backside. Her golden-hued skin shined under the fluorescent lighting and her riveting sky-blue eyes lit up when she saw Callian.

Callian stood up and embraced the beautiful woman. Every inch of their bodies pressed together, and he leaned forward, kissing her airily on both cheeks before taking her in.

"Hey there, stranger, long time no see," she scolded him in a flirtatious manner. "Miss me?" she teased.

"You are hard to forget, little minx," he laughed.

Gods above, is he flirting with her?

She cleared her throat and rose from the table. Callian glanced over at her as if remembering that she was there.

"Kieryn, this is Princess Soraya Kincaid, an old friend of mine," he stated simply.

Princess Soraya? No wonder she looked like a seductress.

Soraya scoffed at Callian, "Ah, is that what we are calling it these days? I didn't realize sharing a bed once upon a time made us *friends.*"

Kieryn tried to control the movements in her face from showing the utter devastation and shock the siren princess's words brought on as they fractured her heart a bit. She saw Callian glance guiltily over at her, but she disregarded him entirely.

Callian watched Kieryn struggle to keep her smile in place, although he saw the brightness in her eyes had dimmed at Soraya's candor about their past.

"It's lovely to meet you, Princess Soraya," Kieryn said courteously with a slight bow of her head.

Soraya peered at her in appreciation.

"No need for titles. If you are a friend of Cal's, you can call me Raya."

Gods, they have nicknames for each other. This is a whole new form of torture.

This close to Soraya, Kieryn could see her eyes were dilated and her golden skin had a dewy glaze.

She's on drugs—Ecstasia if I had to guess.

A powder-like drug that Keresians had created.

The seductive siren sidled closer to her, her hand coming to lightly brush back the lock of hair that had fallen in front of Kieryn's face, her warm gentle fingertips lingering by her jaw. Soraya's lips puckered as she bit down on her bottom lip teasingly.

"She's beautiful, Cal. Did you bring her for me?" she mused.

Callian looked like he wanted to sink into the ground. He'd honestly prefer to fight the Nightwalkers than be here. He choked at Soraya's assumption and quickly steered her away from Kieryn. Kieryn's look of amusement followed him.

"No, she isn't for you. We came here to ask you if you can set up a meeting with your mother?" he prodded.

Soraya gazed up at him longingly. "Ah, so you are here for a favor, not for me."

Callian gave her a look of guilt and remorse. It had been so long since him and Soraya had been a thing. But both had known it was nothing serious. She was adventurous and spontaneous, and it was easy being around her. She didn't ask him questions when he disappeared, and he liked that about her. He could never say no to her, until now.

"I am not here for that, Raya. I missed you, yes, but what happened with us then, that's over," he said soothingly.

"Are you in love with her?"

"It's complicated," Callian returned.

After three full heartbeats, Soraya responded.

"Fine, but you're dancing with me for old times' sake, I want to know everything," before she dragged him away and out of Kieryn's sight.

She watched Callian follow Soraya out onto the dance floor, the siren dancing seductively along the hard rigid body she knew was under those clothes. It did help that Callian's hands didn't linger in certain places. In fact, his hands stayed in the air, hovering above her exposed skin, but not quite touching her. He was, however, whispering in her ear, and she was listening intently to every word he spoke. It made her seethe and her blood boil.

Gods, who am I turning into?

Trying not to remember the faint heat from his breath when he was inches from her lips and begging to have her a mere hour ago, she turned away from them. She was not going to let him ruin her night. She wanted to let go, feel free. She wanted to dance.

She grabbed a glass of Keresian wine off the passing tray and took a huge swig, scoping out the bar and caught the eye of a handsome triton. He was tall, with sandy blond hair that touched his shoulders, and hazel eyes that lit up when he saw her. His eyes showed that he appreciated what he saw, and he made his way through the crowd of people. She watched him approach, her eyes never leaving his.

The first words out of the stranger's mouth caught her by surprise.

"I think you owe me a dance."

"Is that so?" she questioned him. "And what is your reason?"

The stranger didn't hesitate. "Because a beautiful girl like you should never be in the corner of a dance floor." He smiled at her, one side of his lips quirked up, and she laughed, her hand coming up to her mouth, feigning innocence.

I wonder how many times he's used that pick-up line on the women in this bar.

She knew his type, but he was handsome, and she did say she wanted to have fun tonight.

"Does that line actually work on women?" She inched closer to him.

His smile didn't waver, he just continued, "Actually, no—but it did make you laugh, and that's the goal."

She couldn't help but smile at his honesty, and she reached out her hand, laying it on his exposed forearm where his anchor tattoo spilled out of his white tunic, the mark of all *tritons*. Tritons were the male version of sirens; they were seductive in their own right and were the queen's first defense.

"I think you've earned yourself one dance, for a laugh," she bargained.

"I'll take it …" he trailed off.

"Kieryn," she answered.

"Malakai," he replied, and with that, he pulled her by the hand toward the middle of the dance floor, right as the music changed to something upbeat and enticing. With her back to his chest, she threw her hands up and clasped them around his neck, his hands coming down to rest on her hips. They moved their hips side to side in time with the music. She couldn't help her thoughts as she wondered if Callian was with one of those more provocative dancers, or if he was still with the siren princess.

And just as if he heard her thoughts, she found his eyes locked on her from across the room. He was standing alone, in the same spot that Malakai had found her minutes ago. His body was rigid, his muscles tensed, and his fists were balled tightly by his sides. She could see his tattooed arms throbbing under the dimmed lighting as if they had their own heartbeat. When her eyes found him, all that looked back at her was a hostile glare, his lips curled tightly, and his jaw clenched. He looked like he was getting ready to *kill* someone.

Oh shit.

She averted her gaze and turned away, flushed, now facing Malakai.

Was he jealous?

She continued to dance with Malakai, his hands now sliding to her lower back. She was playing with fire trying to rile up Callian, but god, seeing him jealous, spread heat down to her core and an ache between her thighs.

"I suggest you take your hands off what is mine," a familiar voice growled from behind her.

She turned, irritated, ready to get in his face until she saw it contorted like that of an avenging God. The fire in his eyes blazed like thousands of burning suns.

Malakai slipped his hand around her waist, walking the line of protective and possessive.

Callian didn't miss the intentional touch on Malakai's part. He didn't even look at her, his wrath still seeping out of his pores at Malakai's hand still on her body.

"I won't ask again," Callian demanded slowly, his glare predatory. "Remove your hand from what is mine, or I'll do it for you," he snarled.

Malakai didn't flinch. She'd be impressed with him standing his ground if she wasn't scared of Callian's intentions.

"If she's yours, then you shouldn't have left her alone on the side of the dance floor," he threw back in Callian's face. Malakai went to turn towards Kieryn, his hand coming up to grab her arm and steer her away, but he wasn't quick enough. Just as Malakai made to move, Callian lunged for his hand, tearing it away from her, as he brought down his sword on Malakai's hand, his scream echoing through the bar. Callian bent over him, a sneer on his face.

"I warned you to remove your hands from her. Now leave before I decide to chop off your other hand," he demanded. Malakai ran off clutching his arm to his chest, sparing her no second glance.

She rushed at him, shoving him hard.

"You're unbelievable. That was not necessary," she fumed, her temper rising.

How dare he!

He looked down at her, his hand coming up to grip her jaw tightly and his eyes lowered. "No one touches what's mine."

She hated how those words made her body feel like it was being licked up by flames. She could feel the pool between her thighs at the possessiveness in his voice, but she refused to acknowledge it.

He was fast, but not as fast as she was in that moment as she swung her dagger and sliced into his abdomen—not deep, but enough to let him know she was pissed. His sharp inhale told her she had angered him.

Good.

"I am not yours. It would be in your best interest to remember that," Kieryn snapped at him. And with that, she bent down, wiping her blade on the strip of garment still attached to the severed hand. She picked it up and threw it into his chest. "Here, a souvenir for a monster like you."

She turned on her heels and strode through the bar, not caring to look at everyone's bewildered faces, and she didn't care whether he decided to follow her. Once outside in the chilling air, she let the first tear fall and took off towards the inn.

TWENTY-EIGHT

SHE STORMED off in the direction of the inn, her blood boiling at the audacity of Callian's behavior. He was so contradictory. One minute he was telling her he wants her and the next he was dancing with Soraya seductively. Now he'd taken to maiming any man who dared to show her any kind of appreciation or attention. She was halfway up the street when she felt his presence. She turned and faced him, her fists clenched tightly by her sides.

"You are a vindictive little brat, you know that?" he spewed venomously.

She scoffed at him. "That's rich, coming from you."

She turned away from him and headed down the alley to her right, wanting to put as much distance between them as possible. He followed her and pressed her against the wall, pinning her hands behind her.

He continued to lay into her.

"You've got a mouth on you. You're reckless, impulsive, and you are the most irritating woman I have ever dealt with."

If her eyes were daggers, she would have gutted him with her lethal glare. "If I'm too much to handle, then leave. I didn't ask for your help," she hissed, her eyes alight with fury and a wicked gleam.

Removing one hand from her wrist to wrap it around her neck, he leaned in and confessed, "I didn't say I couldn't handle it, *alora.*"

And like a snake striking, his lips crashed down onto hers. He kissed her roughly, as if he was trying to ravage her lips. She hungrily pushed back, her lips parting for his impatient tongue as he explored her mouth. She tasted like peaches, and the warmth of her seized him in its deathly hold. She was liquid fire.

His salvation, his ruin.

He couldn't get enough of her, there was too much space between them, and he quickly rectified that. He pressed his body flush against hers, releasing her hands and exploring the gaps in her dress where her skin was exposed. She could feel his length pressed against her stomach, and she moaned deeply into his mouth, the noise making his entire body shudder with want. She worked her mouth against his, their tongues battling for dominance.

Everything stood still as they kissed passionately in the alley, neither one wanting to break the connection, but he pulled back placing his hands on the wall, closing her in.

"Fuck, *alora* …" he braced himself against the wall, his hands fidgeting, wanting to touch her again and straining to remain flat on the wall. He was losing this battle. That kiss woke him up from the deepest pit of despair that he had dragged himself into.

"That kiss …" he continued, but stopped himself, not wanting to reveal anything more.

"It was what, Callian?" she panted. The sound of his name falling from her lips like that made his cock throb, and he stared at her swollen, pink lips, begging himself to kiss her again. He needed the taste of her, the warmth of her mouth on his tongue once more.

He shook his head, trying to clear the thoughts from his mind as if it would work.

"Nothing, it's not important." He took another step back, one of his hands leaving the wall, but she captured it in hers.

"Don't lie to me … please," she begged. That last word unraveled him. He came undone in front of her.

"You aren't what I was expecting," he revealed, and it sounded like a confession.

She smiled up at him, teasingly. "You've said that before."

He smirked and guided her hand to his chest over his heart. She could feel his heartbeat racing. They locked eyes and time stood still, neither one wanting to break the connection.

"*Gods help me,*" he muttered. "I want to kiss you again until your lips are swollen and the only thing you'll be screaming is my name. I want to touch you and make you forget that any other man ever laid a finger on you, and I want to taste you— your mouth, your skin, your body." He took his hand and cupped her heat throbbing between her thighs, his thumb rubbing over her sensitive bud, causing friction that made her feral. "This dripping pussy," he growled. "I know I shouldn't, but I *need* you," he begged.

Callian never begged and yet here he was, seconds away from dropping to the street on his knees for her. She knew nothing good would come from this, but it was like there was an electric current pulsing through her, an invisible thread connecting them, and she *wanted* him too. Desperately.

She didn't answer him, she didn't trust herself to say anything. Instead, she took his hand and led him back to their room at the inn.

They walked back to the room, and she released his hand, heading straight for the smoky bourbon still sitting on the cart in the corner. She poured herself three fingers worth of the amber liquid and finished it in one gulp. She shuddered, the heat liquifying her insides, and poured herself another. She drained that glass too. There was no fighting her feelings for him anymore, and she would take the repercussions that came later. For now, she just wanted, and she wanted him.

He came up behind her, grabbing her hair in his fist and moving it to the side, exposing her neck. His lips gently brushed her skin on the back of her neck softly, gently, like a butterfly's wings. The heat rose to her cheeks, making them flush,and it wasn't from the liquor.

"Tell me to stop, *alora*. If you don't want this—if you don't want me—tell me to stop and I will."

No words left her lips. She was still holding her empty glass as he left a trail of goosebumps down her flesh where he kissed her. He reached around her, pulling her soft body against his hard stomach, slowly peeling her fingers from the glass and setting it down on the table. He spun her around and enclosed her, the edges of the table pressing into her lower back.

"Tell me to stop, *alora*," he repeated, pleading. She answered him with a moan as his featherlight fingers danced their way up her exposed thigh, inching closer where she ached for them to be.

He slipped his hand over the slit between her legs, feeling the wetness as he thumbed her clit.

"Gods, *alora*, what are you doing to me?" he moaned into her ear, the bulge in his pants stretching, wanting to break loose. His light touch on her clit sent her through a whirlwind, and her toes curled as she lifted to meet his movements, needing more pressure.

"More," she whispered, her voice raspy. Her hands gripped his arms, her dress bunched up high by her stomach, her entire bottom half exposed to the salt air drifting in through the open balcony door. She had decided against panties with the dress she was wearing, and she was glad she had, because the sight of Callian mesmerized by her completely bare for him sent a throb through her core. She watched his eyes lower and he grinned, a grin that even the devil himself would envy. His eyes met hers once more and this time his tone was more demanding.

"Tell me what you want," his thumb stroked, pressing deeper.

She gasped, a moan climbing its way out of her mouth as she finally conceded.

"You," she said breathlessly, "I want you."

His sharp inhale made her ache more. He leaned closer and his lips kissed the corner of hers, his hot breath invading her mouth.

"Then show me."

TWENTY-NINE

SHE DIDN'T THINK, she moved her head slightly, catching his lip in between her teeth and yanking, the growl coming from his throat putting her in a frenzy. He thrust a finger inside her and she cried out, her eyes rolling to the back of her head as he slid his finger in and out, feeling her wetness. She gripped his arms harder as his other hand reached underneath her ass and lifted her to rest on the edge of the table. The leverage made his finger hit deeper, causing more moans to rise to the surface.

She pressed her lips against his, needing the taste of him again. She wanted him to fuck her mouth and his cock. His tongue explored her mouth again, wrestling each other, as she took off his shirt and threw it to the ground. She pulled back and stared at his tanned muscular chest, drinking in the sight of him.

His tattoos continued to snake their way over his chest, right above the jagged scar near his heart. She traced the scar, feeling the hard ridges from it not healing properly, a sudden burst of nostalgia washing over her.

She leaned forward, trailing her lips along the scar. He

inhaled sharply, and she looked up at him then. His eyes glistened, a tear threatening to spill over, but remaining frozen.

He kissed her again, hesitant at first and then rougher. His hand thrust into her hair and pulled, making a heated cry escape her lips. He pulled his finger out of her, but not before he eased another one into her, making her body jolt. The other hand that was wrapped up in her hair slid further south down her back, until it hovered just on her lower back. Gradually, he guided his hand lower and lower, grabbing a fistful of her ass in his hands.

"I could listen to those sounds you make every day," he admitted out loud. "Sing for me, little demon, I want to hear you sing for me. You are mine," he growled, as he circled her other hole, begging for entry. A moan escaped her lips as he added pressure to her entrance back there, and she bucked forward, pleading with him silently to do as he pleased. He didn't need any further instruction as he curled his finger, pushing through. The feeling of him inside both holes made her feel full, but she needed him to move.

He plunged his fingers deep inside her again, her hips rolling to meet the pressure. She bit down on her lip, stifling her moans.

He gripped her jaw, and she opened her eyes, seeing the hunger in his, wanting to drown in them.

"Open that bratty mouth of yours, I want to hear your screams when I make you come."

He watched as her eyes widened, a moan falling from her pretty swollen lips.

"Say it, *alora*. Say you're mine," he demanded as he ripped her open with another finger in both holes, the pressure of feeling absolutely full breaking her apart. The tension pooled from between her thighs, rising higher, sending her close to the edge.

"That's it, baby, come all over my hand. I want to hear my name on your lips. You're mine."

Those words pushed her to the brink, and she rode his hand as she rode out her orgasm, coming undone in his hand. She felt his eyes drink her in and she called out his name, her body shuddering from the high.

Kieryn's eyes came back into focus as she watched him slip his hand out of her thick wetness now coating the insides of her thighs and brought the fingers that were in her pussy to his mouth, sucking on them as if he was a starved man.

"You taste so good, baby. *Fuck.*"

The image of him tasting her sent another wave of heat down through her core. She reached for his hand that was inside her cunt seconds ago and raised it to her lips. He watched her intently, curious, but with hunger in his eyes. She dragged her tongue against each of his fingers, watching his reaction to her tasting herself, and his body convulsed with utter pleasure.

She unbuttoned his pants, freeing his bulge that had been straining against the fabric. She gasped at the length of him, and he chuckled at her, loving the sound of surprise that fell from those "come fuck me" lips.

"I need to taste more of you," he told her as he slowly dropped to his knees before her. "Never say I don't kneel for *my* queen."

The words she was about to say were lodged in her throat as he brought one of her legs to rest on his shoulder, spreading her wide open before him like a feast. Her back bowed as he plunged his tongue into her warm sweetness. Explicit curses left her mouth as he explored every inch of her, memorizing every part of her and finding that spot that made her putty in his hands. He sucked her clit, drawing it out, gently biting before licking it back up, causing her to scream out his name.

If he kept doing that to her, she was going to come again. Sensing how close she was, he stopped thrusting his tongue in her and gazed up at her, the view unsettling.

"Don't you dare come just yet, I am not finished with you," he scolded her, yanking the rest of her dress down, freeing her breasts. He slipped his fingers in her, his tongue slowly circling her already sensitive clit. She squirmed in his embrace, wanting release.

"Not yet," he said in between licks. She felt like she was on fire, crying out for him, begging to come undone. Her hands came up to her breasts and she rolled her nipples in between her thumb and forefinger, squeezing hard until she saw stars behind her eyelids. She bit her lip at the orgasm about to rip from her.

"Let go, *alora*."

"Holy gods!" Kieryn screamed, riding her orgasm, feeling her body catch flame, burning with her desire and feeling euphoric. She clenched the desk hard, collapsing from the aftermath. She had never felt this satiated, and his cock wasn't even inside her yet.

He stood up then, kissing her, fucking her mouth with his tongue. She tasted herself on his lips, and it lit up her insides.

"You like the way you taste, baby? My new favorite snack—peaches." He laughed. "And yes, I am *your* god," he stated.

She answered him in the best way she could. He asked her to show him what she wanted, and right now she wanted his hot, throbbing cock to hit the back of her throat. Kieryn stood up, slowly dragging her dress down her body, enticing him. She took in his devilish grin as he gazed upon her naked body, the dress a pool on the ground.

"Undeserving," he confessed softly under his breath.

She sank to her knees, his eyes going wide at her intentions, as she licked up his length, teasing his tip and smiling to find pre-come on it before swallowing him whole. His grunts were a symphony to her ears as she sucked him off, getting off on his moans. She brought her hand to her sensitive clit and touched herself, loving the sounds that she made fall from his lips. She was so absolutely drenched that she felt the inside of her thighs sticking with the mess he made of her.

"Gods, Kieryn, if you keep doing that I'm not going to last long," he pleaded.

Hearing her name fall from his lips like that was even more incentive to her as she increased her speed, feeling his hands gripping her head, his hands pulling at her hair as he chased her movements. She felt his shudder right before he released his salty, thick liquid in her mouth. She swallowed everything he gave her, her thumb rubbing vicious circles against her clit at how turned on she was.

"Fuck. Holy fucking gods, *alora.*"

He grabbed underneath her arms, pulling her to his mouth and crashed his lips against hers. He reached around her, cupping her ass in his hands, and lifted her into his arms. She wrapped her legs around his waist, their lips never once breaking away, as he carried her to the bed.

Callian lowered himself onto her carefully. His knee sliding up between her thighs. His hand cupped her perfectly perky breasts and he pulled her taut nipple into his mouth, sucking and biting, his hot breath leaving chills on her sensitive, peaked breasts when his mouth released them. The warm flick of his tongue sent another wave of heat and ache to her core.

He guided his hard length into her throbbing pooling heat, and they both trembled with desire and lust. Her tight warmth on his bare cock almost set him over the edge and he hadn't even begun to explore her.

"I'm going to take my time devouring you. I want to hear your moans when I lick your favorite spots. I want to feel your legs shake when you're on the brink of climax. I want to see your face when I make you come repeatedly. Understood?"

She nodded, her lips dry, and she swung her body so that she hovered above him. Her blonde waves fell like a curtain around them, a barrier from the outside world. He reached up and cupped her face in his.

"Your blood sings to me, I need a minute." His breathing was erratic as he tried to inhale through his mouth to fight his inner demon, struggling to gain his composure.

"Take it, Callian. I want you to," she said breathlessly.

He froze, balking at her words, at what she was telling him. She wanted him to mark her, and hearing that stirred something deep and feral inside him. His cock twitched at the thought of tasting her blood again, but yet he refrained.

"Are you sure?"

She nodded, grinding down on him.

He yanked her hair. "I need your words, *alora*."

"Bite me, Callian."

The words had no sooner left her mouth than the beast inside Callian scraped her neck and punctured her skin. She felt the bite of his teeth as they sank in deeper and felt his tongue lapping at the blood coating his mouth. She continued to ride him, the feeling of him drinking from her and the intense force of his cock impaling her and hitting her deepest parts driving her to the brink of chaos and complete and utter detonation.

He released her neck, blood dripping from his lips, and she leaned forward, catching it with her tongue before he could lap it up. She watched him watch where their bodies connected, and she rode him until they both jumped off the edge, falling … falling … falling. His arms came around her back and he breathed her scent in, vanilla and cedarwood. Spice and warmth. One hand cupped the back of her head as he whispered to her.

"Undeserving. So *fucking* undeserving of you. I'm irrevocably yours," he sighed into her hair.

She didn't say anything. She just curled into his side, feeling safe and warm, and finally letting her fears of needing someone in that way go. The last thought she had before drifting into a peaceful sleep was that maybe home wasn't a destination, but a person.

THIRTY

CALLIAN OPENED his eyes to the sunlight pouring in through the open balcony doors, the sun painting Kieryn's bare skin in gold. He turned his head and took in his fill of her. Gods, he could never get enough of her like this. Serene, angelic, wrapped in his arms. She was laying on her stomach, her head resting on his shoulder, and her right arm swung low over his stomach.

She was smiling in her sleep, and he willed himself to remember her like this. He memorized every detail, like the way her eyelashes fluttered, the sound of her light snoring stirring the hair on his chest, and the smell of vanilla and something earthy overwhelming his senses. He was so far gone for her, it was a blessing and his demise.

As he thought that, his wrist started to burn like a thousand wildfires, and he glanced down at the thorn tattoos wrapped around his wrists. His own personal hell. He watched as the thorns came to life and wrapped around his wrists like a snake would its victim. He was at its complete mercy.

He sucked in a short breath, bearing the brunt of the pain as his wrists began to bleed, and he bit down on his lip attempting to breathe through the agony. After an excruciating minute of pain, Callian opened his eyes to the thorns inked delicately around his wrists, no blood to be found, as if it never happened. But, he knew it did. It was a message from *him*, a warning. He was running out of time. He had to make a decision, and soon.

At that moment, he felt Kieryn begin to wake. He watched, transfixed, the warning soon forgotten, as those beautiful emerald green eyes opened. When they found him, her smile grew. She laughed into his chest, a sound so alluring, it was as if an angel had whispered directly into his soul. Callian brought her hand resting on his stomach to his lips and kissed each fingertip softly.

"Good morning, *alora*."

The look on her face would've had him falling to his knees for her if he had been standing. She was breathtaking like this —exposed and vulnerable, a look of wanting and something else hidden beyond those eyes that he couldn't figure out yet.

"Are you ever going to tell me what that means?"

He sighed into the crown of her hair, and kissed the top of her head before he replied to her.

"It means *my beautiful dream*. I look at you and all I see is light and peace. Before I met you, all I knew was darkness. I *was* the darkness. I was the monster that went bump in the night, that parents warned their children about. There was no guiding light for me to follow. I was lost in that dark abyss, but one look at you … and I saw something I never began to imagine I'd find again …" His voice trailed off like the last note of a song.

She sucked in a breath at his confession. "And what was that?"

He grabbed her chin and lifted it so her eyes met his, and with conviction in his voice, he divulged the truth he had been holding onto with a death grip. "Hope."

She kissed him with fervor, his name spilling from her lips, as she licked at his bottom lip, begging to be let inside, and he obliged. Their tongues tangled, and with one graceful move, Callian lifted Kieryn so she straddled him. The early sun's rays lit Kieryn's body like a halo, her golden hair cocooning them like a curtain. The sheet fell away exposing her to him. His gaze traced over every feature in front of him, and the look of lust swirled in his eyes, making her nipples pebble, and he smirked up at her. He took her nipple into his mouth, biting and licking where he had marked her, and she threw her head back, loving how he made her body sing. His hand gripped her hip and brought her closer to him until her lower body hovered over his mouth.

"What are you doing?" she asked breathlessly.

"I'm having breakfast."

And with that, he feasted on her. His tongue parted her lips and he dragged it slowly upward, exactly where she needed him. She whimpered at his touch. She knew he was holding back, that he was savoring teasing her. She grinded down on him, eager for the friction of his stubble on his face. She craved it; she was so close to falling over the edge.

"Don't you dare come, *alora*. Don't you fucking dare. Not yet, I am not finished with you."

He licked at her swollen clit, biting and sucking on it, and when he stuck two long fingers inside her, she cried out and threw her head back, her hands coming out in front of her to grab the headboard.

"Take it, baby, take it all. Take what you need from me," he said as she began to ride his face into oblivion, suffocating him. And when he bit down on her clit, right as he hooked his fingers inside her, she cried out, collapsing forward, her tight grip on the headboard the only thing supporting her weight.

Before she could catch her breath, Callian moved and flipped her until she was on her back.

His arms trapped her hands above her head as his lips brushed the shell of her ear, and he felt her shudder under his touch.

"I'm going to take my time with you, little demon. I want you so full of me,that you're dripping my cum down those legs of yours. I want everyone to know that you're mine. Who you belong to."

His words alone could've made her come again. Her eyes shuddered closed, but Callian gripped her jaw.

"Open your eyes, baby, I want to see those beautiful green eyes looking at me when I slide into you."

She nodded with his hand still locked on her jaw, and with green meeting obsidian, it was catastrophic when he sat himself inside her. Her mouth parted and he took it as an invitation to invade her mouth with his tongue. This time she gave up her control, and allowed him to take the reins. He was gentle, teasing and playful as his hands roamed down her body, his featherlight touches dragging slowly over every inch of her, familiarizing every divot, every curve.

Everywhere his hand was he followed the burning path with his kisses, worshiping her like she was a goddess. He kissed her lips last, softly at first, a kiss that screamed how he felt about her. He showed her in every way possible as he bottomed out inside her.

They moved in sync with each other, a blur of entangled limbs and rumpled sheets. They fed off one another, touching and teasing, their dance like a siren's call—mystical, a powerful force driving them closer. Their souls recognized each other, and they both fell into one another until they drowned together.

It was midafternoon before Callian and Kieryn untangled themselves from each other and dressed to meet up with Princess Soraya, who had promised she'd talk with her mother about a meeting.

They made their way through the town of Capryna, Kieryn's head swaying side to side trying to observe all the things around her—from the smells of the bakery shop, the bookstore on her right that begged her to come inside, to the people milling about the streets. Callian chuckled to himself at the wistful look on her face. Right here in this moment, she felt free, like a child again, but with the freedom of exploration. Callian laid a hand on her lower back and steered them back towards the docks where they'd arrived only the day before. The ship they had sailed in on was already a distant memory.

Kieryn gasped in astonishment. "Where is the water?"

The sea they had crossed on yesterday had receded, leaving nothing in its wake but sand and seashells. It was as if overnight, the sea had split in two, revealing a pathway made of sand, leading directly to Vemond Castle out in the middle of the sea.

"Siren magic. You can only get to Vemond Castle two ways: one way is to sail by boat, and the other is to wait for low tide. Once it is low tide, you can make your way across by the sandbar, but you only have limited time over there before the sea comes back again, and you don't want to be caught out in the middle of it. Tidal waves are known to crash over the stone walls of Vemond Castle, and those are fifty feet high," he answered.

Kieryn's mouth dropped, her eyes zigzagging at the beauty and magic of the island before her. It seemed that each kingdom had its special kind of magic that played a role in supplying its residents. Back in Almeria, the magic was their farmland that always replenished their soils with the richest fruits and vegetables and their coastal town with sea delectables.

Callian and Kieryn made their way over the sandbar. Warm, almost translucent sand wedged its way between Kieryn's toes, as her sandals sank into the grainy texture below her feet. She had opted for an almond-colored sundress that hit just below her knee. It was odd not wearing her usual leathers and boots, but she didn't want to stand out when multiple kingdoms were hunting her.

It took them thirty minutes to trek across the sandbar, Callian spitting out facts about Vemond Castle the entire time. As they got closer to it, she saw everything he had described to her: towering round arches, stonework winding its way around the castle and its province, guarding it from enemies. With the sirens and tritons controlling the sea, the residents never had to worry about their homes being flooded.

The residents who lived on Vemond Castle grounds were those who worked for the queen. Thosewho didn't reside in the castle itself had homes a stone's throw away. It was like its own island—they had their very own taverns and bookstores, apothecary shops and temples.

They passed through the towered walls leading into the village, and Kieryn allowed Callian to take the lead as they walked up the winding stone path towards the castle. Soraya met them at the doors, nodding to the guards standing outside.

Kieryn and Callian followed Soraya through the castle. Spread out before them was an open-air pathway, with pillars that extended to the ceilings, ivy chasing its way over them until it spread out like a spiderweb through the ceiling. Everything about this room was light and airy. The smell of the sea drifted through the open arches, a mix of coconut and salt dancing its way through Kieryn's nose. They passed an alcove on the right where naked sirens bathed in a turquoise-colored pool as their sing-song laughs echoed out into the hall.

"I appreciate the queen meeting with us at the last minute, Princess Soraya," Kieryn said, breaking the silence.

Soraya turned her head to glance back at Kieryn. "I told you, call me Raya, no titles needed."

Kieryn's smile tilted upwards slightly. "Thank you Soraya, this means a lot."

"Well, don't thank me yet. Mother is a cold-hearted bitch with an icy exterior, you are going to need all the luck you can get," she said bluntly, a slight bitterness to her tone.

Callian reached out and squeezed Kieryn's hand, giving her hope before the lump in her throat had a chance to turn to stone. Asking the queen for aid in this war that was about to unleash was critical. Maybe she should've dressed up in her leathers so the queen knew she was serious, but Callian had advised against it

The three entered a grand room decorated extensively with gold and turquoise. The gilded dome ceiling shone brightly on them from above, a crystal chandelier with bright pops of turquoise gems casting dancing light across the onyx-colored marble floor. Oil paintings lined one wall, showcasing the five beautiful islands. One painting portrayed Vemond Castle at golden hour, the waves lapping at the walls, another looked like the island of Layette, known for its unmatched natural beauty. Some had resorted to calling the *Garden Isle* due to its luscious rainforest that covered almost every inch of the island. The island had more waterfalls than land and only a few ventured to make a home on the island.

The third painting was of Palmana, and illustrated a volcano cresting above the clouds, lava rocks coating the top surrounded by hot springs. A beautiful view of the island awaited those brave enough to make the journey to the top.

Astora's painting was a mesmerizing star-filled scene above the cliffside that led to Lovers Leap Beach. Despite the name, it actually came from a story of devastating loss. And the last painting was of Naros, a quaint and idyllic island, with colors bursting in the heart of spring from the painting as if it were alive.

Queen Calista sat in the middle of the room, her dark cherry hair cascading down her back in waves. Her eyes pinned Kieryn where she stood, the color of them just as striking and the same color as the sea they had crossed to get here. Her skin was creamy and translucent, as if she spent most of her days coasting around the inside of her palace and doing anything to avoid the sun, a stark contrast to her daughter, Soraya, who had a glow to her skin.

The queen stood up from her throne, every movement fluid with grace as she approached Kieryn and Callian. She practically floated towards them, her feet barely making a sound on the floor. They bowed low before the queen, and on her way up, Kieryn took in her full appearance. Queen Calista wore a stunning and sheer white dress: two straps of fabric traveled from her shoulders down to her midriff where they stopped, revealing the milky white skin between her breasts. The rest of the dress fell down her body like a waterfall, and two slits crawled their way up her thighs, a thin piece of the fabric hiding what lay underneath. Just over her midriff, where her skin showed, was an intricate design of what looked like vines.

"My daughter here told me you requested my audience," Queen Calista said with a sigh of irritation coating her tongue. "I do not like being summoned, so whatever you have to say better be worth my time."

Queen Calista demanded attention not only with her presence, but in her voice. She was a seductress, yes, but she was also cunning and tight-lipped when it came to where her loyalties laid.

Callian spoke up first, "We deeply apologize for calling this meeting last minute, but it is of the utmost importance." His eyes looked over to Kieryn briefly before he spoke again. "King

Elias is calling for war and he intends to claim power over all residing kingdoms. He will not stop and he has the means to do so."

The queen absorbed his words.

"You mean your father. I know who you are," she said condescendingly. "The exiled bastard prince. Did you think I would not recognize you?" She peered at him with distaste, her eyes then roaming over to her daughter who stood bashfully off to the side, trying to blend in with the walls.

"Although it doesn't surprise me that my daughter befriends the leeches off the bottoms of the barrels." The queen shook her head with disappointment.

The queen's insults wounded Callian, but if Kieryn hadn't known him as intimately as she did, she wouldn't have noticed his slight flare of his nostrils and the light in his eyes starting to dim, his only tells.

"With all due respect, *Your Majesty*," Kieryn said with a bite, "it doesn't matter who he is, what matters is that the king will not hesitate to declare war on you as well, if you do not submit to him and his demands."

The queen finally glanced over at Kieryn and laughed.

"And who might you be," she questioned, not looking for a response. "Wait, yes I know," she said, tapping a finger to her ruby-red lips. "You must be the assassin they are looking for. Well count your days, sweetheart, your time here is limited."

Callian didn't take well to the threat towards Kieryn as his fists tightened and lips thinned.

"Mother …" Princess Soraya spoke up quietly from the corner, before she was accosted by her mother's vicious insults.

"That's enough out of you!" she scolded her. "You disappoint me once again, but why am I not surprised? You were always a stain on this family." The insolent tone of her voice hit Soraya like a force, as if she had been whipped. Words were weapons too. Soraya's lips wobbled at her mother's verbal abuse, but otherwise remained quiet and looked back to the ground.

"Not only have the three of you wasted my time, but you expect me to get involved in a war that doesn't concern me?" She cackled, her lips turning into a sinister smile.

Kieryn opened her mouth to respond, but the queen cut her off.

"Get out of my sight, the three of you are insufferable." And with those words still ringing in the air, she turned on her heel and left the room, leaving the three to stare at one another in disbelief.

THIRTY-ONE

"YOUR MOTHER IS A BITCH!" Kieryn said to Soraya. "She shouldn't talk to you like that, you're her daughter." Kieryn was cold with anger. Soraya shrunk in on herself, her once bubbly and charismatic personality slipping beneath the surface in the aftermath of her mother's venomous behavior.

Kieryn was right, Soraya knew she was, but after years of the non-stop emotional abuse from her mother, she had become numb to it all. There was no doing right by her mother, not when it concerned Soraya at least. She shielded her younger sister, Rylan, the best she could, but she suffered the brunt of it too.

"She wasn't always so ruthless and cruel. She was kind once, when my father was still alive. I think his death changed her, made her cold on the inside." She sighed, defeated. "I apologize …" Soraya started to say, but Kieryn stopped her, with a gentle touch on her arm.

"Do not apologize for her actions. You got us a meeting with your mother, and I am thankful for you trying and for your generosity. This isn't on you, Soraya. It's on her," she said matter-of-factly. "We will figure out another way to stop King Elias."

Soraya gave her a small smile and folded her into her arms.

"Please call me Raya, Kieryn. You're my friend now. Anything you guys need while you are here, please let me know, okay. I will try to talk to her again," she promised, but the smile didn't reach her eyes. They all knew it would be a waste of time. They said their goodbyes in the hall, and Callian and Kieryn made their way out, no one noticing the petite girl with scarlet hair eavesdropping behind the pillar.

They crossed the sandbar in silence, Kieryn quietly fuming the entire way. Callian laid a hand on her lower back, feeling the tension in her ease up a bit at his touch. He tried not to think too much about what that meant. She was trusting him, and she shouldn't. He wasn't a good guy, but he would be for her.

When they got back to the port village, he pulled her in, her silent fuming at bay for a bit when she was wrapped in his embrace.

"I know that didn't go as planned, but let's not give up hope yet. Hopefully your friends had better luck on their end."

She groaned not wanting to accept defeat at this moment. What she really wanted to do was go get her leathers and pay the queen a nice visit.

Callian beamed down at her and she smiled.

"Why are you smiling at me like that?"

"Because I want to show you something. Follow me."

He grabbed her hand and pulled her up the beach until they reached the inn's stable. Callian saddled up his stallion and turned around to help Kieryn up. She grabbed hold of his hand and allowed him to hoist her up.

"Where are you taking me?" she laughed.

He nestled in behind her, pulling her close to him and whispered, "It's a surprise!"

Callian steered them through town before they came across a small path that led them through a canopy of trees. Insects and birds alike sang from the treetops. That and the slight sound of running water were the only things they could hear. Kieryn instantly forgot about the meeting they had with the queen. She took in the wide trees with roots growing from the bottoms like tentacles, some as tall as her and as wide as a carriage. Vegetation grew all around them, from the floor of the jungle to the sky. A light rain settled over them, but the cluster of trees cocooned them in, preventing them from getting wet. The peacefulness of it all was uncanny, like she was intruding on something special.

"Not too far now," Callian's voice came from behind her. "Just up ahead."

She almost didn't hear him over a roaring sound in the distance. As they approached the clearing, she realized they were at a pool and above them, standing as tall as the trees in the jungle, was a waterfall cascading down a mountain.

A breath escaped from Kieryn's lips at the natural beauty before her.

"This is beautiful," she whispered, not wanting to ruin the tranquility of the place. "How did you find this?" she asked Callian.

He dismounted gracefully from his horse, helping her down. He grabbed her hand and guided her cautiously over the wet rocks leading to the towering waterfall. "One of my many adventures that brought me to Keres, I accidentally stumbled upon this while looking for a place to stay. The port village of Saler is just beyond here, but this isn't even the best part," he said, directing her around the back of the waterfall and into the mouth of a cave.

Darkness swallowed them whole as they went further into the cave, but Kieryn felt no fear alongside Callian. *Angel of Death* or not, a warmth in her bones told her she was safe with him. They walked together slowly, hand in hand through the darkness, when she saw a luminescent glow from just around the corner.

Thousands of blue lights shimmered from the ceiling and along the walls of the cave, like stars twinkling in the night sky. Their bioluminescent glow reflected off the hot spring, casting the perfect scene before her.

"This is incredible," she exclaimed, twirling in a circle, taking in the light show around her.

Kieryn finally laid eyes on Callian and his smile was one that she wanted to capture and hold forever in her pocket.

"It's a sanctuary for me, a place where I can just relax and settle my mind. No one knows about this cave, at least I think, but it's my favorite place here on this island." He looked sheepishly down at his boots, before catching her eye once more. "I've never brought anyone here before."

She found herself smiling over at him, something she had been doing more of lately.

"Thank you for trusting me with your secret place."

He nodded and took her hand in his. "Let's go for a swim."

Her laugh echoed throughout the cavern walls and they stripped off their clothes and waded into the hot springs. Callian clutched Kieryn in his hands, lifting her up so that her legs wrapped around his waist. Her forehead rested delicately over his curls as they stared at one another, lost in the other's presence.

"You and your caves," she laughed.

Callian chuckled underneath her, his mouth nibbling along the length of her neck, licking where he bit, soothing the pain. Kieryn arched her neck, giving him more access to her. He grinned up at her as his mouth slowly took in one of her peaked nipples. He bit down and she could feel her legs clench, her muscles coiling at his touch. His hot breath and the lick of his tongue were like a seductive spell. She started to grind on him, feeling his length harden between her legs. His hand fisted her hair and with one thrust, he was moving inside her.

Their bodies moved in perfect tandem, like they were welcoming the other home. She gripped his wide shoulders, nails digging in and drawing blood and with that pain he drove into her harder. As he came, he looked into her eyes and whispered, "*Alora,* my hope." And with those words spilling from the lips of the *Angel of Darkness,* she detonated with him.

They swam over to a spot in the hot springs where they could sit and rest and Kieryn gazed back up at the luminous ceiling.

"What is it? What makes it glow?"

"They're glow wyrms, completely harmless," he answered when he saw her face scrunch up in disgust at the word *wyrms.* "They're rather small, but they build this silk thread that hangs vertically, and insects attracted to the light get caught in the web, similar to that of a spider. It's crazy how survival creates this beautiful phenomenon."

Kieryn pondered at his words, taking in the view of the cave with a new perspective.

Callian glimpsed at Kieryn's bareback, when his eyes went cold.

"Who did this to you?" he seethed, his fingers trailing the slightly faded scars on her back. She gazed down into the water and gulped.

"It was an accident. It happened right before the masquerade ball. There was an altercation outside a bar we frequented in Riyadh. Damien's old pack started a fight, and

Damien was one blow away from possible death, and I refused to stand there useless and watch that unfold," she trailed off.

"So, you took the blow for him, knowing you wouldn't heal like he would," he replied.

"Yes," she whispered in the dark.

"You are one of the most selfless, craziest and courageous women I ever met, you know that?" he confessed, his fingers leaving a trail of goosebumps over her skin. He knew she didn't want to talk about the injury anymore, so he let his eyes focus on getting a good look at the tattoo that flowed down her spine instead. He wasn't familiar with the language of Almeria, but the calligraphy of the words were beautiful in its own right.

"What does your tattoo say?" he asked, changing the topic.

She sighed in relief at the topic change, but a look of sorrow crossed her eyes, as she briefly looked away, getting her bearings.

"It's something my dad used to tell me growing up. It means *'fight off your demons'*. He used to tell me to not let anything affect my ability to be great, that as long as I learn how to acknowledge and understand my inner demons, they can never win. He always said it's better to lose the battle than the war."

"Smart man."

Her eyes glazed over as she stared relentlessly at the cavern wall.

"Yeah, he was," she said.

Callian stroked her arm comfortingly.

"Tell me about them—your parents," he said.

Her face lit up, if only a little, her eyes still portraying the ghosts of her past. And she did tell him about her parents. She told him about her mother's angelic singing and how you could hear her lilting voice in the gardens, that no matter how busy her father was, he always made it a point to be home for dinner. She told him about the love her parents had for each other, how it was selfless and passionate.

"He never left a room without telling her how much he loved her. They'd always be sharing these intimate moments of secret touches and longing looks, whether I was in the room or not. It always felt like I was intruding on a special moment between them, but I loved watching them together. I longed for a love like theirs when I was a little girl."

"But not now?"

It was a simple question he asked, but she can hear the uneasiness underneath his words. Her father adored her mother, and her mother loved him wholeheartedly. They had an easy love. But things changed. She had changed. She saw the ruthlessness of the world. Hel, she was one of the ruthless. She killed for a living, and she never admitted it out loud to anyone, but it was satisfying in a way. It was liberating. Who could love a soulless monster? Who could love someone so tainted by their past, someone who couldn't say goodbye to their ghosts?

"Love is a dangerous thing. Love destroys a person. You can't have your heart broken if you never give it away in the first place."

Callian studied her from behind long lashes, his coal-like eyes a few shades lighter than normal. He inhaled her words as if they were anchoring him to the cave floor, trying to decipher whether or not what she said was a lie or the truth. And quite frankly, she didn't know whether or not her heart believed her mind either.

He dipped his head, dropping the subject. Kieryn basked in the silence, running her fingertips along Callian's forearms, and as she did she felt his body shudder beneath her touch. She ran her fingers higher until they were skating over his tattooed shoulders. Her fingers drifted over an hourglass, the top half featuring a clock, the hand broken, stuck in time, while in the bottom half laid a skull.

"What's this one mean?"

He followed her gaze where it rested lightly on his left shoulder. Her touch was warm, like a roaring fire stroking his skin.

"The broken clock resembles the struggle of life and death. The clock suspended in time at a moment in my life where things … changed, and the skull at the bottom represents death. Time doesn't stop, not for anyone, as much as I wish it did."

Kieryn moved her head closer, the scent of her filling his nose with nostalgia and melancholy. As she peered closer at the broken clock, she noticed the small hand hovered over the three and the longer hand extended out over the seven, 3:35 am, the witching hour.

Her hand slid further down his arm and stopped on the compass on the inner part of his forearm.

"That was one of my first tattoos. I got it in rebellion, to spite my father. I loved to travel and I would find myself on these crazy adventures, despite his disapproval. It was supposed to represent travel and guidance, but it's got more of a darker meaning now of feeling lost and misguided. Trying to find my way back, I guess."

His voice got deeper, slower as he was reminded of the arrogant young prince he used to be.

Kieryn's hand slipped lower still, cradling his forearm in her delicate hands. She gazed at the intricate designs on his arm, a mosaic of artwork on a masterpiece. Her hand gripped the anatomical heart that laid on his skin, a skeleton hand grasping it in its clutches.

"Death has my heart in a tight grip, figuratively and literally speaking. Who I am now has me in a chokehold. The person I am today wouldn't even recognize the person I once was. Death is what I am now."

Her hand moved of its own accord as she twisted his arm to see his outer arm, an eyeball staring back at her, but inside the pupil was a silhouette of a man looking through a doorway.

"A moment in my life that haunts me. I am not proud of the things I did, but something good did come from that night, even if that decision resulted in sacrifice. I can't bring myself to regret what happened, just live with it I guess."

"And the thorns?" she asked.

Bloody thorns wrapped around his thick wrists, twisting around like serpents.

He ghosted over her question, his body tensing up at the mention of the thorns.

"My own personal hell," he simply stated, something deep in his voice conveying he didn't want to talk further about it.

She didn't push him further on the topic. If he wanted to tell her about them, he would when he was ready. Her eyes swung over to his right arm, where an intricate sword was etched deep into his skin, and with exquisite detail. So much so, it looked like an exact replica of the longsword he used in battle. She looked up at him and he smirked.

"Part of my magic, a neat little trick too. My power can call to it," he said this while his other hand went to the tattoo. Upon his touch, the sword rippled beneath his skin, alive. If he wanted to, he could pull the sword from his very skin, like a warrior would with a scabbard.

Kieryn's eyes blew wide at this development, as his magic transferred the sword back into a tattoo on his arm.

"That's incredible," she breathed out, her fingertips tracing over it, a look of amazement and wonder spanning across her features.

As she began to pull back, she noticed the tattooed feathered wings protruding from over his back and running down the length of his sides.

"They don't call me the *Angel of Death* for nothing," he laughed.

They settled back into each other, talking about his tattoos and when he got them, and about life and death in a world like theirs. They both longed for a life worth living for, yet they each had Death at their fingertips.

After a brief lapse of silence, Callian's alluring voice pierced the air.

"Do you believe that someone's soul can be saved?" he asked, his voice barely above a whisper.

She peeked over at him, the look on his face one of consternation. His eyebrows dropped, and his face was stoic as if he was pondering the answer to his own question. She thought it over before answering.

"I think there is hope in the sense of being able to find the light in the darkness. I think that when we don't fight the darkness, but rather embrace it, we can find a light within ourselves. So, can a soul be saved, I hope it can, because mine needs saving too." Her voice drifted, echoing in the space between them, between a light-filled darkness.

He looked at her, a look of adoration in his eyes, and he cradled her face and ever so gently kissed her, the lingering magic of his taste on her lips.

"Here's to saving each other and bringing the light out from the darkness, *alora*."

THIRTY-TWO

GRAYSON MADE good time keeping him and Duchess to the outskirts of the Bloodwood Forest. He had a few close calls along the way; nighttime was always the worst. The screeching sounds of *The Mad King's* creatures kept him awake paralyzed with fear. He slept with his bow on his chest, his hand on his dagger, ready if needed. If it wasn't the terrifying noises of the creatures that lurked in the shadows, he was tormented by the sounds of the dragons calling to their brethren in the air.

He found himself reminiscing more about those days as a Nightraider. The thrill of riding a dragon.. It was an honor to be a Nightraider, but not all those who trained to become one, would officially be one, until a dragon chose its rider. It was a grueling process from the living standards, the training, the danger of it all—as dragons can easily spot the weak, and they damn well made sure you knew.

Grayson was one of the first ones chosen in his class. A black-nosed Hornback picked him, with spikes riding down from his mid-back down to his tail. He was all black, and his red beady eyes glowed like coal in a fire. Once chosen, you were bonded for life, but when he ran, he couldn't bring his dragon, Rajani, with him. When that bond broke, it shattered him, almost as much as leaving *her*. He assumed the dragon had bonded with a new rider, the other alternative he didn't want to think about.

He prayed for the morning, as it beat the pity party he threw for himself at night, or the whiplash he gave himself constantly swinging his head to any slight noise that didn't come from his horse.

They rode in silence together, sometimes Grayson breaking the silence by talking to his horse about his training as a Nightraider. By the fifth day, he felt like he was going to lose his mind, but there before his eyes lay his destination—his old fort.

It wasn't much of a fort, not to the naked eye. But he could tell by the star-shaped stump that he was home. He had wanted a sanctuary away from his father, and between him and her, they built a small place nestled under the cover of trees, if you were brave enough to climb. He took Duchess's reins and led her to a secluded area where the Nightraiders couldn't see her from the skies, and now that they had passed through the Bloodwood Forest, they should be relatively safe.

He fed Duchess a few carrots from his pack, stroking her mane absentmindedly, following the line of the tree trunk vertically until his neck strained. He made his way over to the tree that was home to cherished memories. He pulled up his hood more and angled his boot into a tiny knot into the tree, and began to climb. His footwork was quick, and his hands found hooks and holes in the trees that he knew religiously, as if no time had passed since he was here.

Once his body disappeared through the canopy of leaves, he finally saw it in all its glory. The long, wide branch was ten feet above him, and above that the rope he would climb to get through the opening in the floor of the fort. He hauled himself up the rope, the burn of it on his bare hands making him feel nostalgic. He pushed his way through the opening in the floor and stood up in the wooden enclosure.

It was four bare walls made of Bakrem wood from the trees that were settled at the base of the Alps. There was a thick layer of dust that coated the sidings by the windows, as if no one had been here. She hadn't been here since that fateful night, he would've guessed.

He strode over to the window, peering out beyond the leaves, finding the small gaps in between. His gaze settled on the snow-capped Alps glistening under the evening sun. His thoughts strayed to her, as they always did. Not once did his mind let him forget about her.

He could almost smell her, the sweet smell of roses tickling his nose. The warm, rich honey-like scent engulfed him in sorrow and melancholy. It felt as if she was here with him. He breathed in the scent of her, and as he did he heard the telltale sound of the floorboards creaking and the ghost of the wind of an arrow being nocked into place. He didn't make any sudden movements.

"Turn around slowly," the voice behind him said. It was deep and off-pitch, as if they were masking it.

He turned, hesitant as to how he was going to approach this. As he turned, he faced his enemy head-on. The hood hid the person's face, but they were covered in black leathers with a red dragon emblem over their heart, the sign of a Nightraider. He had been praying that it wouldn't come to this. He didn't want to kill his own brothers and sisters, but he would if necessary.

He didn't give a second thought as he dropped low, the arrow releasing from its hold, grazing his arm as he tackled the target to the ground. They struggled on the dusty floor, specks floating into the air as they went back and forth, wrestling for the upperhand. His assailant kneed him in the balls, striking an uppercut to his jaw. *Low blow,* he thought, as he keeled over briefly. He hopped up, daggers in both his hands, as he swiped at them, his enemy dodging every blow. They ducked under his arm, punching his kidneys as they did, and he faltered as he turned to face them. They were fast and small and at an advantage in this tiny fort, but he had the upper hand, because he knew everything about this place. He faked right and went left instead, and just as he had hoped, the assassin fell for it, tripping over the piece of wood that stuck out slightly because Grayson was too stubborn to fix it back in his youth.

He fell down with the assailant, pulling his dagger back to make the killing blow, just as their hood fell away, beautiful sea glass eyes stared up at him in both alarm and confusion.

"Grayson," she whispered, her warring emotions crossing her face from confusion to sadness to anger.

"Ilyana?"

THIRTY-THREE

IT WAS *HER!* The woman he had left behind, the one his mind could never let him forget, his best friend, his …

He dragged himself off of her, his body falling back into the wall, as if he could melt into it. This was a dream, wasn't it? He had finally lost it after numerous sleepless nights, and this was his angel coming to him in the end. It had to be, because having Ilyana in front of him, in the flesh, was mind-numbingly painful and euphoric.

Her white-blonde hair was the color of freshly fallen snow, and her eyes like sea glass or an arctic blue that you felt like drowning in. She was petite, but strong, probably from her training in the Nightraiders. He couldn't believe she was one of them now. Her almond-colored skin glowed bright, and those damn lips were flushed red from the cold.

He watched her from afar, as she slid away from him, mirroring his movements from the other side of their fort. She was no longer the girl he recognized, she was a woman now, and he took the time to drink her in.

"How are you alive?" She faltered in her words before continuing, "It is you right? You're actually here?"

His eyes fell to his lap where his hands fidgeted, desperate to reach out to her and console her. He answered her without looking at her.

"It's really me, Illy," he said, using a nickname only reserved by him.

Her audible gasp of the nickname he had given her made his eyes dart to her face, and he searched her eyes, for what he wasn't sure—forgiveness, love, acceptance? But what he found was resentment.

"Don't! You don't get to use that name. You lost that right," she said with fire in her eyes. "I mourned you, I felt the loss of you and it *broke* me." She sniffled before reining her emotions back in. A wave of guilt washed over Grayson as he realized the repercussions of his actions all those years ago.

"I had to run and fake my death, all of Calydan Kingdom wanted me dead, Illy." He sighed in defeat. "I had no choice."

She was startled at his choice of words.

"No choice ..." she murmured. "NO CHOICE!" she yelled. She was shaking now. "You had a choice, Grayson. You committed regicide on your own kingdom. The kingdom was in turmoil for months after you fled like a coward. I was taken into custody and questioned," she spat. Her words were like a knife to the chest.

Calydan didn't question, they tortured. He needed names, because he would tear every limb from their forsaken body and make them bleed out slowly. His breathing was heavier, and he stood up abruptly, pacing back and forth at the truth of it all.

She ignored him and continued, "They asked me about your whereabouts, waiting for me to break, but I never said a word, not out of loyalty, although I would've protected you if you had told me the truth, but because I had no idea you had left." Her voice shook with sadness.

"While I was being questioned, word came that you ... that you had fallen from Hangman's Chasm. They confirmed your death, when Rajani felt the bond break and he went into a pit of depression for months."

Grayson remembered that night. In his desperate attempt to escape his kingdom that had so easily turned on him, he did something just as sinful. He sought aid from the mortarri. He paid their price for his freedom: they would fake his death and he in return would kill those who they deemed disposable for them. In the end, Ryvers had discovered him from his indiscretions with this coven, and paid handsomely for him to join the Phantoms, and then he slaughtered that particular clan of witches. He owed Ryvers a life debt.

Ilyana looked down at her hands. They were dainty and small and he wanted nothing more than to hold them again.

"Rajani wasn't the only one that suffered from your loss."

"Ilyana, I'm sorry …"

She stood up suddenly, and faced him.

"I don't need your half-truths and apologies. Not anymore. Tell me why you came here? Tell me why, after all of these years, you came back from the dead?"

Grayson stood there in silence, watching as he lost the woman he loved, twice. It didn't feel any better after all these years. She had to have known his feelings for her. He had left her here with no goodbye, because he couldn't risk losing her out there. He couldn't live with himself if something had happened to her because he made the decision to kill his father, the king. She was better off without him, even though his heart had never repaired itself after the heartbreak of losing her and Rajani.

"I came back to Calydan Kingdom to ask the queen for aid. There is a war coming. They believe my friend Kieryn killed the King of Minas, but it wasn't her, it was King Elias. I am here to try to convince the queen to aid us rather than him, although I haven't yet figured out how I am going to do that when I was a wanted man and now I am a ghost of sorts …"

he trailed off. "Elias can't have access to our dragons, Ilyana. It would be catastrophic and we'd stand no chance," he explained.

"So you're telling me this was a suicide mission?"

"Yup, pretty much." He shrugged nonchalantly, trying to mask his feelings about it.

She sized him up before answering him.

"I can get you a meeting with the queen. You can't be there, they will kill you on sight, but I can go in your place."

Grayson took a step forward, and Ilyana took a step backwards putting up her hand.

"I am not doing this for you, I am doing it for me. The quicker it is done, the sooner you can leave, and this time when you do, I don't need you to say goodbye."

And with those parting words, she dropped down into the hole in the floor and landed quietly on the tree branch.

"Do not leave this fort. I will be back when the moon crests over the Alps, and only then will I sneak you into the city," she called up from the hole in the floor.

And like the ghost-like glow of her hair, she disappeared into the night, leaving Grayson at a loss for words. Because while he may have been the ghost brought back to life in her eyes, she was the one that haunted him, even now, as he stared at the place she once was.

THIRTY-FOUR

THE WORLD WAS CRUEL, this she had always known. Her parents had abandoned her when she was a child because parenting wasn't a thing they wanted to do full-time, so they dumped her at an orphanage. From there, she suffered through the torment of the other children, because she was different. They called her a witch, *Moon Child*, and names she didn't want to think about. Her hair was stark white and bright, and her skin as translucent as her hair. In their eyes, she was a freak. No one wanted her, and eventually the orphanage shunned her as well, because she scared people off with her appearance.

She learned how to survive at the early age of twelve. She stole from the vendors in the street, slept in alleys, ate the burnt food cooks would throw out, until one day, Grayson came across her shivering in tattered clothing, and offered her a helping hand and a friendly, earth-shattering smile. It was the beginning of their friendship.

He chatted incessantly about the Nightraiders and how he longed to be one someday. He was passionate, charismatic, and a prankster. He was only two years older than her, but he was a people-pleaser. He tried to make everyone else happy, but behind those fake smiles he constantly walked around with, she saw the pain etched in his eyes.

He never opened up to her about what he dealt with, but she could see the bruises on his skin he tried to hide. They were best friends, and since that rainy day when he held out his hand for her to take, they became inseparable.

He showed her his favorite place in the world, a fort hidden amongst the trees that he was building, and said that she could claim it as hers too, if she wanted. He offered her friendship, shelter, and food without making her feel like she was a charity case. His friendship came free, although she discovered that he was just as lonely as she was, but the shelter and food he made her work for. She helped him build their safe haven together, and he showed her how to hunt, helping her hone her skills with a bow.

They spent their afternoons chasing one another in the woods, forming games to keep themselves entertained, and then they would hide from the world in their secret place in their oak tree and talk for hours into the night. He was always gone when she woke up, back to the palace, but every morning he left her a parting gift: a rose, fitting for her name, *Ilyana Rose*.

Ilyana ran through the field, toward her dragon that awaited her, and took to the skies, doing her best to escape her past and the special boy with the moss-colored eyes that broke her heart with it.

She followed through on her promise. Just as the full moon was cresting above the snow-capped mountains, her bright hair lit up the darkness and beckoned to him like a beacon in the night. She was still dressed in her Nightraider leathers and a small hint of pride and jealousy swelled in his heart, but he smiled all the same at her.

"What? Why are you smiling at me like that?"

"Proud of you, is all. I never thought you'd become a Nightraider," he said simply. Ilyana pondered his words and drank them in. Her emotions were at war. One second she wanted to throttle him for leaving her, breaking her heart, and the next she wanted to give in to temptation and tell him her feelings for him. But she couldn't, because things were complicated now.

But nothing was more satisfying than hearing someone you loved voice out loud that they were proud of you.

She drowned in everything that was Grayson Hunt years ago, and she never came back up for air, not even now. But he never knew how she felt, and she would keep it that way now, even if that meant pushing away the one man she'd ever truly loved when fate was giving them a second chance.

He would never know she became a Nightraider because it was the only time she felt close to him. The fort only dug up memories she couldn't bear to remember, so she never stepped foot in this place, until tonight. Every night she came back, she made it as far as the tree branch, but could never will herself to cross that threshold, until a feeling in her gut told her to climb that rope tonight.

"When you left and I was questioned, they found my *endurance* of pain riveting. Offered me a position to train with the Nightraiders if I wanted it. After your death, I felt numb— I needed something, anything, even if it was a distraction. I never thought I'd make it through the process. Let alone be bonded to a dragon," Ilyana said with a sense of guilt.

There was more to that statement that she was letting on, but he didn't press her. She wouldn't reveal her secrets to him, anyway. Instead, he diverted the conversation entirely, which she was thankful for.

"Where are we going?" he pressed.

"To my place," she answered before lowering herself through the floor. Grayson followed her, knowing that she could be leading him into a trap, to his possible death, but it didn't matter. He would follow her anywhere.

Grayson led Duchess over to Ilyana. She held up her hand patiently, and the horse sniffed it before nudging her head into Ilyana's open palm, instantly at ease. He helped her up, even though he knew she didn't need it, but reluctantly she accepted his help, trying to forget about the day they met and he offered his hand to her.

He followed suit and took the reins in his hand, but let her guide him. After she told him where to go, he led Duchess into a light walk. The moon's light covered them in an eerie glow, and the tops of trees danced in the wind around them. If their relationship wasn't strained, this would've been romantic, Grayson thought. His mind wandered to the "what ifs" with Ilyana, before she lightly nudged him, pointing to a pathway in the trees. He dug his heels in, and slowed his horse down, reacquainting himself with his surroundings.

The dirt path led them up a hill, where a massive home stood, its structure composed of glass and stone. Even if she was a Nightraider, it didn't explain the size and luxury of her home.

"You live here?" he questioned.

"I do," she said, not giving him more.

"H-How?"

Duchess came to a stop, and Ilyana leaned back into Grayson before landing on the ground. She turned back to him and with barely any emotion on her face, she told him.

"Because I am the Queen's Right Hand." And with that,

she turned toward her house, leaving Grayson to scramble after her.

He chased after her, stepping foot into her home and whatever he was going to say died on his lips as he took everything in. As lavish as the house was, Ilyana had still managed to make the inside feel like a home. The living area housed a comfortable, plush couch the color of his eyes, and a blazing fire was roaring to life beside him, the handmade table next to the fire was worn in, and used with love. He peered over the couch to find stacks of books lining the shelves, the spines gently used. The air smelled like her—warm and floral—and a spicy rich scent he couldn't put his finger on.

She walked through the living room to the kitchen, where she put on a kettle for tea, and he watched her move around her kitchen freely and with a sense of routine. Her kitchen was bright and filled with her personality. It was sprinkled in warm, inviting colors, spices lining her shelves, and her makeshift garden bloomed in its window, bright, like her.

He swallowed the lump in his throat as he imagined himself being here—living here with her. A life they could've shared, if things were different. If he had been born into a different family, perhaps. He looked around at the life he could've had, and the burning resentment toward his father was overwhelming. He felt his chest tighten and his knees became too heavy and he sagged into the wooden chair before him as he clutched his heart.

Ilyana turned to him, the kettle forgotten, and rushed to his side as he hunched over.

"Grayson, what's wrong? Are you okay?" she said, a voice soft with affection, her hands tracing small circles into his back.

He didn't answer her; how could he? He was suffocating in her presence. She was everywhere he looked and what gutted him was that there was no trace of him. There never would have been. Out of all the years he had been at the Keep, it wasn't until this moment, right now in her kitchen, that he truly felt like a phantom. A forgotten soul. A lost memory.

He felt the pull of her delicate fingers lift his chin, and he locked eyes with her calm blue ones, mesmerized at how peaceful they looked. He felt like he was floating as he stared into her eyes, and she stared back at him, unmoving. He placed his palm on her cheek and inhaled deeply. She closed her eyes at his touch and a small sigh left her lips.

"Illy ..." he started to say, but the use of her nickname broke her from her trance and she stood up, away from his touch.

"Here's some tea," she quickly stated, grabbing the kettle that was now steaming, and creating distance between them. He took the tea from her, a small smile making its presence known to hide the panic and chaos wanting to rip from his skin.

Their hands touched and lingered, before she quickly withdrew and faced the cabinets. "There's some soup I made earlier, it just needs to be heated up. You'll find everything you need here. I need to step out for a bit, but I'll be back later," she said softly. "Do not leave this house!" she added with assertiveness and something like worry flitting across her face.

Grayson nodded into his tea, afraid to speak and ruin anything else in her life. He watched her back out of the room. Not once did her eyes leave him, until the last possible second, before she disappeared once more into the night, leaving him alone with his tormented thoughts.

THIRTY-FIVE

IT WASN'T long after Ilyana had left that his agonizing thoughts led him to needing something stronger than tea. He scoured her cabinets until he found liquor stored all the way in the back of one of her cupboards. The grimace on his face came naturally—whiskey. He hated whiskey, but tonight he'd happily accept the poison.

Three drinks in and he began to see why Kieryn enjoyed it so much. The liquid burned going down his throat with each swallow. Another torturous thought about a life he never had, could never have. *Sip.* He paced her living room, trying to find remnants of what her life was now. A life without him in it. She was a Nightraider and more specifically, Queen Ambra's Right Hand. She had made quite a name for herself in his absence, and there were no ill thoughts about that. He didn't expect her to wallow forever, she deserved a good life. She had suffered enough in her childhood, and his death, well his fake death, only added fuel to the fire that was burning her world down.

He tried not to think about that night. The night that he lost

Everything.

He became an orphan that night, not by choice. His father took away that choice when he killed his mother, and after all the bloodshed, all the bruises, all the manipulation and secrets, Grayson couldn't stand by helpless any longer. He was too late to save her, so he did the next best thing and got revenge. For her, and for the lonely and scared little boy that remained stuffed inside that dark closet all these years.

Sip.

He knew it was a death sentence for him, and at that moment he didn't care. He had lost everything, and just as quickly, he realized he hadn't lost everything, he still had her. He still had Ilyana. But just as that thought came, he knew he ultimately would lose her as well.

Sip.

Whether it be from the truth of his actions or not,the world would rip her away from him too. So, he left. He ran and never said goodbye, because he knew if he had, he would've never left her side and then they'd both be dead.

The distinct sound of a key in a lock pulled him from his spiral and he brought the glass back to his lips. *Sip.* He swished the whiskey around the glass, the clinking of the ice lulling him into a stupor, just as she rounded the corner.

"I see you didn't waste any time helping yourself to my things," she said resolutely.

He turned his head slightly to look over at her. "You did say everything I needed was here … well, almost everything." He slung the rest of the contents down his throat. He slammed the glass back down on the coffee table and she flinched, which didn't go unnoticed. He made to grab the bottle, but she got to it first, holding it out of reach.

"I think you've had enough, don't you think?"

He scowled at her remark.

"Not nearly enough, the demons haven't quieted down just yet."

A look of pity cut across her face and her hand lowered the bottle.

"Don't. Don't give me that look," he begged her, "I can't stomach that look on your face."

"What look?" she asked as she placed the bottle back on the table within reach of Grayson, but he didn't reach for it. Instead, he grasped her hand and brought it to his cheek.

"Pity," he murmured into her hand, kissing her fingertips.

That's when he noticed. When the fogginess clouding his eyes vanished as quickly as a summer storm. She had dirt and blood caked all over her hand. His eyes widened in concern, and took in the state of Ilyana. She was leaning to one side, favoring it over the other, and the hard line of her mouth told him she was holding her pain in. And then there was the thin coat of dirt and blood, not just on her hands but her clothes.

"What. Happened?!" he demanded, sobering up.

"It's nothing, just a misunderstanding. I'll be fine."

She squirmed out of his grasp, and limped over to the bathroom, him following her like her shadow.

"I don't believe you. Why are you lying to me?"

She ignored him, taking a wet cloth to her face, wincing at the split eyebrow.

Grayson reached out, covering her hand in his. Her piercing eyes gazed up at him, glistening.

"Let me," he said gently, coaxing her to release the washcloth. She did without a fight, and as delicately as he could, he helped her to sit on the counter. His body fit perfectly in between her legs as he brought the towel back up to dab at her cut. His blood boiled, his hands gripped the wet cloth tightly, and his jaw was clamped so painfully he saw stars.

"Who did this to you, Illy? Do not lie this time, I know when you do."

Her eyes swung up to look at him, and he paused his care-taking to give her his full attention.

"How?"

"How what?"

"How do you know when I am lying?"

A small smirk played at the corner of his lips, as he went back to dabbing the blood and dirt on her face, reaching around her to turn on the faucet to rinse. The river of dark red made his vision swim as death consumed him, which was what he would rain down on those responsible for hurting her. The light touch on his arm helped him to focus on her again, but barely.

"You twirl the ring on your finger and the tone of your voice rises just slightly," he said with an easy casualness.

Ilyana stared at him, bewildered. She never knew he paid attention to the small things about her.

"Of course I paid attention, I always did," he whispered, his forehead coming down to rest on hers. She hadn't realized she had said that last part out loud.

"Now tell me," he continued, "who did this to you, before I burn this kingdom to the ground and kill everyone in my path."

He felt her shake underneath him, and he cupped her face, his heart fluttering like a butterfly in a blizzard when she leaned into his touch.

"As I said, it was a misunderstanding. I'm fine now, it's handled."

"Who are you protecting, Illy?" His words were accusing.

"I-It's complicated," she stammered, tears threatening to spill over.

He shook his head at her, fighting every nerve in his body not to punch the mirror behind her at her willingness to protect this person.

It was his mother all over again.

He pushed through her bathroom door, murder in his eyes, the sounds of her protests dying away behind him. All he saw was red.

"Grayson, stop," she pleaded. He ignored her request.

"Stop and look at me!"

He halted at the door, hand on the doorknob, frozen in place. With a shaking breath, he turned and looked at her, her hair wild, her now clean face and tear marks trailing down her cheeks.

"NO, Ilyana. I will not let you suffer like this. You think I don't know abuse when I see it? That I can stand in front of you, knowing that another woman I love is hurt? I couldn't save her then, let me save you."

Her gasp was audible, and his confession out there now, and quite frankly he didn't give a fuck.

"Who couldn't you save, Grayson?"

Inhale, hold, exhale.

"My mother."

Two words muttered into existence, a knife wound to his heart even after a decade, and it still bled viciously.

"My father, *our king*," he forced out through his teeth, "killed my mother after years and years of abuse. He turned on me, until my mother saved me by forcing me into the Nigh-traiders, and I vowed I would return the favor. I would save her too, and we would escape. But only one of us made it out that night.``

Ilyana's hands flew to her mouth, her sobs tearing from her chest as she finally learned the truth about that night.

"I never wanted to leave you Ilyana, you have to know that." He gripped her face in his hands. "You were the one good thing I had left in my world, but I had committed regicide and I-I couldn't—I couldn't subject you to the same fate."

"That wasn't your choice to make," she scolded with condemnation.

"What I am, Illy, it is not a life. I kill for a living. I am a phantom, an assassin. I am Death. I am *The Grim Reaper.*"

"That's you?" Her head shook like a pendulum swing in his grasp."I never believed you were dead," she confessed. "I refused to believe it even after the broken connection. When I heard about this assassin, the killings, I just felt this pull drawing me towards him, towards you. I can't describe it, I just knew I felt something."

His mouth dropped open in shock at her words.

"I searched for you. In everything. In everyone, for years. I never gave up on you. Not once."

He clutched at his chest, her confession ripping his heart to shreds.

"Illy, what are you saying …"

"You left me alone and heartbroken, Grayson," she whimpered, coming closer to where he stood frozen. "I was so in love with you, and you abandoned me. No explanation. No goodbye."

That one word set him in motion, and his hand wrapped around her head, his other hand gripping her waist.

"*Was* in love?" he asked, trembling at the past tense of her words. "Illy, I am madly, deeply, earth-shatteringly in love with you. I fell in love with you the first day I met you, and I would've fallen in love with you with my eyes closed. You were the only real thing in my life, the light in the darkness and every day without you has been my own personal hell. Ruin me, hate me, hell, kill me, but please don't say you love me in the past tense. I will not survive a life without you in it, not again. Never again."

He gazed into her crystal eyes, the eyes that saved his soul over and over again, the eyes that haunted him for years, the eyes that knew him and loved him, the eyes he wished to spend the rest of his tortured days looking into.

"I don't think I ever stopped loving you, Grayson," she professed, biting down on her lip. "As much as I wanted to."

Grayson closed the gap between them, and swallowed her cry, crushing his lips to hers, savoring the touch and taste of her. Only then did he finally feel the tightening in his chest release, and he felt peace.

THIRTY-SIX

CALLIAN AND KIERYN rode into the town of Saler after a few hours of swimming in the pool, the steady drum of the waterfall the only noise other than their combined laughter. She had braided her hair so that it ran down the length of her back, and she felt sun-kissed being out in the sun all afternoon. A part of her felt guilty that she had enjoyed herself with Callian, but another side of herself couldn't be bothered to care.

The symphony of jungle sounds fell away as they got closer to Saler, a small village Callian had mentioned hosted non-magical folk. As they made their way into the town, Kieryn saw up close how different Saler was compared to the other side of the island. The town was a desolate piece of land, with run-down buildings that had seen better days and streets that were made of dirt rather than stone.

"Why do they live like this?" she asked Callian. "Does the queen not give them aid?"

She felt his body sag into hers, and he dismounted from his horse, helping her down before he answered.

"Unfortunately, Queen Calista has no interest in Saler, even though they are her people. They wield no magic, so they are of little use to her, other than when she needs their services or goods. She's a woman of no heart," he replied, disdain dripping in every word he spoke against the queen.

"Soraya and I have visited every so often and we help in any way we can. Raya would make for a better queen than her mother. She's kind hearted and generous. People around the island may look at her as a party girl who likes to sleep around, but she's more than that. Here she is known to these people as their saving grace.

She comes here at least once a week to help repair people's homes and to give them clothing, all out of her own pocket. The times I've been here, I always came and helped. Even though these people can sense there is something off about me, they always made me feel welcome. It's admirable what Soraya does, and she doesn't broadcast it to her Kingdom for attention, either. Her mother is vindictive and never deserved the crown. Her husband, the king, was kind and Soraya took after him."

Kieryn squeezed his hand, admiring the love Callian had for Soraya. She already liked the stunning siren, but hearing more about the person she was when no one was looking, she commended her for that. Kieryn smiled, thinking Soraya and Ashlyn were very much alike in that way.

"Long live the true Queen of Keres." Kieryn smiled.

They spent the day talking amongst the people of Saler, Kieryn soaking in all the smells billowing in the breeze. The market stalls reminded her of home, back when her father would bring her into the square and she would run free, weaving between the booths. Saler felt nostalgic to her. She bought several things from the stalls, including a few scarves for herself and Ash, striking up a conversation with the vendor about how she made them herself with the help of her daughter.

She found a hand-carved wooden figurine of a wolf that

she bought for Damien, even if he refused her friendship. As for Grayson, he was a bit harder to shop for, until she found a ring forged with dragon fire, the same color as his eyes. She and Callian had stayed around after perusing the market, and Callian had showed her some of the homes he and Soraya had built. He had introduced her to some of the townsfolk, and she told them stories about other kingdoms while they spoke with her about their traditions.

When night fell, the older woman at the vendor stall selling scarves had grabbed her hand and pulled her into the middle of the street to dance, a bonfire lit in the center of the square. Other neighbors had joined, some bringing their own musical instruments and joined in on the fun. Kieryn let a smile slip as she looked around to find Callian sitting on a log with a wide smile on his face as he drank in her happiness.

Being around the people of Saler who still found happiness in the little things and had no magic was humbling, and she hoped she could see them again before her and Callian left the island. By the time they left Saler, her heart felt full and lighter.

The next morning brought a hazy fog that engulfed the island. Kieryn laid awake, her eyes counting the intricate swirls in the ceiling, the satin sheet laid across her bare chest. She and Callian had failed in their attempt to get the queen to side against King Elias. Queen Calista seemed like the type of woman who bet on those she deemed powerful, those who were going to win the war, and clearly she didn't believe that was some lowly assassin and death incarnate. She missed her friends and prayed that they fared better with winning the other kingdoms to their side.

A grunt from her left spurred her out of her trance, and she cocked her head to the side, enjoying the view before her. Callian was shirtless, his muscled chest on display, and she willed herself not to lean over and lick it. His face was serene as she watched him sleep. His right arm was thrown over half his face, and his hair was disheveled from her hands the night before, when she gripped it tightly while he was in between her legs. Her legs clenched at the memory, and she felt the heat pooling there, the cool breeze of the sheets caressing her clit in a kiss that made her shudder.

She gazed back up at his sleeping face, to find him awake and smirking.

"Good morning, *alora.*"

She rolled over to face him, and he scooped her up into his arms, resting her body on top of his. Her hair cascaded around them, and she leaned in slightly to kiss his lips.

"Gods, you taste delicious. I can't get enough of you," he said, bringing her back down to greet his lips. Their tongues explored, sucking and biting until a sharp rap on their door stirred them from their ecstasy.

"I'm going to kill whoever is behind that door," he sighed disgruntledly. She laughed, throwing on her black lace slip. Callian begrudgingly left the bed, throwing on slacks before she followed him to the door. Callian whipped the door open aggressively, ready to lay into the innkeeper, but he didn't expect to see a distressed Soraya on the other side.

"Raya, what are you doing here?" he asked her, moving aside so she could come in.

Soraya came in still dressed in her night attire, her chignon halfway to falling out and day-old makeup streaks running down her golden skin.

"It's … it's … I …" she stammered.

"Take a deep breath, Raya. Tell me what happened," Callian said soothingly, dropping into a crouch before her. He rested his hand on her knee as she took in a few deep breaths trying to calm down.

"It's Saler, Cal … a triton reported to my mother that one of King Elias's warships was encroaching on our island. Alistair said that he was able to sneak close to the ship, when he caught wind of a conversation between members of the crew. They were told there was a sighting of Kieryn there yesterday …" her voice faded off before she caught her breath again. "Cal, they were moving cannons into position and their target was Saler. My mother refuses to take action to protect them."

Soraya brought her face to her knees and started to whimper. Callian had gone deathly still, but Kieryn had tuned out after King Elias. Her feet moved of their own accord, and by the time she was done dressing in her leathers and tying her hair back, she caught the tail end of Soraya's devastating news.

"I'm going to Saler," she stated.

Callian whipped his head around so fast that the angle seemed almost unnatural.

"The fuck you are," he seethed. "You won't make it in time, and I can't lose you," he commanded in a cold tone, a voice she was sure would stop people in their tracks. But she wasn't afraid of death, of him.

"They have no magic, Callian. They are helpless and I have to try, I have to do something." Her eyes pleaded with him to understand.

"Kieryn, even if you got there in time, what can you do? It's an entire army. I won't let you …"

There it was.

Let.

"You don't get to decide what I do or don't do. I can warn them, I can help get them to safety. But I won't stand by and let him obliterate an innocent village while the queen does nothing to defend them. They don't deserve that."

She pushed past him, grabbing her daggers and sheathing

them along her thighs and chest. She strapped *Makaria* across her back and swung open the door.

Callian reached out to her once more, grabbing her wrist tightly, but not enough to bruise.

"*Alora*, don't … please," the *Angel of Darkness* begged her.

Kieryn lashed out with her shadows, pinning him to the wall of their room.

"Do not try to stop me. I'm deeply sorry for this," she mumbled as she stepped over the threshold and ran for one of the horses in the stable.

The shock that fell upon Callian's face threw her off balance. To be honest, she was shocked, too. She had never used her shadows like that, and she hadn't even given it a moment's thought. It was like they acted independently from her. A part of her felt drained by the use of them, as if the shadows had taken a piece of her soul with it.

As she ran towards the fields, she realized there was no way Callian's stallion would allow her close enough to him. She skirted around the townspeople milling about town, not a care in the world that the other half of their island was about to be wiped out. She hopped the fence, making a dash for one of the horses grazing in the fields. She didn't bother with a saddle, she just took a running jump and threw herself on the brown mare. She got her bearing, swung her leg over, and grasped the midnight black mane before her. She kicked her heels into the mare's sides, heading in the direction of Saler.

She hoped her memory would help guide her there as she raced through the jungle, pushing the mare to her absolute limit. She could hear the rush of the wind slapping around her, her golden hair flying behind. She heard the pounding of hooves behind her, and knew without glancing back that Callian was racing after her. Whether to stop her, or aid her, she wasn't sure, but she'd ram her own sword through him before letting him stop her.

She pushed onward, leaning as far forward as she could, maneuvering the agile mare around tree roots and low hung branches. A rapid succession of booms resonated from ahead, the ground shaking beneath her. The horse struggled to stay balanced, and she smelled the ash before she felt the scorching heat.

"NO!" she screamed.

She made it through the clearing, and what she saw before her was catastrophic.

In front of her was nothing but smoke and flames. She jumped off the mare and raced toward what was left of the village. The entire village has been razed to the ground by King Elias's fire bombs. They had no warning, no time to attempt to escape. There would be no survivors.

She could have saved them, instead she signed their deaths away. It was her fault they were killed, and now she would bear that burden on her shoulders. The continent may think her a Kingslayer after the masquerade ball, but now she'd prove them right. She was coming for King Elias' blood, and she would make sure he died painfully and slowly.

She ran through the flames, not giving herself time to think.

Callian crested the hill, screaming out of her name.

"KIERYN!" Callian screamed, his voice hoarse from the smoke filling his lungs. He looked for any sign of her as he tried to fight his way through, but the flames burned so high, they cut off any access he had to the village.

Did she make it to the village just as the king unleashed his fire bombs?

No, he refused to believe that. He refused to believe he had lost her right when he finally had her. The *Reaper of Souls* sank to his knees, a look of absolute devastation and hopelessness on his face.

"KIERYN! ANSWER ME!" The words were a hollow scream leaving his throat.

"Please," he whispered into the empty void.

He stared in a daze at the burning flames, waiting …

Finally, the flames danced and began to take shape. Suddenly, Kieryn walked through the flames. No, that wasn't right, he thought. Not through, the flames had parted around her, her shadows whipping out like weapons cutting through the path, her hair floating upwards as if she was underwater, and *Gods,* her eyes, they were glowing black. Soot clung to her skin, and she was covered head to toe in ash.

He ran to her, grasping her face in his hands, checking her for injuries. Her shadows released her from whatever state she was in and she reared back from his touch.

"Don't. Touch. Me!" she yelled.

Her eyes went dark and cold, as she stared into the flames. She was numb to the carnage around her, the sights that she had seen beyond the flames. She would become Death herself and inflict pain on King Elias and anyone that defended him.

"*Alora* …" he started to say.

"No, don't. Do not use that name with me right now. I could've saved them," she cried out. "I could've made it on time, to at least warn them to run. They never saw it coming. They were incinerated on impact. Some who were further away from the sea died from severe burns, and the ones who were alive and were suffering," she wheezed, her throat constricted, choking on her next words, "begged me to kill them to put them out of their misery."

At that last part, Callian peered down at Kieryn's hands, the dagger in it dripping blood.

He reached out to console her, but she dodged his touch.

"Don't, I … I can't be near you right now. Don't follow me. If you do, I won't hesitate to drive this dagger through your heart."

Her hands shook at her admission, but the fire in her eyes

blazed, the golden specks glowing like a phoenix rising from the ashes.

And with those parting words, Callian watched her walk over to the mare, and gallop back through the forest.

He stared after her, the flames behind him burning stronger and brighter. Before he had left the inn to chase after Kieryn, he had gotten through to Soraya to gather any siren and triton she could and bring them to Saler. That fire would ravage the forest between Saler and the rest of the island, and if the queen cared about anything at all, it was protecting her luscious land and not its people. The tritons and sirens would use their water magic to put out the blaze.

He tried to see past the flames, a village filled with innocents he had come to know over time, that had accepted him willingly and wholeheartedly, gone in a blink of an eye. His steps wavered at the massacre before him. His father did this. Elysium called him evil, and he may be tainted with blood, but evil resided in his father and Queen Calista. They were the wolves in sheep's clothing.

He looked back towards the forest, every bone in his body wanting to go over after Kieryn, but the bloody thorns on his wrist said otherwise. At that moment, he knew he had to reach out to the contact Soraya had mentioned to him at the club that night. He had no other option. It was time he made a decision.

"FUCK!" He let out a blood-curdling scream, throwing his fist into the tree, making bark fly everywhere. He hopped onto his stallion's back and made his way back to town, hoping that Kieryn would come back to him.

THIRTY-SEVEN

KIERYN GALLOPED THROUGH THE TREES, the mare's hooves thundering against the

jungle floor, the sound reverberating in her ears, and the telltale sound of her racing heart thumping along with it. A kaleidoscope of greens and browns blurred past as she soared through the dense vegetation. If she could outrun her thoughts and the wreckage she witnessed today, she would.

Flashbacks assaulted her mind with the wooden stalls that caught ablaze and spread like wildfire, demolishing everything. The putrid smell of the burning bodies was nauseating and she could still taste that thickness on her tongue. She hadn't felt the flames licking at her skin, or the ash and smoke filling her lungs at the time, all she knew was death and agony. She had a feeling her shadows had something to do with how she managed to not succumb to the flames.

She had found the woman that danced with her that night, the one that sold her the scarves, laying haphazardly on the dirt ground, covered in burns from head to toe. She had tried to shield her young daughter, but she too had been a victim of the king's revenge. The woman turned to face Kieryn, pain in her wide, bloodshot eyes. It had taken every ounce of her energy to mutter the words to Kieryn.

"End it, my child," her throat raspy, her lips non-existent. Her skin was bone and melted flesh, and Kieryn swallowed her bile as she knelt down next to the mother.

"May the blessed gods be the light to guide you home," she said, her voice barely above a whisper.

Kieryn shook her head trying to clear the memory that would haunt her for the rest of her days.

Why do I get to live while all of those innocent people died?

They had died because of her. Just like her parents.

Kieryn came to a stop at the clearing that Callian had shown her the other day, the waterfall a steady drum in the night. The night sky looked like it was going to buckle and fall from the skies. Pregnant black, malicious clouds rolled in above her, and bright white streaks of lightning danced across the skies, the explosion after like a sonic boom. She shrank in on herself at the sound of the thunder, reminded of the cannons that fired on the village. Rain poured from the heavens in an onslaught, but Kieryn didn't mind. It seemed that even the gods were crying over the slaughter left behind.

Kieryn hopped off the mare and headed towards the tidal pool. She sank to her knees in the wet sand, thrusting her hands and dagger into the water, trying to clear the images and the blood from her skin. She frantically scrubbed at herself until she was raw, her shallow breathing labored as tears slipped from her eyes.

A strong gust of wind whipped her hair, the golden strands falling around her as the storm raged on. She peered down at her shaking hands, when out of the corner of her eye, she saw the water ripple. She leaned in closer, trying to get a better look, when she saw a faint light coming from the depths of the aquamarine water. Kieryn skimmed the top of the water with her hand, just as a force from below pulled her under. The vise on her wrist was ghost-like, no creature was before her, but something had her in its grip and she was falling, falling, falling …

When she landed, she wasn't underwater, nor was she in Keres. She was everywhere and nowhere. She couldn't decipher where she was, just a vast land lay before her. She turned in circles, but found no one, not even the ghost of the hand that forced her down. Her eyes darted around the area wildly, searching for any kind of life.

"*Makaria*, sweet child, welcome to *the Veil*," a beautiful, silvery voice graced her ears. Kieryn turned toward the voice, and saw three women before her.

The woman who had spoken to her had long, wavy hair the color of espresso beans that were tied loosely in braids that hung over her chest. Horns grew from the crown of her head, and her face was sharp angles with rosy cheeks and full lips. In her hands, she held what looked like a ball of twine. The midnight-blue gown she wore shimmered with every step she took, like waves kissing the shore.

"My … my name is Kieryn," she stuttered, struggling to find her voice.

"If that's the name you choose. I am Klatho," the sweet, melodic voice sung out to her.

"These are my sisters, Lachesys …" Her petite hand waved over to a slim white-haired woman. She wore a dress with a deep plunging front that was the color of stardust, her ice blue eyes drinking her fill of Kieryn, a spindle spinning between her tiny, delicate fingers. "And this," Klatho continued, "is my sister Atra." She was referring to the scarlet-headed woman on her left hand side.

She had stunning, yet calculating, mossy green eyes that Kieryn got a feeling of unease from, as if they could see into her soul. Atra balanced shears between her fingers as she gazed, transfixed, at Kieryn. Atro wore a slim-fitting gold strapless top that exposed her midriff, and a skirt with slits that rose high to her hips on both sides, a tiny strip of cloth lying lazily between her legs.

"We are *The Fates*, and you may ask us one question each and we will answer truthfully. Be careful with your questions, young one," Klatho said with a controlled smile. "You won't ever get the chance to ask again."

Kieryn's mouth dropped open at the words she heard. She was face-to-face with *The Fates*, the three goddesses of destiny. She had always thought they were a myth, a story people told for amusement and wonder, but this was real. They were tall and elegant, and their presence exuded power. She didn't know if she should bow or get on her knees before them. Probably both if she was honest.

From the stories she had heard, they were the weavers of souls, as they held a person's life in their very hands. One represented the past, *Klatho*, the present, *Lachyses*, and the future, *Atra*.

Her body stilled at the task that they had bestowed on her. She had three questions she could ask, and they'd answer truthfully. The pressure built in her chest at the realization of her situation. She didn't know where to begin. Her mind raced at who she should ask her first question to, and the three women before her waited patiently, discreetly eyeing her.

"Who killed my parents?" Her first question was directed at Klatho.

Her striking gray eyes narrowed slightly, darting between her two sisters as if she was consulting with them on how to proceed answering. The two sisters gave nothing away, but Klatho smiled sadly with acceptance.

"The evil that killed your parents is the same evil you battle today. Look to the beginning, try to remember that night, scars tell stories," she said vaguely.

"I remember everything about that night, every detail, it's

hard to forget the worst night of your life," she spoke with conviction and grief in her tone.

Klatho nodded, but did not speak again. She had said her piece.

Kieryn looked over to Lachyses, her eyes falling to the spindle, the spinning motion distracting her.

Finally, she had her question and it slipped from her lips before she could think twice.

"My shadows—where do they come from?"

She had wondered about this, and she had hoped Callian was wrong about Shade being the only one who had the same power, but she didn't dare voice that out loud. She was afraid to admit the truth—that she already knew. And she was terrified of that.

Lachyses spun the spindle faster between her fingers, her eyes closing as she did. When she opened them again, her eyes glowed a rich, red.

"Are you sure you want to ask that question, a question you know the answer to?" she prodded.

Kieryn took a deep breath in, knowing that as soon as the words left her mouth, she couldn't go back after that. The answer would be out there, confirmed. She didn't want to hear it, but she knew she had to hear it for herself. She nodded her head.

Lachyses shook her head in defeat, a somber look crossing over her face.

"Your shadows come from the Shadow Realm. the power to wield shadows, make them bend to your will is a *very* rare power indeed. Not many have the ability to do so, and it's one you should try to conquer before it conquers you."

Kieryn couldn't help herself.

"Who did my shadows come from?" she demanded.

Lacyhses only shook her head, but it was Klatho that answered.

"She cannot answer that."

"Can't or won't?" Kieryn pressed on.

"Both."

Kieryn's eyes roamed over to Atro, who's piercing eyes never strayed. Kieryn studied her back just as openly as she did. She radiated power, just like her other sisters, but the three of them together were a deadly combination. While she felt safe standing next to Callian, she felt frightened and on edge before them.

"How will this war play out with King Elias? Is there any hope at all?" she couldn't help but sneak in the second question, more so to herself.

Atra's voice was resonant, yet hypnotic when she spoke. A chill ran down Kieryn's spine at her words.

"You ask the wrong questions, child. You say you are at war with the king, but you will soon discover you are at war with something much worse than him. The future for you is still …" She hesitated, "Unclear. I know how long each mortal's lifespan is, but you … I can't see your future. It is still being written, I'd assume."

Her steps faltered at *The Fate's* confession.

The revelation of her past and future weighed heavily on Kieryn, as she soaked in what she had learned. *The Fates* couldn't lie, they were bound in truth, but their answers were riddles that left a lot to be discovered and interpreted.

Klatho didn't give her much time to process their truth, before she spoke once more. As she spoke, the three *Fates* began to shimmer, becoming translucent, as if this was all a vision and Kieryn was fading away.

"You are strong and more powerful than you think, Kieryn. There will come a time when you will know what you have to do, do not be afraid when that time comes. I have a feeling we'll meet again."

As the last word fell from Klatho's thin lips, they disappeared completely, as if they were never there, and a force pulled her up, up, up ....

Kieryn reared back from the tidal pool, as if she had been holding her breath. She shook her head, still in a daze and trying to come to terms with whether or not that actually had happened or if she was truly losing her mind. Despite it all, she was left with more questions than answers.

PART THREE

THIRTY-EIGHT

RYLAN'S ivory skin stood out like a beacon as she tried to wedge herself behind a statue and a wall, eavesdropping on the conversation between her older sister, Soraya, and the queen. She was a petite thing, so her small, lithe frame was able to hide behind the giant stone statue. She was used to not being seen. She could be present in the room with her family now, and her mother wouldn't even notice her. She stood in Soraya's shadow, even though she was only three years younger, so more often than not she was overlooked in everything—her beauty, her status, her power. This was when Rylan enjoyed not being seen, because she could eavesdrop on conversations she normally wouldn't have been privy to.

She heard the yelling echoing down the hall, and she leaned forward so her face peered out from the corner of the wall. She had a small face, with freckles dusting her nose and cheeks, and a long nose. Her features came from her mother's side, while Soraya was blessed with the more golden skin of their father.

"How dare you!" Soraya screamed at their mother.

"How dare you speak to your queen like that, let alone your mother!"

"To be honest, I don't see either in front of me. A mother would have noticed that her daughter paid weekly visits to that village you just incinerated. I could've been there at the time of the attack—did you ever think of that?!"

Rylan could hear the shaky whimpering in her sister's voice, so she knew she was on the verge of crying.

"And a queen would have defended her people, regardless of their power or status!" she spat, before continuing. "And you did neither. You watched as your own people burned up in flames, and for what, a sighting of Kieryn?" she scoffed at her mother then.

"And how did they know she was here, *mother*?" Soraya said the last word with revulsion in her tone.

"I sent word to King Elias about Kieryn. She is an infectious thing that needed to be handled. I wasn't aware of his plans until the warship came into our harbor, but then he was taking care of two problems for me, so I didn't stop him," the queen said matter-of-factly, picking at her nails.

Soraya stood there, shocked at her mother's admission. A cold nausea ran through her entire body at the despicable words that fell from her mother's lips. The person who stood before Soraya was not her mother, not anymore. She hadn't been a mother in years to either her or Rylan. She was selfish, cruel and manipulative, and this was the thing that would break them apart for good. Her relationship with her mother was strained beyond repair, but this - this was unforgivable. She didn't care about the innocent lives she had slaughtered, nor the fact that her *own* daughter could've been one of those victims.

"You could've aided Kieryn. King Elias annihilated an entire village of ours off the face of the map. What is to stop him from turning his back on us if he wins the war? He's not a man of negotiation, and he won't hesitate to betray his allies. He turned his back on his own flesh and blood and sold him."

The sound that came out of Queen Calista was foreign to Soraya's ears. The queen bent at the waist with a loud, unrestrained laugh.

"And who is going to command the navy fleet? *You?*" her mother asked, laughing maniacally. "Keres' *Party Princess* is going to lead them into war. You will easily be leading them to their own slaughter, silly girl. No one will take you seriously."

Rylan stepped out from the shadows and walked briskly to stand next to her sister.

"I will," she said confidently. "I have been shadowing the trainers—I know how to navigate by the stars and read maps. I can lead the fleet. Father has been training me for this my entire life."

The queen's horrified expression said it all. Her head fell back, and she chuckled at the preposterous idea.

"That's rich, the party princess and the ghost of a child trying to lead an army. You are no children of mine. You are as weak-minded as your father. He coddled you girls, but I am the one that must deal with your insolence. You are nothing but a disgrace to this family. This is not our war!"

With a deadly calm in her voice, Soraya made her choice.

"And you are not my mother, and you are *certainly* no queen of mine. You will pay for what you have done. Rylan and I deserved better than you as our mother, because you are nothing but a monster. Enjoy your throne, alone."

She felt the bite of her mother's hand on her cheek, the sound of flesh on flesh resonating throughout the Throne Room. Soraya's head whipped to the right, and she felt the hot pain searing her skin as she brought her hand to her left cheek.

The startled gasp of her younger sister pulled her back inside her body.

Mother and daughter faced off and Soraya felt the slide of her younger sister's hand squeeze hers.

With no words left to say to her mother, Soraya brought Rylan into her side and led her from the Throne Room, forcing herself to remain facing forward and to not give her mother the satisfaction of a second glance.

"What are we going to do?" Rylan asked her once they were out of earshot of their mother.

Soraya looked down at her sister, the scent of her lavender perfume blanketing the space between them. She inhaled the floral scent, trying to remain calm and collected.

"I'm going to do what I do best—defy the queen's orders." She smiled down at her sister then. "Are you in?"

"You're going to do what?" an appalled Callian asked.

"I like the idea," Kieryn said happily.

"We cannot drug the queen and forge papers that will lead a Kingdom into a war—it's treason," Callian explained.

"It'll work, Cal," Soraya declared.

"My partying ways will be a benefit for once as I can get the toxin that will put her to sleep until I decide to give her the antidote. We will lock her in her room, I'll be made interim queen, and Rylan will command the fleet. They know her and respect her. It's simple."

"It's not, though," Callian said, laying his strong hand delicately on her arm. "What happens when the queen eventually wakes?"

"I will deal with it, but that is a problem for then, not now."

She sensed something off between Callian and Kieryn as soon as she entered the tavern they were meeting at. Callian looked like someone had kicked his puppy, and Kieryn looked every bit the *Deathbringer* she was known to be in Elysium.

She was guarded, her muscles pulled tight, and she kept glancing at the door as if she wanted to run. While Soraya had broken down and given into her feelings, Kieryn had run into the fight, with no regard for her own life, to save people she had only met once. Soraya had known them, had known their families and their names and their problems, and she couldn't even show up when it mattered the most. She was a mess that morning and the pounding headache from the party she was at the night before didn't help. Sometimes she wondered if her mother was right. She was just the "party princess" and maybe that's all she ever would be, all people would associate her with. But there was hope for Rylan, that she was certain of.

"Are you okay, Kieryn?"

Kieryn's head snapped up, and she looked at her with a haunted look in her eyes.

"Yeah, I'm fine," she lied.

"I think it's a great plan," she added, deflecting the talk about her. "You had me on board when you said incapacitating the queen. We have to get word to my friends."

Rylan stepped forward.

"I can bring your friends the message. Where are they?"

Kieryn explained to her where they'd be and where she could find them. Rylan nodded and headed off back to the castle to wait for the moment when Soraya's plan would take place.

"This will work," she said to Callian. "It has to." She said the second part more to convince herself than him.

It had to work, otherwise she was committing treason.

THIRTY-NINE

DAMIEN AND ASH stayed silent most of the trip back towards Riyadh. They had ultimately made the decision to not go back to the Keep until they knew if there was a traitor in their midst.

Was the King of Phantoms given bad intel, or was he aware that he was sending them into a trap?

Regardless, Ashlyn pushed the thought aside, and the two assassins stayed off the grid at a small inn just outside Dakar. Damien was not quick to forget about the last time he had stepped foot in this kingdom, and the repercussions Kieryn had suffered that night. The thought of her confused him. A part of him ached for her voice, her soothing touch in the night when he had broken down and unleashed his demons for her to bear.

Another side of him hated her for betraying him. She knew what Natalie had meant to him. Seeing her again had been like lightning through his chest—he felt alive in her presence. *You also felt that with Kieryn,* his subconscious argued with him. He wasn't ready to die, he knew that now. But standing in front of Natalie after all that time, feeling her touch, tasting her lips, he would've gone into the depths of the shadows and followed her willingly into the afterlife.

He felt guilty, a feeling he knew quite well over the years. After Natalie, it was a while before he was intimate with another, but with every lover he had it was just physical. He never developed feelings for anyone. Until Kieryn. And if he felt guilt at just being physical with another after Natalie, his conflicting feelings for Kieryn gutted him. He had become her friend almost instantaneously, and for a while it was just that— friendship. But, the more he got to know her over the years, her unparalleled beauty, her daring attitude, it all reminded him of Natalie. Deep down, maybe he was trying to fill the void Natalie had left him with. There would be no one after Natalie. Once a wolf found its mate, there was no one else. But Kieryn, she made him forget, if only briefly.

But when Natalie had kissed him, he felt remorseful. He couldn't remember what she had tasted like, he had forgotten, and while he kissed Natalie, all he could think about in the back of his mind was Kieryn, and how she tasted like sunshine and whiskey. When he felt the pull and saw Kieryn's tear-stained face and wisps of shadows retreating into her like branches of a tree, he blamed her for his guilt, for his confused thoughts on what he was experiencing.

And like always, he sabotaged his only source of happiness he had left and retaliated. He was ruthless toward her, and yet he knew she would forgive him, because that was who she was. He had pushed the one woman who he had deemed worthy of his heart, what was left of it anyway, away, and right into that dark and mysterious stranger's arms. While she may forgive him, he knew their relationship was altered forever because of the truth they hid from each other. But maybe that was what was best for both of them. He knew deep in his heart, he could never love Kieryn as he had Natalie, and that wasn't fair. So, just like with everything else, he swallowed his misery and pain.

"Are you ready for this?" Ashlyn asked from the bed where she sat with her hands in her lap. She was dressed in their assassin leathers, her weapons hidden away, ready for whatever may come. She looked over at him, a look of worry and hesitation in her eyes.

"I have no other option, so am I ready, no I am not. But will I do it? Yes," he said matter-of-factly.

She stood up and grabbed his hands, holding them in hers.

"Whatever happens, I have your back."

He nodded solemnly, not risking words out of fear he might lose it in front of her. She didn't know his torment, but he had a feeling she was going to find out soon enough. He only hoped she liked a good ghost story.

Damien and Ash arrived at Exile, painful memories slamming into Damien at the sight of the pool table immediately. He reminisced about when he showed Kieryn how to play pool, the chalk staining her chin. He smiled fondly at the thought of her smile and laugh before the havoc broke loose.

How was that just over a week ago?

They made their way over to the bar before pulling up barstools. Damien didn't sit, but rather hovered near Ash, a shield of what was to happen. They ordered their drinks and waited, knowing word would get to Emmett. The barkeep gave him a side eye as if to say, "I remember you."

They didn't have to wait long before Damien knew Emmett and his pack had arrived. The bar went quiet, no one daring to make a sound. Damien slammed back the rest of his drink and turned to face Emmett head-on.

Emmett stalked over to him, death settling in his eyes as he focused on him. Emmett fisted Damien's shirt and yanked him onto the bar, glasses scattering and shattering to the floor.

"I thought I warned you that if you stepped foot back into Riyadh, I'd kill you and whoever got in my way," he seethed, his eyes roaming over to Ash, where she stood defensively.

"I see you didn't bring that hot blonde of yours, That's a shame. I was hoping to show her a good time as promised." He grimaced.

Damien snarled at his comment.

Emmett sneered at Damien before throwing him across the room. He crashed into a wood table, breaking it in half. The patrons sitting there scattering in either direction. Damien stood, shaking off the broken glass.

"I am not here to fight you, Emmett. I heard what you said the last time, but things have changed and I…" he looked over at Ashlyn, her silent nod encouraging him to go on. "I need your help," he finished, chest heaving, his pride sinking into the pits of his stomach.

The pack surrounding Emmett howled and doubled over laughing.

Emmett's smile was one of hostility and arrogance.

"Is the great Damien begging for my help?" he mocked, the rest of his pack chuckling. Damien gritted his teeth in response and nodded.

"I don't think I heard you, Damien."

"Yes, I am begging for your help," he muttered, breathing out through his teeth. Emmett shook his head, relishing in Damien's begging.

"Not good enough," he announced loudly to the room. "I want you on your knees."

Damien stood tall and didn't move, refusing to play into Emmett's game. When he didn't fall to his knees, two of Emmett's men yanked him by his arms and forced him to kneel, digging their feet into the backs of his knees, so he stayed there. He saw out of the corner of his eye Ashlyn move towards him, before one of Emmett's guys pinned her body to his, preventing her from reaching him. He shook his head at her.

"That's better." Emmett grinned. "Now, how badly do you want my help?"

Emmett's men dug their heels into Damien until he growled up at them, shards of glass prodding into his skin.

"You want to hear me beg, Emmett? Fine. Well, here I am begging on my knees for your help. Is that what you want? We used to be brothers, man…" he trailed off, his head hanging low.

Emmett rushed him, forcing his chin up, demanding Damien look at him.

"You don't get to call me a brother anymore. You gave up on me, on the pack, to get your revenge. You don't think I miss her, too? She was my fucking little sister! Don't forget I was there too that night when we found…" he choked, his throat bobbing and swallowing before continuing, "When we found Natalie. I saw what they did to her, too. I wanted their death by my hands, too. I wanted revenge. You took it too far. Your plan was what got her killed in the first place…"

"You don't think I fucking know that!" Damien spat. "I have had to live with that regret every day of my life. I had to bear that burden of not only losing my mate but the actions I carried out that night, that I made you and the pack carry out. I'm no better than he was. And I know Natalie would be ashamed of the man that I have become in her absence," Damien snapped back at him, tears coating his eyes.

He continued, letting the tears finally run down his face.

"You want me to beg on my knees? Well, here I am. You want me to admit that it's my fault Natalie is dead? I won't argue with you on that. If it weren't for me, she may still be alive. You want me to say that it is my fault I annihilated an entire pack? I am guilty as can be and no god will forgive me for that. I know there is no afterlife for me in *the Veil.* No one hates me more than I do myself, trust me."

Emmett turned away from him, his body going rigid and his fists opening and closing.

"If that's true, prove it. Turn," he demanded.

The silence in the bar was deafening.

Damien looked up at Emmett, a subtle shake of his head. He knew he would ask this, and he had prepared for it, but when it came down to it, he just couldn't. He didn't think he could survive that pain.

Emmett scoffed down at him.

"Just what I thought. You're a coward. You haven't turned since the night she died, have you? You don't want to feel that invisible string go taut and snap. You refuse to feel the loss of her completely, because you know when you do, it's final. You think the pain you feel now hurts? Try feeling it tenfold for a decade. You weren't meant to lead this pack, never could."

He started to walk towards the exit, his pack following behind after shoving Damien to the ground.

Emmett glanced back once at Damien. "Only when you turn, will I consider helping you."

Ash ran over to him after Emmett and his pack left the bar and helped him to his feet.

"Damien, I say this as your friend who cares about you. I may not know your story, but you need to swallow your pride and do as he asks. Everyone suffers from loss, trust me I know," she said, her eyes glistening and shying away from him, before collecting herself once more. "We can't change the past. I know suffering and the grief that accompanies it, but if you can't take this last step toward healing and redemption, more innocent lives will be taken. Do something that will make Natalie proud of you."

Damien glanced up at her, soaking up her words. He sighed in defeat, braced himself on his knees, and rose from the sticky floor to follow Emmett.

Damien swung open the door, charging after Emmett, the wooden door slamming into the wall with his force. Damien could feel his heart pumping, his anxiety rising to the surface. His hands shook and his skin felt clammy. He could taste the tang of his blood on the tip of his tongue.

Emmett turned to face Damien, and the rest of the pack, on edge, lowered themselves to defensive poses, ready to protect their Alpha. Damien stared directly into Emmett's eyes before forcing himself to face his demons, and with an agonizing yell that turned into a somber howl, he shifted into his wolf form after ten years.

FORTY

DAMIEN'S back arched with the transformation, his bones breaking and bending to mold into his wolf form. The transition was usually painless, if you turned often, but after ten years, he felt every snap of his bones, every pull and twist as they reformed.

Don't you dare show them any weakness, came a whisper of a voice in his head.

The sun reached out its rays to bathe him in light—the voice of Kieryn. He swallowed his pain down, and he pawed at the ground. He stared down at where his hands once were, that now had been replaced with two furry paws with five claws protruding from his skin instead of fingernails.

He lifted his head, and what Ashlyn saw before her was a magnificent, beautiful creature. His fur coat was a grayish-white, with specks of gray on his head and white cascading down his legs and chest. He stood taller than her, and she took a step back, trying to take in the scene before her. Ivory teeth appeared between his jaws, and saliva clung to his lips. He pawed at the ground, his hackles raised, waiting.

Damien let out a howl as he gave in to his emotions, and

one by one, they slammed into him. *Natalie's naked body torn to pieces.* His legs started to tremble underneath him as he swayed in place. *Her blood, written on the walls.* His body convulsed and his front legs collapsed from under him, bringing Damien to the ground. He started to whimper at the onslaught of his memories from that night. He lived every last detail of that night. Ashlyn moved to console him, but Emmett intervened.

"Don't," he warned her, blocking her path to him with his arm, "he needs this."

Damien writhed in pain on the forest floor as images of his life swam before his eyes, each image of Natalie burning into his brain.

The memory of them meeting out at the lake, their ceremony and how she had made him wait until after the wedding to make love to her for the first time under the moon, at the place that they had met. The moments of her cooking in their kitchen, to their fights in between about their barrier protection and the pack, and the one he tried to forget the most because it scared him too much to talk about. Starting a family. She had wanted to start a family so badly, and he kept pushing it aside. With them on the brink of war, it wasn't the greatest time for that. He had to protect them all first. But life was cruel, and the day she died was the day he found out she was pregnant with his child. Only a few weeks along, but when he discovered her lifeless body and what they had done to her and carved into her body for, he went numb. He blacked out and went *feral.*

It was that action alone that brought down the King of Wolves, as he made that decision to end an entire wolf line, and he felt every burn and sting of that memory. He felt every death, whether it was by his hands or his pack's, but each death hit him like a tsunami. He cowered into himself, bracing himself for the impact of their agonizing and brutal deaths. He dug his claws into the earth, trying to ground himself and to not get swept away in the graveyard of his memories. He breathed in through his nostrils, tasting the scents around him. He could sense Ashlyn, off to the side, her cool, sweet scent of jasmine filling his head with warmth, and he clung onto her familiarity as his soul ripped into two in front of everyone.

Ashlyn watched as Damien faced his demons, tears spilling down her cheeks at seeing him in torment. She sank to her knees, wanting to reach out to him, to hold him and let him know he wasn't alone. He never was.

After Damien crouched for what felt like eternity, he lifted his head, unashamed of the tears forming in his eyes, and looked back at Emmett and his old pack before he howled in surrender, the last tether of Natalie fading away into the night. Emmett and the rest of the wolves shifted and joined in. The chorus of howls did not stem from a place of malice or mockery, but solidarity. A welcoming home of their lost brethren.

Ashlyn watched it unfold before her eyes, and wished more than anything that Kieryn could have been here to witness Damien in this moment, but she knew she would be so proud. So she brought her arms up and hugged herself, overwhelmed with emotions at the scene before her.

The howls faded out, and the pack took off running through the woods, leaving just Ashlyn, Damien, and Emmett alone in the clearing. Emmett shifted back from his all black wolf form and walked over to Damien, who had yet to shift back. The two were at eye-level, and the look exchanged between them was familiar. It was the look she had shared numerous times with Kieryn, one stemming from a bond that was unbreakable. She hoped for Damien's sake, this was the beginning of making amends with his old pack.

"Meet me back here tomorrow, same time, and you can fill me in. You better convince me, Damien," he said, and this time there was no anger in his voice, just the truth.

Damien nodded and bent his head low, as if he was bowing

to him. Emmett stood taller and turned away, but before he shifted into his wolf form to follow his pack, he looked over at Damien.

"Natalie would be proud. She's always been with you; don't lose that through all this," he muttered to him, and with a running leap, he transformed back into a black wolf and raced through the opening in the trees.

After Emmett had left, Damien sank to the ground once more, wallowing in his pain. He had forgotten Ash was there until he felt her sit next to him, placing his head in her lap. She stroked behind his ear in a slow, calming rhythm. She didn't speak, but her presence alone was comforting enough as he coped with feeling everything tenfold.

It wasn't just the attack of his memories from back then, but Kieryn getting injured during his last altercation with Emmett, and how he felt that night opening up to her. His feelings for her, as confusing as they were, only terrified him even more. The night of the ball, his actions and her heartbreak over his words caused his heart to crack. He didn't know how much more loss he could endure. He was beyond his limits.

They sat there in silence for a while, the rest of the world moving around them. Patrons still entered Exile, doing everything to avoid them out there in the clearing. Finally, Ash interrupted the tranquil moment.

"I lost the love of my life too," Ashlyn blurted out into the inky night. Damien sniffled, lifting his head, and stared up at her questioningly.

She didn't look at him, just kept nodding. She felt him move and shift beside her and took her hands in his.

"Her name was Ivy, and she was the most alluring woman I had ever met," Ash continued, getting lost in the ghost of her.

"She had silky, light hair that flowed down over her shoulders, and these cute freckles above her nose, and I knew the second I saw her, I needed to know everything about her. We trained together with the Alessians, and when they paired us up in the ring, it was hard not to feel a connection with each other.

"We snuck around for a bit, even though relationships were never frowned upon. We just wanted to soak each other up for a little while longer, before anyone knew. Ivy had dated girls in the past, but me … I struggled with my feelings my whole life. Boys never caught my eye as much as girls did, and for the longest time I thought there was something wrong with me." Her voice trailed off.

She cleared her throat before continuing, "It wasn't until I started training with the Alessians and I saw girls together like that that I realized it wasn't just me. I wasn't alone in this."

Damien squeezed her hand in understanding.

"I hate that you had to hide who you really were with us. Did you think we wouldn't accept you?" he said with concern in his voice.

She glanced up at him. "No, it was never that. I knew you guys would, but after what happened back then, it's hard for me to be myself out in public. I fear it'll happen again."

At this confession, she started to cry. Damien held her like she had for him.

"I am here, Ash. Whatever you need."

She let a few more tears fall before she took a deep breath. If Damien could face his demons and try to heal, then she could do the same for him.

"One night a few of us were finishing up part of training on the border of Eretum. We had all gone for drinks at a local pub, and most of everyone had left, but me and Ivy hung back so we could have some time together." She swallowed, and it felt like glass ripped through her throat.

"As we were leaving, we snuck a kiss over on a side street. We thought we were alone, too lost in the moment, caught up in each other, that we were startled once we heard the catcalling and whistles. Six men cornered us in the street, making snide remarks about wanting to watch, begging for us to kiss more. They were drunk and looked dangerous. We were still at the beginning of our training and we weren't prepared."

Damien tensed up, afraid of knowing where this story was going to lead. He held her hand tighter, his eyes glistening along with hers as she dredged up her trauma.

"We fought the best we could, but they caught us off guard. There were just too many of them. They forced themselves on us and then beat us within an inch of our lives and left us bruised and bleeding in the streets. When we didn't show back up at camp, the Alessians warriors we were with came looking for us and helped us back. Her words started to come out more vehemently as she continued. "They brutally raped and beat us, all because we wouldn't give them the time of day," she spat angrily.

Damien seethed through his teeth, as he tried to stomach the trauma that his friend had endured back then. At the cruelty of what those monsters had done.

"What happened after?"

"The rest of the Alessians wanted revenge, but Elijiah, Kieryn's dad, warned us against it. He was sympathetic, yes, but he didn't want any more of us getting involved and hurt. He said that they would get what was coming to them. But Ivy didn't take that decision lightly. She was livid, and with every right. As was I, but back then, all I felt was numb. They took something from me that night. They had taken a piece of me I could never get back. They altered me in a way that has forever changed how I view people and myself. Ivy was the opposite. She couldn't just sit on her hands. I begged her not to go, and she promised me." She went quiet for a bit before screaming into the void, "She promised me that she would stay!"

Ash looked out into the distance, counting the stars in the sky.

"She snuck away in the middle of the night. I woke up the next morning to an empty bed. When I told Elijiah, he sent a search party out for her. They came back hours later, and when I saw a limp body in Elijiah's arms, the sway of her golden hair now dull falling across his arms, I knew my life had ended. Without her, I ceased to exist. I screamed and cried, I ripped at my hair, praying that who he held was not Ivy, but I knew in my soul she was gone."

She took in deep gulps of the night air.

"We gave her a burial. We burned her body as an offering to the Gods that day. I was so distraught and broken, I couldn't even get out of bed to attend my own girlfriend's burial," she scoffed.

"Elijiah found me and told me that Ivy found the men responsible. She was able to kill two before they jumped on her and slit her throat. After that, I went through the motions of grief. Day in, day out, the same routine, and I hid from the world. I shut down completely. The one person who got me, understood and loved me, had been ripped away from me. I had to live through two traumatic events back-to-back, and some days I refused to continue. I just wanted to be with her," she whispered.

"Even though I tried to join Ivy in the afterlife, something always went wrong and I think it was her warning me that I was where I was supposed to be. That I had to live for the both of us, and so I did. I became an Alessian warrior, but it didn't feel right. It was our dream, and without her, I didn't know what to do anymore."

She finally looked into Damien's eyes and saw the sadness in his eyes for her.

"I became an assassin for Ryvers, and I never looked back. I tracked down the remaining four men who burned my world to the ground and I gave them a proper slow and painful death. I haven't been with anyone since Ivy. I don't know if I could ever get back there. I just … I don't know how to let anyone else in, let alone share with the world who I really am. It's better when I'm invisible."

Damien gripped her arms, a commanding tone in his voice.

"Ashlyn, don't you dare hide yourself from the world. This world is a better place with you in it. You are a fierce Alessian warrior, and the mysterious *Wraith*. People tremble at the sound of your name, and with good reason. But you are also Ash, my kind, loyal friend who has taken care of our group for as long as I can remember. You have a kind soul, and anyone would be honored to know you." He lifted her chin with his hand. "The real you. Don't dim your light because of those monsters. What they did to you and Ivy was inexcusable, and your revenge was just, but don't let them dictate how you live your life moving forward. You are giving them control. Take back your life, for you and for Ivy. She'd want to see you happy, not hiding."

Ash cried out, wrapping her arms around Damien's neck, and they sat there, embracing their ghosts. Damien picked Ash up off the forest ground and held her hand.

"Are you ready to head back?" he asked.

She nodded over at him, a wave of relief falling over her shoulders. Both she and Damien had taken a huge step in their healing process and she knew her friendship with Damien was stronger because of it. The thing about losing someone you love was the grief never left you alone. With every day came the overwhelming emotion of never being able to look to that person and share in the experience of a new milestone. Never being able to feel the warmth and light of their hug. Never being able to tell them you loved them, just one more time. She knew her words were only a bandage of comfort, that words alone would not heal a broken heart, just like his wouldn't for her. Time and healing could only patch up the cracks so much. But, in solidarity of their lost loved ones, she held onto his hand as they made their way back to the inn, the demons of their pasts still shackled to them, slowly trailing after.

FORTY-ONE

RYLAN WAITED in the shadows for Soraya's signal that everything was set to go. Sitting through dinner with their mother was brutal, and she could only imagine what her sister was feeling after their last altercation. Soraya sat there stoically, pushing her food around, eyes cutting to Rylan's every now and again.

Soraya had received the toxin from an old contact a few days ago, but it was Rylan who had snuck into the kitchens to mix it with her mother's wine right before the staff had brought it out. Halfway through dinner, their mother started to show signs of illness, and excused herself from the table.

Thank the gods, too, because she thought Soraya was going to explode or better yet, stab their mother with her fork. Their mother didn't waste time at dinner continuing to sling insults at them, so when her words started to slur and the fork fell from her grasp, it was a blessing in disguise.

Soraya had left not long after that to talk with her hand-maidens to make sure nothing looked suspicious. They would call the royal doctors, and Soraya wanted to be there for it. She had informed Rylan that the toxin was untraceable, and the toxin that was used not many people knew of, since it was used more in the Eretum area. Rylan knew the rumors of her sister that spread like wildfire through the streets of Capryna. They labeled her the party girl, and while she knew her sister was more eccentric and untamed, she was fiercely loyal, compassionate, and strong-willed. Soraya was never one to shy away from her feelings. She loved with her whole being, and if you were on the receiving end of it, you knew. To be loved by Soraya was life -altering, even if it was a death sentence.

Rylan admired her sister for living fiercely and without fear. She lived her life to its full extent, and she wondered if the curse was why Soraya refused to give her heart away. Rylan never knew love or lust. She was so young when her father died that the memories of her parents together were jagged fragments. While her sister was loud and confident, Rylan was quiet and private. Rylan was good at hiding in the shadows and staying hidden, but when it came to her father's fleet of tritons, she was a quick learner.

After her father's passing, his lifelong friend's son, Captain Devereux, took over leading their fleet, and he always allowed Rylan to accompany him to training whenever he caught her sneaking around. She learned a lot from him over the years. He was the one that showed her how to read the stars as a guide, how to steer a ship, the training drills he put his men through, and the intricacies of war and strategies. She looked up to him, and they shared a unique bond growing up without parental figures. While he was stern with his training, he was a good leader and a man of respect. She knew her father would have been proud of the both of them.

Rylan was so lost in her thoughts that she almost didn't hear Soraya stride up next to her where she stood on her balcony overlooking the sea. For a while, both Kincaid sisters stood idle, shoulder to shoulder, staring out at the waves barreling into the jagged rocks below before Soraya's melodic voice shattered the sense of calm Rylan desperately tried to cling to for a little longer.

"The doctor said she was poisoned, but he has no idea what she was poisoned with, so we are in the clear. I told them that the town of Saler was just decimated the other day and a triton had reported it to the queen that it was Elias's crew. They are planning on calling a meeting to report that mother being incapacitated is a full -on threat by Eretum, and they are waging war against them."

Rylan's knuckles went frigid and white, a complete contrast to the dark stone wall.

"Our plan worked, then? We're going to war?" she asked with a falter in her words.

Soraya nodded.

"It did. And yes, we are. As soon as they make the announcement, I am to be crowned the interim queen, and I will make it known this is an act of war not just against the queen, but against the people of Keres and to all of Elysium. I will be sending some warships up the coast towards Riyadh Kingdom, where you will be in charge of the fleet. Be ready for my command."

Rylan couldn't help the smile that graced her face. She had been waiting to prove herself for so long. To not sit idly in the shadows, but to finally stand in the sun, where she felt free, on the floorboards of their ships.

Her sister continued, "You will make a great warrior, little sister. Make me proud out there. I will follow you soon enough," she said, embracing her in a body-crushing hug. When she pulled away, Rylan could see the proud tears that clung to Soraya's bottom eyelids.

Soraya turned away before she could see the tears fall, but as soon as she crossed the threshold back into Rylan's bedroom, Rylan spoke from behind her.

"Keres Kingdom is lucky to have their rightful queen in

power. You will do great things, Soraya. Know that above all else, your heart is your biggest strength."

Soraya raised her head, blinking back the tears that wanted to spill over, and without facing her sister, for fear she would break down completely, she nodded and continued to walk forward, leaving her sister and their secrets behind on the balcony.

That night, Soraya was dressed in a sapphire blue gown that cascaded behind her like a wave. The sheer fabric of the gown reminded her of the deeper parts of the Kalani sea. The parts that were left to be discovered by those who dared to be brave enough and venture that far, that deep below the surface.

The color of the gown made her blood-red hair stand out vibrantly. They had piled her long locks on top of her head, the curls weaving themselves intricately around each other, so that it looked like a crown itself. She donned her normal crown —she wouldn't be crowned with the queen's until a formal coronation. But to the people of Keres, she looked the part.

The gown hugged her body like a second skin, the A-line, off-the-shoulder cut of the dress lifting her breasts higher. There was a slit that ran the length of her left thigh, and the back of the dress was practically non-existent, swooping to just above her lower back. The fabric was sheer and with each twirl of the dress. it glimmered under the lights.

Keres women were known to be bold in their dress attire, albeit some chose to wear as little as possible. Here in Keres, women were coveted, a treasure amongst the men. Their bodies were temples and the women loved showing off every asset.

Soraya did a final twirl in the gown and stepped up to the

full-body mirror, taking in her appearance. She looked like a queen on the outside, but deep down in her core, she felt like a fraud. She couldn't help but think that her people would think the same of her. She could hear her mother's insults in the back of her mind. *Party Princess*. How would her people react to her announcement about being the new queen? They'd probably laugh at her for playing dress up.

Her sapphire eyes stared back at her in the mirror, assessing her, mocking her. Her eyes glowed and appeared bright beneath the charcoal liner they rimmed her eyes with. She was a woman to be reckoned with, a force to not underestimate, and with one big breath, she exhaled and walked as a queen to her balcony doors to address her people.

Soraya took in the crowds below her. A sea full of her people stood restlessly, all their gazes directed at her, waiting with bated breath. She took a deep breath, and on the exhale she locked eyes with her sister in the crowd, her hair a beacon of hope for Soraya, one she latched onto tightly with both hands.

"People of Keres, I am here before you to regretfully inform you that Queen Calista has been poisoned and is undergoing treatment as we speak, with the hopes of making a full recovery."

She paused, taking in as many of the faces of her people before her, their reactions all the same. Shock, bewilderment, anger. They were confused; she knew they were. Some voices rose to her from below, statements of "This is an act of war!" and "Who poisoned the queen?"

"Yesterday morning, Eretum soldiers were spotted along our coastline by one of our *tritons* headed directly for the small coastal village of Saler." Soraya's voice stalled briefly thinking

about the heartbreak that ate away at her chest for all the innocent lives that were lost.

All the friends she had made.

"It pains me to say that there were no survivors. Eretum decimated the entire village, and if that wasn't enough, they sent an assassin to incapacitate the queen. They failed in killing the royal bloodline, but we will not take this lying down."

"This is an act of war on our queen, on our kingdom, and on you. We will not go quietly. We will fight back with every-thing we have. The last thing Eretum and King Elias will know before their deaths will be our names on their lips."

The crowd roared beneath her, ripples of their echoing cries bouncing off the castle walls.

"Long live the queen, long live the kingdom," Soraya cried out, her voice solid and regal.

"Long live the queen, long live the kingdom," her people responded back, chanting it over and over again.

She locked eyes with her sister in the crowd, Rylan's smile wide enough that she could see it from her balcony. She smiled back, before slowly stepping backwards into her room, where she felt the onslaught of the crushing weight of a queen's reign as she sank to the floor, the gown swallowing her whole.

FORTY-TWO

CALLIAN AND KIERYN walked in silence back to the inn after they had met with both Soraya and Rylan after Queen Soraya's announcement. Rylan was set to sail the following day, where she would eventually meet up with Damien and Ashlyn. From there, she would make sure word made it to Calydan Kingdom where Grayson was.

Kieryn was lost in her own thoughts, her mind still reeling from her conversation with the Fates. She was intrigued even more about her shadows, and she wondered how deep her power actually resonated.

The Fates' reply about the scars still baffled her, and as she was trying to put the pieces together, she felt a slight tug on her arm from Callian.

"Talk to me, *alora*. I can't bear the silence from you. It is deafening," he pleaded with her, his onyx eyes studying the golden hues speckled throughout her eyes for any answer she would give.

"What do you want me to say, Callian?"

She ripped her arm back, the slight twitch of Callian's eye

the only indicator that the loss of touch wounded him. She cringed on the inside, knowing she was hurting him, but she just couldn't stop. She felt this raging inferno inside burning her, wanting to be let off its leash. Something had changed inside her after yesterday. Her shadows were becoming more desperate to be free. They danced with the fire within, and she was losing control of all of it. She wanted to scream at the top of her lungs into the shadows of the night, wanting to find some type of release. Instead, she took it out on Callian. He didn't deserve her wrath, but he would take the brunt of it for her.

"The king annihilated an entire village, filled with innocent humans, who had nothing to do with this war. They died in my name, because … because they always do. People die because of me and I am so sick and tired of feeling helpless. I am the *Deathbringer*. People of Elysium hear that name and they cower at it. And yet, the title is fitting, isn't it," she rambled on, her laugh becoming hysterical. "Everywhere I go, death follows me like a shadow."

Callian wanted to reach out to her, help her, console her, gods, anything to take away this pain she harbored. But he stood there taking it, taking whatever she needed to say.

"You should've had my back. Together we maybe could have warned them, saved enough to…" She broke down then, her hand coming up to cover her mouth, as she held back the sobs. He reached out to her then, and although she struggled at his touch, he folded her into his arms, and she eventually gave in. She let go.

She let go of everything she was holding on to. All her doubts, all her fears, all the questions she had yet to find the answers to, of all the lives gone because of her, of the people that she irrevocably hurt because of who she was. She let it all go, and Callian became her crutch.

He cradled her in his arms, a firm barrier between her and the outside world, as if he could block whatever evil came her way, and she sank into him, despite wanting to pull back at how close they'd grown over the last week. History would repeat itself, and she couldn't bear the thought of losing him.

When her cries quieted down, and the only sound was their mingling breaths and the rapid beating of their hearts, she finally stood up straighter so she could peer up into his eyes.

"I know you are hurting, *alora*. Give me your pain, I can handle it. Give it all to me. This is not a burden you need to carry alone. I wish there was something I could have done, but you know deep down, even if you had left just a minute or so earlier, you would never have reached them in time. Their deaths do not rest on you. Elias is to blame, and he will pay for that, we will make sure of it." He slid a hand into hers, and he cupped her chin with the other before sliding it around to grasp the back of her neck, pulling her taut to his body, so her neck arched.

"But know this." He gripped her harder. "I'd watch this place burn to the ground, and I'd walk through the flames as it crumbled to ash. I'd endure a thousand cuts upon my skin and lay myself on the blade if it meant your life was spared. I'm not the hero you're looking for. I've always been the villain. I'll always choose you, *alora*."

Shadows danced in his eyes as Kieryn felt the impact of his words, something fluttering in the pit of her stomach at his proclamation for her. She was at a loss for words. She threw herself at him, their mouths colliding and tongues fumbling to get deeper, closer. She needed him more than she needed anything at that moment. She felt the urgency in his touch, saw the lust fill his eyes as he held her closer.

He slid both hands under her backside and lifted. Kieryn's legs came up and locked behind him, grinding herself along his length, the moans elicited from her lips a symphony to Callian's ears, and he bucked his hips into her viciously.

"Fuck, baby, I need you. I need the taste of you on my tongue."

"Whatever you need, Cal, it's yours, take it." She breathed heavily into his mouth, her tongue darting out and nipping at his lip.

Callian looked around at where they were, and made a swift decision before he backed them into an alley. Kieryn's back met the cold brick wall, and she shuddered at the temperature. Her slim-fitting dress did nothing to warm her, but she didn't need it to. Callian's touch ignited her skin like a blazing fire.

"Hold on to the bars above you, little demon."

She glanced up at the lights that hovered above them, two small bars protruding out from the wall, leaving her enough space to grab onto. She smiled down at him, just as he lifted her higher and she latched on tightly as he ripped her underwear right off her body and discarded it somewhere behind them. Before she could protest about how that was expensive, he shoved his face between her thighs and began to feast on her, making her slam her head back into the wall and cry out his name, over and over. His tongue lapped her up, all the way from her slit to the top where he bit down hard on her clit, making her see stars inside her head, the beauty of them battling the ones that watched them with envy from above.

He gripped her ass harder in his hands and as he sucked on her clit, he moved one hand back to her opening, prodding the skin there. He dragged his fingers slowly and tortuously to her front, where she was absolutely doused in her own juices, and used her own slickness to penetrate her other hole. She bucked her hips closer to his mouth, eager to have both his fingers and tongue inside her.

He chuckled at her impatience, his hot breath blowing on her clit, sending shivers through her body, as he happily obliged. He worked two of his fingers inside her, and she met his thrusts, eager for more, eager for him. She was in a frenzy and chasing the lust-filled high he had her in, and right as he twisted his fingers inside her and bit her clit, she shattered.

And just as she erupted with her orgasm, her head whipped back, not in ecstasy but with a force she couldn't describe and had no control over. Her eyes instantly filled with a vision of blood, black feathers, and shadows. And just as the vision faded, she lost her grip on the bars and fell limply into Callian's arms.

She heard a faint echo of someone calling her name, and she slowly opened her eyelids to the frantic look of Callian, holding her in his arms, his hand coming to caress her cheek in a gentle manner.

"Kieryn, what happened? Did the orgasm I give you truly make you black out?" he laughed, but his smile didn't truly reach his eyes.

"I … I don't know what just happened. It was like I had a vision. It felt so real, like it was a future promise of what was to come." She didn't meet his eyes.

"What did you see?"

She swallowed the bile that rose in her throat at the scene she had witnessed.

When she looked up at him, all Callian saw was the utter devastation on her face.

"I saw you, bound and stripped bare. You had blood pouring from wounds … there was so much blood … and I, I… saw black feathers on the ground by your feet."

His eyes grew wider in that moment, as he was slowly processing what she was saying. A guilty look crossed his face. A twitch of his mouth told her he wasn't being truthful, and as he went to speak, a look of terror came across Callian's face at something behind Kieryn.

She felt the cool tip of the blade at her throat too late, and the putrid smell of the vile creature that she saw at the corner of her eye. Eretum soldiers had surrounded them, and a *Helhound* lay in wait by her leg, waiting for its master to give the command. Kieryn didn't fear much. She didn't fear the blade at her throat, but the Helhound she did.

She glanced down at the monster, one of Elias's creations, or maybe this was one of Callian's suggestions. The Helhound's jaw was unhinged and hung loosely at his jowls, its elongated, sharp teeth snapping close to her skin. Its long talons pawed at the pavement as if it was sharpening its weapons. It was crouched in a fighting stance, not even at its full height, which would be that of a small horse. It was an ugly thing, its patches of fur few and far in between, the spots of skin festering with bugs and bloodied scratches.

No, what Kieryn feared the most were its teeth; one bite would be a death sentence and no antidote would be enough to save her. She would succumb to death almost immediately, and that was if the Helhound didn't finish its meal.

Her eyes found Callian, and she almost wished she hadn't. His face had gone stone cold, and he was deathly pale, for he wasn't staring at the dagger at her throat but at the beast that posed the biggest threat to her life.

They hadn't prepared for this.

Helhounds were scent trackers, and it wouldn't have taken them long to find their scents in town and ambush them after Saler burned down.

The soldier that had the dagger to her throat spoke directly to Callian.

"Your Master requests both of your presence. It is time for your reckoning."

His Master?

But she didn't have time to think more of it, because the last things she saw before the soldier clocked her with the hilt of the dagger were Callian's face and black feathers.

FORTY-THREE

KIERYN WOKE to realize three things. One, she was bound with impenetrable obsidian steel. Two, she was somewhere cold and alone. And three, she had a terrible migraine. She could feel the side of her head throbbing with heat from where the soldier had hit her, and she swore to herself. She slowly lifted her body to a sitting position and leaned up against the prison wall. There was minimal light, nothing but darkness and shadows. She tried to Shadow Walk, but she realized soon after that the obsidian steel must act as a deterrent to magic.

She was in a small cell, with small metal bars preventing her from escaping. Not even the window above her head offered her ample room to sneak through. She didn't know how long it had been, but she didn't think she was out for that long. She called out Callian's name, but heard no reply. All she could do was wait for her kidnapper to make an appearance, and until they did, she'd bide her time and wait. Wait until the right moment where she could strike back.

After what felt like a few grueling hours, Kieryn heard the faint click of a door opening and shutting down the corridor. She got to her knees and then stood, waiting to face her enemy. An Eretum soldier greeted her with a malicious grin, with three other soldiers standing resolute behind him. She guessed she should feel a thrill of excitement that the king thought he needed four of his men to escort her even though she was detained. She smiled despite the situation she was in. Her smile made the soldiers uneasy. They knew that the *Deathbringer* stood before them, and if given the chance, she would tear them limb from limb. They were wise to be wary of her.

"Let's go." The first soldier sneered at her, grabbing her roughly by the arm, pushing her up against the bars of the cell.

"Maybe if the king is easy on you and keeps that face pretty, I'll make you feel better later," he huffed into her ear, his body pushing her tighter against the bars. Her hands being bound behind her back put a strain on her shoulders. His body on hers repulsed her, and she tried to control her breathing before the panic attack set in. The rest of his men sneered.

The soldier behind her glided his hand along her thigh, and with an alarming terror, she realized she was still in the dress she had worn when she was with Callian, her underwear shredded to pieces back in Keres. Her whole body tensed up when he forced her dress higher, revealing the underside of her backside, his erection rubbing her bare skin.

"I'm going to take my sweet time destroying you," he whispered into her ear, the smell of his body odor causing Kieryn to choke. He took that as an invitation to bring his restless fingers closer to her opening.

"I can feel the warmth of that pussy. Pretty soon it's going to be eager for my cock." He smiled cruelly, shoving his hand down to cup her sex. Her body went rigid as he violated her, her dress moving higher with his movements, putting everything below her hips on display for the other men before her.

"Not so scary now, are you, *Deathbringer*, when you're tied up? It's a good thing I like them broken."

She ground her teeth so hard she felt as if they were going to break.

"You just signed your death warrant. Doesn't surprise me that the only way you can touch a woman is when she's bound," she spat. "Better pray to your gods, because the second I am free, you will be the first one I gut," she promised with lethal conviction, and then she rammed her head back into his face, feeling the snap of bone and his swearing from behind.

The other soldiers swarmed her, shoving her into the wall, the stone scraping the side of her face. The first soldier ordered his men to turn her around to face him and when she did, she smiled with her eyes, a threat that she would follow through on her promise to end his life. And when he punched her and she felt the blood in her mouth, she spat it at his feet, her smile now bloody and menacing.

"I'll make you bleed for that later, whore."

The soldiers marched her through the cell door and down dimly lit hallways before they came through a side room. She stood straighter as they opened the door into the throne room, but she wasn't met by the king.

No, this person stood tall, facing the fire that roared in its hearth. He had one arm propping himself up, toned muscles rippling with the strain, even through his black long-sleeved shirt. He had dark hair, and his body was elegant, god-like. Her stomach turned at how familiar he felt. He turned and if she wasn't being held up by the soldiers surrounding her, she would have collapsed where she stood. Her knees felt weak, and she was blindsided by the man that stood before her.

"It's you," she gasped, the man standing before her leaving her speechless.

"It is. You clearly didn't heed my advice. Your feelings will get you killed, and love blinded you to it all," the man's haunting, deathly voice spoke.

"I am here to collect that debt you owe me. But your powers fascinate me," he said, walking up to where she stood. He took her in like a hunter would its prey. "You may be more valuable to me alive than dead."

The delicate touch of his hand slid across the back of her arms. A slight shiver ran down her body, and she tensed at the contact and how it made her feel. It felt off, but natural. And with a flick of his wrist, she felt the obsidian steel fall from her bound hands.

"Show me that darkness in you that I know you crave to surrender to," he said provokingly.

Kieryn brought her hands to her front, rubbing her wrists gently, massaging the area that was tender.

"Who are you?" she asked him, knowing the answer.

The man turned to face her again, his smile devastatingly beautiful.

"You know the answer to that, Kieryn. Say my name."

Her eyes widened, and she knew that once she spoke his name into existence, it would feel real.

"Shade," she whispered.

With a stealth only the God of Death could embrace, he stalked over to her, wrapping his hand around the back of her head, and pulled her close, almost as if was going to kiss her.

"In the flesh," he whispered seductively into her ear. " Now…show me what you can do."

He shoved Kieryn away, and she stumbled before catching herself. She felt that inferno singing in her veins and she felt the shadows humming below her skin. Shade saw it too.

"There she is." Shade smirked. "Beautifully unhinged. Give into your darkness, Kieryn."

She tunneled deep into her core and freed her mind. She

gave up control, and she allowed her shadows to consume her, falling willingly under their control and power.

"*Mercy!*" the *God of Death* muttered.

She caught her reflection in the mirror behind Shade's head, and the vision of herself was terrifying. Her once bright emerald-colored eyes had faded, and instead, opal eyes stared back, her hair floating upwards, and a curtain of black hugged her frame, her shadows billowing out behind her like flames.

"You are an exquisite creature, indeed," he practically sang.

Her head fell back as she absorbed the power within her, flooding her senses. She had never felt this alive, this powerful, this free. Her shadows had never reacted like this with her, except when she was in that dimensional world, before Shade, how her shadows sang for his shadows.

She found her victim instantaneously, and with a cry, she cast her shadows, pinning the four soldiers from earlier with a death grip around their necks. The tendrils of shadows snaked their way through their limbs, binding their feet and hands together, and she watched while three of them choked until they were blue in the face, and then she let those bodies crash to the floor. She walked directly up to the first soldier who had violated her.

"I told you that when I was free, I'd make you suffer. The minute you put your hand on me, you were already dead," she seethed.

"Guess you won't get to see me bleed for you later, instead I'll be watching you bleed."

She slashed her arm through the air, and she watched as the man's eyes started to bleed, a trail of his blood running down his face. Next, she made his lungs fill with blood as he choked.

In a voice that didn't feel like her own, she commanded more.

"Now, drive your dagger through your heart."

The man that hovered in the air before her, locked in by her shadows, released his hands, and he reached for his dagger strapped to his waist, his hands shaking the entire time, fighting the compulsion wracking his whole body. He hesitated, and Kieryn pushed harder with her mind, and she heard the piercing scream leave his lips as he drove his dagger through his heart.

Only when Kieryn saw the life leave his eyes did she call her shadows back to her. As soon as they settled home beneath her skin, she slumped slightly, physically exhausted. Where darkness lingered, she would rise like a phoenix from its ashes.

"Beautifully unhinged, indeed… Ah," Shade said, his voice filled with excitement. "Hello brother, just in time."

FORTY-FOUR

KIERYN STUMBLED back into her body, and when she turned, she felt the world give out beneath her. This time she didn't have the soldiers to bear her weight, so she sank to the ground, her head feeling heavy, her heart shattering into two.

Because before her stood Callian, in all his glory. He was in black leathers, and behind him, two beautiful black wings sprouted from his shoulders. He was death incarnate, and he was beautiful. Shade had called him his brother. She felt sick as she braced herself for impact.

When she felt the *Angel of Death* near, everything slowed. She lost all senses. She didn't dare to breathe and she willed her heart to stop beating for him. She was frozen in shock on her knees before Callian, and the look in his eyes was not who she roamed the Kingdoms of Elysium with, this was not the Callian that took an arrow for her, not the Callian who opened up to her about his past and his tattoos. She had seen his scars, and she saw him, she … and as if a spring storm had opened up on her, Kieryn stood to face Callian, realization dawning as her eyes flickered down to his heart, where a scar lingered beneath the shirt.

Scars tell stories.

No, no, no, no.

The same word thrashed around in her head. It couldn't be.

"It was you that night," she said, her voice dropping, a deeply pained look crossing her face. She stared into Callian's onyx eyes, and as if the truth had set him free, the true color of his eyes revealed itself, changing to the piercing sapphire blues that had haunted her for all of these years.

She reared back a step, preparing to throw all of her power at him, for betraying her trust, for lying to her.

Did he even care about me?

Was everything he said a lie to get me to trust him?

Were any of the stories he told me true?

She had a hard time distinguishing what was real and what was a lie.

"*Alora,* I…" Callian began to plead.

"Don't you fucking call me that. Don't you dare," she yelled.

"I can explain, Kieryn. It's not all what you are thinking," he tried again.

"No? So it doesn't look like you convinced me to trust you, open up to you, give myself to you? Only to hand me over to your evil brother? You're too late, anyway. I already did."

Callian's look of shock was genuine.

"You what?"

"The night of the ball, I signed my soul away to him in exchange for Damien's life."

Callian clutched at his chest, stepping backwards as if a violent wind had tried to knock him down. He spun around and looked over at his brother with unrestrained emotion on his face.

"I told you I was handling it. Why? Why would you subject her to that?" his anger in full force.

Shade glanced lazily over at his brother.

"You seemed to be enjoying playing house, rather than completing the task I assigned to you. Were my messages not clear enough?" he snapped, his eyes briefly glancing down at Callian's wrists, where the thorns moved to the sound of its master's voice.

"Don't do this, Shade. I could have convinced her. You didn't have to take away her choice."

"You are blood bound to me, Callian. Do not forget where your loyalties lie."

Shade brought his hands up, as if pushing an invisible force upwards, and it wasn't until Kieryn glanced back over at Callian that she saw his feet dragging him closer to Shade, and making him kneel before him.

"Do not forget who you yield to, who commands you."

Falling for him had been at the cost of her own self - destruction and it had made her weak. It was the end of being trusting and powerless. He'd been her shield—but now it was time to become the sword.

"What do you want with me?"

"Well, dear, I'm going to make you one of us, and then I am going to take great pleasure in breaking you."

Everything after that felt like it was in slow motion. Callian forcibly tried to get off his knees and run to her, but the weight of Shade's command held him in place. That didn't stop Callian from continuing to try to fight his compulsion by attempting to crawl to her. Shade's shadows swarmed the room, and above them through the skylight on windows, the moon eclipsed the sun, and bathed the world in darkness, just as Shade drove an obsidian dagger through Kieryn's heart.

She clutched at the dagger protruding from her chest and ripped it out, her knees slamming against the marble floor once more. She would die just like she was supposed to all those years ago, and before her eyelids closed, her last image was

Shade walking out of the room, and Callian crawling over to her, his compulsion gone, cradling her in his arms, his apology spilling from his lips.

She realized then that the only pain worse than death was betrayal.

@VIIMORTEART
@VIIMORTE
PATREON.COM/VIIMORTE

GLOSSARY

Alene - *Goddess of the Hunt and Moon*, one of the goddesses sleeping in the Veil. She was one of the gods that sacrificed herself for the realm of Elysium in the Gods War - gifted her powers to Riyadh Kingdom

Alessian Warriors - An elite army of dangerous and lethal women who were known for their brutality and strength. Prayed to the twin sister goddesses, Cahira and Irina.

Almeria Kingdom - One of the six kingdoms located in the southern region of Elysium and ruled over by Queen Nyla

Ambra Petrova- Current Queen of Calydan Kingdom, known to Elysium as *The Savage Queen*

Arlo - Former Alpha of the Shadow Crescent wolf bloodline who led the massacre against Damien's pack

Ashlyn Delgrer - Former Alessian warrior turned assassin for

Phantom's Keep, originally from the kingdom of Almeria, known to Elysium as *The Wraith*

Basalto - A small village located in the kingdom of Riyadh, and was home to the massacre of Damien's pack and mate

Bajna Castle - Residence of Queen Ambra, also the home to the *Nightraiders* and their dragons

Bakrem Alps - Snow-capped mountains that travelers have to pass through on their way to Calydan Kingdom

Bjorn Aros - Current King of Riyadh Kingdom, known to Elysium as *The Blood King*

Bloodling - A rare dark magic ability - they possess magic that can manipulate blood, ultimately controlling any living thing. While it is an ultimate weapon in battle, it is very draining and the dark magic wielder needs to feed on blood to recuperate to full strength

Bloodwood Forest - A sinister forest that separates Eretum, Calydan and Minas Kingdom - it is home to *The Mad King's* vile creatures of the night

Cahira - *Goddess of War,* one of the goddesses sleeping in the Veil. She was one of the gods that sacrificed herself for the realm of Elysium in the Gods War - gifted her powers to Almeria Kingdom

Callian Ashwood - Exiled Prince of Eretum Kingdom, but known around the realm of Elysium as *The Angel of Death, Reaper of Souls or the Prince of Darkness*

Calydan Kingdom - One of the six kingdoms located in the northern region of Elysium and ruled over by Queen Ambra

Calista Kincaid - Current Queen of Keres Kingdom, known to Elysium as *The Siren Queen*

Cardosian Mountains - Mountains in Calydan Kingdom, Bajna Castle sits perched on top.

Clarke Ryvers - The King of Phantoms, rules over Phantom's Keep

Coventry - A countryside town located in the kingdom of Almeria, and where Kieryn grew up until she was sixteen, nicknamed the "Green Heart" for its vast lands of green

Dakar - A small mountain town located in Riyadh Kingdom

Damien Conall - Former Alpha of the wolf bloodline, Crimson Fangs turned assassin for Phantom's Keep, originally from the kingdom of Riyadh, known to Elysium as *The Executioner*

Dreamdive - A power that Shieiks possess that allow them to dive into a person's dreams

Eliana - *Goddess of Revenge and Retribution,* one of the goddesses sleeping in the Veil. She was one of the gods that started the Gods War - gifted her powers to Calydan Kingdom

Elias Ashwood - Current King of Eretum Kingdom, known to Elysium as *The Mad King*

Elijiah Rhodes - Father to Kieryn Rhodes, and former Chief Commander of the Alessian warriors

Eretum Kingdom - One of the six kingdoms located in the eastern region of Elysium and ruled over by King Elias

Exile Bar - A bar Kieryn and her assassin friends frequent, located in the kingdom of Riyadh

Folk-healers - Elemental witches who use the resources nature provides to heal

Grayson Hunt - Former *Nightraider* and Prince of Calydan Kingdom until he faked his death, currently an assassin for Phantom's Keep, known to Elysium as *The Grimreaper*

Hangman's Chasm - Deep fissure that ran through the Bakrem Alps, it is the easiest traveling route to reach Calydan Kingdom

Helhounds - At the command of Shade, they are the size of a small horse and have unhinged jaws, elongated sharp teeth, and long talons, their bite is deadly and there is no antidote

Ilyana Rose - Friend of Grayson Hunt, currently employed as Queen Ambra's Right Hand and a *Nightraider* in her aerial fleet

Irina - *Goddess of Peace,* one of the goddesses sleeping in the Veil. She was one of the gods that sacrificed herself for the realm of Elysium in the Gods War - gifted her powers to Almeria Kingdom

Kano - *God of the Sea and Sky,* one of the gods sleeping in the Veil. He was one of the gods that started the Gods War - gifted his powers to Keres Kingdom

Keres Kingdom - One of the six kingdoms located in the southern region of Elysium - nicknamed *Tidal Islands* and is comprised of five islands Layette, Capryna, Palmana, Astora and Naros - and ruled over by Queen Calista

Kieryn Rhodes - Current assassin for the Phantom's Keep, known to Elysium as *The Deathbringer,* she is the daughter of Elijiah and Adeline Rhodes and possesses the rare ability of Shadow Walking

Kalani Sea - Body of water that separates the kingdom of Keres from the other kingdoms

Luc Ambosio - Former King of Minas Kingdom, known to Elysium as *The Beloved King*

Lux - *God of Light and Life,* one of the gods sleeping in the Veil. He was one of the gods that sacrificed himself for the realm of Elysium in the Gods War - gifted his powers to Minas Kingdom

Maddox Young - Weapons Master for Phantoms Keep

Mila Thorne - Potions Master for Phantoms Keep

Minas Kingdom - One of the six kingdoms located in the eastern region of Elysium - nicknamed *The Floating Island* and is constructed of hundreds of canals and bridges that crossed throughout - and ruled over by King Luc

Mortarri - Coven of witches that combined their magical powers and unique skill sets to create stronger and bigger spells

Nightraiders - Prestigious dragon riders for Calydan Kingdom in Queen Ambra's aerial fleet

Nightwalkers - One of King Elias's creatures - they can take the form of whatever the person fears the most, and have no exact shape as their chosen skin is visible only to the person whose dread they are representing, they roam the Bloodwood Forest

Nyla D'Amore - Current Queen of Almeria Kingdom, known to Elysium as *The Fair Queen*

Phantoms Keep - The residence for the assassins, built into the side of mountains

Riyadh Kingdom - One of the six kingdoms located in the western region of Elysium - ruled over by King Bjorn

Rylan Kincaid - Princess of Keres Kingdom, the younger sister to Soraya Kincaid

Saler - A small village on Capryna and is full of non-magic folk

Santuario del Corona e Sangue - The Sanctuary of Crown and Blood is the name of the school for assassins, its location secret and protected by the wards of the Gods, they do not answer to any king or queen, and the assassins are known as Phantoms

Seers - Magical witches who were empaths and could predict people's futures with Tarot readings or through touch

Selkies - Ghastly creatures who lived in the deepest and darkest depths of the water, they are the distant and estranged cousins to sirens - they are skeletal with webbed hands and feet with no teeth, instead they have a mouth consisting of a pronged tongue like a razorblade

Shade - *God of Shadow and Death,* banned to the Shadowrealm by the other Gods while they sleep peacefully in the Veil, he was the leader of the gods that started the Gods War - gifted his powers to Eretum Kingdom, besides his shadow powers

Shade Walkers - A very rare and unique power - they are force wielders that can conjure the darkness and shroud themselves in shadows, giving them immeasurable power, only two in existence share this unique ability, the rest were killed off in the Gods War

Shieik - Dark magic wielders that practice mind altering, forcing someone to perform an action unwillingly - they can also dreamdive - dive into people's dreams

Sirens - Beautiful and alluring creatures that are seductresses with their body and mind, they can also control the element of water

Soraya Kincaid - Princess of Keres Kingdom and older sister to Rylan, known in her kingdom as *The Party Princess*

Tritons - The male counterpart to sirens and the first line of defense to Queen Ambra's naval fleet, they can control the element of water and air as gifted to them by the God Kano

Venetu - Capital of Minas Kingdom and where the king resides

Veritas - Capital of Almeria Kingdom and where the queen resides

ACKNOWLEDGMENTS

I never thought I would get to this exact moment. As I sit here writing this acknowledgements page, I realize it is true when they say it takes a village. There are so many people to thank, and words truly can't express how grateful I am, but I will try.

To start, thank you to my readers. If it wasn't for you picking up my book, this wouldn't be happening. Since I was a little girl I had always wanted to write a book. When they asked you what you wanted to be when you grew up back in elementary school, my answer was simple - an author. I was told that it was an unrealistic goal. That there were so many authors out there in the world, and my chances were slim. I doubted myself for the longest time. I wrote poetry and short stories for a while in my free time, never picturing the day I would publish a book of my own. This bookstagram community has truly been a blessing in my life. The unconditional support and love you have shown me here has been incredible. It was your words that pushed me to take that leap of faith and bring this story to life, so thank you, truly, from the bottom of my heart.

To Kaitlyn, it all started off with me sending you this story in chunks. The first ever person to read this book and fall in love with these characters almost as much as me. And now you have become one of my closest friends. You are my biggest cheerleader and the best hype woman a girl could ask for. I am so blessed to have found a friend in you over these last two years. You were a part of this journey every step of the way, and you are an absolute gem of a person. I love our audio exchanges every day. You are the first person I bounce my ideas to and you have been crucial in helping me get to where I am today.

To my beta readers, Amber, Courtney, Nolani, Courtney and Rhianna - the five of you were the best beta readers I could have ever hoped for. You'll never know how truly humbled I am that you took a chance on this book back in its very first stages, before the edits. Your reactions and feedback is what helped shape this book into its final stage and because of that I am beyond blessed to have you on my team and for your friendships. I apologize in advance for the roller coaster of absolute hell I will be taking you on in this series.

To my family - thank you for all of your love and support along this emotional journey, especially my mother who read this book, and listened to me over and over for years about this book idea. To those who asked me how the writing process was going and telling me you'll buy the book and happily display it "loud and proud" even though I know most of you don't read, I appreciate you all.

To my Grandma Sassy - you were one of the first ones to read my book in its entirety in the first draft phase in only a few days. Thank you for passing on your passion and love for epic stories. As promised, I made sure the very first print was signed and yours to keep.

To my editor, Taylor - I knew when I finished my first draft of my debut baby, I wanted you to edit my book, and I was so happy I did. You have been an amazing person to work with. Every question I had, you answered. When I couldn't think of the right words, you did. I have enjoyed working with you and I loved seeing your comments in the margins. Here's to working on many more projects with you in the future.

To my absolute dream team - Sarah, Hannah, Kristen and Vii. Sarah, I am still blown away by the cover art of my book. I fell to my knees, quite literally when I first saw the final product. You have truly outdone yourself with this one, and you have brought this vision to life. Can't wait to see what ideas we come up with for the rest of the series. Hannah, I knew when I wanted a map illustrated for this book, you were my go to girl. You were so easy to work with and you took my chicken scratch of a map and turned it into this beautiful map I want to frame in my house for the days to come. Kristen, you have been a godsend in this process. From answering my questions and helping me finish this book in its last moments before the final reveal, I am so happy I chose you to help design the interior. And to Vii, you have brought these characters to life in ways I can't explain. They are absolutely beautiful and even better than what my mind had imagined. You have such a gift, thank you for sharing it and bringing my vision to life.

To my ARC team, thank you for taking a chance on me and my book. I will always be thankful for you and the friendships I have gained along the way. I hope you stick around on this epic journey of mine, as I have so many fun projects I have coming in the next couple of years.

To those who have made it this far, I know the words thank you aren't much. But, just know I am humbled and grateful to anyone who has picked up my book and gave me a chance, I am indebted to you. Writing a book is not an easy feat. This was three years in the making. It started off with a dream, literally. The masquerade ball scene in particular. It was a recurring dream for months, until a friend of mine convinced me to write the damn story. And so I did. After ending a three-year long relationship, I sat down at my computer and wrote my story back in April of 2022. It has been a long emotional roller coaster writing this book. There were many times I doubted myself and thought that I was a fraud, that no one would read this book. There were months where I had writer's block and felt lost. I wanted to make sure this book was perfect. After 1.5 years of writing this book, this book was complete. And now just over a year later from finishing this book, it is now in your hands and that feeling is euphoric. As an author, it is an amazing feeling to have my debut baby in your hands, but it's also a scary moment as well. If my words and these character's stories have resonated with just one person, I know I have done my job as an author. I hope you'll stay and stick around for this journey of mine.

ABOUT THE AUTHOR

Born and raised in a small town in Connecticut, Leslie Bates always had her nose buried in the pages of a book.

Leslie works full-time as a wedding coordinator. She is also a dark fantasy/romance writer who loves a good villain story with just the right amount of spice and morally gray characters. When she's not writing her newest story, you can catch her exploring the world one passport stamp at a time, curled up with a good book, or spending time with family and friends.

For updates on future projects, follow her on social media!

instagram.com/_butfirstbooks
tiktok.com/@_butfirstbooks
goodreads.com/_butfirstbooks

THANK YOU

To all my readers who took a chance on my debut novel, thank you so much for taking the time to read Where Darkness Blooms!

It would also mean the world to me if you could leave a review on Goodreads or Amazon because as a new indie author they help tremendously.

Don't forget to follow my social accounts. My DMs are always open, so come over and say hello.

www.ingramcontent.com/pod-product-compliance
Lightning Source LLC
Chambersburg PA
CBHW031847310726
48972CB00005B/1446